Anders de la
MOTTE
END of
SUMMER

Anders de la Motte is the bestselling author of the Seasons Quartet; the first three books of which – *End of Summer,* *Deeds of Autumn* and *Dead of Winter* – have all been number one bestsellers in Sweden and have been shortlisted for the Swedish Academy of Crime Writers' Award for Best Crime Novel of the Year. Anders, a former police officer, has already won a Swedish Academy Crime Award for his debut, *Game,* in 2010 and his second standalone, *The Silenced,* in 2015.

To date, the first three books in the Seasons Quartet have published over half a million copies. Set in southern Sweden, all four books can be read as standalones.

Anders de la MOTTE
END of SUMMER

Translated by Neil Smith

ZAFFRE

Originally published in Sweden by Bokförlaget Forum in 2016
First published in the UK in 2021 by
ZAFFRE
An imprint of Bonnier Books UK
4th Floor, Victoria House, Bloomsbury Square, London WC1B 4DA
Owned by Bonnier Books
Sveavägen 56, Stockholm, Sweden

Translation by Neil Smith

'End of Summer' copyright 1953 by Stanley Kunitz, from
The Collected Poems by Stanley Kunitz. Used by
permission of W.W. Norton & Company, Inc.

A CIP catalogue record for this book is
available from the British Library.

ISBN: 978-1-78576-823-1

Also available as an ebook and an audiobook

1 3 5 7 9 10 8 6 4 2

Typeset by IDSUK (Data Connection) Ltd
Printed and bound in Great Britain by Clays Ltd, Elcograf S.p.A.

MIX
Paper from
responsible sources
FSC® C018072

Zaffre is an imprint of Bonnier Books UK
www.bonnierbooks.co.uk

To my father, for everything you tried to teach me

I stood in the disenchanted field
Amid the stubble and the stones,
Amazed, while a small worm whispered to me
The song of my marrow bones.

Blue poured into summer blue,
A hawk broke from his cloudless tower,
The roof of the silo blazed, and I knew
That part of my life was over.

Already the iron door of the north
Clangs open: birds, leaves, snows
Order their populations forth,
And a cruel wind blows.

From 'End of Summer' by Stanley Kunitz

Prologue

Summer 1983

The baby rabbit was crouching in the tall grass. Its coat was wet and shiny with the dew that had accompanied dusk into the garden.

He should really go in. His mum didn't like him being out on his own, especially not when it was getting dark. But he was a big boy now, he would be five in a few weeks, and he liked dusk a lot. Soon all the night animals would start to appear. Hedgehogs would peer out cautiously from beneath the big bushes, then set off across the grass in funny, zigzag paths. Bats would start to swirl about between the tall trees, and from the avenue of chestnuts on the other side of the house he could already hear the first cries of the owls.

It was the rabbits he wanted to see most. Having one of his own was right at the top of his wish list. A fluffy baby rabbit, just like the one sitting over there in the grass. The little creature looked at him, twitching its nose as if it wasn't sure about his smell. If he was dangerous or harmless. He took a couple of careful steps towards it. The rabbit stayed where it was, it didn't seem to have made up its mind.

He had been looking forward to his birthday for a couple of months already. He was hoping to get a kite from Mattias. He had watched his big brother spend hours making kites out in Dad's workshop. The way he carefully measured the canes for the frame, stretched twine between the ends and covered the whole thing with taut, shiny fabric that he had pinched from the boxes up in the attic. Clothes that had once belonged to their grandmother, that Mum hadn't got round to getting rid of.

Several times this summer he had watched as Mattias and his friends held competitions with their homemade creations. Mattias's kites always flew highest, every time. Hovering above the fields just like their feathered namesakes.

The rabbit in the grass was still looking at him, so he took a few more steps towards it. He stopped when the animal raised its head slightly. He felt like running straight at the rabbit to grab hold of it. But Uncle Harald always said that a good hunter didn't rush things, so he waited, standing perfectly still and thinking about his wish list.

He was hoping to get a red car he had seen in the shop in the village from his big sister. It had big flames on its sides, and if you pulled it backwards and then let go, it would race off on its own. It was probably expensive, but Vera was bound to buy it for him anyway. Dad would give her the money. If she asked for it. He didn't really know if she had forgiven him for the business with the hawk's eggs, but he didn't want to think about that. Mattias had forgiven him, but it was harder to tell with Vera.

The baby rabbit lowered its head again and started to nibble on a blade of grass. Its whiskers were twitching so cutely that he very nearly broke Uncle Harald's rules. But he needed to wait a bit longer. Wait for the moment the rabbit relaxed and was no longer looking in his direction.

He had asked for a bicycle from Mum and Dad. He had already started practising on Mattias's old one, even though he wasn't actually supposed to do that on his own. The other day he fell off and grazed his knee. Not badly, but enough to draw blood. He had started to cry, and went and hid in the treehouse. Uncle Harald had found him and gave him a telling off. 'What did your mum say? Don't you understand that she gets worried?'

Yes, he understood. His mum worried about him pretty much the whole time. 'Because you're my little mouse,' she always said. 'Because I can't bear the thought of anything happening to you.' That was why he had hidden himself away and didn't go back into the house. After telling him off, his uncle had put a plaster on his knee and told Mum that he had fallen over on the gravel path between the barn and the house. *Easily done if you're running in wooden-soled shoes.* The lie was for his mother's sake, not his. So she wouldn't worry. Since then he hadn't been allowed to wear wooden-soled shoes like Mattias and Vera. He thought that was unfair.

Suddenly the baby rabbit moved. It took a couple of short hops in his direction, in search of longer grass. Instead of running towards it he stood perfectly still. Waiting, just like Uncle Harald said.

Uncle Harald was the best hunter in the area, everyone knew that. There were almost always dead animals hanging from the roof of his boiler room. Pheasants, deer, hares, with empty eyes and stiff bodies. Uncle Harald had rough hands. He smelled of tobacco, oil, dogs and something he couldn't identify. But he guessed it was something dangerous. A lot of people were scared of Uncle Harald. Vera and Mattias were, even if Vera pretended not to be. She sometimes contradicted him, but you could hear the wobble in her voice. Mattias, on the other hand, didn't say anything, just stared down at the ground and did as he was told. Fetched Uncle Harald's pipe or fed his dogs. They weren't the sort of dogs you could play with. They lived outside in big pens and travelled on the back of the truck rather than inside it. Rough coats, anxious eyes that followed Uncle Harald's every movement. The other week he went to the swimming pool with Dad and Mattias. He had sat in the sauna listening to the old men talk. When Uncle Harald came in everyone moved out of the way, even Dad. Clearing the best space for him, right in the middle. Looking at him the same way the dogs did.

The only person who wasn't scared of Uncle Harald was Mum. Mum wasn't scared of anyone, except maybe God. Sometimes she and Uncle Harald had arguments. He had heard them say things to each other. Harsh words that he didn't really understand, but he knew they weren't nice.

All the same, Uncle Harald's birthday present was the one he had the highest hopes of. A little rabbit that would be his alone, that's what his uncle had promised. Maybe just like the one sitting a few metres away from him. If he could catch that one, he'd have two. And Uncle Harald would be proud of him. Proud of him for being a proper hunter.

He'd waited long enough now, so he took another careful step forward. The baby rabbit went on chewing the long grass, didn't even notice him getting closer. He took another step and slowly reached out his hands. It might just work.

'Billy, time to come in now!'

The rabbit raised its head, it seemed to be listening to the voice from the house. Then it turned and scampered away.

He felt disappointment tug at his chest. But then the rabbit stopped and looked back at him, as if it was wondering where he'd gone. He hesitated. Mum would be worried if he didn't go in. The owls were hooting louder now, and the outside lights had come on, making the shadows in the garden deeper. The rabbit was still looking at him. It seemed to be saying: *Are you coming?*

He took a couple of steps, then a few more.

'Billy!' his mum called. 'Billy, come inside now!'

The hunt was on. The rabbit scampered away from him, and if he was really lucky it would lead him to its burrow. Somewhere full of baby rabbits with big eyes and soft fur. Rabbits he could take home with him. Which could live in the cage Uncle Harald had promised him.

'Billy!' Mum's cry disappeared in the distance. The baby rabbit was still running ahead of him, and even though he was wearing his best running shoes it could probably easily outpace him if it wanted to. Perhaps the rabbit *wanted* him to catch it? Hug it, make it his.

5

He followed it through the rows of gnarled old fruit trees. Then in amongst the overgrown bushes. He didn't really like this furthest part of the garden. Earlier in the summer his friend Isak had found a jawbone on the ground under the dense branches, a white bone with four yellow molars attached. Uncle Harald had said that Grandfather used to bury things there. Things he wanted to get rid of for good. That the jawbone probably belonged to a pig, and that you had to bury some things very deep to stop the foxes finding them.

He had only ever seen one fox in his life. That was when Uncle Harald, Dad and the other men laid the results of their hunt out in the yard last autumn. Narrow eyes, a shimmering red coat, sharp teeth that stuck out beneath the bloodstained nose. The dogs kept their distance from it. They seemed unsettled, almost frightened. Uncle Harald had said that you always shot foxes if you got the chance. That it was the duty of every hunter, whenever the opportunity presented itself. Because foxes were cunning, just like in fairy tales. They knew how to move without leaving a trail.

'They've got incredible noses,' he said. 'And foxes love the smell of rabbits and little boys. So make sure you stay inside the fence, Billy!'

Then Uncle Harald had laughed, that rumbling laugh that sounded jolly and dangerous at the same time, and after a while he had started to laugh too. But he hadn't been able to stop thinking about foxes digging for skeletons in the garden. He even dreamed about them at night. Sharp teeth, paws digging in the soil, damp, shiny noses sniffing the air. Sniffing in the direction of the house for a little boy.

He had avoided that part of the garden since then, and hadn't protested when Isak wanted to take the pig's jaw-bone home with him, even though it should really have been his.

But right now neither skeletons nor foxes could stop him. The rabbit scampered round the dry bushes and he followed it deeper into the undergrowth. A low branch caught his sleeve and he had to stop for a couple of seconds. By the time he had pulled free the rabbit had disappeared.

He hesitated for a few moments, wondering if he should turn back and go up to the house. But he was still caught up in the thrill of the chase. That gave him the courage to go on. Further in amongst the bushes. Like a proper hunter.

More branches reached out towards him, feeling for his clothes with thorny fingers. Somewhere up ahead in the gloom he thought he could see a little white tail bobbing about. Perhaps he'd reached the burrow now? The thought made him speed up, and he almost ran straight into the tall fence that marked the end of the garden.

He stopped abruptly. Just a metre or so beyond the wire fence a dense crop of maize was growing. It wasn't going to be harvested for a while yet. Not until it had dried and turned yellow, Dad said.

Crickets were chirruping among the leaves, weaving their song into a crisp carpet of sound that almost drowned out his thoughts. The rabbit was on the other side. It was sitting right beneath the green wall of maize plants, watching him. Waiting for him.

The fence was tall. Maybe even taller than Uncle Harald, and certainly too tall for him to be able to climb over. The hunt was over. He wasn't going to see the rabbit's burrow. Even so, he couldn't help feeling a bit relieved. He had never been this far in the garden on his own before. There was only a thin streak of evening light left in the sky, and the shadows among the undergrowth had turned to dense darkness almost without him noticing.

He decided to go home, and was about to turn back when he caught sight of something. A small hollow had been dug out beneath the fence, just big enough for a small boy to crawl through. He looked over towards the rabbit. It was still sitting there.

A gust of wind blew through the field of maize, then the rusty links of the wire fence and the dark bushes behind him. He looked round, then got down on his knees, then his stomach. He wriggled carefully under the jagged wire fence, stood up and brushed the dirt from his hands and knees. He was tingling with excitement. He was out now, beyond the garden, for the first time on his own. He would tell Isak about it on Monday. Maybe Mattias and Vera too. Tell them how brave he was when he caught a rabbit of his very own, only they mustn't say anything to Mum.

There was a rustling sound among the maize and at first he thought it was the wind again. Then he saw the white tail disappear among the tall plants. The rabbit wasn't scampering anymore, it was running, fast. Its ears were tucked flat against its head and soil was flying up from its paws. It wasn't until the rabbit had disappeared from view that he realised what had happened. That the animal's sensitive nose had picked up a smell belonging to someone other than him. Someone who had burrowed under a fence. Someone with a red coat and sharp teeth who loved the smell of rabbits. And little boys . . .

His heart was beating fast, racing as if it belonged to a frightened little rabbit. The maize plants loomed above him like dark, swaying giants, pushing him back towards the fence. He felt a sob rise in his throat. From the corner of his eye he caught a glimpse of something moving, something red. He turned round and realised at the same moment that the crickets had fallen silent.

Mum! he had time to think. *Mum!*

Darling,

This is the start of our story. Yours and mine. I've tried to resist, tried to keep you away from me and not let myself fall, but now I'm letting go, my darling, and I'm relying on you to catch me. Will you? Or are we both going to fall?

I hope not. I'd like to imagine that our story has a happy ending.

Chapter 1

S he's an autumn person, always has been. Or almost always. Once she wished that summer would never end. That the light, warmth and clear blue sky would last forever. But that's a long time ago now. Another place, another life.

The clock on the wall says that there are eleven minutes to go before the start of the session. So far everything has gone well. She and Ruud have made sandwiches and filled the pump-action thermos flasks with coffee. They've arranged the chairs in a neat circle on the grey carpet. Twelve worn, folding metal chairs – probably more than they need, but not so many that there'll be big empty gaps in the circle – with a couple of cheap paper napkins on each seat.

When everything is ready Ruud unlocks the double doors from the foyer, letting in two early arrivals who bring the smell of warm, rain-wet tarmac in with them. Of all the city's smells, this is the one she likes most. Possibly because there's something cleansing about it. A new beginning. Just like this day is supposed to be.

The first participant Ruud let in is a man in his thirties, like her. He has tattooed arms, crumpled clothes and a head that seems slightly too large for his body. Probably because of the beard. It's bushy, unkempt, and he has a dull, bloodshot look in his eyes. He's unlikely to be alone in that today.

The second participant is older, a grey-haired woman almost as old as Ruud. Her hair is gathered in a long plait down her back. The eyes behind her glasses are kinder than the tattooed bearded man's, but there's still something similar about them.

Ruud shepherds them gently towards the coffee, and she's on the point of going over to introduce herself when it hits her. The feeling that she's made a big mistake and that everything, all this, is going to go horribly wrong.

Shit!

She rushes out into the kitchen and reaches a chair just before her legs give way. Face in hands, head between her knees, deep, slow breaths.

In.

Out.

Iiiin.

Ouuut.

The sound of Ruud's polite small talk filters through the swing-door. Curls round her heart, merging with the rhythm in her temples.

'Did you get the bus here?' *Thud, thud.* 'Oh, the metro.' *Thud, thud.* 'And you drove as usual, Lars? Did you manage a parking space OK? Yes, you have to be careful round here, the traffic wardens are really aggressive.' *Thud, thud, thud.*

She can hear other noises now, more participants dragging their feet across the worn carpet, stopping, squinting up at the

14

fluorescent lights until Ruud notices them and brings them into the group using bait that very few people can refuse: 'There's coffee and sandwiches over here.'

Hesitant, shuffling steps, the click of plastic cups being pulled apart, followed by the wheeze of the flask. Her breathing gets easier, but she daren't sit up just yet. She looks down at the tiled floor. Lets her eyes follow one of the cracks, which is beige-grey with grease and dirt. Everything in here is greasy, even the air. Thirty years of ingrained cooking smells, leaving a sticky, salty taste at the back of your throat.

The chatter in the other room is getting louder, echoing slightly in the large space. *Bus, metro, parking? Nice to get a bit of rain. Good for the lawn. It's been a lovely summer, though, don't you think? Almost like the Mediterranean. Got any plans for the weekend?*

She's regretting it now. Regretting not taking the redundancy payment they offered her. Anyone sensible would have taken it. Left everything behind and started again somewhere else. It doesn't really matter where. A different city, a different part of the country. Why not even a completely different country?

It isn't too late yet.

The back door is right there in front of her. She's got the keys in her pocket. Outside is a flight of concrete steps and some bins, then the street. It wouldn't take a minute to sneak out. But she's signed their papers, assured them that she's worth a second chance. Convinced herself that it's the last one she's going to get.

The noise in the other room is getting louder and louder. The flask goes on wheezing, louder as the amount of coffee inside decreases. The conversation is starting to stall.

Goodness, yes. You really can't complain about the weather, you really can't . . .

She sits up, glances at the back door. Shuts her eyes. Her fingers find their way to her lower right arm, her nails scratch the thin fabric of the shirt and the cuff starts to slide up towards her elbow. In less than a minute she could be outside on the rain-wet tarmac. Free. Heading away from here.

The door swings open. It's Ruud. He crouches down. Touches her knee.

'Is everything OK, Veronica?'

His big hand is warm, the liver-spots clearly visible. How old is he really? Closer to seventy than sixty. He's worked here for twenty years, has seen and heard all the misery that can be seen and heard. Has definitely earned his pension. Yet he's still here. Why? *For the free coffee*, she's heard him say, and the laughter that always follows saves him from further questions. A smart trick. Something she ought to try herself.

She looks up at him and forces herself to smile. Tugs her sleeve down over her wrist. Ruud thinks she's scared, and at one level he's absolutely right. She's terrified. Utterly terrified. But that isn't the whole truth.

'Fine. I'm just trying to gather my thoughts a bit. Run through the routine,' she says, tapping the notepad on her lap.

'Good.' Ruud holds his hand out and helps her to her feet. 'How long has it been since you were last at work? Three months?'

Even though they've spent almost a week together he's still pretending he doesn't know every last detail of the arrangement. As if he isn't the one who has to make sure she sticks to it.

And, just as before, she plays along.

'Two months, two weeks and four days. Not that I'm counting.'

Ruud laughs. 'That's more like it. You'll soon see that this isn't much different to where you used to work.'

He leads her out into the meeting room. Drops his careful grip of her elbow just before the participants turn round.

Nine people, a few more than she was expecting on a Friday afternoon. Evasive glances, tentative smiles, brief nods of greeting. A feeling of hopelessness hangs over the room like a sticky veil, huddling in the dark corners where the fluorescent lights can't quite reach, stopping any oxygen getting in.

She forces herself to smile again, sits down on one of the chairs and opens her notepad. Her heart jumps into her throat, making her feel slightly sick. She can feel Ruud watching her from over by the wall, but doesn't look in that direction. She tries not to think about why he's here.

A deep breath. She feels inside her chest. Finds the ice without any problem.

'Hello, and welcome. My name is Veronica Lindh, and I'm a conversational therapist specialising in the treatment of grief. I worked for the Civic Centre for four years, but this is my first day with you here in the southern district.'

She is surprised by how steady her voice sounds. Alien, almost as if Veronica Lindh's voice isn't hers, which of course is partially true.

'This support group is for those of us who have lost someone close to us, someone we loved.'

All eyes are focused on her. Her heart is thudding against the layer of ice just below her ribcage. She imagines it growing slightly weaker with every beat. Beat after beat, until a crack opens up and the black water beneath becomes visible.

'I lost my mum when I was fourteen years old. One night she filled her coat pockets with stones, then walked out onto an ice-covered lake.'

She mustn't hesitate now. Mustn't stop, mustn't look up. Another breath. The cold gradually spreads through her chest.

'There was a man on the other side of the lake. He said Mum walked straight out, even though the sound of the ice cracking was unmistakeable. When he called out to her she stopped in the middle of the ice and looked at him. Then she was gone.'

She forces herself not to think about the gap in the ice. Imagines the ice closing up again, above her mum, above the crack in her chest. It freezes to solid armour.

She clears her throat and gently hugs the notepad. No one has the chance to see her hands shaking, not even Ruud.

'Mum chose to leave us,' she says. 'She left my dad, my older brother and me, and we had to cope on our own. It was many years before I was able to forgive her. Before I stopped asking the question you're all asking.'

She swallows a couple of times, feels her blood resume a texture far more pleasant than cold water. She's done it. She's offered herself up, and now it's time for the longed-for reward. She counts silently to ten, then turns to the person sitting closest to her. The grey-haired woman with the plait.

'Please.'

She nods to the woman and hears her take a deep breath. A different story, yet still very familiar.

Daughter, cancer, not yet thirty.

She puts on her sympathetic expression, makes notes on her pad. The pen moves quickly, turning the grief to ink. The grey-haired woman is crying. Tears roll quietly as her story unfolds, stopping for a moment at the rim of her glasses before carrying on down the woman's cheeks. More words.

Not fair, her whole life ahead of her. Miss her so much.

When the grey-haired woman has finished she takes her glasses off and wipes them with one of the cheap paper napkins. Then she folds it neatly and puts it in her handbag, carefully, as if her tears are made of glass and she wants to take them home. Put them in a glass-fronted cabinet like tiny, translucent pearls of grief.

The thought makes Veronica lose her concentration, and the next person has already stared talking. Lars, the man with the beard. More words, a harsher voice. She hurriedly makes some notes. Sucking up his story with her pen.

ANDERS DE LA MOTTE

Wife, car accident, drunk driver, brain damage, wrong treatment, never recovered.

No tears, just anger. Bitterness. She adds that to her pad. Her hand is moving more easily across the page now.

Hatred, fantasises about revenge, causing pain. Eye for an eye ... They all need to be punished, all of them, the drunk driver, the doctors, everyone!

Lars falls silent and takes a deep breath. At first he looks relieved, then ashamed. He mumbles something Veronica doesn't hear, then looks down at his hands. They're rough, callused, the skin cracked so deeply that the dirt and oil won't wash out. Dad's hands, Uncle Harald's. Her own hands are soft and smooth. Long fingers, better suited to a pen. Writing hands. Mum's hands. She pushes the thoughts aside and nods to the next participant to start talking.

They go clockwise around the circle, leaving the speakers sniffing and sobbing, fumbling with the paper tissues. Her pen scratches the page, faster and faster, just like the pulse pumping reward hormones through her body.

Tragedy, our family will never get over it. Never.

The minute hand moves mechanically round the yellowed clock-face on the wall. Every fifth minute the hand sticks slightly and stops for a couple of seconds before pulling free with an audible click.

When all the stories have been told, the word that everyone always says is at the bottom of the last page, in capitals. The question that hovers over the room, and which none of them can ever answer, no matter how many times they tell their stories.

WHY?

Veronica underlines it, rewrites the letters, the question mark, until the pen goes through the paper. She doesn't stop until the minute hand on the clock clicks one last time and the session is over.

The relief is immense, mixing with the endorphins that have already taken over her brain. Her left hand feels for her lower right arm again, scratching idly over the cotton and the long scar hidden beneath it.

Is it over already? she thinks. Then: When can I have more?

Chapter 2
Summer 1983

It was good rain, really. Not a storm that flattened crops, but soft, mild rain that gently moistened the ground and would stop at sunrise, so that the ears and leaves would be dry by lunchtime. Harvest rain, as the farmers around there called it. Good rain, and on any other summer night Chief of Police Krister Månsson and the men standing with him in the yard at Backagården would have welcomed it.

He pushed his cap back and ran his hand over his forehead. Even though he had loosened his tie a good while back, his blue uniform shirt was still sticking to his neck.

He had conducted searches before, he told himself. Or had at least practised them when he'd done his officer's training a few years ago. It was all a matter of planning, organisation and leadership. Of methodically ticking off every imaginable alternative until you found what you were looking for. But in darkness and rain that was easier said than done.

Some of the men had left their cars running, parked in a circle around him in the yard in front of the Nilssons' house.

Their headlights illuminated the growing crowd of people, turning them into silhouettes, their legs and lower bodies clearly lit up, but their faces ghostly and difficult to make out. But he didn't need to see them. They all recognised each other. They all knew each other.

Månsson looked around at the faces. He tugged slightly at the creased jacket of his uniform, a little too tight and on the point of succumbing to the rain. He adjusted his cap and raised his hand.

'OK, listen up!'

Neither his words nor the hand gesture managed to still the buzz of voices around him. He wondered if he should climb onto the back of the pick-up beside him, but realised that the metal sides were too high and slippery to risk his dignity. So he tried raising his voice and sounding more authoritative instead.

'Everyone, listen!' The result was only marginally better.

'Shut up, for fuck's sake! Månsson's got something to say. We're wasting time while you stand around talking shit.'

The harsh voice belonged to a lanky man who had jumped up onto the pick-up behind Månsson without any problem. Harald Aronsson, the boy's uncle. The chatter stopped at once and the men crowded closer around Månsson and the pick-up.

He cleared his throat and nodded appreciatively at Aronsson, but got no reaction.

'Most of you have already heard what's happened, and I can understand that you're eager to get on with the search,' he began. 'But to make sure we're all on the same page, I'm going to give you a brief summary of what we know at present.'

He paused to give the late arrivals the chance to come closer.

'So, we're looking for little Billy Nilsson, almost five years old. He was last seen by his mother just before eight o'clock, meaning that he's been gone . . .'

Månsson looked at his watch, a square digital contraption Malin had given him to mark their twentieth wedding anniversary. The only one of the four protruding metal buttons he understood was the one that made the little screen light up, which was actually quite handy in the dark.

'. . . almost five hours now. His family have already searched the garden, the house, the barn and outhouse . . . I mean, cowshed,' he quickly corrected himself, 'before they sounded the alarm at eleven o'clock. Just before midnight the police started searching the garden with a tracker dog.'

He gestured towards the house at the other end of the yard, and to his satisfaction most of them turned their heads.

'The dog found a gap beneath the fence leading to a field of maize at the far end of the garden. Unfortunately it lost the trail there, probably because of the rain, or because Billy's parents and brother and sister had already been there.'

He lowered his hand and waited until everyone was looking at him again.

'So it looks like the boy crawled under the fence and got lost among the vegetation. As you all know, the maize is as tall as a man at this time of year, so it's easy to get lost out in the field, especially in the dark. This is where we need your help. We're going to form four search parties . . .'

When Månsson had finished the briefing he noted with relief that everyone in the yard followed his instructions. They quickly split into teams and left the farm either on foot or in their cars, each group led by one of his uniformed officers.

They were all keen to get going as soon as possible. Most had children of their own and could easily imagine the hell the Nilsson family must be going through. But it was also about the collective relief the whole district would feel when little Billy was reunited with his mother – wet, frozen and frightened, but alive. Because that was obviously what was going to happen. They were all counting on it, and some of them may even have been feeling a measure of excitement, Månsson thought. They were also looking forward to the possibility that they might be the one who found the boy. Whoever found Billy Nilsson would never have to pay for his own drinks, either in the local pub or at the park pavilion, Harald Aronsson would see to that.

Månsson had been chief of police in Reftinge for four years now. He moved down here with his family when he got fed up of the nightshifts, drunk drivers and crazies in Norrköping. He was tired of being overtaken in his career by younger, hungrier officers. In Reftinge, right on the edge of the Skåne Plain, he was free from all that. He was in charge of twelve police officers and two civilian employees – women who answered the phone, received reports and issued weapons licences.

He himself had grown up in a similar agricultural area on the Östgöta Plain, and knew how things worked in the countryside, which was presumably one of the reasons why he'd got the job. In his experience, people who lived in the country worked hard and helped each other out. They largely stuck to the Ten Commandments, which meant that Reftinge's crime figures mostly consisted of burglaries, illegal hunting, drink-driving and traffic offences. As far as the last two were concerned, he knew his officers were more inclined to be lenient than strict. There was a sort of tacit agreement between the inhabitants and the forces of law and order that had been established long before his time. Out in the countryside people needed their cars. No car meant no job, and no job meant no food on the table. And he didn't want to be the person who stripped a family of both employment and food. Being an outsider was hard enough as it was, not just for him but for Malin and the children. It took time to settle in and be accepted, not least when you had a different dialect.

He had certainly done his best. He had got used to being called *Månn-senn* rather than *Måån-sson*. He had switched from Gevalia coffee to Skåne Roast, and had learned to call lunch dinner. He, Malin and the children had all joined the local football club, and he went to the swimming baths at seven o'clock every Thursday to sit in the sauna with the old boys. His efforts had paid off. Last season Malin was appointed vice-treasurer of the club, and he became head coach of the under-fourteen boys team. And early last spring he had been invited to join one of the big hunting teams. He was looking forward to the autumn, he genuinely couldn't wait.

Before then things were likely to liven up a bit, towards the end of the harvest when the men were worn out and fractious. Fights, drunkenness and criminal damage, an assault or two if things got really bad. But it didn't usually get any worse than that. In fact before this evening there hadn't been a single incident that had demanded much of him at all in his four years as chief of police, which suited him fine. He preferred to keep a low profile. Drink his morning coffee in peace and quiet while he read the local paper and magazines about country life and hunting. Go to meetings of the local chamber of commerce, the Red Cross and the local council. Burn a bit of hash at parents' evenings so that all the parents knew what to look out for in case any enterprising youngster managed to bring a lump home from Denmark. Run annual bicycle and traffic awareness courses in local schools. That was the sort of police work he preferred. The sort he was good at.

The realisation that all eyes were now on him had hit home when the reserves they'd called in were gathered in the yard. An anxious lump had formed in his stomach, and only grew larger as the number of men rose. Everyone was looking to him, trusting he would help them put an end to the Nilsson family's nightmare.

Månsson looked back at the main house, where every lamp seemed to be lit now. Two children, a girl and a boy, the same ages as his kids. He tried to remember the names of Billy's siblings. He had known their father's name, Ebbe, for some time. Ebbe Nilsson was a calm, thoughtful man who didn't make a lot of fuss, one of the ones who used to sit quietly on the lower benches of the sauna while other men talked. His brother-in-law, Harald Aronsson, for instance.

And everyone knew the children's mother, Magdalena Nilsson, née Aronsson, of course. The very first beauty queen in the district, whose black and white coronation photograph was still hanging in the lobby of the council building even though it was over twenty years ago now. That was probably as much to do with Magdalena's surname as her beauty. The Aronsson family were a big noise in the district, which didn't exactly make the current situation any easier.

Månsson was still trying to remember the names of the two children up there in the window, but no matter how hard he tried they wouldn't come. Without really knowing why, he raised one hand in a wave, but neither of the children showed any sign of responding. They just stood perfectly still in the window, watching him. Waiting for him to find their little brother. Make everything right again.

Chapter 3

Veronica generally regards herself as a good person. She sorts her recycling, pays her bills on time and gives money to deserving causes now and then.

She hasn't been to church for many years, though. She doesn't like the memories that religious buildings summon up. The same memories that mean she only calls her dad once or twice a month. She keeps putting off phoning, until her guilty conscience gets the better of her. It always takes at least eight rings before he answers. Then comes the click as he lifts the receiver and the seconds of silence when they both, against all reason, hope to hear a different voice at the other end. Then the disappointment as reality sinks in, a disappointment that neither of them quite manages to hide and which no amount of small talk in the world can dissipate.

She hasn't been home to Reftinge for years, not for any birthdays, christenings or funerals, even though she really ought to have gone. She knows that the people there pay attention to that sort of thing. Talk about it.

That irritates her, just like it irritates her that she still thinks of Reftinge as home, even though more than fifteen years have passed since she left.

She and Ruud are standing on the broad flight of steps in front of the grey, 1960s bulk of the Civic Centre. It's stopped raining, and the heat stored in the tarmac, metal and concrete around them has already dried out most of the moisture. The fresh smell earlier on has vanished, replaced by the stench of rubbish, food and exhaust fumes. Normal summer air in the city. She closes her eyes for a few seconds, enjoying the feeling of wellbeing that is only slowly ebbing away.

'Thanks for today. See you next week?' The grey-haired woman's farewell is a statement that somehow manages to sound like a question. As if the woman isn't altogether sure if there are going to be any more meetings.

Veronica nods, squeezes the woman's hand. It's as fragile and bony as a baby bird.

'See you next week.'

The grey-haired woman goes down the four steps, half turns and gives a noncommittal wave. Then she clutches the handbag containing her pearls of grief tightly to her chest before setting off along the pavement.

They stand and watch as the woman walks towards the metro station.

'How do you think it went?' Ruud says, without looking at her.

She shrugs. 'OK.' Her answer is almost as true as it is a lie.

'Hmm.' He pulls out a tub of chewing tobacco and tucks a portion behind his top lip. Nudges it into place with the tip of his tongue. 'You didn't ask many questions.'

She shrugs her shoulders again.

'I didn't want to break the flow.' She glances at him, regretting her slightly abrupt tone. A bit of self-awareness is probably in order. She's the one under evaluation, after all. 'But obviously I'd appreciate any feedback,' she adds.

He pulls a face, unless he's merely adjusting the chewing tobacco.

'If you ask questions, then the others usually dare to do the same,' he says. 'It's important to get a conversation going within the group, not just a series of monologues. So that everyone can participate. That's the whole point of group therapy.' He turns towards her with a slightly wry smile. 'But you know that already, of course. You're just a bit out of practice. After a couple more sessions everything will run smoothly.'

She nods, and stops herself from meeting his gaze so he won't see how relieved she feels. The grey-haired woman has disappeared from view, slipping away between the buildings like a frightened mouse.

'What you said about your mum,' he says in a low voice. 'I didn't know anyone saw when she . . .'

'One of the workers was out looking for her.' Veronica is still surprised by how steady her voice is. That she manages to reply to his question and simultaneously make it clear that she'd rather not be asked any more.

Ruud doesn't let himself be put off. 'Terrible story . . .'

He obviously wants her to say more, confide in him even though they've only known each other a week or so. But she has no inclination to challenge herself any further today, not for Ruud's or anyone else's sake. She carries on looking along the street instead. After a while he gets the hint and turns away to spit through his teeth.

They stand in silence for a while as the shadows cast by the buildings grow longer. The afternoon traffic is rumbling on the motorway a couple of blocks back.

'You're going to get through this, Veronica,' Ruud says quietly. 'What happened in the spring was an unavoidable bump in the road that you just had to get past. Just take it calmly and focus on the job and everything will soon be back to normal again.'

She still doesn't respond. In some ways she's relieved that the charade they've been acting out for the past week is over. That he's finally stopped pretending he doesn't know the reason why she was transferred. But that doesn't mean she wants to talk to him about it. She's already turned herself inside out a hundred times in the past few months.

Why do you think you reacted the way you did, Veronica? What can you do to avoid this sort of situation arising again? What emotions do you associate with what you did?

A motorbike turns into the street in front of them. The sound of the engine is a subdued hacking. The biker is wearing jeans and a brown leather jacket. His helmet is matt black, the dark visor impenetrable. The bike glides slowly past them, barely moving enough to stay upright. Just as it passes them the rider turns his head. Looks straight at her.

She's no model, whatever that might mean. But she keeps herself in shape, has long legs, and a look about her eyes and mouth that she inherited from her mum, and which becomes more pronounced when she wears make-up and has her hair down. A sort of vulnerability, a hint that there might be something wrong with her. A surprising number of men think that kind of thing is attractive. When she was younger she used to exploit it. But that's all in the past now, in a different place, a different country. These days she keeps her mouth straight and her head high. Speaks softly but firmly, and looks people in the eye. Even so, it still takes surprisingly little to get men going. A gesture, a tilt of the head. Sometimes just a glance.

The man on the motorbike goes on looking at her as he rides past, seems to nod slightly, as if they know each other. Ruud evidently seems to think so.

'Someone you know?' His tone is meant to sound amused, but she detects a note of irritation.

'No.' She shakes her head to convince both him and herself, but for some reason her heart has started to beat faster.

She watches the man as he rides off, staring as he heads down the street. Suddenly he accelerates. The roar of the engine makes her start. It echoes between the buildings, sounding like the roar of a wild animal.

The noise fades as the motorbike quickly disappears from view.

'Perhaps it's someone trying to pluck up courage? Wanted to see how dangerous you look before daring to join the group?' Ruud nudges her in the side with his elbow and grins.

She nudges him back, feels the tension ease and smiles at him gratefully.

'If you help me lock up, I'll give you a lift home,' he says. 'Deal?'

'Deal.'

He turns and starts to walk back towards the door. She stands where she is for a couple of seconds, looking off in the direction where the motorbike disappeared. The sound is still just about audible as a distant growl.

Chapter 4
Summer 1983

Månsson had set up his command post on the raised terrace at the back of the house. From there he had a view of what little that could be seen of the garden in the darkness, and could hear the occasional cry from the search parties out in the fields around Backagården.

Bi-lly

Biii-llyy

He had spread a large map out across the garden table and had got hold of a paraffin lamp that he'd hung from the awning above his head. His police radio was tuned to the designated channel, and as the search teams passed the reference points they had agreed on he marked them off on the map. Just as he had predicted, the tall maize, darkness and rain were making it difficult for the teams to orientate themselves, and the police officers who were leading the search had to keep stopping to change course or gather in lost members of their teams.

The terrace door behind him opened quietly and Ebbe Nilsson came out. He was carrying a tray containing a flask, some mugs and a plate of sandwiches that he put down on the part of the table that wasn't covered by the map.

'I thought you might need something to warm you up.'

Månsson gratefully accepted a cup of coffee, then felt a pang of guilt. Ebbe Nilsson's little boy was missing, the whole family was in shock, but the man had still taken the time to make coffee for him. And had even thought to bring him something to eat. He studied Nilsson discreetly as he bit into one of the sausage sandwiches.

The man's eyes were wet, his face white and deeply lined. The shadows and weak light from the lamp emphasised his harrowed appearance. But he was standing tall and seemed fairly composed.

'How's it going?' he asked.

Månsson gestured towards the garden and maize field.

'We're doing what we can. The darkness and rain aren't helping. But we're going to find him, you'll see.' That last sentence slipped out before he managed to stop it. He knew better than that. He'd been in the police long enough to know that you didn't make any promises about things that were beyond your control. Yet that was pretty much what he had done. Out of sympathy, he told himself, but he suspected that wasn't the whole truth.

His radio suddenly crackled and he turned round. No message, just a burst of static that stopped almost as soon as it had started. Månsson swallowed the last of the sandwich.

'How's Magdalena?' He nodded towards the upper floor.

'She's sleeping,' Nilsson said curtly. He must have realised, because he quickly changed his tone. 'She was so upset she took a tranquiliser. In her confusion she took a double dose, so now she's fast asleep. Maybe it's just as well for her to get a break from everything. Billy means the world to her—' Nilsson's voice broke and the rest of the sentence was swallowed by the drumming of the rain on the awning.

'And the other children?' Månsson said, then realised that the question could be taken several ways. But Månsson picked the right one.

'Mattias and Vera have gone to bed, but to be honest I doubt they're asleep. If it weren't for them I'd be out there too.' He pointed towards the maize field where the light from the torches occasionally flickered.

One of the search parties must have turned back towards the farm. Månsson consulted the map and let out a sigh when he realised that team B was searching an area beside the fence that had already been searched earlier in the night. He picked up his radio, but stopped with it in his hand. Nilsson's shoulders had slumped, his eyes were staring at the ground and his mouth was half open as if he was about to say something. But no sound came out. The man suddenly looked completely crushed, ready to collapse at any moment.

Månsson cleared his throat. Tried to think of something to say.

'You're more use here, Ebbe,' he said. Then, after hesitating for a few seconds, he patted the man rather feebly on the shoulder.

'Any of us can go out and search, but you need to take care of Magdalena and the children. Besides, someone has to be here when we find Billy.'

Again, he had promised more than he should, but at least his words and gesture seemed to have some effect. Ebbe Nilsson closed his mouth, then slowly nodded his head.

The police radio crackled again.

'Are you there, Månsson?'

'Listening!' he said.

'Berglund here, search team B. The dog-handler's found something out in the field, approximately twenty metres away from the gap under the fence.'

'What?' Månsson held his breath. He looked at Ebbe Nilsson. The man straightened up and seemed to regain some of his energy.

The radio stuttered a couple of times, cutting off Berglund's voice.

'—hoe,' was all they could make out.

'Say again!' Månsson said, leaning over the map and trying to identify the location. 'What have you found, Berglund?'

The radio crackled again.

'A small blue and white shoe.'

Chapter 5

Ruud stops his Volvo outside her building. The smell of the pine air-freshener hanging from the rear-view mirror is so pungent that it makes her nose itch. He unfastens his seatbelt and for a moment she wonders if he's trying to invite himself in for coffee.

She's on the point of stammering a feeble excuse when he digs about in his trouser pocket and with some effort pulls out his tub of chewing tobacco before fastening the belt again.

'See you on Monday,' he says. 'Breakfast meeting, nine o'clock.'

'See you then.'

She's out of the car before he has time to put the tobacco in his mouth. She stops with her hand on the car door.

'Thanks,' she says.

'No problem, it's not far out of my way.'

She's about to say something else, then sees him wink at her.

'It will be easier next week, Veronica. I promise.'

Her flat could belong to anyone. Forty square metres furnished with a mixture of flea-market finds and IKEA. Kitchen and living room to the right, bedroom on the left.

Practical, clean, unfussy. No family photographs, pictures or posters. No scented candles, no rashly purchased Buddha statues, dried flowers or fridge magnets with inspirational slogans like 'Carpe diem' or 'Today is the first day of the rest of your life'.

Surprisingly impersonal, as an idiot with tattoos on his neck whom she had dated a long time ago, way before Leon, called the flat. He was one of those you-just-have-to-take-me-as-I-am people. The sort of people who think they're more genuine than everyone else simply because they lack something as fundamental as basic manners. And his way of fucking was pretty much what you'd expect. Selfish and unimaginative, as she pointed out when she dumped him.

He didn't take the criticism terribly well. Her battered old car ended up with long scratches along the driver's door from his keys, but by now the rust had almost made them blend into the paint. An indistinct souvenir of an old mistake.

The air in the flat is warm and stuffy. She undoes the top button of her blouse, opens one of the living-room windows and leans out. Through the leaves of the trees outside she sees Ruud's Volvo slowly drive away.

It's only a couple of degrees cooler outside than inside the room, and the air is just as stagnant. She opens the other window as well, then the narrow window in the bedroom facing the courtyard at the rear, in a vain attempt to get some sort of through-draught.

The fridge light flickers in a disconcerting way. Probably about to give out. Something else to add to the to-do list.

The fridge contains half a bottle of Ramlösa, a few sachets of soy sauce and an old ready meal with an unpromising best-before date. She stands in front of the open fridge door for a while, enjoying the cool before she takes out the bottle of Ramlösa. The mineral water has gone flat, and tastes almost salty.

An unavoidable bump in the road.

Ruud means well. He and the HR department think they know exactly who she is and what's best for her. Whereas in fact they have no idea.

So why has she submitted to their authority? Why didn't she accept the terms the union managed to negotiate and just leave?

Good questions, and all the more relevant after today, but the answers remain the same. Because she made up her mind to stop running away the moment anything gets difficult. That sounds good – mature and responsible – but the main reason she's stayed and has agreed to all their demands is considerably less noble.

She glances at the phone on the kitchen worktop. The red light isn't flashing. No messages. She wasn't expecting anything different, but there's still something about that unflinching red light that depresses her. The buzz from the therapy session has faded now and her body feels weak and sad. She briefly considers picking up the receiver. Letting her fingers dial the forbidden number just to hear Leon's voice when he answers. But of course she doesn't. She's not an idiot, and she gets annoyed with herself when she thinks about the fact that she daren't get a mobile phone, seeing as text messages almost write and send themselves.

She goes into the bathroom. Clothes in a heap on the floor: the long-sleeved white shirt that makes her look like a nun, the black trousers, cotton underpants she buys in packs of five from H&M. Cheap, plain garments, pretty much as impersonal as her home.

The water is tepid even at the coldest setting. She lets it run down her body, down the jagged red scar that runs almost all the way down her lower right arm. Within a few years that too will have faded, blended in, like the scratches on her car. An indistinct souvenir of an old mistake.

Afterwards she feels better, as if the water has washed her gloomy thoughts away. She wraps herself in the white towelling dressing-gown she and Leon stole from the cosy little hotel in Trosa where he told her he loved for the first time, then takes her cigarettes and an ashtray and goes and sits in the alcove by the open window facing the street. She's supposed to have stopped smoking. That's part of the treatment plan she's worked out for herself. No stimulants, no tobacco or alcohol. Especially not the latter.

The streetlamps have come on now. She can see clouds of insects buzzing around them. For a moment she thinks about the moths back home that would sometimes slip in through the terrace door and dance round and round the kitchen light, wings buzzing.

Then the anxious look on Mum's face that their dance prompted.

The memory catches her by surprise and she lights a cigarette, blowing the smoke out into the summer night. Tries to think of something else. Not follow Mum out onto the ice.

She comes to the end of the cigarette sooner than she expects, so she stubs it out in the ashtray and considers lighting another. Before she can make up her mind she notices something a little way along the street. A faint light flickering for a few seconds before it goes out, replaced by a glowing pinprick. A neighbour who's snuck out for an evening smoke, probably.

Curious, she leans a little further out the window, staring through the foliage of the trees along the street in an attempt to get a glimpse of who it is. The only indication that there's anyone there is the little glowing point of light that gets stronger then weaker as the person smokes.

She guesses that whoever it is has crept outside for a surreptitious cigarette even though they promised their partner that they'd stopped a long time ago. She imagines them blowing the cigarette smoke away from their clothes, with a packet of mints in their pocket to conceal their deceit.

The thought makes her smile. She likes the idea of sitting up here, silent and invisible, while the smoker down below is trying to protect his or her secret. It gives her a sense of having the upper hand, of control – excitement, almost – similar to what she felt earlier in the therapy session.

The glow flares again, then falls in an arc towards the gutter. The cigarette break seems to be over, time for the smoker to go back inside. But nothing happens. The smoker doesn't seem to have moved. She leans out a little bit further, and thinks she can see the dark silhouette of a figure through the leaves. A paler patch appears, a face tilted upwards in her direction. She starts and quickly pulls back. Feels suddenly exposed. Caught out.

Darling,

I've never felt so alive as I do now. It's as if I've just woken up from a long sleep, as if I've spent far too long in some sort of no man's land, somewhere between sleeping and waking. I'm awake at last now. With you at last.

I live for our drives together. Our brief excursions together, when we can be ourselves.

People talk about you sometimes, as I'm sure you know. Say things that aren't nice. I can't help smiling at them in secret, because I know they're wrong. I know you better than anyone, I know who you are behind that hard mask. But we have to be careful, my darling. All eyes are focused on us, and no one wishes us well. No one.

Chapter 6

Summer 1983

'OK, we've been at this for over an hour now. High time to stop for a drink, what do you say?'

'I wouldn't say no.' Sailor looked on as Rask pulled the drag-anchor out of the water and hung it over the railing of the little plastic boat. The younger man slapped the back of his neck and wiped the mixture of dead gnats and sweat on his trousers before pulling a vodka bottle from the bag on the deck between their feet.

'Hot as Africa,' he declared unnecessarily, and passed the bottle to Sailor. Even though the overgrown pool of water was no more than ten metres in diameter, and therefore almost always shaded by the trees growing around it, the heat was oppressive. Insects danced across the stagnant surface, occasionally braving the small patches where the sunlight pushed through the vegetation, changing the colour of the water from black to dark green.

Sailor didn't respond. He unscrewed the lid and took a couple of large swigs. He noted that it was homemade. He handed the bottle back to Rask and leaned over the short oars. The younger man drank roughly twice as much as him, but Sailor didn't say anything. It was Rask's bottle, after all, his moonshine, and making comments about the thirst of the person being generous wouldn't be appropriate.

'Ah, that hit the spot,' Rask said. He stretched his hands above his head, showing the sweaty patches under his arms. 'I can hardly notice the stink of this fucking puddle now. We should have had a drink before we started.'

Sailor murmured in agreement.

'You should be feeling right at home,' Rask said. 'When did you get back from sea?'

'Last spring.'

'How long were you away this time?'

'Seven years.'

'And before that?'

'I left in '62, when the mine closed. Last time I was home was '76, when my mother died.'

'That's a long time to be away. You must have had a woman in every port. A proper Fritiof Andersson.'

Sailor shrugged his shoulders. He knew Rask was teasing him. Most people in town did. Made fun of how introverted he was, how awkward. Of his fondness for drink. He glanced furtively at the bottle between the other man's boots.

Rask took out a tub of chewing tobacco and nodded towards the green strip between the field and the water just a few metres away. Among the nettles and grasses lay the muddy remains of a bicycle, two half-rotten logs and a rusty bucket.

'Fucking impressive catch so far. These old marl pits have been used as rubbish dumps since the war. I don't know why Aronsson didn't fill them in years ago. He's not usually the sort to cling on to the past.'

Rask tucked a generous portion of tobacco under his lip but showed no sign of sharing this time. Sailor glanced at the bottle again, thinking that he'd rather have another drink anyway.

'Aronsson's probably waiting for the council,' Rask went on. 'Hoping they'll stump up the money for it.'

He put the tub of tobacco away again and wiped his fingers on his check flannel shirt.

'You got any idea why Månsson wanted us to drag here in particular? Do the police seriously think Nilsson's little lad made his way through two kilometres of maize in the dark and rain, climbed over three stone walls and a tarmac road, then carried on through the sugar-beet for another hundred metres?' He gestured over his shoulder with his thumb towards the field, where the trail left from dragging the boat was clearly visible against the green plants. 'Every little kid round here knows to watch out for fire defence ponds and marl pits. My dad used to scare the shit out of me with stories about them. He said they were bottomless and full of leeches.'

Sailor let out another grunt of agreement. He was still casting glances at the bottle. Maybe Rask would pick up the hint? Decide they should have another swig before they carried on. Sadly his attention seemed to be fully occupied with his thoughts about the Aronsson family.

'Then there's the whole business of the maize. If Ebbe Nilsson had sown peas on that strip behind the house like any other farmer would have done, the boy could never have got lost. But obviously that was Aronsson's decision. Nilsson's never taken a decision for himself in his life. Christ, he's probably not even allowed to go for a shit without asking his brother-in-law, or maybe his wife.'

Rask cleared his throat and hawked a gobbet of yellow-brown saliva into the dark water. Sailor said nothing.

'Did you notice how few of us there were this morning? Not even half as many as the first few days. No one wants to be the one who finds the boy. Not now. So they let people like you and me do the shit work. Because we're dependent on Aronsson. The only people still looking for the boy are Aronsson's workers or his tenants. Or customers of his. Or people who owe him money.'

Rask spat again. The heavy globule hit the water with a splash, scaring away some pond skaters and forming a couple of lazy rings that were almost immediately swallowed by the sluggish water. He picked the bottle up from the deck.

'There's something else I've been thinking as well.' Rask sat there with the bottle in his hands.

'What's that?' Sailor said when he realised that the lid wasn't going to come off until he answered.

'We've been scouring the countryside for almost a week now, the police have been out with dogs, and that walking disaster Månsson even managed to get a police helicopter here from Malmö. And apart from that shoe we haven't seen any trace of the lad. It's like the ground's swallowed him up.'

Rask opened the bottle and took a couple of thoughtful swigs instead of offering it to Sailor.

'Mm . . .' Sailor licked his lips.

'I can't help thinking something else must have happened.' Rask took another swig and looked up at him invitingly.

Sailor tried to figure out what he was supposed to say. It took him a few seconds before he realised.

'You mean someone might have taken the boy intentionally? Who, though?'

Rask shrugged and finally handed the bottle over. Sailor took a couple of large swigs. Then another one, just in case there wasn't enough for another round. The alcohol burned his throat, bringing with it a wonderful warmth as it made its way to his stomach.

'There are plenty of people who don't like the Aronsson family,' Rask said. 'Most of the money Harald Aronsson used to buy up all the land round here came from his father's dealings during the war, everyone knows that. Assar Aronsson was a tight-fisted sod, he never made a bad deal. Harald's more polished than his father. I've heard he's got contacts in the bank, he knows exactly who's short of cash and would have no choice but to accept a disgracefully low offer for a bit of forest, farmland or property. He's getting rich at others' expense. But despite that, the whole family sit in the front pew in church. Aronsson, his sister, her miserable wretch of a husband and their kids. Water-combed hair, fancy clothes, sanctimonious as hell. But no one ever dares say a word. And as for his sister – that's another whole story no one ever mentions.'

Rask made an impatient gesture and Sailor reluctantly handed the bottle back to him.

'I went to school with Magdalena Aronsson. She was pretty damn attractive even then. Red hair, long legs, well developed in all the right places. There were plenty of us who tried our luck. Magda wasn't exactly unsullied goods, if you know what I mean.'

Rask grinned, revealing some of the chewing tobacco. Sailor did his best to smile back.

'Magda liked to be courted, she liked flirting. And old man Aronsson and her big brother watched her like hawks. Anyone who came a bit too close got a serious seeing to from Harald and his gang. I had to lie about how I got those black eyes when I got home, say I'd fallen off my moped. But Magda went on encouraging me. Leading me on. When old Aronsson died I wasn't the only bloke who hoped the path was clear at last.'

He spat for a third time.

'But Magda took off to Copenhagen. Presumably looking for something better than us peasants. So it's something of an irony that she ended up marrying Ebbe Nilsson, her brother's best friend, which is about as close to in-breeding as you can get, right?'

Rask drained the bottle, then tossed it into the water. Sailor looked on with regret.

'So, yeah . . .' Rask grabbed the rope, unhooked the anchor from the railing and dropped it back in the water. 'There are plenty of people round here who'd have good reason to want to give the Aronsson family a bloody nose. If our chief of police had any balls at all, he'd have made a list and ticked them off one at a time instead of making us do pointless stuff like this. And you and I both know who he should have started with, don't we? Your hunting buddy, Tommy Rooth.'

Sailor didn't respond, just watched the line run between Rask's hands, little by little, until the anchor reached the bottom far below in the muddy darkness. He took hold of the oars and pulled rather lazily at them. The boat glided half a metre through the water, then stopped abruptly when the rope pulled tight.

'Got something,' Rask said. 'What sort of crap do you reckon it is this time, then? Fish, fowl, or something in between?'

He started to pull at the line but it barely moved.

'Back up a bit,' he commanded. Bracing himself against the bottom of the boat, he tried again. Whatever the anchor had got hold of, it didn't want to budge. 'Damn!'

Rask stood up and took the strain again before trying to pull the line.

The movement caused the boat to lean and for a moment Sailor thought it was going to tip over. Then it suddenly righted itself.

'Whatever it is, it's big,' Rask groaned as he went on tugging. 'A log, probably.' He carried on pulling at the line. Sticky green slime was sticking to it as it was hauled back into the boat.

Sailor could see the water starting to move. Reluctantly, as if it didn't want to let go of whatever was caught in the anchor. He realised he was holding his breath.

'OK, here we go,' Rask said with a groan.

The water started to bubble. Something dark came into view below the surface, followed by something lighter. An object that made Sailor's stomach clench. Head, shoulders, something that looked like an arm.

Without warning the drag-anchor suddenly let go of the bundle and Rask tumbled backwards. He hit his head on the bench and the boat rocked wildly to starboard. Dark water poured over the side and Sailor leaped to his feet to shift the weight the other way. Too late. The water dragged the side of the boat down and the thick, stinking sludge swallowed the boat, Rask and Sailor himself.

Chapter 7

She knows she's an addict. Between the ages of eighteen and twenty-five she tried most things: ecstasy and coke at parties, weed and benzos to come down afterwards. And since then she hasn't been entirely clean either, if she's really honest. But it wasn't until she started training to become a therapist that she discovered the sort of drug that worked best for her. Other people's grief.

The Friday group consists of eight people. Most of the same people come on both Fridays and Mondays, so she's managed to learn most of their names by now. Apart from grief therapy, the past week has also offered two groups of alcoholics, a group for addictive gamblers and another for depressed unemployed people. Even if that sort of misery isn't the same as pure grief, the months she was away have left her sufficiently receptive for the endorphins to flow. And she's in almost complete control of the ice now. She can open up a crack, just enough for the group to see that she's one of them, then quickly close it again before she risks being dragged down into the depths.

Ruud is still hovering at the edge of the room from time to time, but he's eased up on the monitoring and spends most of his time in his office. That suits her fine, it gives her more of an opportunity to focus on her own interests.

Elsa, the grey-haired woman with the pearl tears, has been talking again about her daughter who died of cancer, and her grief has gained another half page in the notepad.

Sture, a pensioner with a thin combover and flaking skin, has just started to speak when the door opens and a blond man in his mid-twenties walks in. He doesn't hesitate by the door like all the others, but walks straight across the worn carpet. He seems to know exactly where he's going and why.

Sture is talking about his grief at losing his brother, but Veronica is no longer listening. There's something about the new arrival that catches her attention. He's undeniably handsome, broad-shouldered and slim. His skin is tanned, his eyes are bright blue, and when he notices her looking at him he smiles. One sleeve of his T-shirt is rolled up, and beneath it she can make out the rectangular outline of a packet of cigarettes. He must have picked that up from a James Dean film, but unlike most people who try it, he's got the confidence to carry it off.

For a moment she feels a tingle just below her midriff and a dry voice in her head announces exactly how many months it has been since she had sex with anyone but herself.

The man nods at her, pulls out one of the chairs and sits down. She forces herself to look away, to focus on Sture and his dead brother again. Forces her pen to carry on sucking up his story. But all of a sudden it doesn't feel anywhere near as satisfying as it did a few minutes ago. The grief doesn't seem to want to stick to the page now, and she finds herself glancing repeatedly at the blond man. He's leaning forward on his chair with his elbows on his knees, and appears to be listening intently to what Sture is saying. His aura is so different to the others' that the rest of the group's attention is drawn to him like the moths drawn to the streetlamp outside the window of her flat.

Eventually even Sture realises what's going on. He falls silent and stares dumbly in front of him for a few moments, as if he's not sure what to do. She comes to his rescue before it all gets too embarrassing.

'Thank you, Sture.'

The other participants murmur quietly. It should now be Mia's turn to speak. Her husband died in a workplace accident, the tragic nature of which would ordinarily have warranted almost an entire page of the pad. But everyone is looking at the blond-haired man, even Mia, so she decides to bend the rules slightly.

'I see we have a new member – welcome! My name is Veronica Lindh, I'm a conversational therapist.' She nods towards the man and is rewarded with a smile that looks a little too relaxed in the circumstances. 'You probably already know, but everyone in this group has lost someone close to them. By sharing our grief, we try to work through it so that we can start to move on. We ask each other questions, but never about details, just about how we feel. We're careful to show respect and empathy towards each other.'

She pauses, half expecting his smile to fade, then for him to stand up and apologise for getting the wrong time and group.

But instead he carries on smiling his slightly too charming smile, as if to confirm that he is exactly where he should be. She turns to a new page in her pad, glancing around quickly to see if Ruud is present, but fortunately he's nowhere in sight.

'Would you like to introduce yourself and tell us why you're here?'

She puts pen to paper and waits.

'Hello, everyone. I'm Isak . . .' The man leaves a brief pause, as if he isn't sure if he should give his surname. 'When I was five, six years old, I lost my best friend. He disappeared and I never found out what really happened. Nothing was the same after that, not for my family or the little village where we lived. It was as if there was a big vacuum that no one could quite fill. I still think about him a lot. Wonder what happened to him.'

Isak's accent suggests that he comes from somewhere further north, but there's something about the rhythm of his speech that doesn't entirely support that. He glances at her, as if waiting for guidance before going on. But she sits motionless. The sense of wellbeing conjured by the earlier stories is gone now, and she can hear the ice start to move.

Isak waits a little longer for her to say something, and is about to go on when the bitter bearded man called Lars opens his mouth.

'You're saying your friend *disappeared*?' His tone is sharp but still interested. Lars has never addressed anything said by another member of the group before, preferring instead just to voice his own anger and revenge fantasies.

Isak leans back in his chair. The expression on his face is no longer quite as confident, and his smile looks slightly strained now.

'Well . . . He was out playing one evening. When his mum called him in, he didn't come. The whole village spent over a week looking for him, but he was never found. He was just . . . gone.'

The sound of the ice is growing louder, swallowing the last remnants of gratification provided by the earlier speakers. She is about to move on to another participant when Lars asks another question, one that changes everything.

'You mean like Billy Nilsson?' Lars sounds almost excited. He turns to address the other members of the group. 'You remember him, don't you? That boy who went missing in the early eighties?'

A murmur goes through the group. She ought to intervene, take control of the conversation. But she can't.

Lars gets to his feet, and now there's life in his otherwise vacant eyes. He steps forward into the circle, seeking support from the others. 'The story of Billy Nilsson's disappearance was treated like a soap opera by the tabloids. People hardly talked about anything else. Billy was almost five years old, lived out in the sticks in Skåne. Is that who you're talking about? Was Billy your friend?'

Isak is squirming uncomfortably now, trying to catch her eye. Lars has broken the rules. He's encouraging the others to do the same, and she should have stepped in and stopped him already. Instead she is sitting perfectly still on her chair. Her head and body are stiff with the chill pumping through her veins.

'He was abducted, wasn't he?' a high-pitched voice says from her right. It belongs to an acne-scarred woman in her fifties. Annika, or possibly Anita. Veronica's brain has suddenly lost their names.

Lars throws his arms out eagerly to encourage someone else to speak. Several voices chime in as the crack in her chest goes on growing wider.

'My parents wouldn't let me go out on my own for months after that.'

'Did they pay a ransom?'

'Did they ever find out who took him?'

She realised that Isak is staring straight at her. The expression in his eyes is almost pleading now, but there's something else there too. Something she can't identify. Pain, perhaps, possibly even sympathy?

'Bloody awful business.'

'His poor family.'

The crack grows wider, freeing up the dark water beneath. She opens her mouth, gasping for the air that will let her scream. Yell at them to shut up. That she doesn't want to go through the ice. That she doesn't . . .

'Sit down, Lars!' Ruud's firm voice brings the cacophony of voices to an abrupt halt. Lars remains standing, and stares defiantly at Ruud as he slowly approaches the circle.

'We can ask questions, can't we?'

'You know the rules. Questions about feelings, not details.'

'OK, sorry.' Lars holds his hands up. Then turns towards Isak and points at him with a rough, callused finger. 'How did you *feel* when your friend Billy went missing? Do you know who took him?'

Veronica tries to force her body to obey her, tries to say or do something, anything. But all she and all the others in the group can do is stare at Isak.

Ruud strides into the circle and stops between Lars and Isak. 'That's enough, Lars.'

Lars glowers at Ruud. His eyes are bloodshot, the skin around them puffy and translucent. His cheeks are covered by a fine tracery of broken veins and the tip of his nose is mottled pink and blue.

The two men are about the same height, but Lars is thirty years younger and in considerably better shape. Even so, Ruud doesn't appear to be remotely scared of him.

'You've been drinking, Lars,' Ruud says quietly, in an almost friendly voice. 'You know that isn't allowed. I'm going to have to ask you to leave.'

Lars opens his mouth, clenches his fists and takes half a step forward. For a moment it looks like he's going to hit Ruud. Veronica holds her breath, the rest of the room seems to be doing the same. Ruud doesn't move. Just goes on looking impassively at the other man. Lars's gaze starts to waver. He glares at Isak, then at her, then Ruud once more.

'You can all go to hell!'

He turns on his heel and knocks two of the folding chairs over, breaking the circle. They skitter off across the floor like huge autumn leaves made of grey metal.

Ruud waits until the door has slammed shut behind Lars.

'The rules exist so that everyone can feel safe,' he says. 'Each of you chooses what you want to share, and how much. No one has the right to question or cross-examine anyone else. Is that understood?'

He looks around the remains of the circle, and is met with embarrassed nods of agreement from each of the participants.

'I think it might be time to bring today's session to an end, what do you say, Veronica?'

The sound of her name breaks her paralysis. She manages a murmur of agréement, takes a deep, cold breath and adds mechanically: 'See you next week.'

She gets to her feet and takes a couple of unsteady steps. But by now Isak is already halfway to the door.

'Sorry, Veronica, but I've got a question.' It's Sture with the combover, who has evidently realised that he never got the chance to finish talking about his dead brother. He holds her up for five long minutes, and because Ruud is watching her she does her best to look like she's listening carefully. She doesn't actually hear a word of what Sture is saying. All she can hear is a ringing metallic sound, like the hum of the rails in the metro the moment before a train arrives. The sound of thick ice about to crack.

Chapter 8

Summer 1983

'And you're absolutely certain of what you saw?'

The two men sitting on the grass in front of Månsson were wrapped in yellow blankets from the ambulance. The summer heat had had a couple of hours to dry them off, but they still looked like a pair of drowned rats. Their faces were streaked with grey, their hair and clothes soaked with a mixture of mud and algae that made them stink worse that chicken shit.

'It was the boy,' Rask said. 'He's down there. Isn't that right, Sailor?'

The other man didn't answer, just gave a non-committal shrug of his shoulders.

'You don't seem quite so certain, Olsson,' Månsson said, leaning closer. Sailor avoided meeting his gaze and looked down at the grass.

'We're sure,' Rask said curtly. 'Why would we lie?'

Because you're two of the biggest drunks around, and you still stink of drink despite the stench of the mud, Månsson thought. But he decided to keep that thought to himself for the time being. Reminded himself that even a broken clock tells the right time twice a day.

Behind him some other men were trying to salvage the boat with the aid of a tractor. It was almost entirely submerged in the mud. Another larger boat was positioned in the middle of the marl pit, and for almost three quarters of an hour the men on board had been dragging the pond with double hooks at the spot Rask had pointed out, without finding anything.

Månsson had leaped into his car the moment he got the news. He had organised another boat with dragging equipment within an hour. The movements of the men out in the new boat gave a clear indication that their initial determination had been replaced by nagging doubt, which was pretty much what he felt.

'We saw him as clearly as we can see you now,' Rask said, having evidently realised that his credibility was in question. 'But that marl pit's bottomless. He could be way down there.'

'Three metres,' Månsson said.

'W-what?'

'It's barely three metres at its deepest, according to the guys out there.' He gestured towards the boat. 'Didn't you notice when you went for your little swim?'

Rask pretended not to notice the sarcasm. 'So it can be pumped out, then? Get the fire brigade and drain the shit out of it.'

'Maybe,' Månsson muttered. He had already considered that, as well as calling in a team of divers. He doubted if anyone would volunteer to go into that sludgy water to fumble about blindly over the bottom. Who knew what sort of rubbish had been dumped in the marl pit over the years? And even if any-one did volunteer, he wasn't sure if it was worth the risk based solely on the claims of these two witnesses.

Månsson glanced at his watch, then looked sternly at the two men once more. Sailor was still staring vacantly down at the grass, and even Rask looked less certain now. Another half hour, he said to himself. Then he'd call off the operation and send these two drunks home.

Movement in the corner of his eye made him turn round. The men in the boat were moving differently now. Quick, resolute movements. A taut line.

'We've found something,' one of them called. 'Something big.'

Månsson took a few steps towards the water. He shaded his eyes with one hand to see better. The boat was no more than four metres out, and he looked on as the men tried to attach another drag-anchor to the object below. After a couple of attempts they succeeded.

'OK, let's get it up!' The two lines stretched tight as they were slowly hauled in.

Rask was on his feet now and came to stand next to Månsson, so eager that one of his feet ended up in the water.

The lines were slowly pulled in. The boat rocked with the weight of the object caught in the anchors. Rask spat nerv-ously on the grass. Månsson felt his heart start to beat faster.

The lengths of rope were getting shorter. The water surrounding the boat started to move, reluctantly giving up its secret.

'Th-there!' Rask gasped. 'There he is!'

A dark figure, covered with brown sludge, but still recognisably human, emerged from the water. A torso, two arms. Månsson took a deep breath. His heart leaped into his throat.

They'd found him! They'd found little Billy.

It was like a weight being lifted from his shoulders. Billy's death was an accident. A terrible, tragic accident that no one around there would ever forget. But at least he had done his job. Resolved the issue. And no one would be able to claim otherwise.

The body was pulled slowly from the water until it was hanging over the side of the rocking boat with its legs still in the water.

Månsson suddenly realised that something wasn't right. The proportions were all wrong. This wasn't a young boy. More like a grown man. Or something that looked like one. The head was a hessian sack, and there were no hands. Stuffing was poking out of the worn overalls in places.

'A scarecrow,' one of the men in the boat shouted. 'It's a fucking scarecrow.'

Chapter 9

The box is on the top shelf of the clothes cupboard in the bedroom, and Veronica has to stand on a stool to reach it. There's a thick, furry layer of grey dust covering the lid, and the cloud of dust motes disturbed when she pulls the box towards her, together with the half bottle of wine she's drunk to pluck up courage, almost make her fall.

She puts the box down on the coffee table, then sits and looks at it for several minutes. The red wine is combatting the chill inside her, and she takes another few mouthfuls before she feels brave enough to open the lid.

On top is a bundle of yellowed newspaper cuttings held together by a paperclip. The headline and grainy images on the first one drives an icicle straight through the warmth of the wine.

Who took little Billy? The mystery that's still tormenting a rural community fifteen years later.

She pours herself some more wine and almost downs it in one gulp. The warmth returns. The cutting is dated summer 1998. Which means five years have passed since she last opened this box. Five years since she last added to her private treasure trove of grief. That must have been just before she moved here. Before she started working as a therapist. Long before Leon.

Obviously she should have thrown all the cuttings out instead of dragging them here and hiding them in the cupboard. Her therapist would no doubt have been able to tell her precisely what psychological mechanism is stopping her, but even though they've seen each other twice a week throughout the time she's been off sick, she hasn't told him about Billy. She doesn't talk about Billy to anyone. She's kept him and her mum hidden under the ice, and has thought herself safe.

She puts the crinkled cuttings aside without reading any more of them. Beneath them she finds the brown envelope. She quickly empties her glass. Waits until the wine has softened the room before opening the envelope.

The first picture was taken by a photographer back home, and shows her little brother dressed smartly and sitting on a white antique chair. Blond hair, inquisitive, bright blue eyes, a hint of a snub nose. He's laughing towards the camera, probably because the photographer was pulling a face. There are similar pictures of her and Mattias further down in the box, taken when they were roughly the same age. The same chair, the same grey-brown backcloth, the same carefree laughter. She turns the photograph over. It's dated 3 February 1982, eighteen months before he went missing.

The bottle of wine has somehow emptied itself, so she goes into the kitchen to get another. The red eye of the telephone glares judgementally at her.

She turns her back on it and goes over to the sofa.

The next photograph is a family portrait, probably taken at the same time. Mum is sitting on a chair, with her and Mattias on either side of her and Billy on her lap. Dad is standing behind her with one hand on her shoulder. The stilted pose was the photographer's idea, her parents definitely never used to touch each other like that. The proud look in her dad's eyes is, however, genuine, as it stares out through the photo. Mum is glancing down at Billy. She must be thirty-three in the picture, almost exactly the same age as Veronica is now. They're even more alike than she remembers, almost frighteningly so. Hair colour, shape of face, posture. The tender way her mum is looking at Billy feels painful to see. She closes her eyes for a few seconds, telling herself that the similarity goes no deeper than appearance. That she and Mum are very different people.

To the right of her mum stands Mattias, looking uncomfortable. He turned fifteen a week after the photograph was taken. His shirt, suit and tie were all new, and at least one size too large, and Mum made him shave off the little moustache he was so proud of, making his top lip look slightly pink. He didn't protest. Didn't say a word. Because Mattias is an obedient boy, always does what's expected of him.

Billy is beaming at the camera, just like in the other picture. With his blond hair and blue eyes, he's the focus of the photograph. His clothes are light in colour, newly bought, and fit him perfectly.

As for Veronica, she's staring out angrily from beneath her strawberry-blonde fringe. The dress she's wearing is baby-blue, with little white bows along the hem and on the chest. Aunt Helga, who is actually her mum's aunt rather than hers, made it. The dress may have looked pretty on an eight-year-old girl, but in the picture she's just a few months away from thirteen. She has long, coltish legs, and you can just make out two small bumps beneath the front of the dress. They argued about the dress before the photograph, and as usual when she and Mum argued too long, Dad took her aside and asked her to do whatever made her mum happy.

Veronica leans over, squints and inspects herself more closely. Her face is turned towards the camera, her chin lowered. She notices that she's not looking straight ahead, at the photographer, she's looking at her mum and Billy. She blames the age of the photograph for the dark look in her eyes. All the bright colours in the picture look slightly subdued, and the darker tones, like her eyes, seem almost black in contrast. If she looks at the picture from a distance, it's almost like someone's placed a thin, dark veil across it. Like a warning, a premonition of what was to come.

She puts the photograph down and shakes the feeling off. Just her imagination, of course. An intoxicating cocktail of alcohol and hindsight. Even so, she can't quite tear her eyes from that twenty-year-old moment.

Her glass needs filling again, and she reaches for the bottle. She only realises she's drunk when she misses the glass and spills some wine on the coffee table. Instinctively she wipes her sleeve over the spillage, letting the washed-out cotton soak up the liquid. Then she lifts her arm and studies the growing stain with fascination. She can feel the moisture against her skin, against the scar beneath the fabric. She suddenly realises that the wine looks like blood. She shudders, quickly drops the photographs back in the box and stands up, rather unsteadily.

She goes out to the kitchen to get the dishcloth and wipes up the rest of the spilled wine. She stops at the telephone, its red eye still glowing, now more in sorrow than reproach. She still has Leon's last message on the answerphone, even though she keeps promising herself that she's going to delete it. She's got rid of everything else: his clothes, toothbrush and razor. The little notes he left on the kitchen table, the things he bought her on their trips. She burned it all in a layby an hour's drive south. She drenched it all in lighter fluid until the flames devoured the whole lot. Extinguishing all traces of what they had once been.

She taps in the code, fast forwards and listens to the last sentence.

'You need to stop.' Leon's voice doesn't even sound angry, just resigned. 'Please, Veronica. You need to stop now.'

Chapter 10
Summer 1983

Månsson had put it off for as long as he could, trying to find other things to do, important things. But the truth was that he couldn't postpone the conversation any longer.

By then they had already searched every field, meadow, barn, shed, marl pit, ditch and culvert within a five-kilometre radius of Backagården, many of them more than once. His officers had spoken to all the neighbours and anyone else in the district who might possibly have any involvement. Now Månsson realised that he was going to have to go and tell Ebbe and Magdalena what everyone already knew. That the police had failed to find the slightest trace of their young son, apart from the shoe in the field of maize.

He got up from the chair at his desk and tilted the blinds. The diffident reporter from the local paper had been joined by others in the past few days. Summer meant a shortage of stories, and people were fed up of reading about submarines in Swedish territorial waters. As luck would have it, if that wasn't a terrible thing to say, a large forest fire was raging up in Småland, which had given him a few days' grace. He didn't usually have a problem with journalists, and had done his best to answer their questions, at least to start with when the search was still going on. But recently the evening tabloids had been full of rumours that the investigation was about to take a new turn. They had been contacting the Nilsson family's neighbours and relatives at all hours of the day and night, and people were even turning up unannounced at Backagården with cameras and long lenses, which had forced him to station a patrol car in the drive. His overtime budget was already shot to shreds, and this twenty-four-hour protection soon swallowed up the little that remained. As if that wasn't enough, the reporters had started hounding him as well, and Malin had eventually unplugged the phone in the house. That had helped for a while, but that morning two reporters had been waiting for him outside the staff entrance, and refused to go away until he promised to hold a press conference. And before that happened, he needed to talk to the Nilssons, to warn them about what was coming.

He walked towards the exit and glanced cautiously through the window in the door, checking that the coast was clear before he went outside. He jogged the short distance to his blue Volvo.

A wave of heat hit him when he opened the car door. He slid quickly into the driver's seat without giving it time to cool, started the engine and reversed so fast that the tyres squeaked on the soft tarmac. The plastic steering wheel was burning his hands, but he didn't wind the windows down until he had built up a bit of speed.

He turned the radio on and switched between Radio Malmöhus and Radio Kristianstad, both of which were playing Carola Häggkvist, before finally settling on P1. They were broadcasting live from the forest fire in Småland.

'We're doing what we can,' the exhausted fire chief was saying in an interview. 'But sometimes that just isn't enough.'

Månsson stopped in the drive leading to Backagården to talk to the officers stationed in the patrol car. He realised too late that he should have brought them something, a flask of coffee, some Danish pastries or a couple of cold cans of Coca Cola. Something to alleviate the heat and boredom, to show that he looked after his staff. Instead he kept the conversation brief so they would think he was far too busy to let himself be distracted by that sort of thing.

In the yard, the door to the cart shed was open. Ebbe Nilsson's car was parked inside, and next to it he could see Billy's brother and sister. He knew their names now. Vera Nilsson, fourteen years old, and her brother Mattias, two years older. Vera was in the parallel class to his eldest boy.

When Månsson got out of his car the girl walked slowly towards him. She was shading her eyes with her hand, but lowered it when she saw who it was. Vera looked a lot like her mother, Månsson noted. Tall and thin, with strawberry-blonde hair and fair, freckled skin. There was something about her nose and mouth that looked simultaneously vulnerable and resolute, and there was an intense look in her eyes that was hard to interpret.

'Hello, Vera. Are your parents home?'

The girl nodded and gestured towards the main house.

'Have you found something?' Her voice was high, still a child's.

Månsson shook his head. He rubbed the back of his neck, trying to think of something to say. Something that would sound both hopeful and comforting.

'Not yet,' he eventually said. It was better than nothing. 'But we're doing what we can,' he added, and realised he sounded almost exactly like the fire chief he had heard on the radio.

The girl looked at him without saying anything.

'How's your mum? Is she feeling any better?' he tried.

Vera shrugged her shoulders and looked over towards the cart shed. Her brother was still in there, crouching down next to his moped with his back to Månsson, looking a little too busy to be strictly plausible.

Månsson leaned a little closer to the girl, smiled and lowered his voice.

'His moped's been souped up, hasn't it?'

Vera's eyes opened wide and she suddenly looked almost frightened. Månsson quickly held one hand up, he hadn't meant to alarm her.

'Don't worry, I won't say anything. Everyone needs a few little secrets, don't they?' He winked at her. 'Would you like to know mine?'

She looked at him for a few moments. Then she relaxed, gave him a crooked smile and nodded.

'I usually pinch those little packets of sugar you get in restaurants. I've got loads in a drawer back at the station. It's not as if I actually need them, but I can't seem to help myself.'

Vera's smile grew wider and turned into a giggle. Månsson smiled back, like they were two friends sharing confidences.

'Mattias wanted a motorbike when he turned sixteen. He saved up the money, but Mum wouldn't let him. So he's souping up his moped instead.'

'Well, just tell him to be careful.' Månsson suddenly thought of something. 'The night Billy went missing, you and Mattias got home at the same time. You said you cycled home . . . ?' He raised his eyebrows slightly.

'He pulled me,' Vera said without hesitation. 'Mattias rode alongside me on his moped and I held on to his arm. I usually let go in the drive and let him get home first so Mum and Dad don't see. I know you're not supposed to do that – you won't say anything, will you?'

'Of course not.' Månsson smiled again. There was something unusual about Vera Nilsson. She acted nonchalant and indifferent, but he was pretty certain that not much got past her.

'What happened when you got home? You left the bike and moped in there . . .' He pointed towards the cart shed.

Vera nodded. 'Dad came rushing out with a big torch, saying he and Mum couldn't find Billy. He asked us to check in all the outbuildings. We sometimes play hide-and-seek with Billy.'

'So you looked in all his usual hiding places?'

She nodded again. 'The cart shed, the cowshed and the barn. We were very thorough, took our time, just like Dad said. Mattias unlocked the old milking parlour, even though there was no way Billy could have been in there.' She stopped and almost seemed to shudder. As if the thought of the milking parlour had unsettled her.

'But you didn't find anything,' Månsson concluded.

'No.'

'What happened after that?'

'That was when the first police car arrived.'

'Do you know what time that was?'

Vera shook her head. 'Not exactly. Mattias and I got home at half past nine on the dot, like we'd promised, so it would have been a while after that.'

'I see.'

Månsson already knew all this. The first patrol that arrived at Backagården at quarter past ten had conducted exemplary interviews with Ebbe Nilsson, then the children. But he had to be careful not to rush things if he was to find out what he really wanted to know.

'When you were on your way home, you and your brother . . .' Månsson hesitated, then decided to go on. 'Did you see anyone?'

'A car, you mean?'

'Car, cyclist, moped. Someone out walking their dog, maybe?'

She thought. 'A couple of cars. One was the Lindgrens' blue Saab, I'm sure about that.' She frowned. 'The other one might have been red. I don't really remember, I was busy trying to . . . well, you know.' She smiled again, and held her hand out as if she was holding on to her brother's shoulder.

Månsson returned the smile. 'And you don't remember anything else?'

'No.' She looked at him in that rather probing way. She suddenly seemed to figure out what his questions were getting at. 'Why are you asking?'

Månsson was about to reply when he caught sight of Ebbe Nilsson coming down the steps from the house, striding quickly towards him. He wondered if the man had heard what they were talking about.

'Vera, can you and Mattias go inside and start dinner?'

The girl nodded, and gave Månsson one last anxious glance before she slipped away to her brother.

Månsson shook Ebbe Nilsson's hand and waited to be invited up to the house. But Nilsson just stood there in front of him. He looked even more tired than he had done the night Billy disappeared. His bloodshot eyes seemed to have sunk further into his skull. His face was both pale and suntanned at the same time. His checked shirt hung from his drooping shoulders and the knees of his trousers were dark with dirt, as if he had been kneeling and praying to the Lord for help. Månsson knew that the Nilsson family, like so many others in the area, went to church on Sundays. He had managed to get Malin and the boys there just once, in yet another attempt to become part of the community. But only the once. Malin was usually fairly amenable, but she preferred to spend the day of rest in her dressing-gown with a large cup of tea, as she took pains to explain to him. So the Månsson family only went to church at Christmas and Easter. He wasn't really that bothered. He wasn't exactly religious. The deeds of men occupied him considerably more than the unfathomable ways of the Lord.

But Månsson could easily picture Ebbe Nilsson on his knees, his hands clasped together, looking up to the heavens and praying for his little boy. He'd probably have done the same in Ebbe's shoes.

Månsson cleared his throat and tried to focus on why he was there. He had prepared what he was going to say, practising it several times on the drive over.

'Well . . .' he began. 'I'm thinking of holding a press conference tomorrow. Or rather, the regional police chief thinks that would be best. Damn reporters . . .'

He gestured with one hand and grimaced slightly, but didn't receive the support he had been expecting.

'In which case . . .' He swallowed. 'I'm thinking of saying that we're calling off the search for the time being. That we're investigating other possibilities.'

'What possibilities?' Nilsson's voice was gentler than he had anticipated. Even so, there was still a sting of sharpness there.

Månsson glanced to his side, and discovered that the girl and her older brother were standing in the open doorway watching him. He wondered if they could hear the conversation.

'Maybe we could talk about it inside?' Månsson held his hand out towards the house. 'Magdalena should probably be part of this.'

Ebbe Nilsson slowly shook his head. 'She's resting. The doctor was here again this morning.'

'I understand,' Månsson said. That explained why Nilsson hadn't asked him in. He had heard that Magdalena Nilsson had shut herself away in her bedroom. That she couldn't even get out of bed without help. Evidently that wasn't just a rumour.

He swallowed again and composed himself. He looked once again at the two children before he said the words that he really didn't want to have to say. 'Over the past few days we've started working on the hypothesis that something else may have happened. That Billy didn't get lost, but that someone might have taken him. Someone who wanted to hurt him or you.'

Chapter 11

I sak arrives punctually this time. But only just, so he's missed the coffee, sandwiches and small talk. He didn't show up for the Monday meeting, and Veronica has spent the whole week waiting impatiently for him. Crossing off the days while she tried to concentrate on her other therapy groups. Evidently with mixed results, judging by the look on Ruud's face.

The regular Friday attendees are already gathered in the circle, with the exception of Lars. Ruud has called to tell him that he's not welcome back for a month. He didn't take it very well, claimed the whole thing was her fault, in terms Ruud was unwilling to repeat.

Isak sits down on the same chair as last time and nods amiably to her. His eyes are bluer than she remembers. He smiles, and she finds herself smiling back.

'Welcome,' she says, and notices that her breathing has grown shallower.

'Thanks.'

He goes on looking at her as he leans forward. He opens his mouth to say something, but before he can speak Ruud appears out of nowhere and pulls up a chair beside her.

'I thought I'd sit in today. You don't mind, do you.' A statement rather than a question.

'Of course not.' She turns back towards Isak, but he's straightened up and is looking away. *Damn!* She tries to hide her disappointment before Ruud notices it.

The conversation flows well. The participants share their grief and she interjects with the usual questions when they need a bit of help. Her pen moves over the pad, but just like earlier in the week it isn't as effective anymore. Instead of soaking up the sorrow and pain, it mostly just darts about, the usual kick doesn't happen.

She can feel her frustration growing, and realises that she wants the other participants to finish so she can move on to Isak. Ruud's presence means she has to stick to the procedures, keep herself under control and let everyone have their say. Leif, a businessman in his fifties who lost his entire family in a car accident, is taking far too long. He cries and sobs his way through far too many minutes, and Veronica has to make a real effort not to sound impatient when she prompts him.

When it's Isak's turn at last there are only a few ticks of the clock left. She quickly turns to a fresh page in her pad, aware that her hand is trembling.

'Hi, my name's Isak,' he begins. Like last time, he doesn't say his surname. 'When I was young I lost my best friend. He disappeared and I never found out what really happened. I've thought about him a lot over the years. Sometimes I still have dreams about him.'

He seems to have finished, because he looks around for the usual nods of acknowledgement.

'How do you feel after those dreams?' she says. She tries to keep her voice neutral even though her heart is beating hard against the ice in her chest.

He looks up and shrugs.

'It varies.'

'Can you give an example?' The question is ambiguous. It might well refer to his feelings, but she hopes Isak misunderstands her and gives her details which she hasn't actually asked for.

'Sometimes I dream that we're playing hide-and-seek in his garden.'

He smiles to himself, looks down and slightly off to the side, as if the grey carpet is a projection screen for his memory.

'The garden's really big, or at least it is the way I remember it. Overgrown, almost like a forest. I close my eyes and count to a hundred. I can hear which way he's running, the bushes rustle as he moves through them.' Isak pauses and looks up.

'Then what?' she says. Her throat is dry, her pulse throbbing in her neck. She feels Ruud looking at her. She's crossed the line, but she can't stop now.

'When I finish counting and start to look, I can't find him, even though I try all our usual hiding places. The hollow elm tree, the treehouse his older brother and sister built in one of the old fruit trees, even the hayloft. Then I give up and call out. I stand there calling his name, over and over again.'

Isak takes a deep breath. There's a heavy silence, everyone is looking at him. Her pen has long since stopped moving, and for a moment her heart seems to have done the same. Isak slowly opens his mouth, as if he's about to call out, just like in the dream.

The minute hand on the clock lets out a loud click, indicating that the session is over. But she doesn't notice. Isak's eyes seek hers. His lips move, and seem to form a soundless word. Two silent syllables that she recognises all too well. Which break the shell over the abyss.

Bi-lly!

She sits perfectly still, frozen to the spot. Unable to speak or move. After a few seconds Ruud comes to her aid.

'OK, thanks for sharing, Isak. That's all we've got time for today.'

The chairs scrape around her, the participants get to their feet, but the paralysis doesn't let go until Ruud puts one hand on her shoulder and asks how she's feeling. She doesn't answer, just stands up and stumbles towards the door.

'Veronica,' Ruud calls. But she ignores him. She has to catch up with Isak, she has to find out more.

The afternoon sun out on the steps blinds her, making her raise her hand to shield her eyes.

Something goes past outside. A motorbike roars, grainy and dazzling, before disappearing down the street.

Chapter 12

Summer 1983

Things had got off to a good start. Britt, the reception-ist, had booked the little primary school hall, which was sometimes used as a Friday night cinema, for the press conference. Fourteen reporters and photographers had responded, but an hour before the start a live broadcast van suddenly pulled up in the small yard in front of the school. Antennae were erected and cables laid all over the place, and the school caretaker was bombarded with questions about voltage boxes and three-phase power supplies. And some-how the agitated atmosphere had spread through the village. People started queuing outside the hall half an hour before the press conference was due to start.

Månsson hadn't envisaged that the locals would be inter-ested in attending, so hadn't instructed his staff to turn anyone away. So instead of looking out at two rows of seats occupied by reporters he was now standing in front of a packed hall, with people crowding outside the doors trying to hear what was being said. It must have been over thirty degrees in there, and even as he stepped up onto the little stage he could feel the first trickles of sweat run between his shoulder blades. The spotlights in the ceiling were shining in his eyes, making it hard to make out any faces beyond the first few rows. All he could see were clenched faces and tense features.

He cleared his throat and looked down at his notes – stiff, official phrases he had practised saying in front of the mirror. A camera flash went off, followed by another. A man with a bulky television camera on his shoulder took a few steps forward.

'As you all know, just over a week has passed since Billy Nilsson went missing.' He paused for breath. Another flash went off. 'And after a thorough and meticulous search we have now reached a point where further efforts of that nature can no longer be regarded as justifiable.'

He hadn't planned to pause for audience reaction, but found himself doing so anyway. A murmur ran through the room, and grew to a buzz.

'I have therefore decided to call off the search,' he added. 'We will however be continuing with other lines of inquiry.'

'Do you still think Billy might have got lost?' someone in the front row called out.

He tried to see who the man was, but more camera flashes blinded him.

'Well ... We're keeping an open mind and aren't ruling out any scenarios.'

The murmur grew to a rumble of voices.

'Do you think the boy was abducted?' another reporter called.

'As I said . . .' Månsson felt his shirt sticking to his back. He held his hands up to quieten the voices in the audience. 'As I said, we're keeping an open—'

'Do you have a suspect?' someone interrupted. Månsson shaded his eyes, trying to see if the question had come from another reporter.

'W-we . . .'

'Of course there's a suspect. The whole damn village knows who did it by now. The only question is why Tommy Rooth hasn't been arrested.'

Månsson recognised this voice at once. Harald Aronsson. Before he had time to respond the noise level increased further still, and more people started to shout out, agreeing with what Aronsson had said. Several of the journalists stood up and pushed closer to the stage to make themselves heard.

He held his hands up again and asked in vain for everyone to sit down so he could answer their questions one at a time. No one seemed to listen. People were yelling at him from all sides. Questions mixed with confident statements.

'So you have got a suspect?'

'Bring the bastard in, Månsson!'

'What hypotheses are you considering?'

'Rooth's a dodgy fucker! Always has been!'

'Is this about money? Have there been any ransom demands?'

'We daren't let our kids out of our sight as long as he's on the loose!'

'Do you believe Billy's still alive?'

In the end Månsson realised that he'd lost control of the situation and decided to give up.

'Bloody hell,' he muttered to himself as he left the stage behind one of his sturdiest officers. 'Fucking bloody hell!'

Chapter 13

S he isn't a particularly good daughter. Nor a particularly good sister, either. She's so unsure of Mattias's home number that she has to dig her dog-eared old addressbook out of a drawer to check before she calls him.

The year Billy disappeared and Mum died, she was fourteen, Mattias sixteen. They grew up in an area Mattias once called the Shadowland. She likes the expression, and has thought about it a lot. Only more recently has she come to realise that he must have heard it in a film.

The Shadowland is vast, yet you hardly ever hear about it in the news except when something terrible happens. The rest of the time it's hidden behind the names of stations swishing past outside the train windows, or exits on the motorway that you never take, all the half familiar places you pass on the way to somewhere else.

Two types of people grew up in the Shadowland, according to Mattias. Those who leave, and those who stay. And the two of them would be leaving as soon as they possibly could.

Mattias got into the Police Academy in Stockholm the year he turned eighteen, one of the youngest in the intake. He left her behind in that big house with Dad and the empty rooms for two slow years. She was angry with him for that. Even so, she used to long for the weekends when he came home. Longed for him to talk about the flat in Stockholm that they would share, the things they would do together. She counted the days, ticking them off on a calendar like a convict counting down her sentence.

'HellothisisCeciliaNilsson!'

The voice on the phone sounds like a happy exclamation. Cecilia is her sister-in-law. Mattias's first and only girlfriend. Against all the odds, Cecilia managed to get their relationship to survive his move away. She was smart, didn't make any demands, just offered him a bed and a warm embrace whenever he wanted. And Mattias was stupid enough to want it.

When there were only five days left to cross off on the calendar, Veronica found herself standing on the steps outside the church throwing confetti over Mattias's graduation uniform and Cecilia's meringue wedding-dress. Shiny white fabric stretched over a slightly protruding pregnant stomach. Mattias had got a permanent job at the police station in the village, and Uncle Harald gave them a terrace house as a wedding present. The wedding photograph is somewhere towards the bottom of the box in the clothes cupboard, but she doesn't need to get it out to know that Mattias's expression is more or less the same as the one in the family photograph. Because Mattias is an obedient boy, and always does what is expected of him.

A week later Veronica packed her suitcase and left everything behind. The Shadowland, Mum, Dad, Billy. And Mattias.

'Hello, this is Veronica.' The alcohol on her breath bounces off the phone.

The silence that follows is several seconds too long.

'Vera,' she adds.

'Of course, hi! I didn't recognise your voice.'

A lie, naturally. What her sister-in-law is actually saying, in her passive aggressive way, is that they no longer speak with the same accent. That's part of the game, like forcing Veronica to introduce herself with a name she hasn't used in over fifteen years.

'Is Mattias there?' she says before her sister-in-law has a chance to add any predictable remarks about her not being in touch for such a long time (true) and that the girls are missing their aunt (pure lie).

Cecilia takes a deep breath, presumably annoyed at having been thwarted.

'He's working late. A big surveillance case with the police in the city. Franzén's letting Mattias run most of it. He's going to be leaving next year.'

'Mattias?' Veronica realises her mistake the moment she says it. Blames the stress hormones and alcohol swirling round her brain. Or possibly wishful thinking.

'No, Franzén, of course! Early retirement.' Cecilia lets out a laugh, pleased to have gained the upper hand again. 'Mattias will be replacing him, the youngest local police chief in the whole province.'

'That's great,' she murmurs. 'You don't know where I could get hold of Mattias? I need to speak to him, it's pretty urgent.'

'Have you tried his mobile? Perhaps you don't have the number?' Obviously Cecilia already knows the answer to that even before she asks. One-nil to the solid, dependable wife.

Veronica has no choice but to bite into the rotten apple. 'No, I'd be very grateful if you could let me have it.'

Mattias answers on the third ring. She's surprised by how hard and grown-up he sounds. But his voice softens a little when he hears that it's her.

'Vera, hi. I didn't know you had this number.' He sounds pleased to hear from her. A bit, anyway.

'Cecilia gave it to me. Is now a bad time?'

'Not really, we're just on a stakeout. Don't expect anything to happen before midnight. How are you doing? It's been a while.'

'Fine.' She hears how false it sounds. So does he.

'Has something happened?'

She takes a deep breath and composes herself.

'Do you remember Isak Sjölin?'

'Who?'

'Billy's best friend . . .' As usual, their younger brother's name makes the crack in the ice open slightly, not just inside her.

'Only vaguely. Why?'

'I think I've met him.'

'Where?' The police tone is back in his voice.

'Believe it or not, but he's in one of my therapy groups. Grief counselling.'

'And how do you know it's this particular Isak Sjölin?'

'I don't. But considering what he's said, I don't know who else he could be.'

A few seconds of silence follow. Mattias's voice comes closer to the phone.

'What did he say?'

'That he lost his best friend when he was little. That he just disappeared, and nothing was ever the same afterwards. He spoke about our garden, the hollow elm tree, the treehouse, the hayloft.' She takes a sip from the wineglass to stop herself talking, and holds the receiver away from her so Mattias doesn't hear her swallow.

'Did he mention Billy? Did he say it was him?'

'No, not directly.'

'What do you mean?' His questions came quickly, giving her no time to reflect.

'Another member of the group asked if he was talking about Billy, but Isak neither confirmed nor denied it.'

'So you don't know for certain?'

'Don't know what for certain?' Her brain was being sluggish again.

'If it was Isak Sjölin. And if he was actually talking about Billy?'

She doesn't answer. Her brother the policeman has remorselessly uncovered the weakness in the story. Not even the silent name she imagined she had seen on Isak's lips can change that, which is why she doesn't mention it. *Suppositions aren't evidence. Assumptions aren't the same as facts.*

Rather than assert a dry police statement of fact, he asks another question. One that catches her by surprise. One that she hasn't had time to think about.

'Do you think he knew who you were?'

She pauses, forces herself to think.

'I don't actually know. I mean, how could he? I've changed my name, and no one from home knows where I live and work.'

Hardly even my own family, she adds to herself.

Mattias murmurs something, and she knows what he's thinking. Policemen never believe in coincidence.

'What did he look like?' he asks.

'Blond, average height. Blue eyes.'

'How old?'

'Twenty-five or so, just like . . .' She stops mid-sentence, and Mattias finishes it for her:

'. . . Billy would have been.'

They say nothing for several seconds. She hears him moving about, then the crackle of a police radio.

'I've got to go,' he says. He sounds annoyed. As if he would rather have carried on talking. 'The Sjölin family moved away a long time ago, but I'll try to find out where they went.'

'Thanks.'

The police radio crackles again at his end of the line. A car door opens, followed by a woman's voice whispering.

'I have to go now,' he says. 'Stay away from this Isak until I've found out who he is and what he's after. He could be a reporter trying to worm his way in, or in the worst case some sort of nutter. It's almost twenty years ago. Anniversaries always get people going.'

'OK.'

'Good. Look after yourself, Vera. I'll do some digging and call you as soon as I know anything. It's good to hear from you.'

The call ends abruptly, so she doesn't have to think of an appropriate response.

She puts the handset back on its base. Drains the last drops from the wineglass as she walks to the window. Her eyes are drawn to the spot where the smoker had stood. She can't see the glow of a cigarette this time. Oddly enough, she can't help feeling a little disappointed.

Just as she is about to lower the blinds she sees something moving right below her window. She realises what it is before she has time to feel worried. An animal, padding softly through the darkness with its nose pressed to the ground.

At first she thinks it's a dog, but then it reaches the light of the streetlamp. It stops, looks up towards her window and tilts its head slightly, as if it's looking right at her.

A black nose, white chest, red fur.

A fox.

Chapter 14

Summer 1983

Månsson didn't get back to his house on Algatan until just after ten o'clock that evening. His talkative neighbour's water sprinkler was on, and he thought he could hear someone moving behind the neatly trimmed conifer hedge next to the drive, so he hurried inside as quickly as he could.

He had stayed at the police station until the main television news was over and the clip from the unfortunate press conference had been broadcast for the last time. The regional chief of police had called just a few minutes later, as Månsson had expected him to. He had made all the right noises, making it sound like he was sending a few detectives over just to help out. Månsson had thanked him for the initiative. Said he was looking forward to working with the regional detectives, and that any extra resources that could help solve the case were of course very welcome. But he knew what it was really about. They were taking Billy's disappearance away from him. His case.

Malin was waiting for him in the kitchen. She was making toasted sandwiches, which he realised she must have put in the oven the moment she heard the car. The smell of melted cheese, pineapple and ham made his stomach rumble, and he suddenly realised that he hadn't eaten anything since lunch-time. He sank down onto one of the kitchen chairs and took a sip from the glass of milk his wife had placed on his mat.

'Are the boys asleep?'

Malin nodded. 'They wanted to wait up for you, but I said you'd probably be home late. Johan wants you to wake him up, he wants to tell you about the match.'

'Of course . . . how did it go?' In truth he had no idea what match they were talking about. He suspected that his wife knew that, but she played along.

'Two-nil, he scored one of the goals.'

'That's great. And Jakob?'

Malin pulled a face that was all too familiar. Månsson sighed.

'Have they been getting at him again?'

'He won't say anything, just shuts himself away in his room.'

'Hmm.' Månsson took another sip of milk. 'Who was it?'

'Probably the same gang as last time. The shopkeeper's two boys, Patrik Brink and another one.'

'Should I call the parents? Sören's a sensible man, so is Olle Brink, most of the time.'

'I don't think that would help. Not right now, anyway.'

'Maybe not,' Månsson mumbled.

The children are merely repeating what they've heard their parents saying at the dinner table, he thought. That he and his colleagues are never going to find Billy. That he hadn't had the guts to bring in the only plausible perpetrator. That he was actually frightened of Tommy Rooth.

Månsson was perfectly aware of the source of all this. Brink and the shopkeeper both belonged to Harald Aronsson's inner circle, and calling them to control their little brats would only diminish him still further in their eyes.

Malin pulled out a chair and sat down beside him. 'I saw you on the local news,' she said in the same tone she used to console the boys when they were little. 'How are you doing?'

Månsson felt her hand on his arm and muttered something into the glass of milk. His first instinct was to say that it was nothing to worry about. That everything was under control and there was no need to her to be concerned about him. Malin would accept that and not ask any questions. Just tilt her head to one side in that slightly sad way she did when she knew he wasn't telling the truth. So he spared them that and changed the subject.

'The Nilsson family,' he said. 'Magdalena's in a bad way, she's not even getting out of bed now. The doctor's there every day. And Ebbe looks like a ghost. As for the children, they . . .'

He looked down again, turning his glass and watching the last drops of milk roll about the bottom. Malin squeezed his arm without saying a word.

Månsson glanced at his wife. They had been together for almost twenty-five years, knew each other inside out. Malin's face was a little fuller than when they first met, her body too. The lines at the corners of her mouth and between her eyebrows were more pronounced, and if you looked really closely you could see little flecks of grey in her hair. She looked more and more like her mother, which of course it would never occur to him to point out. He loved her more at that precise moment than he had ever done. The fact that she was sitting there, just holding his arm in silence.

All of a sudden he was filled with a sense of immense gratitude. He and Malin were sitting there in the kitchen while Johan and Jakob were tucked up in their beds, safe and warm. He almost said as much to her, told her he felt ashamed, not of his efforts as chief of police and lead investigator, but because he felt relieved. Relieved it wasn't his little boy who had been swallowed up that August night, plunging his family into darkness. But before he had time to say anything he was interrupted by the egg-timer on the cooker, announcing that his supper was ready.

Månsson devoured three toasted sandwiches in rapid succession, and had taken a first bite of a fourth when his indigestion caught up with him. He discreetly stifled a burp with his hand. The acid reflux burned in his throat and he put his knife and fork down and leaned back.

'The Nilsson children,' he said. 'You've seen them at school, I suppose?'

'Yes.' Malin stood up and cleared his plate and cutlery away. 'Mattias Nilsson finished Year 9 this spring. A nice boy, well behaved, doesn't exactly draw attention to himself.'

'Is he going on to sixth form in the city?'

'Yes. The two-year social studies course, I seem to recall. I think he was hoping to join the police, or maybe the fire brigade.'

'And the girl? Vera?'

Malin sat down beside him again and shook her head gently. 'As a careers advisor you don't really see the students until they reach Year 8. Obviously I know who she is, I see her in the corridors. Hear what her teachers say about her.'

'And what do they say?'

'That she's smart, she gets good grades.' Malin sounded a little circumspect all of a sudden.

'But?' He knew her as well as she knew him. He knew when it was time to ask a follow-up question.

Malin shrugged her shoulders. 'That she can be a bit difficult at times.'

'In what way?' He could see the girl in front of him. Those coltish legs, the voice that was still a child's.

Malin looked off towards the hall, as if she was worried one of the boys was standing there listening. She leaned closer to him.

'She's evidently something of an early developer. Boys, alcohol. The counsellor's been involved, but I don't know any more than that.'

Månsson nodded. He was thinking about the expression in Vera Nilsson's eyes. Intelligence, alertness, and something else. Something unsettling.

Darling,

Do you remember the first time we met? Even then I knew you were the one for me. I knew it the moment our eyes met. Maybe that sounds silly, like some teenage infatuation. But it's how I feel. You mean everything to me. Everything!

I dreamed about you last night. That you were here, beside me, in my arms. Forever. Instead I have to make do with brief moments of happiness. Right now I can live with that. I'll wait patiently for you because I know that our time will soon be here.

Chapter 15

For the first time in a long while she dreams about her mum. The same dream, and when she wakes up on Saturday morning her head feels sluggish and her body heavy.

She goes for a quick walk to get herself going, and checks for evidence of the fox she saw the previous evening. She can't find anything. *Because foxes are cunning. They know how to move without leaving any sign.*

When they were little Uncle Harald used to tell stories to her and Mattias. Always in secret, when Mum couldn't hear. The stories were terrifying, about children getting into trouble. Children drowning, starving or freezing to death. Sometimes the stories made her wake up in terror in the middle of the night, her nightdress wet with sweat. Even so, she and Mattias never told their mother the reason for their nightmares. They knew Uncle Harald never forgave anyone who couldn't keep a secret.

She follows the pavement to where she saw the smoker standing the other night. The smoker wasn't as cunning as the fox, because she finds cigarette butts in the gutter. Five of them, all with a red crown printed on the paper just above the filter. Red Prince, the sort her mum smoked.

She thinks about the packet of cigarettes in Isak's carefully rolled up James Dean sleeve. Imagines that it was white and red, then the strong smell of tobacco on his breath, which oddly makes her feel a bit excited. She tosses the cigarette butts on the ground and hurries back home.

The eye of the phone is winking at her invitingly when she gets in, and she finds herself hoping it's Leon. But when she taps in the code she hears Mattias's voice.

'I've found Isak. Call me.'

Her excitement grows as she calls him back.

'Hi, Vera, hold on.'

She hears voices in the background, then footsteps and a door closing.

'That's better. Right, I've tracked down the Sjölin family. Like I said, they've moved away. Their dad lost his job when the brickyard closed down, and they ended up in Kristianstad . . .'

Her curiosity gets the better of her and she interrupts him.

'What about Isak?'

'Studying architecture in Oslo for the past two years. I've got his number, but I haven't got hold of him yet. According to the mother, they don't often talk about Billy, but she remembers them discussing a newspaper article about his disappearance when Isak was home last spring. It evidently upset him.'

'So it could be him?' Her pulse begins to quicken again.

'It's not impossible. Just to be on the safe side I asked his mother to fax me a picture of him. I've got it in front of me now.'

'What does he look like, is he blond?'

'The fax is black and white and the picture isn't great quality, so it's hard to tell. But he certainly looks like he's got fair hair.'

Frustration makes her bite her bottom lip. Then she has an idea.

'Listen, we've got a fax at work. I'll head over now, and call you when I get there.'

The metro gods are more helpful than usual and in little more than thirty-five minutes she's switching off the alarm in the Civic Centre. The big meeting room looks even sadder when it's empty.

Ruud's office is at the far end of the room. Although you couldn't really call the windowless little room he hangs out in an office. Cubbyhole would be closer to the truth. The lino floor can't be more than five square metres in area, and the noticeboards covering all the walls are plastered with lists, pictures and folders relating to different seminars, meetings and groups.

It feels a bit unnerving, walking into Ruud's private sanctuary without asking for permission. The room even smells of him. Chewing tobacco, coffee, and something else she can't quite describe.

The desk is dominated by the keyboard and a huge computer monitor which is almost completely covered with Post-It notes. The fax machine is perched on a small filing cabinet, and she calls Mattias from Ruud's phone and gives him the number on the Dymo label stuck next to the on button. Then, while she waits impatiently, she looks at the sheets of paper on the noticeboards. Instead of getting rid of anything out of date, it looks like Ruud just pins new information on top of older material, making his noticeboards into a sort of retrospective collage of the history of the Civic Centre. She stops short when she sees her own picture on a folder from the northern district. *Veronica Lindh, conversational therapist.* The photograph is several years old, taken when she first started the job. The thought that this photograph of her exists in hundreds, possibly thousands of folders, is oddly unsettling. Unless it's the memories of Leon and her old workplace haunting her.

A sudden noise makes her start. The fax machine has woken up and is slowly spitting out a sheet of paper. She goes and stands in front of it, waiting. Almost holding her breath.

Mattias was right. The photograph is blurred, and doubtless hasn't been improved by being faxed a second time. But one thing at least is abundantly clear, and doesn't change no matter how much she stares at the warm paper.

She breathes out and sits down heavily on Ruud's desk chair, then picks up the phone. Mattias answers on the first ring. He doesn't even bother to say hello.

'Well?'

She looks at the picture one last time. Isak Sjölin looks perfectly ordinary. A side parting, slightly protruding ears and a kind, almost shy look in his eyes. There isn't the slightest similarity between him and the blond man in her therapy group.

'It isn't him.'

'You're sure?'

'No doubt at all.'

'OK.' Several seconds pass, as Mattias seems to ponder what to say next. 'How many times has this man come to your sessions?'

'Two, most recently yesterday.'

'Has he spoken directly to you? Asked any questions?'

'No.' She shakes her head, which is obviously ridiculous seeing as Mattias can't see her. 'He leaves as soon as the sessions are over.'

She wonders about mentioning the motorbike and cigarette butts on her street. Once upon a time she used to tell Mattias all her secrets. But that's a long time ago now. Before he stayed and she left.

'When's the next session?'

'Monday.'

'Can you ask to switch groups?' He's looking at the problem in practical terms, just as she expected. Get out of the way, hide for a while and it might all sort itself out.

'No.' She comes close to shaking her head again.

'Why not?'

'I just can't.' She has no inclination to tell him that she has no room for manoeuvre right now. He would immediately ask why, and she doesn't feel like telling him about her breakdown. About Leon, the therapy, and the fact that she's under Ruud's supervision. So instead she changes the subject abruptly.

'I dreamed about Mum last night. The hawk's eggs up on the silo.'

He says nothing, but she can tell that he's uncomfortable. She almost imagines she can hear his chair creak anxiously.

'Look, Vera . . .' He sounds far less decisive now. Unsure enough to let himself be interrupted.

'Why do you think she did it?'

'Because what we did was wrong. Because you don't break birds' eggs.'

'Not that. The lake, the ice. Why do you think she committed suicide? I mean, her doctors said she was getting better.'

'How the hell should I know? Mum lost interest in me long before the little prince . . .'

He regrets saying that immediately, she can tell. But it's too late now, the words are already out. Lingering on the phone line.

'What I meant is that we weren't exactly close. I was only sixteen, I had no idea what was going on inside her head.' He clears his throat. 'Anyway, you're the therapist in this family. Why does anyone commit suicide?'

'Because they don't have anything to live for.' Her answer comes instinctively, before she has time to think about it.

Silence again. The line crackles, as if he's sitting up. She hears him take a breath, it sounds like he's about to say something.

Then there's a distant knock, followed by the sound of a door opening. A woman's voice says something she can't quite hear.

'OK,' Mattias says. 'Get the car and I'll see you round the front.'

Then he's back on the line.

'Listen, something's come up, I'm going to have to go. Call me if this guy shows up again on Monday, and don't say a word to him about Billy. OK?'

This last bit sounds like a police officer giving orders, not a brother talking to his sister. Before she has time to tell him that, he's hung up.

She sits quietly at Ruud's desk for a few moments. The blond guy isn't Isak Sjölin, which in some ways is a bit of a blow. Deep down she'd been hoping that he was. Hoping to hear what he remembered about Billy. And maybe Mum too.

But that isn't going to happen now. Because the blond guy isn't an old acquaintance, he's a stranger. Someone whose motives and intentions are unclear.

A thought suddenly hits her. Mattias had said that Isak Sjölin and his mother had discussed an article about Billy back in the spring. She turns Ruud's computer on and waits impatiently for the search engine to appear.

It takes her a while to find the article, and she scrolls quickly down to the by-line without reading the text. The author of the article turns out to be a woman, not the young, over-eager blond man she was expecting. She scrolls back up to the headline again. It's unusually fitting. Summarises the whole tragedy in just five words.

The summer that never ended.

Immediately beneath the title were three pictures. One is the photograph of Billy that she's got in her box at home. The police must have used it in the investigation seeing as the newspaper had got hold of a copy. The second photograph is of Tommy Rooth, probably from his driving licence. It shows a fair-haired man with intense eyes and an arrogant smile. She has to admit that he looks handsome, in that bad-boy way that some women like. The way she used to like them.

The third picture is computer-generated, a man who looks human but is still missing something that would make him look properly real.

She stares at the picture, then at the caption beneath it. The room lurches, then it does it again, and she grabs the desk to stop herself falling.

What Billy Nilsson would look like today.

The blond man on the screen stares at her with lifeless eyes.

Chapter 16
Summer 1983

Månsson was shuffling the papers covering his desk. Sorting them into piles, mostly to convince himself that he was actually doing something useful.

On the far left was a large bundle of memos about work that had been carried out, including the searches with police dogs and the helicopter he had requisitioned from Malmö. Next to the memos was the large heap of reports from the search parties. On top was the well-thumbed map where he had marked the areas that had been searched. A third pile contained all the interviews that had been conducted – the boy's father, older siblings, neighbours. And anyone else who might have something of value to contribute, which wasn't many people.

Then finally, on the far right, the pile of tip-offs from the public. Ninety-five per cent of them from people who had never set foot in the area or seen Billy Nilsson except in photographs. An unholy mix of crazies, armchair detectives, self-proclaimed experts and loners who just wanted someone to listen to them for a while.

The rest of the tip-offs weren't much to write home about either. A few reports of unfamiliar vehicles or people behaving oddly, and then a list of suggestions from locals as to who they should be investigating and why. As if he didn't already know. Tommy Rooth's name appeared in practically ever other sentence, and Månsson was well aware why. Rooth was a regularly recurring name in the police station, and by now Månsson knew the whole of the man's life story. Restless and a bit of a troublemaker at school, souped-up mopeds, criminal damage, all the usual. Then, later on, unlawful driving, drunk and disorderly conduct, fights in public places and clubs. Usually clashes with jealous boyfriends of the girls he was hitting on, unless they were the ones hitting on him. Rooth was undeniably good-looking. A chiselled, tanned face, fair hair that kept falling across one eye. And there was something about the look in those eyes. Self-assured, almost arrogant, just like his behaviour. Out here in the countryside, where the men were mostly taciturn and withdrawn when they were sober, it wasn't hard to understand why women were attracted to him.

Rooth went off to sea as soon as he came of age. He returned in 1974, after his father died, together with a woman he had hooked up with in Malmö. They moved into the family farm and started their own family. In spring and summer he did seasonal work, laying tarmac and helping with the pea harvest. In autumn and winter he supported himself as best he could with whatever odd jobs he could get, and with what he could make from his own smallholding. Rooth didn't follow the unspoken rules of the area, he refused to accept his place in the hierarchy, and that sort of thing wound people up, and they started to talk. About the theft of diesel and poaching, about Rooth's mother being a gypsy, and that he had been thrown out by his father. That he had even killed a man when he was at sea.

Månsson dug out the short interview that had been conducted with Rooth. His scornful tone was clearly discernible in the dry typed transcript.

> I'm only here because of what happened with Aronsson's car last autumn. Your boss does what he's told, just like everyone else in this godforsaken place. Anyway, why isn't Månsson here in person, doesn't he have the guts to talk to me? I thought we knew each other pretty well by now.

The penultimate sentence made Månsson flush slightly with embarrassment, both at what Rooth had said, and the fact that it had been kept in the transcript. But perhaps most of all because there was a grain of truth in the allegation. Rooth had no respect for authority, and that included the forces of law and order. Månsson found people like that difficult. He didn't like conflict, especially not conflicts he didn't think he could win, which was why he had chosen not to be present when Rooth was questioned.

He leafed through the main file containing all the material relating to the case, going through it yet again, comparing it to every document in the other piles. And, just like the twenty-five times he had done this before, the result was the same.

He had followed the procedure to the letter. Had searched every possible location, expanded the search area so it stretched considerably further than a five-year-old boy with only one shoe might have been able to walk in rain and darkness. He had interviewed anyone who could possibly have any involvement, even following up tip-offs from people claiming to be in touch with 'the other side'. Despite all that, he had failed. Billy Nilsson was still missing, and he wasn't the slightest bit closer to solving the mystery than he had been when he stood under the canopy on the terrace at Backagården and promised Ebbe Nilsson that he would find his little boy.

Månsson took a swig from the mug on the desk and regretted it immediately. Lukewarm coffee was hardly what he needed right now. His unsettled stomach had been telling him it was high time for lunch for a while. That was usually a part of the day he looked forward to. The local pub served sturdy portions of traditional Swedish food, but today he didn't feel any inclination to go.

He stood up and opened the door to the corridor and conference room. The two detectives the regional police chief had sent over were sitting in there eating takeaway pizza. The smell made him put his hand on his stomach. Bloody gastric catarrh, one minute he was feeling sick, the next hungry enough to eat a horse.

Månsson watched the men surreptitiously for a few seconds. Detective Inspectors Bure and Borg, so similar in facial features, hairstyles and dress, that he had trouble telling them apart. Unless that was just because he hadn't really made any effort to do so. A sort of petty revenge for the fact that he had been side-lined. And the fact that these two men in suits had taken over his conference room, investigation and police station.

Månsson clenched his jaw. His stomach rumbled again. The evening papers had established their own local headquarters in the two pizzerias, which meant that he couldn't go there, unlike Bure and Borg. He could always go home for lunch, of course, but Malin was at work and his own culinary skills left a lot to be desired. Or he could send one of the receptionists out to get food for him. But he had already done that several times in the past few days, and he was pretty sure that his staff were on the point of seeing through him.

That left either the hotdog kiosk at the edge of the village, or the pub over the road. Scylla or Charybdis.

Chapter 17

On Monday morning Veronica gets there well before she needs to. She even beats Ruud.

'Early bird,' he declares, before going into the kitchen to switch on the coffee machine.

She ought to be feeling guilty about using his office without permission, but that's drowned out by the tumult in her head. She can hardly remember how she got home on Saturday. Or how she's managed to pass the hours between then and now. All she knows is that there are three empty wine bottles in her kitchen, and that her hangover is tinged with excitement and confusion. Strangely, none of this seems to be outwardly visible. Ruud chats away as usual, and even though she turns away feeling nauseous when he unlocks the door to his office and bustles about in there, he doesn't seem to notice anything.

The usual Monday participants appear, and this time she stands by the door and shakes them all by the hand. Every now and then she wipes her hand discreetly on her trousers so it doesn't feel too clammy. Even though she's well aware that the blond man has only attended the Friday sessions so far, she still feels disappointed when it gets to nine o'clock and he hasn't shown up. *The blond man*. That's how she thinks of him after her conversation with Mattias. *The blond man*, not Isak.

She sits down in her place, takes a deep breath and leafs through to a blank page in her pad. Her movements are impatient and frustrated. She nods to Elsa with the grey hair and pearls of grief to start talking about her daughter. The woman looks back at her in surprise, and she doesn't realise until Elsa has started speaking that she forgot to introduce herself and tell them her own story the way she usually does. She glances towards the wall, hoping that Ruud hasn't noticed. Better than that, he isn't even there.

Elsa is halfway through her daughter's story when the door opens and the blond man walks in. He's wearing the same clothes as before, and when her initial surprise has subsided she realises that she's staring at his face.

He nods apologetically and slips onto one of the empty chairs, and she forces herself to look away. She quickly turns to the faxed picture of the computer-generated face that she's tucked in the back of her notepad.

The similarities are still striking, even if her raddled brain may have exaggerated them since Saturday. If you looked closely enough, you could see that his nose and forehead were slightly different, and the eyes were a little closer together on the photofit picture. But if you saw the picture from a few metres away, most people would probably say it was the same person. She can't test that right now, though. All she can do is glance at the blond man while she pretends to listen to what Elsa is saying. She tries to conjure up Billy's expressions and mannerisms and compare them with the blond man's. But he's sitting still, doesn't make any gestures that might help her. Besides, she's also trying to compare a child with a grown man.

It takes her several seconds to realise that Elsa has stopped talking. She apologises and manages to pose a couple of awkward questions before moving on to the next participant. She sits painfully through another seven stories, trying all the while not to stare at the blond man. Even though she hurries them along – and on a couple of occasions brings things to a somewhat abrupt end – once again there are only a few minutes left when it finally gets to his turn.

By now her shirt is sticking to the small of her back, and her hands are as clammy as her mouth is dry.

The blond man repeats his usual story. *Hello, my name's Isak. My best friend went missing when I was little. Nothing was the same after that* . . . and she can tell that he's about to conclude at roughly the same point as last time. She even sees him glance up at the clock. So she does what she absolutely isn't supposed to do. She interrupts him with a question about the background to his story.

'Where did you grow up, Isak?'

He stops, and for a moment looks rather surprised. Then he smiles at her. His smile is lovely, and she hardly notices herself mirroring it almost immediately.

'Out in the country. A long way from here.'

'And your parents, did they ever talk to you about your missing friend?'

'No, not at all. I grew up in a foster family. All that business with . . .'

He makes a gesture and she takes a deep breath, thinking he's about to say her younger brother's name, but he doesn't.

'. . . my friend happened before I was adopted. It's mostly just fragments of memory, a mystery that was never really explained. Maybe that's why I'm having trouble letting go of it.'

The last sentence hits her in the chest like a shard of ice. The man fixes his bright blue eyes on her, and it's as if the whole room dissolves. The folding chairs and other group members are gone, and the two of them are all that's left. Her eyes fill with tears and she feels her mouth open.

'That's all we've got time for today.' Ruud's voice is brusque, and she looks up at him, surprised and frightened; she sees a similarly stern expression on his face.

Ruud collars her before she has a chance to go over to the blond man. He takes her arm gently but firmly, and makes her stand up. He smiles at the group members as they leave the room, and she forces herself to do the same – and not stare at the young man's back as he walks out. Not try to see if the cigarette packet he pulls out just before the door closes is a pack of Red Prince.

'We need to talk, Veronica,' Ruud says.

Chapter 18

Summer 1983

Månsson realised his mistake the moment he opened the door to the pub. He ought to have checked the cars in the car park, worked out who was inside and taken that as the basis for his decision about where to have lunch. But he had been in a hurry, and wanted to avoid the reporters, so he had pulled a civilian coat over his uniform and almost jogged across the square.

And now he was standing here in the doorway with pretty much every face in the pub turned towards him. Naturally he recognised most of them. Möller the grocer, Kurt the painter, Kristin from the bank and her colleague with the long red nails. A couple of people from the council office a bit further away. But it was the group at the table right next to the door that worried him most.

Harald Aronsson, Billy's uncle, was sitting there with his foreman, Brink, and the Strid brothers. The four of them seemed to be in the middle of an animated discussion when he walked in.

Månsson took a deep breath and set off towards the far end of the room where he had spotted a free table. He nodded to Aronsson and his gang, adding a 'Good morning' which he hoped sounded simultaneously authoritative and relaxed, but which of course did neither.

'Månsson!'

He stopped and turned round reluctantly. Aronsson was pointing towards a free chair at their table. 'Grab a seat!' It sounded more like an order than an invitation.

Månsson hesitated for a moment, trying to think of a good excuse not to join the men, but Aronsson pre-empted him.

'Alf,' he called to the landlord. 'Can you get the chief of police the dish of the day, please. On my tab.'

Aronsson gestured towards the chair again and raised his dark eyebrows slightly. His deep-set eyes and prominent nose always reminded Månsson of a buzzard.

He sat down opposite Aronsson and unbuttoned his coat. The landlord put a plate of hash in cream sauce down in front of him, a dish he would usually have devoured with relish, but suddenly he didn't feel anywhere near hungry. He felt the other men's eyes on him and forced himself to eat some.

Brink was a thickset man of about fifty, almost completely bald. The Strid brothers were some ten years younger, red-haired, in good shape and the closest thing to local celebrities the village could come up with. They had both been successful wrestlers, one of them had even been Swedish champion. In latter years they had taken over the running of their father's engineering workshop and had expanded it significantly. They were currently building three big wind turbines for Aronsson. A ridiculous idea, according to most people in the village.

'How are things going? Looked like you got into a bit of hot water the other day,' Aronsson said.

From the corner of his eye Månsson could see the other men smirking.

'We're continuing with the investigation.' He finished chewing, then washed the mouthful down with a swig of low-alcohol beer. 'The regional police chief has sent over a couple of detectives from the city—'

Aronsson interrupted him with a wave of his hand and a look of irritation.

'That's all in the papers. I want to know what you're actually doing to find whoever took my nephew. What lines of inquiry you're working on, who you're talking to.' Aronsson leaned closer. 'And when you're going to arrest the man who did it.'

'Well,' Månsson said, avoiding Aronsson's eyes, 'details of the investigation are confidential.'

Aronsson slammed his fist down on the table.

'I don't give a shit about fucking confidentiality!' His exclamation silenced the room instantly.

Aronsson's eyes were black, and a blue vein was throbbing in one of his temples. Månsson swallowed again, drily. He cursed the fact that he hadn't been able to stifle his reflex reaction.

'We're still conducting interviews, following up various leads . . .' he began, without really knowing where the sentence was going.

'Have you questioned Tommy?' one of the Strid brothers asked.

'Tommy Rooth,' Brink added. He leaned over the table towards Månsson. 'Have you questioned him? Everyone knows there's bad blood between him and Harald. All that business last year about poaching, and Harald's windscreen getting shot out.'

Månsson looked at Brink, then back at Harald Aronsson.

'We've questioned Rooth. He denies any involvement. Says he doesn't know anything about Billy.'

'What about his farm? Didn't you find anything there?' the other brother said.

Månsson closed his eyes and took another mouthful of hash to gain a bit of time. He should have kept quiet, he should never have sat here in the first place. Shouldn't have been so damn desperate to please people. He put his fork down.

'Old grudges aren't enough to get a search warrant. Anyway, he was acquitted of the shooting incident. We tested all his rifles without getting a match. Rooth's smart . . .'

Månsson stopped himself. He held his hands out and stood up.

'I have to stick to the law, especially now Regional Crime are involved. Without something that definitely connects Tommy Rooth to Billy, I can't do more. Thanks for lunch, Aronsson, but I have to get back to the station.'

He had been sitting at his desk for around ten minutes, trying to settle his stomach with some dry biscuits from the staffroom, when the phone rang. His direct line. 'Hello, this is Laila down at the petrol station. I've got something I want to tell you.'

Månsson tried to summon up a picture of the woman in his head. Short hair, glasses, a little bit plump, not unlike Malin. Always friendly, with a lively glint in her eye. He usually referred tip-offs from the public to the receptionists. But something in Laila's voice told him he should take this call himself.

He brushed the crumbs from his desk, and reached for a pen and paper from one of his drawers.

'What was it you wanted to say?'

The line went silent for a few moments, long enough for him to register her hesitation.

'It's about Tommy Rooth.'

Chapter 19

S ometimes when she repeats certain words over and over
again to herself, they start to sound strange. As if the syllables were scratching against each other, shifting the meaning
and somehow making the word into its own opposite.

This time it isn't her words that change but Ruud's.

*Everything's going to be all right. Everything's going to be
all right.*

. . . be all right.

. . . be all right.

He says lots of other things too. That she called the forbidden number from the phone in his office on Saturday, and
that she had therefore breached the ban on contact, even
though she has no recollection of that at all. A completely
stupid thing to do, of course. Unlike her home phone, the
telephone in the Civic Centre hasn't got a 'withhold number' function, so calling from there is a sure-fire way of
getting caught. He doesn't ask what she was doing in his
office on a Saturday, though, which she's grateful for. But on
the other hand, she can't help wondering why. Maybe he simply doesn't want to know the answer?

Ruud says he'll try to persuade the HR department to give her one last chance. But she'll have to see the therapist again, convince him that the phone call was a one-off, not a relapse. She agrees without realising that Ruud means right away. She doesn't appreciate that until he pulls up outside the clinic and tells her one last time that everything is going to *be all right*.

Her therapist, who isn't really hers seeing as her employers are paying him, is called Bengt, and he's tall in a slightly hunched way. As if he's ashamed of his own height and tries to look shorter by leaning forward, which brings his face far too close to hers.

'Tell me what's happened, Veronica.' He's sitting on the leather armchair opposite her. Smiling kindly, the tip of his tongue visible at the corner of his mouth. She hears his fountain pen scratch on his notepad as she tells him about her call to Leon, the call she really shouldn't have made. She's fighting the urge to dig her fingernails into the skin of her lower arm, clawing deep gouges in her flesh. Punish herself for her utter stupidity.

Ruud drives her home afterwards. He doesn't ask any questions, lets her just sit there in silence staring out through the side window. He even turns the radio on, just loud enough for the silence to feel less oppressive.

'You're off work for a week,' he says when, after what feels like an eternity, they turn into her street. 'Bengt has promised to send a report early next week. As soon as HR get it and we've had a chance to talk it through, I'll be in touch. I promise I'll do everything I can to help you. OK?'

'Great,' she mumbles. Then, a few seconds later, she adds, 'Thanks.'

He slips into a loading zone, then turns towards her.

'You need to pull yourself together, Veronica.'

This unnecessary exhortation sounds simultaneously pitying and concerned, and she doesn't know which she likes least.

'No alcohol, not even a glass of wine at the weekend. And absolutely no more phone calls to Leon Santos, because then I won't be able to do anything to help you. And stay away from the Civic Centre, OK?'

She knows Ruud means the blond man. Maybe he's got it into his head that she fancies him. Maybe he's even a bit jealous. Or angry. Because she's had the nerve to do something like that right in front of him.

She can't be bothered to reply, so just gets out of the car. She glances instinctively along the street to where the smoker had been standing. And, just as before, there's no one there.

Chapter 20
Summer 1983

T he small, windowless room was hot, and well on its way to becoming airless. There were four of them in there, which was at least one too many. Månsson put his fist in front of his mouth and stifled a belch. His gastric catarrh had turned into a full-blown attack now, and he hadn't slept much last night. But nothing was going to stop him from taking part in this interview.

'Right, then, let's get going,' the slightly shorter of the two detectives, Borg or Bure, said, leaning back against the wall.

His colleague pressed the button on the recorder and moved the microphone so it was closer to the man sitting opposite him.

'Interview with Tommy Rooth, date of birth 21 October 1947. Present are myself, Detective Inspector Bure and Detective Inspector Borg from Regional Crime, and Police Inspector Månsson.'

'Chief of Police.' Månsson put his hand over his stomach.

Bure looked up and exchanged a quick glance with his colleague.

'Chief of Police Månsson,' Månsson repeated, louder and firmer this time. They didn't actually want him there, he was well aware of that. They had even implied that it might make the interview more difficult. But he had still insisted on being present.

'Chief of Police Månsson,' Bure said, correcting himself with ill-disguised sarcasm.

He opened a folder he had put down next to the microphone. Then looked up the man opposite him.

'OK, Rooth. You've been through this before, so I daresay you know how it works?'

Tommy Rooth shrugged his shoulders.

'Two convictions for assault, one for threatening behaviour. Resisting arrest, violence against a public official, vehicle theft. For a while you seem to have been quite a regular here at the station.'

'That was a long time ago now, before I went to sea. Youthful misdemeanours, ask anyone.' Rooth's tone was provocative, as usual. As was his body language.

'That's exactly what we've been doing,' Borg said from over by the wall. 'We've asked loads of people if there's anyone who might have a grudge against the Aronsson and Nilsson families, and guess which name kept popping up? You don't seem to be very popular locally.'

'People round here talk a load of crap,' Rooth snorted. 'They always have done. That's all well in the past now.'

'Well in the past?' Bure turned a sheet in the folder. 'It says here that on 5 October last year you paid a visit to Harald

Aronsson's home. According to the report, you were intoxicated and threatening.'

'Intoxicated and threatening? Fucking hell, Aronsson's such a liar. He's just pissed off that someone put him in his place for once. Everyone around here does whatever Harald Aronsson says, including Månsson here.'

Månsson looked away, avoiding the men's gaze.

'So you admit you were there, then? And that you and Aronsson had an argument?'

Rooth gestured towards Månsson. His hand had long, strong fingers, tanned as brown as his face.

'We've already been through all this, me and Månsson. Most recently last week. No, hang on, it wasn't Månsson who questioned me, it was one of his puppets. Månsson didn't dare do it himself.'

Månsson clenched his teeth.

'We know you've already been interviewed,' Bure said. 'But now it's us asking the questions. Did you go to see Harald Aronsson at his home on 5 October last year?'

Rooth raised his eyebrows in a fake grimace of resignation.

'Sure, I was there. We argued. The bastard bought the Northern Woods from the estate last autumn and revoked my hunting licence there and then. Claimed there was no written contract and wouldn't even let me hunt to put food on the table, even though I live next to the forest. My grandfather used to be gamekeeper on the estate back in the day. My dad inherited the hunt from him, and then it passed to me. We never needed a contract. The forest is what we live off half the year. That's how I provide for my family, so believe me, I was pissed off.'

'Pissed off enough to put a bullet through the windscreen of Aronsson's car that same night?' Bure asked.

Rooth folded his arms over his chest and pulled one corner of his mouth up in an arrogant smirk.

'That's already been investigated. The bullet didn't come from any of my guns. Ask Månsson, his people tested all my rifles. None of them housed that bullet. The investigation was dropped, wasn't it?'

'That's correct,' Månsson muttered, unable to stop himself. He knew what the detectives were thinking, he could see it on their faces. *Useless fucking rural police.*

'The car was parked in the yard,' Bure said. 'So the shooter must have been very close, using a silenced weapon. The sort of rifle poachers use.'

Rooth's smile grew even broader, and his eyes glinted.

'I wouldn't know anything about that.'

'So you don't go poaching in the Northern Woods? You and your seafaring mate, Kjell-Åke Olsson, more usually known as Sailor?'

Rooth let out an exaggerated sigh. 'You city types don't understand how anything works around here.'

Neither of the detectives said anything. Rooth leaned across the table.

'Look, it's like this. Harald Aronsson is pissed off because I sit on my side of the boundary of the Northern Woods and shoot deer he'd rather sell to trophy hunters from Denmark.

I hunt whatever the hell I like on my land, especially animals that eat my crops. Game belongs to whoever owns the land where it falls. Everyone knows I'm within my rights, but no one dares say anything because they're so bloody terrified of getting on the wrong side of Aronsson.'

He leaned back in his chair.

'I'm not frightened of Harald Aronsson. He can go to hell. Who knows, he could well have shot his own windscreen and tried to blame me, to give Månsson a chance to snoop around my farm and take a look in my gun cabinet. Aronsson was probably hoping I'd have illegal weapons there, so I'd lose my guns and licence. That would have solved all his problems. But I'm not that bloody stupid. You should be investigating Aronsson instead. There's a lot of stuff about that family that could do with being dragged out into the light. But obviously no one's got the guts to do that. Not even hot-shot city cops like you.'

Rooth grinned again, then crossed one leg nonchalantly over the other. Månsson saw Borg straighten up over by the wall. He could almost feel how angry he was, and sympathised with him. But Bure kept his cool, and seemed to decide it was time to change the subject.

'You didn't join in with the search for Billy Nilsson. Why not?'

'I was busy. It's the middle of harvest.'

'Where were you the night he went missing?'

'I've already answered that, several times. In the forest, probably, or out in my fields.'

'Is there anyone who can confirm that?'

Rooth shook his head. 'The dogs, maybe. You could try bringing them in for questioning.'

Another grin, but Bure refused to let himself be provoked.

'Several witnesses say they saw your car in the vicinity of the search areas on the days following the disappearance. What were you doing there?'

Another shrug. 'I didn't know I wasn't allowed to move around the place where I live. I suppose I must have had business that way, and was a bit curious. Especially when time started to run out. I couldn't help wondering what on earth the police were doing if they couldn't find the lad.'

Månsson gritted his teeth again and clenched one hand behind his back.

'The boy, yes. Billy Nilsson. Were you curious about him, too?' Borg took a step towards the centre of the room.

'How do you mean?' Rooth turned towards Borg. He suddenly seemed more wary.

'Have you ever spoken to Billy Nilsson?'

Rooth shook his head. 'Never.'

'Never? You've got a boy the same age. Haven't you ever run into Billy and his family in the village, exchanged a few words? You're quite sure about that?'

'Yes. Nilla looks after the kids. I've only seen the lad from a distance, I know who he is.'

Borg and Bure exchanged a glance. Here it comes, Månsson thought.

'We have a credible witness who saw you and Billy Nilsson together the day before he went missing,' Borg said.

Rooth's expression changed. It was so fleeting that afterwards Månsson couldn't help wondering if he'd read it correctly. But for a couple of seconds in that stifling room, he could have sworn the man looked scared.

'That's a lie.'

Borg and Bure exchanged another glance, and Månsson understood what it meant. They had uncovered the fact that Rooth was lying. And where there was one lie, there were usually more.

'You spoke to Billy down at the petrol station just after five o'clock when his mum was inside paying,' Bure said. 'He was sitting in their car, and you spoke through the open window. The witness says it looked like you pulled the door handle and were trying to persuade Billy to get out of the car. That you'd probably have persuaded him to go with you if his mum hadn't shown up.'

Rooth said nothing for several seconds. The mocking smile was gone. His mouth was a thin white line. Månsson held his breath.

'I want to talk to a lawyer,' Rooth finally said. All of a sudden he sounded tired, almost resigned.

Afterwards the two detectives were giddy with delight. They slapped each other on the back and shook hands. Their tone was friendlier now, more comradely. Månsson mostly felt bemused, and couldn't quite figure out what he thought.

Borg called the duty prosecutor while Bure poured shots of Gammel Dansk from a hip flask. The atmosphere in the room was elated, but Månsson had trouble sharing the men's excitement. He thought about Rooth's hard eyes, his long, strong fingers. And little Billy Nilsson. The spicy liquor burned his throat, its warmth spreading through his chest and out into his blood.

In the background he heard Borg's conversation with the prosecutor.

Has a grudge against the family . . . Suspected of previous offences against the boy's uncle . . . Has shown a keen interest in the search . . . Tried to get the boy to go with him the evening before he went missing . . . Rooth's car has been washed, and looks like it's been cleaned up inside.

That last line was a lie. Bure had already taken a look in the car using the keys they had taken from Rooth. He had concluded that the rust-red Volvo Amazon estate had been tidied up, but on closer inspection they had found what might well be traces of blood in the back.

Bure was still trying to convince the prosecutor: *Rooth has lied under questioning, and has previous convictions for violent conduct.* And then the nail in the coffin: *He doesn't have an alibi for the night of the murder.*

The night of the murder, that's what they had started to call it now. The evening Billy Nilsson went missing. The evening Billy was murdered.

Månsson's shirt was sticking to his back. He suddenly felt short of breath, and had to loosen his tie and undo the top button. Borg hung up, grinned and gave them the thumbs up.

'Rooth is formally under arrest, as of now. And we've got warrants to search his car, home, business premises and surrounding areas, so call in Forensics and all the police officers we can get hold of. Two days, maximum three, before we find where he's buried the boy.'

Bure poured more Gammel Dansk and they drank another toast. More alcoholic warmth. Månsson coughed, then let out a belch.

Borg slapped him on the back. He was one of the gang now. One of the team who had cracked the case. He felt suddenly overwhelmed by relief. The tight band around his chest gave way and for a couple of seconds he thought he was about to burst into tears.

Chapter 21

She dreams about the sound made by the door of the crooked little wardrobe in her room – which would later become Billy's – when it is slowly opened. Claws scraping drily on the floor. Noses sniffing to find a young child.

She pulls the covers over her head and screams until the air runs out and her head is spinning from lack of oxygen. Someone grabs hold of the duvet and pulls it away. And then her mum is there, the wardrobe door is closed and for a brief moment everything feels better. She huddles into her mother's embrace, squeezing her as hard as her five-year-old arms can manage. But then she notices the streaks of grey in the long, strawberry-blonde hair, sees the absent look in her eyes and recognises the smell of medication, cigarette smoke and institution. This is her mum after Billy disappeared.

Mum says nothing, she hardly ever does in dreams. Just strokes her cheek and looks at her in a way that expresses both disappointment and sadness. As if it's Veronica who has let her down, who has made her mother sad, and not the other way round. The words burn in her throat, but as usual they don't emerge until the dream is starting to dissolve.

I did my best, Mum. I looked everywhere, but I couldn't find him.

It wasn't my fault.

I love you.

And then, at last, the question. The question that all the participants in her therapy group can't stop asking:

Why?

It's scorching hot inside the car when she wakes up. She winds the window down a few more centimetres to release the smell of hot plastic, but there's barely any breeze, like most days this summer. The air is quivering above the tarmac, and on the other side of the road, in front of the grey concrete box of the Civic Centre, the weeds are yellow and dried up. It is almost five o'clock on Friday afternoon, still a long time till dusk, when the heat becomes more bearable. She shifts position on the seat and tries to shake off the dream. She couldn't have been asleep for more than a few minutes, but her clothes are still sticky against the seat.

She goes through the dream in her head. Can't help smiling a little at first. Why did Uncle Harald tell such terrible stories? What did he get out of frightening little kids? She wonders if he told the same stories to Billy when she and Mattias had grown too old. If he does the same for his own son, now that he's belatedly become a father. If Timothy too wakes up crying and needing to be comforted by his mum.

She reaches for the bottle of water between the seats, drinks a couple of mouthfuls of the tepid liquid and watches the usual members of the Friday group walk up the steps, one by one. Elsa with the pearls of grief, Mia with the dead husband and old Sture with the combover. Still no sign of the blond man who says his name is Isak.

The past few days have been sheer torture, and she's had to throw herself into all kinds of activities just to get the time to pass. Cinema, jogging, television, sessions in the gym that left every muscle aching. And now she's sitting here, unable to stay away.

She carries on waiting, taking little sips of the water so she won't need to go to the toilet and interrupt her surveillance. *Drink because you're thirsty, not because you're bored.* Leon used to say that when they were out on trips together. Dalarna, Värmland, the Kingdom of Crystal in Småland. Leon liked driving. Likes driving. He isn't dead, after all, just out of reach. Unobtainable.

She's not particularly fond of cars herself. Her rattly old Golf is ten years old and has a tendency to overheat if she forgets to top up the radiator.

At two minutes to five she imagines she can hear a motorbike and adjusts the rear-view mirror in an attempt to see where it is. She sits motionless for several seconds, then opens the window a bit more to try to work out where it's gone. But the sound is drowned out by the rest of the traffic and there's no sign of a motorbike in the street.

Five o'clock, ten past, quarter past. By now at least two group members would have had time to tell their stories. There's no sign of the blond man.

Her drinking tactic doesn't seem to have worked, because her bladder is making itself impossible to ignore. At twenty past five she starts the car and sets off for home, looking in the rear-view mirror more often than she needs to.

She's in luck, and finds a parking spot just round the corner from her flat. She rushes up the stairs, throws the front door open and only just manages to pull her trousers and underpants down in time. She sits on the toilet with the door open and shuts her eyes as the smell of warm urine spreads through the little bathroom. The blond man hadn't shown up. She didn't get a chance to see what brand of cigarettes he smokes, make a note of the licence number of his motorbike, perhaps even follow him to wherever he lives. And the next therapy session isn't until Monday. Can she manage to wait that long?

The other question is whether she's still going to have a job after the weekend. It all depends if slightly-too-tall Bengt has allowed himself to be persuaded.

A sudden noise inside the flat makes her jump. A faint, irregular sound, a bit like rain on a windowsill.

She holds her breath. There it is again, and this time she hears it more clearly. There's someone there. Someone or something. Because she imagines that she recognises those clicking footsteps. She hears them in her nightmares. Claws scraping on the floor.

She gets to her feet, pulls up her trousers and lunges for the door, slamming it shut and locking it. Her heart is trying to break out of her chest and her vision blurs. She leans back against the wall and sinks down onto the floor. She forces herself to take deep, slow breaths. She can feel the small vibrations as someone walks across the floor outside. Coming closer and closer. She feels like turning the light out, because she has no duvet to pull over her head, but immediately realises that the darkness and enclosed space would only make her more frightened.

There's no window in the bathroom. The door is the only way out, and then there are three metres of hall before you reach the front door and freedom.

The cautious footsteps stop outside the bathroom door. She leans forward, trying to see under the door. She can make out a dark patch on the floor. The shadow of whoever or whatever is standing outside.

She stares at the door handle and the feeble brass lock above it. Holds her breath. Shuts her eyes.

Nothing happens. And when she opens her eyes again, the shadow outside has gone.

She doesn't know where she gets the strength to unlock the door, throw it open and rush for the front door without looking round. She thinks she hears noises behind her. Heavy breathing, feet with claws scraping on the floor.

She fumbles with the lock, instinctively keeping her head lowered. She's expecting to be bitten, to feel warm breath on her skin, teeth biting into her. Or, more likely, a strong hand grabbing her by the shoulder and dragging her back into the flat.

The front door opens and she rushes headlong into the stairwell, colliding with a man in a dark motorbike helmet and black leather jacket who's standing right outside. He's big, and looms over her like a giant. She screams, kicks and flails her arms. Hands grab her wrists, holding her clenched fists away, and he pulls her to him. The smell of leather and petrol fumes is nauseating.

'Vera,' the man yells in her ear, but the helmet makes his voice muffled and unclear. 'Vera, it's me.'

And suddenly she recognises the voice.

Mattias.

Darling,

We both know that this is dangerous, that we stand to lose everything. Yet we still can't stay away from each other. We're like two moths being drawn towards a lamp, circling the flame, round and round, while our fragile wings get hotter and hotter.

Are we going to be consumed by the flame? I don't know, and I'm not really worried about that. All I know is that I have to be near you.

I'm yours. Yours alone. Now and forever.

Chapter 22
Summer 1983

Rooth's farm was at the end of a narrow gravel track, just a few hundred metres from the edge of the Northern Forest. Three small buildings arranged in a horseshoe as protection against the wind. Walls and roofs made of dirty brown fibre cement, leaky windows that could have done with being replaced a long time ago.

A couple of grey mongrels were roaming the paved yard, barking and baring their teeth, forcing the officers to stay in the car until Rooth's wife had shut them in the run at the end of the barn.

Nilla Rooth was shy, and seemed keen to avoid direct eye contact. Månsson had met her in town. He had said hello to her in the store, or in the tailor's where she sometimes worked, but had never exchanged more than a few words with her.

The small kitchen looked out onto the yard, and smelled of fried food and damp. Two flaxen-haired children, a girl of seven and a boy around the same age as Billy Nilsson were sitting at the table, and stared up at them wide-eyed when they stepped in.

'We're here to search the house,' Bure said, unnecessarily brusquely. 'You'll have to stay in here in the meantime, is that understood?'

Nilla Rooth dried her hands on her trousers and mumbled something with her head bowed, while the children went on staring at them.

With Rooth's keys at the ready, Bure and Borg set off across the yard towards the stable and barn. They unlocked the door, then struggled to open it – the wood seemed to have swollen in the frame. Månsson stayed in the kitchen. He looked at the children and smiled as warmly as he could. The girl looked down at the table, but the boy shyly returned his smile and Månsson tried not to think about Billy Nilsson and Tommy Rooth's strong fingers.

'A cup of coffee would be great, if you've got any,' he said to Nilla Rooth. 'Perhaps the children could go up to their rooms while we're here.'

Månsson let the two city police officers get on with it while he drank his coffee. He already knew that the only things out there were empty pigsties and a filthy workshop, but Bure and Borg were welcome to find that out for themselves. Rooth never used the farm to store things that could link him to anything criminal, Månsson had figured that out last autumn, after the business with Aronsson's car. Rooth was an arrogant bastard, but he was evidently smart enough to keep his legal activities separate from those that were less legitimate. Which was why Bure and Borg weren't going to find anything today. Not here, anyway, Månsson was sure about that.

Nilla Rooth reappeared with the coffee pot and Månsson raised his chipped mug.

'Thanks, I wouldn't say no to a bit more. It's good coffee.'

Nilla Rooth blushed and looked away. She clearly wasn't used to compliments.

The last time Månsson was at the farm, Rooth had been home. He had followed them as they searched the house, mocking them when they got their uniforms dirty. Nilla and the children had mostly stayed out of sight, only visible as frightened faces in the upstairs windows.

Månsson looked at the woman standing beside him. Once upon a time she had probably been very attractive. But that was before she ended up out here with Rooth, before her body had borne the burden of childbirth and monotonous labour. Nilla Rooth could hardly be much more than thirty, even though she looked at least ten, fifteen years older.

'What does Tommy do with the animals he shoots?' Månsson said.

The hand holding the pot trembled, spilling some coffee on the table.

'I know he doesn't keep them here on the farm, he's too smart for that. So what does he do with them, Nilla?'

The woman turned her back on him. She put the coffee pot back on the hotplate and started to busy herself with the washing up, unnecessarily noisily.

'We're not actually bothered about the poaching. We're here because we think Tommy might have done something really stupid. That he might have harmed Billy Nilsson. After all, everyone knows what Tommy thinks of the boy's uncle.'

He paused for a few seconds, letting his words sink in.

'Tommy sometimes loses his temper. Sometimes he does things he later regrets, doesn't he?'

She stopped moving. Månsson made his voice as soft as he could.

'We have to find Billy. His mother is beside herself, she's shut herself up in her bedroom and won't talk to anyone. You have to help me, Nilla. Imagine if it was your son. Your little ...' Månsson couldn't remember the boy's name, so he gestured towards the ceiling and said: '... lad.'

He fell silent. Nilla Rooth stood motionless with her eyes fixed on one of the crooked cupboard doors.

'Tommy will never know that you've said anything,' Månsson said quietly. 'Never, I swear. Please, help me.'

Nilla's shoulders slowly sank. When she breathed out, it sounded almost like a sob.

Chapter 23

Veronica is sitting out on the landing with Mattias's motorcycle helmet in her lap. Her hands and thighs are shaking. Her breathing is jerky, and she hardly knows what to do with herself as Mattias goes into the flat with his pistol drawn.

Through the open door she hears him move inside the flat, methodically checking the rooms. Bathroom, kitchen, living room. And last of all the closet at the far end of the bedroom.

She doesn't hear any shouting, no commotion, no shots from the pistol. Just the sound of his cautious footsteps. She fiddles with the helmet, pushing the dark visor up and down. When did Mattias start riding a motorbike? And what is he doing six hundred kilometres from home with a pistol tucked inside his jacket?

Mattias looks out of the doorway. And says what she's already realised. 'There's no one here.'

Veronica gets to her feet and walks back inside the flat on unsteady legs. She follows him into the living room.

'Can you see anything that's missing?'

She looks around. The television is still there, and the cheap little stereo system she hardly ever uses. In the bedroom her chest of drawers looks untouched, and when she opens the top drawer the little boxes containing her few pieces of jewellery are exactly where she left them.

Everything seems to be the way it should, but she still knows that it isn't. Something about the room feels wrong.

'Do you normally leave this open?' Mattias is pointing to the narrow window in the far bedroom wall.

'Sometimes. Why?'

'It isn't properly closed.'

He's right. The window is shut, but the two metal catches on one side are pointing upwards rather than sitting in their clasps. He opens the window and sticks his head out. There's a fire-escape ladder outside which leads down to the dark inner courtyard. He seems to study the ladder carefully. Then he goes back to inspecting the catches and windowsill.

She tries to remember the last time she left the window open. Last night, probably. The through-draught is the only way to cool the flat. She shuts her eyes, takes a deep breath and tries to remember if she closed the window.

'No signs of forced entry on the frame,' Mattias says, and closes the window. 'No evidence that the ladder has been used either. You're sure you heard footsteps? It couldn't have been the window banging in the breeze?'

She almost snaps at him, saying she's certain there was someone inside the flat. But she stops herself, realising that just a few minutes ago she thought she was being chased by monsters from nightmares she had when she was a child.

'What the hell are you doing here?' she says instead.

'Up for a meeting. Do you think you might have forgotten to shut the window properly?'

'Maybe. What sort of meeting?'

'A narcotics case we're working on. National Crime wants to be kept informed, so they asked me to come up. It could be connected to one of their cases.'

'You're on your own?' She doesn't really know why she's asking. She sees him stiffen slightly.

'Me and a colleague. It was all very last-minute so I didn't have a chance to tell you beforehand.'

He turns his back on her and checks the other bedroom window, the one looking out on the street. Then he goes into the living room and does the same with the windows in there. They're all closed, and she lives on the third floor.

'I just thought I'd call by and see if you'd heard any more from that Isak. If you'd found out who he is and what he's after.'

His police voice is back. Unless it's his older brother voice. Whichever it is, it makes it clear to her that she shouldn't ask any more questions about why he's there and who he's with.

'No, he wasn't at the last meeting,' she says, which of course is perfectly true. The fact that she wasn't there either, and the reasons for that, are none of Mattias's business.

He sits down on one arm of the sofa. She can see the strap of the holster under his leather biker's jacket. Mattias's shoulders sink, and his tense jaw relaxes slightly. He's lost weight, she notices now. He looks fit and agile. His hairstyle is different too. She likes it, and tries not to think about how long it's been since they last saw each other.

'Are you absolutely certain there was someone in here?'

He tilts his head a little, the way he always used to when he was worried about her. She hasn't seen the gesture in years, and it makes her feel warm inside. Mattias has good reason to be worried. Her behaviour over the past few days has hardly been healthy. Bordering on crazy, to be honest. What would have happened if he hadn't appeared? Would she have banged on the neighbour's door? Called the police? Ruud?

She looks down. Mutters a vague apology about maybe mishearing. That the draught when she opened the front door might have made the back window slam, which then set her imagination off. At the same time she tries to convince herself that all the rest of it – the sound of footsteps and the shadow outside the bathroom door – were just figments of her imagination caused by stress and lack of sleep. Even so, she can't quite shake the uneasy feeling. Something about the flat is different. Something she can only detect as a faint tingle in the hairs on the back of her neck.

She tries to persuade Mattias to stay for dinner. She'd like to be able to tell him about the photofit picture of Billy, which looks like the blond man who says his name is Isak. She'd prefer to do that calmly, in a way that doesn't sound crazy. Besides, she doesn't want to be left on her own in the flat.

But Mattias has a prior engagement. He doesn't specify what, clearly indicating that he's not going to answer any further questions. So she walks outside with him.

His motorbike is big, black, and looks very new. The saddle has two seats, they look like little armchairs, and when he opens one of the panniers she glimpses another motorbike helmet. He sees her looking and quickly shuts it.

'Call me if you need anything, you've got my mobile number.'

She nods, then gives him an awkward hug.

'Are you free this weekend, Vera?'

'Sure.' She hopes he's about to suggest lunch or dinner, and doesn't realise she's walked into a trap before it even has time to spring shut.

'You don't feel like coming home for a couple of days? It's been so long. Dad would be really pleased. It's Mum's birthday on Sunday. You know what that means to him.'

'Maybe,' she mumbles, realising that none of her usual excuses feel entirely appropriate. It's much harder to lie to his face than it is over the phone.

'Great,' he says, as if the matter were settled. 'Well, see you there tomorrow afternoon, then we'll have time to talk properly. I've got to go now.'

He starts the engine before she has time to protest. He folds the visor down and waves to her as he slowly rides away.

She stands down in the street for a long time. It takes her almost ten minutes to pluck up the courage to go back upstairs. The unsettling feeling is still there, like an invisible mist. She opens the windows in an attempt to air it out. She gets out her cleaning things and mops the floors until the flat stinks of detergent. The effort leaves her in a sweat, and she goes into the bathroom and takes her shirt off. She stands at the window in just her bra. She leans on the windowsill for a couple of minutes until the tension has eased. The scar on her right arm looks an angry red, but it isn't actually itching at the moment.

In a while, an hour, maybe, she'll call Mattias and tell him that she won't be able to make it after all, that she can't go home to mark their mother's birthday this year either. He won't be surprised, barely even disappointed.

She goes into the closet to fetch a clean shirt. The little steps from IKEA are standing beneath one of the shelves, even though she's sure she put them back in the corner.

One corner of the box containing her grief collection is sticking out over the edge of the shelf. And when she lifts it down with trembling hands she sees that the lid isn't on properly.

Chapter 24

Summer 1983

The little gravel track was almost impossible to spot if you didn't know exactly where to look, Månsson thought. Two barely visible tyre tracks that ran alongside a stone wall between two fields. There were plenty of similar, half-overgrown tractor paths around here, and almost none of them were marked on any map.

One of the wheels drove into a hole, making the bottom of the Saab scrape along the strip of green in the middle of the track.

Bure swore. 'Damn, this car's almost new. Are you sure Rooth's old woman isn't winding us up?'

Månsson shaded his eyes with his hand and gazed off towards the dark strip of forest at the end of the field.

'There!' He pointed at the outline of a low roof, barely perceptible beneath the canopy of trees.

They left the car in the middle of the track and walked the rest of the way. They found clear tyre marks in the mud next to a puddle – probably from Rooth's Amazon – and while

Bure photographed the imprint Månsson took the chance to look around. The little pump house was right on the boundary between field and forest, just as Nilla Rooth had said.

The walls were yellow-brown brick, which had taken on a greenish tone over the years. The roof had sunk beneath a covering of moss, and the foliage brushed the tiles in places. It looked almost as if the building was huddled up. As if it was hiding, crouched in the shadows.

Something about the windowless little building and the dark forest behind it made Månsson feel uneasy, and it took him a while before he realised why. The silence. No chirruping from crickets, no birdsong, not from the fields, and not from the forest either. Only a faint rustling as the wind blew weakly through the treetops.

They didn't hear anything until they were approaching the door in one end of the building. A rattling bark, almost a scream, from somewhere in the gloom of the forest. The two detectives stopped.

'What the hell was that?' Borg said.

'A fox,' Månsson said. 'Nothing for a grown man to worry about.'

Borg glared at him sullenly and his colleague grinned. Månsson felt the sweat starting to run down his back again. The heat was oppressive, this whole summer felt like one long session in the sauna.

There was a steel bar across the door, fastened with a sturdy padlock, but Borg found the right key on Rooth's keyring at the first attempt. The door swung open without a sound, letting out cool, damp air and a cloying smell that Månsson recognised at once. Rotting meat.

He looked at the others without saying anything. Bure switched on the torch he had taken from the boot of the car and went first.

The pump house was approximately thirty square metres in size, and the roof was open all the way to the beams. The pump had been removed, probably back in the sixties when the farms in the area were put on the water-grid. But the damp and cold from the well far beneath the foundations was still clinging to the walls, mixing with the smell of blood and decay.

There were three animal carcases hanging from the roof. Stainless steel hooks had been driven into their thin necks before the animals were hoisted up with the help of chains and pulleys attached to the roof beams.

Their chests and abdomens gaped emptily, their hooves hanging scarcely any distance above the bloodstained stone floor. The glare of the torch reflected off empty, glassy eyes, and the two city detectives stopped.

'Two roe deer calves and one red deer,' Månsson declared. 'None of them legal to hunt at this time of year.'

The beam of the torch swung round, and Bure must have found a light switch because there was a click and a couple of old fluorescent lights flickered into life. There was a battered old freezer along one side of the room, and a low door at the far end. Bure put the torch away and pulled out his camera. The click of the shutter echoed off the stone walls.

Månsson went over to the freezer. It was big enough to hold a grown man, so it could take a five-year-old boy with no problem at all. The white lid was covered with bloody fingerprints. Månsson took a deep breath. Steeled himself. Raised the lid cautiously.

The freezer was divided into two large compartments. In the right-hand one were a couple of dozen neatly marked paper parcels of various sizes: *Pheasant July '83, Roe deer saddle July '83, Red deer fillet June '83, Red deer haunch June '83.*

The other end contained large transparent plastic bags. He picked one up and found a black and white badger pelt. Borg looked over his shoulder.

'Well?'

Månsson shook his head despondently. 'Just a load of meat and skins that Rooth hasn't managed to sell yet.'

Along the other wall there was a stainless steel bench, also covered with bloodstains, and above it hung a selection of tools, ten knives and meat cleavers of various sizes. There was a large saucepan on top of an electric hotplate. Borg lifted the lid and immediately jerked back.

'Jesus fucking Christ, what the hell is that?!'

Månsson looked down into the pan. A pair of horns were sticking up out of the grey-black porridge-like sludge. The stench was overwhelming.

'A red deer skull,' he said. 'The antlers look pretty good. Bronze or silver, maybe. Rooth's boiling the flesh off so he can mount and sell them.'

'Mmh.' Borg's grunt suggested he had just learned something new, which pleased Månsson. It was thanks to him that they were here, after all. It was thanks to him that they were getting close to solving the case, and it was high time the two detectives recognised that.

'Come and look over here!' Bure had opened the low door at the far end of the room. Inside was a small room, no more than five or six square metres in area.

The light from the other room wasn't strong enough to reach inside, so Bure had switched his torch on again. He was pointing it at an old metal bedstead covered with a stained mattress and a blanket. Beside the bed was an electric radiator, and beside that an empty vodka bottle and a bundle of adult magazines, their edges curled with damp.

The fox barked out in the forest again. Closer now, more shrill. It sounded almost like a child's cry and Månsson shivered in spite of himself. Bure swung the beam of the torch towards one end of the bed, where a metal object was fastened around one of the posts.

A pair of handcuffs.

Chapter 25

O ne of the first things she notices when she emerges
from the forest onto the great expanse of the plain is all
the wind turbines. White steel towers, almost one hundred
metres tall, in regimented lines, their red eyes winking in
sequence at night. Wind giants, that's how she usually thinks
of them. On breezy days their heartbeat can be heard several
kilometres away. A dull, pulsating rumble that makes her feel
unsettled.

When she was a child there weren't any wind giants. Back
then the silos were the tallest things around. Big, shiny metal
cylinders, one or two per farm, sometimes more. She used
to think of them as silver towers silently watching over the
fields, farms and people. Now the towers look tiny in the
company of the giants, shrunken, like so many other things
from her childhood.

Mattias took her up onto their silo once. It was before Billy
disappeared, in the days when Mattias was still her best friend
and she never wanted summer to end. They waited until Billy
was having his lunchtime nap, didn't want to have the little
tell-tale following them.

She can still remember how she felt as she climbed the rusty steps. The vibrations in the warm metal, the excitement of doing something that wasn't allowed, and the fact that Mattias trusted her.

'Keep looking up, Vera. Just look up.'

She followed his advice. She didn't look round until they had reached the gently domed top of the silo and the height turned her stomach into a knot of terror and excitement.

Mattias pointed everything out to her. The church tower in the village a few kilometres away. Ängsgården, which Uncle Harald had taken over from Grandfather, with three times as many silver towers as anyone else. The ridge and Northern Forest which blocked the view way off in the distance like a dark, jagged line. When she turned and looked south, there were no such obstructions. Just a patchwork of green and yellow fields all the way to the horizon, and above them a blue sky that seemed endless. It was the first time she realised just how big the world actually was. The first time that anxious, nagging feeling hit her.

The birds' nest was built from sticks, twigs and bits of green paper from seed sacks. It was tucked between two of the silo's roof struts, tucked beneath a loose sheet of tin that protected it against wind, rain and crows. There were three eggs, greenish blue-white, in the middle of the nest.

'Goshawks,' Mattias said confidently. 'They catch chickens and ducks. Pheasants too, Uncle Harald told me. Poachers.' He spat over the edge of the silo and nodded towards her.

It took her a few seconds to realise what he meant. What he wanted her to do.

Afterwards she swore never to tell anyone. That it would be their secret for ever and ever. It wasn't until they got down and saw their younger brother running towards the house as fast as his legs would carry him that they realised that wasn't what was going to happen.

The car radio crackles, wavering between static and music before finally opting for the former. She turns the dial until she finds a local station playing old favourites. An Abba track is playing and she turns the volume up. Then she winds the window down a bit further. Her car doesn't have air-conditioning, so she has to try to find the right balance between maximum airflow and being able to hear the music.

'Hasta Mañana.'

She can hardly remember anything about the first two hours of her drive the previous evening. She has a vague recollection of throwing a few essentials in a bag, rushing down the stairs and jumping into the car. She remembers passing Södertälje and realising that she was heading south. She stopped in Linköping, completely exhausted. She spent the night in an impersonal motel with noisy air-conditioning and cheap sheets. But that was still better than staying at home. Because someone had definitely been in the flat. An intruder who had climbed in through the window facing the court-yard and gone through her belongings, so carefully and qui-etly that he had left hardly any sign that he had been there. If it hadn't been for the steps and moved box, she might almost have been able to persuade herself that he'd never even been there. That her home was still a safe place.

He must have been caught by surprise when he heard the door to the flat open. Snuck into the hall to check he'd heard right, realised she'd locked herself inside the bathroom, then left in a hell of a hurry.

She could have called Mattias and told him all about it, that there really had been someone there, that she hadn't imagined it. That there was proof that even he couldn't dismiss. But Mattias is no longer her best friend. And these days he has his own secrets, the sort he doesn't share with her. That thought sours her mood and she turns the radio up a bit more and joins in.

It was one of her mum's favourite songs, on one of the albums she used to play for her before Billy was born. She wonders if the records are still there in the cupboard under the record player. Probably. Dad never moves anything. Especially not Mum's things. So the records are almost certainly still there, along with the James Last albums she and Mattias gave him every Christmas after Billy, and which he hardly even plays. The last time Veronica was home was when her dad turned fifty-three. She tries to tell herself that was only last year, or possibly the year before. In fact it was just over five years ago. Half a decade. A bit longer than Billy was alive. Or perhaps not.

The song comes to an end. It's followed by adverts, so she turns the volume down again.

By now she has had the chance to think everything through carefully, put the pieces of the puzzle together in a way that seems more or less logical.

Fact: she should have been leading a group therapy session at the Civic Centre at the time of the break-in, so the flat ought to have been empty.

Conclusion: the intruder is someone who knows her routine. Someone who has mapped out her movements, maybe even been watching her.

She thinks about the smoker outside her flat. And the fact that she never saw whoever it was enter or leave any of the other buildings. All she saw was a dark silhouette, the glow of a cigarette, then later a few butts in the gutter. Red Prince, enough to suggest that the smoker had stood down there in the street on more than one occasion. Smoking in silence, possibly while he looked up at her windows.

The blond man smokes. He should have been at the therapy session yesterday, just like her. He's in his mid-twenties, has memories that correspond with both Billy's disappearance and the garden back home. If you added the strange attraction she feels towards him, not to mention his disconcerting similarity to the photofit picture – what conclusions dare she draw from that?

She's been through her reasoning several times, but she's still having trouble accepting it. If Isak is Billy – and she sticks with 'if' mostly to stop herself getting carried away – that would turn her whole life upside down. It would turn *all* their lives upside down, which is the main reason why she has set out on this roadtrip. Because she could have driven back home this morning instead. She could have changed the locks on the door, got an alarm, made sure she kept the bedroom window properly shut. But she didn't.

Obviously she's thought about Billy over the years. Wondered who he would have become if he'd had the chance to grow up. If he would have been good at sport like Mattias, or liked writing like her and Mum. Maybe Billy would have inherited Dad's gentleness, his interest in cooking and gardening? Dreams and speculation, at least up until now. Because suddenly there's a possibility of getting answers to those questions.

The first thing she realised when she woke up on that hard motel bed was that she needs to talk to Dad. Tell him that his youngest son is probably alive, and that even if everything isn't going to be fine from now on, it will at least be much better. And she has to do it face to face, like a good daughter. For Dad's sake, she tells herself for the umpteenth time. Even if she knows that isn't the whole truth.

'*Hasta mañana*,' she sings to herself. She raises her voice to drown out the noise from the open window.

Chapter 26

Summer 1983

Månsson had stood up and was about to pack up for the day when there was a knock on the half-open door to his office.

Britt from reception was standing in the doorway. He pulled his jacket from the back of his chair to demonstrate that she had come at a bad time, but she didn't let herself be deterred.

'You've got a visitor,' she said curtly.

Månsson threw his hands out. 'Now? I was just about to go home. I haven't eaten dinner with my family for two weeks. Or supper, even,' he added.

He was being treated to cod with mustard sauce, and he'd been looking forward to it all day, just as he'd been looking forward to spending a bit of time with Malin and the boys. The chance to spend a few hours not having to think about that dank pump house and its horrific contents.

Britt nodded. 'It's probably best if you see this visitor.'

Månsson sighed.

'OK, but can you do me a favour? Come back in five minutes and say that the Regional Chief of Police is on the phone, please.'

Månsson put his jacket aside and sat down on his worn office chair, thinking about the dinner that risked being delayed. It struck him that Britt hadn't said who the visitor was, and obviously he should have found out before he agreed to stay.

There was another knock on his door, and before he had time to react Harald Aronsson walked into the room.

'I want to see him,' he said abruptly, without bothering with any introductory pleasantries.

Månsson sat up straighter. 'Well . . .' he began, but Aronsson cut him off.

'Tommy Rooth. I want to see him. Now!' Aronsson folded his arms and stared at him.

'I see . . .' Månsson said, mostly to gain a bit of time. He glanced towards the door in the hope that Britt might be about to come to his rescue.

Aronsson went on staring at him with his bird of prey's eyes, and Månsson couldn't help squirming uncomfortably. He thought about his dinner again, and Malin and the boys waiting for him.

'OK. But it'll have to be quick.'

Månsson slowly tapped in the code to open the sturdy door that separated the station's offices from the custody unit. He had realised that this was a bad idea during the short walk along the corridor. He should have refused Aronsson's request point blank. But he hadn't, and now it was too late. He wished Bure and Borg had been there. It would have been far easier if one of them had confronted Aronsson, but he hadn't seen either of the detectives all day.

There was something about Harald Aronsson that scared him. All his resolve turned to doubt the moment the tall man fixed his eyes on him. Månsson wasn't alone in that. There weren't many people in the village who dared to oppose Aronsson, but that was scant comfort just then.

Kant, the officer on duty in the little glass-sided office in the custody unit, stood up when the two men walked in. He took a couple of steps forward and raised his eyebrows slightly. Månsson gestured to indicate that everything was fine. He needed to stay calm, and stop the situation from getting out of control.

'Rooth,' he said. 'Which cell is he in?'

'Has something happened?' Kant didn't move, just kept looking between Aronsson and Månsson.

'No, we're just going to check on him,' Månsson said. 'Which cell is he in?'

The policeman gave Månsson another long look.

'Four.'

Månsson turned and gestured to Aronsson to follow him. He walked as slowly as he could along the grey linoleum.

The custody unit only had four cells, and Rooth's was at the end, in the corner. Månsson stopped outside. He paused for a couple of seconds before opening the eye-level shutter in the door.

Rooth was sitting on the bunk inside the bare room. He barely bothered to look up when he heard the sound of the hatch. He looked deflated, and there was no sign of his usual arrogance. When he caught sight of Månsson he straightened up a little and his eyes regained some of their defiance.

Månsson turned and nodded towards the hatch, at the same time pressing his back against the door handle and lock.

'There you go. He's in there.'

Aronsson stared at Månsson with those bird of prey eyes. He made no move to look through the hatch. Aronsson was a head taller than him. His stare burned into Månsson's face, and he realised why the man was there. And knew what would happen if he backed down again.

He lowered his chin and folded his arms before meeting Aronsson's gaze. Through the various smells of the custody unit he suddenly became aware of the odour of sweat, and realised it was coming from him. Aronsson went on staring silently at him.

Månsson felt a trickle of sweat run down one temple. He pursed his lips. Forced himself not to look away. He mustn't back down.

'Well, he's in there. Do you want to look or not?'

Aronsson didn't move. Månsson almost imagined he could hear the seconds ticking by. He counted them off silently to himself as the sweat poured down his back.

When he had got to eight Aronsson suddenly turned his head and leaned forward to look through the hatch. Then he slowly straightened up. The clenched set of his mouth and chin had suddenly softened a little.

'Happy?' Månsson said. His uniform shirt was so wet that he was almost sticking to the cell door.

The corners of Aronsson's mouth rose in what could be taken to be a smile, but he still didn't speak. He didn't open his mouth until they were back out in reception.

'Thank you, Krister.'

'Don't mention it.' Månsson did his best to sound relaxed. As if what had just happened inside the custody unit was perfectly normal.

He waited a few moments for Aronsson to leave, but instead of walking off towards the glass doors he just stood there. Aronsson held out his right hand, and after a brief hesitation Månsson shook it. Aronsson's grip was firm, and he held on to Månsson's hand, then nodded and looked at him with an expression that Månsson couldn't interpret at first. Then he suddenly realised what it was. Something he had worked hard for, but had begun to doubt that he would ever achieve.

Respect.

Månsson straightened up. He cleared his throat and squeezed Aronsson's hand a little harder.

'Just doing my job, Harald.'

Chapter 27

The turning is getting closer, she sees the sign and eases her foot off the accelerator pedal. All of a sudden she feels nervous. Five years since last time. But it doesn't feel like it. Maybe that's because everything still looks almost exactly the same. First the rectangular boxes of the pea factory out in the middle of the fields. The weekend shift's cars are parked outside. Ten, twelve, no more. Far fewer than when she had a summer job there. Most of it's probably done by machines now. More efficient, cheaper. More money for the shareholders. The company logo on the flag has changed since last time, but the sign at the top of the corrugated wall is the same: PEAFAC – PROUD SPONSORS OF MISS PEA SINCE 1965.

She thinks of her mum, who won the very first Miss Pea contest when she was just seventeen years old. In spite of the title, and no matter how rotten the whole notion of beauty pageants is, her junior-school self still feels rather proud of that. That her mum was more beautiful than everyone else's. But she would never admit that, barely even to herself.

After turning left at the junction she passes the big red building of Reftinge Brickworks. From a distance it looks almost attractive, but as she gets closer she can make out the boarded-up windows and barbed wire fence, where plastic bags have got caught and are now fluttering in the wind. On the cracked cement yard there are four long white cylinders waiting to be joined together to form new wind giants. They belong to Strid Engineering, which is based next door to the brickworks and has been specialising in wind turbines since the 1980s.

She remembers the Strid brothers pretty well. Two stocky men with bull-necks who used to hang around the drinks table at Uncle Harald's parties, occasionally casting longing glances at her mum when they thought no one was looking. How old had she herself been when men started to look at her that way? Fifteen, maybe, or sixteen. No older than that.

Immediately beyond the workshop and petrol station is the sports ground with the wooden stand that was the ultimate hang-out for smoking and snogging in the eighties. The space under the stand was locked, but you could easily climb over the gate into the darkness. She remembers the excitement, the smell and taste of cigarettes, of another person. The feeling of doing something forbidden, something Mum and Dad wouldn't like. Of having your whole life ahead of you, when anything was possible. She smiles at the memory, but that all fades away as she reaches the steep slope leading down towards the village itself.

Reftinge lies in a hollow, a long geological depression that cuts across the plain. At one end the hollow rises almost imperceptibly until it reaches the level of the surrounding land about ten kilometres south of the village. At the other end it narrows as it disappears into the Northern Forest, where it ends in a steep ravine high up on the ridge where coal was once mined. The mine is the reason Reftinge's coat of arms features both an ear of corn and a pickaxe. She heard the explanation at some local festival, and tries to repeat the words in her junior-school teacher's nasal voice in the rear-view mirror. The result is good enough to prompt a small smile.

A river – more of a stream, really – runs lazily through the village along the bottom of the hollow, with the railway running parallel to it. A ten-metre-long bridge is enough to connect the west part of Reftinge with the east.

At the bottom of the slope, at the start of the main street – called, of course, Main Street – you pass between two almost identical signs: PIZZA – KEBAB – SALAD. When she was at school the larger of the two pizzerias was owned by the family of her classmate Lidija. Lidija was really too plain and over-weight for the boys to be interested in her, but she was cocky and quick-witted enough to stop anyone teasing her. And she had a video recorder, a SodaStream and a popcorn machine at home, which, along with the free pizzas her dad always pro-vided, made Lidija one of the most popular kids in the class.

She wonders what Lidija is doing now, if she's one of the ones who stayed or left. Probably the latter.

A bit further on, past a three-storey block of council flats, is the centre of the village. The council offices, police station, health centre, library and school. Then the square, with the pub, the florist's and the only remaining grocery store. She's fairly sure it's still run by Aunt Berit and Uncle Sören. She can't really imagine them doing anything else. The shop looks a lot smaller than she remembers as she drives past. Maybe her memory's playing tricks on her, unless they've actually decreased the floor area, slowly winding down in line with the rest of the village. The bank and post office disappeared in the early nineties, the photographer who took the family photograph in her grief-box has gone, and the furniture store had to close when IKEA opened in the nearest city. The squat building now houses a flea-market run by the sports associa- tion, open every other Friday, according to the printed sign in one of the windows.

She winds the side window right down and leans her elbow on the door. The street in front of her is deserted apart from an old man who's cycling so slowly on a woman's bike that it ought really to be physically impossible. There isn't much going on in Reftinge on a Saturday afternoon in the middle of summer. Nor any other time, to be honest.

Almost at the end of Main Street – before you go past the railway station where the trains haven't stopped since the seventies – is the fast-food kiosk which is the real hub of the village. Here at least there are signs of life.

On the patch of gravel in front of the kiosk she can see two tractors and three pick-ups, all the same green colour. The logo on the doors is familiar. ARONSSON FARMING. Uncle Harald's business, given that name after he went on a research trip to the USA in the late eighties. It's been a recurrent topic of conversation ever since. *In America, you know, they . . .*

A few men in flannel shirts with the sleeves rolled up are standing in the shade of the projecting roof. They're staring at her car. Uncle Harald's employees are working in the heat even though it's Saturday. The crops don't distinguish between the days of the week. Out here summer and autumn are one long sequence of harvests, from strawberries and new potatoes in June through to the sugar beet in November.

She drives across the bridge, past the small fire station and carries on through the residential district. Rows of matching single-storey houses built of the red Reftinge bricks that are no longer produced, and beyond them split-level houses from the seventies with darker, gloomier façades. Around half of her old classmates lived here. The rest were fairly evenly distributed between farms and council flats.

The road to the church leads her back up to the plain. The little white church balancing on the eastern edge of the hollow dates back to the twelfth century, the authoritative junior-school teacher's voice in her head says, and she quickly turns the radio up before it has time to go on. She finds herself listening to Laura Branigan's 'Self Control', one of her favourite songs.

They used to go to church every Sunday, the whole of the Nilsson-Aronsson clan. Her, Mum, Dad, Mattias, Billy, even Uncle Harald. Smartly dressed up, the way Mum wanted. No one ever dared object. So she and Mattias would sit through the hymns and sermons, glancing up at the little painting on the ceiling that could only be seen from the first few rows. A goat's head with curved horns. The creepy little head had probably been left uncovered by one of the workers who painted over all traces of Catholicism in the 1700s, possibly as a joke. That's what she and Mattias chose to believe, anyway. But that grinning head could just as easily have been a warning. A reminder that even if you could hide the past away, it was still there.

Dad stopped going to church soon after Billy went missing, so she's only been there a couple of times since then, for Mum's funeral and Mattias's wedding. Different ceremonies, but equally horrible.

She thinks about the ice again, about Mum. And turns the radio up even more to drive the thoughts away. For a few moments she's back in the comforting darkness under the spectators' stand. In the feeling of being young and optimistic. Immortal.

Halfway round the S-bend by the church she realised that she should have stopped to visit Mum's grave. But before she has time to ease her foot off the accelerator she decides to put that off until tomorrow.

She passes the vicarage and parish hall at the top of the rise, leaving the village behind as she emerges up onto normal ground-level again. The road narrows, loses the line running down the middle and slowly straightens out, becoming what feels like an endless long straight between the fields of grain and giant wind turbines.

Here and there gravel tracks lead away from the road, marked by green mailboxes that prove there are other houses between the village and their own farm. There were ten mailboxes when she was a child, seven when she left home. Now there are four. She sees several combines and tractors at work. Almost all the same colour and bearing the same logo as the vehicles at the kiosk. Uncle Harald's empire is evidently still growing.

A little more than three kilometres from the village she sees the crooked post of the familiar mailbox and slows down. Even so, she turns off unnecessarily quickly and the car skids slightly on the loose gravel. The roof of the main house is just visible through the trees a few hundred metres away. These days the roof is the highest point at Backagården. The silo where she and Mattias found the goshawks' nest was dismantled a long time ago.

On the way to the farm she passes yet another green pick-up. The driver is wearing a trucker's cap, aviator sunglasses and is talking on a mobile phone. He nods to her as the vehicles pass each other with barely any gap between them. She recognises him vaguely. Patrik something. One of Mattias's former classmates, and now another teenage memory pops up. A party, a slow track on the record player. A taste of saliva, tobacco and alcohol, hands fumbling over her body. She has quite a lot of memories of that sort, and forces her mind to change track before it summons more of them up.

The fields between the road and the farm have already been harvested. Large round bales lie scattered across the sharp stubble. The heat is making the horizon hazy, and two kites are circling on the thermals in the sky. Round and round, as they stare down at the ground looking for prey. She thinks about the goat's head again and stifles a shudder. High time she pulled herself together. She's starting to get wound up, the way she does before a therapy session. Apprehension, anticipation. Possibly even excitement. She's doing this for Dad's sake, she tries to tell herself again.

She drives into the shade of the avenue of chestnut trees that leads to the farm. One of the trees looks almost dead, its dry, bare branches reaching up towards the sky.

The buildings are laid out in a U-shape around the yard. The main house on the little hillock is flanked by buildings that used to be cowsheds and barns, but which have stood empty for the past twenty-five years, with the exception of the cart shed, where Dad parks his car, and the workshop behind it. She looks at the buildings. The door to the cowshed has a new steel bar across it, and a shiny, heavy padlock. She can't help thinking about the little milking parlour in there. The smell, the darkness, the raw smell. The panic when she realised she couldn't open the door.

The roof of the old cart shed seems to have sunk even lower. The tiles are grey, and the overall impression makes the building look tired and resigned. Grass and leaves are sticking up from the gutters, and there are tall weeds and nettles growing beside the buildings.

A large green diesel tank bearing the Aronsson Farming logo catches her eye. It wasn't there the last time she was home. The metal tank annoys her, it doesn't fit in, it's far too industrial and modern. Another sign that Uncle Harald is everywhere.

The front door to the house is locked. She knocks a couple of time without anything happening, which worries her slightly. Her dad knows she's coming, she called him from the motel this morning. He usually leaves the door unlocked when he's home.

The spare key is in the usual place, in the front of the window box hanging under the nearest window. She unlocks the door and is met by the familiar smell. The one which transforms her in a fraction of a second from Veronica Lindh to Vera Nilsson. The smell of home. She hates it, or at least tries to. And today that's even harder than usual.

'Dad? Hello!'

No answer. She goes inside, closes and locks the door behind her. Despite the heat outside, the old stone house is cool and the sudden change in temperature gives her goosebumps.

To the left is what used to be the gentlemen's room, where the smell of Grandfather's cigars still clings to the wallpaper. Behind that is the best parlour, with its heavy furniture and Mum's piano, which has stood silent for twenty years. She turns right, through the dining room and into the kitchen. The newspaper is open on the kitchen table, and beside it is a half-drunk cup of cold coffee. No sign of Dad.

The house is almost silent, the only sounds the ticking of the clock on the wall of the dining room and the buzzing of a large fly in the kitchen window. The fly keeps hitting the glass without understanding why it isn't getting anywhere. Every so often it falls to the windowsill and lies there exhausted until it summons up the energy to make another vain attempt to escape.

She goes and looks in the study. The desk is covered with papers and documents. Most have the Aronsson Farming logo on, but some are from an energy company and the council. Some seem to be contracts and documents relating to planning consent.

The battered leather sofa is still standing along one wall, but the bulky television is new. A big screen, in that new widescreen format that she still isn't used to. She wonders when her dad got that? Beside the sofa is a pile of blankets and pillows, and there's a medicine bottle on one of the armrests. She can't resist the temptation to take a closer look. Sleeping pills, prescribed little more than a month ago. Odd, because as far as she knows, Dad's never had any trouble sleeping. She tries to remember how it was just after Billy, but she can only remember Mum. She was the one everyone tiptoed around. Mum, who couldn't bring herself to get out of bed and for whose sake they all had to whisper when they were in the house. They carried on doing that for weeks after Mum had been taken off to the home, which was the word they absolutely had to use. The home. Not the description everyone in the area usually used for that sort of institution. The mental hospital.

The window is slightly ajar and she hears an indistinct sound from the garden. The tall poplars that edge the garden are hardly moving at all. Even out here on the plain there's unusually little wind. She hears the sound again, a bit louder this time. A metal tool hitting soil and stones.

She goes back out into the kitchen, opens the door and walks out onto the raised terrace that runs along the rear of the house. She leaves the door open to give the fly one last chance of freedom.

From here she can see most of the garden. The overgrown lawn, the fruit trees, the treehouse she and Mattias built, and the hollow elm the blond man mentioned in the therapy session. She's having trouble thinking of him as Isak, but she isn't yet ready to start calling him anything else.

Beyond the fruit trees is the wild shrubbery that reaches all the way to the boundary, and beyond she can see the field of maize. On the horizon are the tops of two wind giants, the first ones in the village, which Uncle Harald put up just a few months after Billy went missing. She steps down from the terrace so she doesn't have to see them.

To the right is the walled rose garden. It faces south, and if she remembers rightly it was established as a kitchen garden by her great-grandfather. Dad restored and replanted it the spring after he and Mum got married. He raised the height of the wall to provide better protection against the wind, built the cold-frames and summerhouse, set out the paths and, not least, planted all the beautiful roses as a belated wedding present. Mum loved roses. And this way she would be able to see and smell them simply by opening her bedroom window.

Veronica used to like that story, the idea that the rose garden was a symbol of Dad's love for Mum. After Billy went missing and Mum died, the garden became Dad's sanctuary. Somewhere to hide. Perhaps she'll be able to change that now?

The wooden gate in the wall is closed, but there are noises behind it and it isn't locked. She pushes it open and peers in.

The heavy scent of roses hits her, bringing her up short. This was just how Mum's bedroom used to smell.

Inside the tall walls there's no sign of the decay that reigns in the rest of the garden. In the neatly edged beds, expertly pruned roses climb either up the wall or metal frames. There's no hint of any weeds between the slabs in the path, and along the short side of the garden, closest to the house, the summerhouse sits almost entirely enclosed within perfectly maintained foliage. The little building has no solid roof, but the roses are twined tightly across the cross-beams.

Beyond the summerhouse, in the corner below Mum's bedroom window, Dad is on all fours, half covered by one of the biggest rosebushes in the whole garden.

She stands and watches him for a few moments. He's only fifty-eight, but ever since Mum's funeral his movements have been slow, deliberate, as if everything took an immense effort of will. But right now he is moving quickly, almost nimbly. His gloved hands move back and forth, pulling out tiny weeds and tossing them on the rug beside him. He runs a small rake over the shingle. Smooths it out until the small stones are lying perfectly. They're gleaming almost as white as the roses above his head.

She pushes the gate open a bit further and takes a step into the garden, and opens her mouth to call to him, but before she can do that one of the old hinges makes a creaking sound.

The sudden noise makes her dad turn round sharply. His eyes are open wide, but the look of surprise on his face vanishes the moment he realises it's her, replaced by the gentle smile she knows so well.

'Hello, Vera, are you here already? I thought you weren't getting here till this afternoon?'

He gets up onto his knees and then, with some effort, to his feet. He brushes off his trousers and walks towards her along the narrow path. His movements are once more heavy and deliberate.

'It's almost two o'clock,' she says, hugs him and kisses him on the cheek. He smells of soil, aftershave and something else, something that makes her sad. The smell of an old man, maybe.

'Really? I must have lost track of time. Have you eaten, would you like me to get you something?'

'No, thanks, just coffee would be great.' As usual, her accent changes without her even thinking about it.

He puts his arm round her and guides her slowly towards the door. But she doesn't want to leave, not just yet. She stops in front of the bush covered with pink flowers that's planted next to the summerhouse and covers the whole of the roof.

'How beautiful it is now,' she says. 'Big, too.'

She looks at the little brass sign that's stuck in the ground beside the plant. MAGDALENA. Mum's very own rose, bred by Dad. A rose he's spent the last twenty years nurturing.

'That white one's lovely, too.'

She points at the big bush he has just been weeding so carefully. She knows he's proud of his garden, and complimenting him on it is an easy but perfectly legitimate way of getting him in a better mood.

'That's one of yours as well, isn't it?'

'Mm.' Her dad nods happily.

She's been able to feel his grief from a distance, she could feel it from the gate, maybe even from the other side of the wall. It doesn't give her any sort of kick, because his grief is also hers. Dad has let his grief become his whole life. Screening it behind garden walls where he nurtures it tenderly, as carefully as the roses. She prefers other people's.

All of a sudden she realises that she misses the group therapy sessions. It's like a sort of withdrawal, and it only grows stronger as she stands there beside her dad breathing in the scent of the roses. She looks away, shuts her eyes, tries to shake off the feeling. His hand pats her back rather feebly. It helps, at least a little. She opens her eyes, leans her head against his shoulder and surreptitiously studies him.

He seems the same as usual. But there was something about the look on his face when he turned round, just before he realised it was her standing by the gate. She can't recall having seen it before, but perhaps the shadows under the rose bush were playing tricks on her.

They start to walk towards the house, and by the time they reach the kitchen door she's almost managed to convince herself that it was all just an illusion, a figment of her imagination.

Because if she didn't know better, she would have said that the look she saw on his face was fear.

Chapter 28

Summer 1983

Månsson managed to get all the way to dessert without either thinking or saying anything about Billy's case. He devoured three helpings of cod while he listened attentively as Malin and Johan talked about their days at school. He even managed to come up with a few polite questions in between mouthfuls. The telephone, which he had finally dared to plug back in the other day, remained silent out in the hall.

All in all it was a perfect evening, even if he might have wished that Jakob had been a bit more talkative. He had tried, tentatively, to find out if his schoolmates' teasing had stopped now that Tommy Rooth was behind bars, but he didn't get a clear answer.

Jakob would soon be fourteen, so he was hardly at an age when you confided in your parents. Månsson still felt he was doing his best, providing crisps and drinks whenever Jakob and his friends played games down in the basement in the evenings. He made an effort to appreciate the monotonous, industrial music he listened to, and had stopped asking why he had to have a tuft of hair left uncut at the back of his neck. But usually Jakob just rolled his eyes and grunted when he tried to talk to him. Månsson had found out from Malin that this season would probably be Jakob's last in the football team, which was a disappointment he was going to have trouble hiding, especially seeing as he was the team's coach. He wondered what had happened to the little boy who slept with his toy pistol in bed with him and wanted to catch bad guys just like his dad. He wished he'd made more of an effort to enjoy that time.

This evening Månsson wasn't going to let himself be deflated by his shortcomings as a parent. He was just happy to get the chance to spend some time with his family without interruption at last.

'So, how's it going?' his wife asked when the boys had cleared their dishes away and were sitting in front of the television down in the games room.

'Well. We're waiting for the test results from the pump house and Rooth's car. But that's mostly a formality. We've got him.'

Månsson realised that he had borrowed the last two sentences from Bure or Borg. He liked the two city cops better now. A sort of reluctant respect had developed, and had only grown stronger when they refrained from trying to persuade the District Police Chief to have Rooth transferred to the city prison. He had been pretty sure they would do that, snatching the suspect from the Hicksville cops to grab the glory for themselves.

'Rooth was probably planning to blackmail Aronsson. Force him to compensate him for the hunting licence and income he believed had been stolen from him. But something went wrong and Billy died. I imagine the body's buried somewhere in the forest behind the pump house. We're busy searching right now.'

'And Rooth still hasn't confessed?' Malin spooned another pear in chocolate sauce onto his dish.

Månsson shook his head. 'I don't think he's going to either.'

'Why not?'

'Because some crimes are so terrible that the perpetrator never confesses, even though he knows he did it. There are two reasons for that.'

He put his dessert spoon down and held up one finger, just as Bure had done the other day when he explained the same thing to him.

'One: if you confess to something as terrible as killing a child, that makes you a terrible person. An evil person. Your friends and family have no choice but to cut you off and distance themselves from you. At a stroke you lose whatever support network you might have left.'

'But they'll still see the evidence. If you're found guilty in court, that's usually because you *are* actually guilty.'

'Of course, but this is about emotions, not logic. People find it really hard to accept that someone they know well, maybe even someone they have kids with, might be capable of doing something terrible. That they've lived with someone like that without noticing anything.' Månsson lowered his hand and drank a sip of coffee. 'As long as there's no confession, anyone who feels so inclined can regard it as a miscarriage of justice, that they're not the ones who make a mistake. People see what they want to, basically.'

'Mm.' Malin refilled her own cup. 'That argument is based on the idea that everyone thinks people are either good or utterly bad. That it isn't possible to be a good friend, a good husband, and simultaneously a serious criminal. Which surely is perfectly possible,' she added, half as a question, half as a statement. 'A bank robber can be a good dad. A murderer can be a good friend.'

'Of course.' Månsson nodded.

'But it can't be a fear of losing his loved ones that's stopping Rooth from confessing, can it?' Malin raised one eyebrow slightly. 'He hasn't got any friends, and hardly any family to support him. Half the village were pointing the finger at him long before you arrested him.'

'True,' Månsson said. 'Rooth belongs to the second category.'

'Meaning what?' Malin said, before he had time to raise a second finger.

'That the crime he's suspected of is so terrible that he can't cope with admitting it, even to himself. That's far more common among people like Rooth who have an inflated sense of their own importance.'

Malin put her cup down.

'So you're saying that Rooth, no matter how much evidence you present him with, will never say what he did to Billy Nilsson because that would mean admitting to himself that he's a monstrous child killer?'

Månsson nodded slowly, and was about to say something when Jakob came into the kitchen. He was holding an empty bowl in his hand, and waved it about vaguely.

'Are there any more crisps?'

'In the larder,' Malin said. 'You're taking more for Johan as well, aren't you?'

Jakob muttered something in response. Månsson looked at his eldest son's back and suddenly remembered that he had meant to ask him something.

'Jakob?'

'Mm.'

'Do you know the Nilsson kids? Mattias and Vera?'

Jakob went on rummaging through the larder for a few moments before he turned round.

'What do you mean, *know*?'

Månsson tried not to let himself get wound up by the aggressive tone. Jakob glowered at him, then gave in.

'I know who they are, but we're not friends, if that's what you're wondering.'

'What are they like?'

Jakob shrugged his shoulders. 'Mattias is keen on sport.'

'And Vera?'

Another shrug, possibly even more reluctant than the last one.

'What about her?'

'What's she like?'

Jakob pulled an ambiguous grimace. 'She's hard to miss. Look, *Hill Street Blues* is about to start, so . . .'

He squirmed a little and took a couple of steps towards the door.

'Does she have many friends?'

Jakob stopped in the doorway. 'Not among the girls,' he said with a slight smile. 'But the boys like her.'

Darling,

At the end of the summer we're going to get away from here. You promised me that a long time ago. Do you remember? Promised it was going to be just you and me. Forever.

I know there are sometimes others. I can smell them on your skin. It doesn't matter. At least I try to convince myself that it doesn't, but it's getting harder and harder. You don't come to our meeting place as often anymore, and you don't take me out in your car like you used to. Have you got tired of me? I don't want to believe that. You're not like that. Are you? Is all of this a big mistake?

Chapter 29

'Vera. Vee-raa!'

Mum's voice wakes her. Makes her sit up in the middle of taking a breath. She looks around for a few confused seconds. Her heart is thudding with joy, with loss. Then her brain catches up. She's in the room she used to share with Mattias. But she's no longer a child. And this winter Mum will have been dead twenty years.

She and Dad sat for a long time down in the kitchen earlier. She tried to summon up the courage to pull out the photofit picture and tell him what she'd concluded about the blond man. But all of a sudden her courage and resolve had vanished, and they mostly talked an awful lot about nothing. About how hot the summer was, about the harvest, about how long her drive had taken. They were like two skaters circling round each other. Taking tentative little steps so as not to break the thin ice separating them from the cold, dark depths.

When her dad suggested she might like to go upstairs and have a rest before they went to get food for the evening meal she jumped at the idea. Told herself it would be better to talk this evening, when they've both had a bit more time to get used to each other.

She's got no idea how long she's been asleep. The old clock radio is showing four zeroes. She wonders about trying to put it right, then realises she's forgotten how it works. Everything in the room looks the way it always has, just smaller and sadder, much like the village itself. Mattias's dusty model aeroplanes are still on their shelf, and above them the wallpaper is slightly creased up by the picture rail. The poster from *OK* that she pinned up above the desk sometime in the mid-eighties and never bothered to take down looks bleached, and one corner is hanging loose.

She and Mattias shared this bunk bed after Billy was born. They carried on during the years following his disappearance, even though her own room was no longer being used. No one suggested otherwise, not Dad, not Mattias, not her. Later, when Mattias started at the Police Academy, the room and the bunk bed became hers alone, apart from the weekends when he came back to visit. But to be honest he mostly slept at Cecilia's then, which is another reason why she hates the stupid cow.

She's already tried the doors to both Billy's and Mum's bedrooms. They're locked, as usual. Dad moved down to the leather sofa in the study the night Billy went missing, so that Mum wouldn't be disturbed. Two decades later he's still sleeping downstairs, and those doors have remained locked. She hasn't been inside either of the rooms since then. Before the blond man appeared she hadn't given the rooms any thought at all. Not even on the few occasions when she came home. She wonders what they look like. If her memory is accurate, and if the blond man would recognise them if he saw them.

She swings her legs off the edge of the bed and pulls the photofit picture from one of the side pockets of her bag. Maybe it's just common sense catching up with her, but she sees more differences between the picture and the blond man than she did before. Unless she's merely looking for a good excuse not to have to say anything. Her uncertainty is exacerbated by the silence of the house, echoing through the landing between the locked doors.

The sound of a car engine interrupts her thoughts. Dad's back from the shop. She hears him open the front door, then the sound of him putting things away in the kitchen.

'Food'll be ready in half an hour,' he calls.

Mattias shows up in time for the meal. In a car this time, and thankfully without wife and children. His presence makes everything more difficult, and she decides to postpone her conversation with Dad until the following day.

It doesn't take long for her to realise that Mattias and Dad have dinner together fairly often, just the two of them. She gets the impression that Mattias even spends the night here, which would explain the rolled-up military sleeping bag on the top bunk in their old room.

They eat at the large oak table in the kitchen, with space for six people around it. Even so, they sit unnecessarily cramped together at one end, as if they were clinging to each other and wanted to avoid the emptiness around the rest of the table at all costs. A spiral flycatcher hangs above the lamp. It looks new, probably the only thing in there that's been swapped or changed. The flecked wooden floor, the rag rug, the yellowing wallpaper, the kitchen cupboards that could have done with being repainted years ago – everything is the same. The fly that was trying to get out through the window earlier is stuck to the brown glue of the flycatcher. She thinks it's the same fly, anyway. The green and black insect has stopped moving.

Halfway through coffee she changes her mind. The cognac her dad has served may be responsible for her newfound courage.

'I've been dreaming about Mum,' she begins, feeling the nervousness in her throat.

'Oh.' Dad's voice has a wary tone to it, as usual.

'I often talk about her with one of my groups. Grief therapy. There's a man there, he's about twenty-five years old. Blond hair, blue eyes.'

'Vera . . .' Mattias is glaring sullenly at her but she looks away.

'This man says his name is Isak. He talks about himself, about memories from when he was a child. About a five-year-old boy who went missing, and a garden with a treehouse and a hollow elm . . .'

Dad looks up. His eyes are more alert now, and he's even more wary.

'It all seems to fit. And then I saw this.' She reaches for her back pocket, and feels her cheeks flush.

'OK, Vera . . .'

Mattias is properly angry now, but her blood is up and she refuses to let herself be deterred.

'Look!' She puts the photofit picture down on the table triumphantly. She waits until they've both had a chance to read the caption and understand what the picture is.

'This man, Isak, this is what he looks like. Almost exactly. He looks like Billy would have looked.'

Silence. Dad takes his reading glasses from his breast pocket and pulls the picture towards him. She continues to avoid looking at Mattias. Her heart is hammering against her ribs. She stares at her dad's face, waiting for the reaction that must surely come. Tries to imagine it. Joy, tears, sadness, maybe even anger. But nothing happens.

After what feels like an eternity, but which couldn't really have been more than a few seconds, her dad pushes the photofit picture away.

'That isn't your little brother,' he says in such an unexpectedly harsh voice that both she and Mattias are taken aback. 'Billy's never coming back, Vera. I reconciled myself to that a long time ago. I thought you had, too.'

She walks out to the car with Mattias. Dad has long since said goodnight and shut himself away in the study. The light of the television flickers through the crack under the door. Her movements are heavy with disappointment. Even if she has tried to tell herself that this has all been for Dad's sake, it was just as much for hers, if not more. She wanted to be the good daughter who found Billy, who solved the mystery once and for all. Ridiculous, she can see that now. It takes more than a few vague memories and a computer-generated image to have any effect on Dad's grief. And bearing in mind everything she knows about grief, she ought to have had the sense to realise that she shouldn't talk to him until she had firm evidence. Instead she had jumped the gun and made him angry.

It's almost completely dark outside now. A nightingale is singing from the avenue of chestnuts. The sound is melancholic, echoing faintly off the neglected buildings. Mattias leans on the bonnet of his jeep, pulls a crumpled packet of cigarettes from his pocket, offers her one, then lights it between cupped hands.

'I didn't know you smoked.'

'I don't.' He grins and blows the smoke from corner of his mouth. 'Promise not to tell Cecilia.'

'About you smoking?'

Mattias gives her a long look but doesn't rise to the challenge. 'When did you find that photofit picture?' he says instead.

'A week or so ago.' She tries to sound indifferent.

'When were you thinking of telling me?'

'I just did.'

She shrugs her shoulders but doesn't look away this time. They try to outstare each other for a few moments until she changes tack.

'Do you ever think about him? Billy? Who he might have become?'

Mattias looks away, which in itself is an admission.

'You need to be careful, Vera,' he mumbles.

'What do you mean?'

'I mean that you can't just show up like this and stir things up.'

'What do you mean, show up?' she snaps. 'You were the one who suggested I come down.'

'To commemorate Mum's birthday, yes. Not to blurt out to Dad that you think Billy's still alive.'

She looks away and takes an angry drag on the cigarette.

'I know you mean well,' he goes on. 'You just need to think a bit more. Not jump to conclusions before we've had time to look into it properly. Sometimes we want something to be true so badly that it makes us blind to the actual truth.'

She glares at him, wondering whether to go on being angry. But his voice doesn't sound as bossy now, and besides, he said *we*. We, as in him and her.

They each sucked on their cigarettes. She can't really get over the fact that he's a secret smoker. Mattias is the most honest person she knows. Or at least he used to be. She thinks about the box in her closet. Suddenly gets it into her head that it could have been Mattias who opened it. It's not as unimaginable as she'd like to believe. She heard him look in there, after all. But why would Mattias poke about among her things?

'I saw the sleeping bag in our room,' she says, without really knowing why. Maybe she wants to punish him, but regrets it at once. 'How bad is it?' she goes on in a gentler voice.

He doesn't answer, just picks a flake of tobacco from his tongue. She feels ashamed. She's crossed the line, sticking her nose into something that's none of her business.

'Cecilia and I are having couple's counselling.'

'Right,' she says, which is a stupid thing to say. But oddly enough, in spite of the fact that Mattias is having problems, she mostly feels pleased that he's confiding in her. Before she thinks of anything better to say he stands up, drops the cigarette butt on the ground and steps on it.

'Go and get some sleep. Dad's asked Uncle Harald, Tess and Tim to come over tomorrow to mark Mum's birthday. I'll be back with Cecilia and the girls. Stay calm and please – don't mention Billy again. Once this weekend's over I promise I'll find out who that Isak really is. OK?'

She nods silently. Then stands and watches as the rear lights of his car disappear down the dark driveway.

Chapter 30

What do you do when you've done your absolute best but still failed? If you can't draw a line under it and move on, and find yourself clinging to something or someone for so long that it eventually ends up being the only thing you've got left, the only thing that keeps you going? Veronica wishes she had the answers to those questions.

She's lying on the bottom bunk of the bed once more. The house is silent and dark. The only light comes from the four flashing zeroes on the clock radio. They make her think of the answerphone in her flat, the message she still hasn't deleted.

She doesn't really know why she can't let go of Leon. She'd had other relationships before him, with other men. On most occasions she knew in advance that they weren't going to last more than a few months, sometimes less than that. And when they came to an end, it was always at her initiative. Her relationship with Leon was different. It was her first real attempt at something serious, and she really did try to make it work. Maybe that was why it went so wrong? Because she gave so much of herself that it later became impossible to let go, even though they clearly weren't good for each other. And another, even more important question:

is she on her way to becoming obsessed with the blond man instead of Leon? She feels undeniably drawn to him, and not necessarily in a strictly brother and sister way. Is that was this is all about? A new obsession?

What she would like to do most of all right now is go back to Stockholm. Put this failed visit behind her and concentrate on more important things instead. Such as keeping her job, and not throwing away the fragile life that she's made such an effort to construct. But she can't leave now, not before they've marked Mum's birthday, which means she's stuck here until after dinner tomorrow evening at the earliest. Dad will say it's not a good idea to drive at night, that she ought to stay until the following day, but he won't insist and try to make her. Nor will Mattias, to judge by their conversation earlier. Her big brother has changed, and she wonders if he's thinking the same about her. If he's thinking about her at all. If that *we* of his actually referred to someone other than her.

She shuts her eyes and takes a deep breath. Her thoughts wander off, and gradually end up somewhere between sleep and wakefulness.

Keep looking up, Vera. Just look up.

She's back on the ladder with Mattias. Him behind her, the vibrations in the warm metal. The colours blur, sounds change. Mattias's voice becomes Mum's. Louder, upset.

'Do you realise what you've done? You've killed the baby birds!'

'Uncle Harald says there's only room for one hunter in the forest. That a proper hunter doesn't—' The palm of Mum's hand strikes Mattias's cheek, then the top of his head. Once, twice, three times, more.

'Harald isn't the one who decides what you do. He's not your father.'

Mattias's sobs get louder. She hunches up, gets ready. But in place of her mum's agitated breathing she hears a different noise. A long rattling sound that turns into a bang.

She's awake in an instant. That last noise wasn't in her dream, she's sure of that. She gets cautiously out of bed and goes over to the window. The blue nights you get in early summer have been replaced by deep, black August darkness. The sky is clear and the moon, which is almost full, is spreading a silvery light that makes the tall poplars cast long shadows across the grass and the far end of the garden. The red eyes of the wind giants' warning lights are flashing above the dark fields.

Years have passed since she was last down there. Even before Billy went missing she used to avoid that part of the garden. The half-dead, jagged shrubs used to scratch and catch in your hair. And sometimes you found bones on the ground, the skeletal remains of animals that had been buried there long ago.

The noise that woke her isn't repeated. She opens the window carefully, but all she can hear is the crickets and the distant cry of a lone owl. Just as she's about to go back to bed she catches a glimpse of something moving out of the corner of her eye. She turns her head sharply, but all she manages to see is a change in the shadows. An animal, probably. A deer that has snuck in to eat the windfalls. Or one with a red coat, black nose and sharp teeth, one that likes digging for old bones.

Then she hears another noise. A faint creak she recognises from earlier. The hinges on the gate to the rose garden. She shifts position, trying to get a better view. Only a small portion of the white wall is visible from the window where she's standing. In Billy's or – even better – Mum's room she'd have a far better view of the garden, so just to be sure she goes and checks the doors, even though she knows they're locked. She stands on the landing for a few moments. The clock on the wall says it's quarter past two.

Without switching on any of the lights, she goes downstairs and knocks gently on the door to the study. There's no light coming from beneath it.

'Dad, are you awake?'

No answer. She tries again, a bit louder.

'Dad, I think there's someone in the rose garden.' Still no answer. She knocks a third time, tries to open the door, and discovers to her surprise that it too is locked. There's no sound from within. Her dad's probably taken one of his pills, sleeping so soundly that he can't hear her. But why has he locked the door? She thinks back to the frightened look on his face earlier. The front door had been locked when she arrived, which was unusual, and now the door to the study as well.

She creeps into the kitchen, trying to find a window from which she can get a better view of the wall of the rose garden. It takes a few moments for her eyes to get used to the odd brightness outside. And then she realises that the gate to the garden is standing open.

Her heart is thudding hard. There's someone out there, someone who's just snuck into the rose garden. An intruder, just like in her flat. The feeling from the day before is back. Impotence, a sense of not being able to defend herself. She feels like running back upstairs, calling Mattias and locking herself in the bedroom. Hiding under the covers until all danger is past, just like when she was little. But what could she do if the intruder decided to come inside the house?

Suddenly she thinks of an answer to that question. She runs lightly into the hall and opens the cupboard under the stairs. She lifts the loose plank in the panelling aside and sticks her arm into the hole. At first she can't find anything, and feels vulnerable standing there with her back to the dark hall.

She reaches her arm further into the cavity, so far that she feels the tendons creak. Her nose picks up a faint smell of gun oil, and then to her relief her fingers touch wood and cold metal.

She pulls the shotgun out from its hiding place and breaks it open with a practised gesture. The gun isn't loaded, but she finds two shotgun cartridges wrapped in yellow waxed paper on a ledge in the cupboard. The cartridges are homemade, by her grandfather, and one of them sticks a little and she has to force it in. The gun belonged to her mum, which is why her dad leaves it undisturbed. He hates guns, anyway. He can't even bring himself to touch them.

She snaps it shut, puts the butt against her shoulder and aims it along the hall, trying it out. Her fear is fading now, replaced by a different emotion. A feeling of security and power. Control. Uncle Harald taught her how to handle a gun. How to breathe, how to squeeze – not pull – the trigger. She wishes she'd had the gun the previous evening. Then she'd never have allowed herself to be frightened away from her own home. No way!

She lowers the shotgun, makes sure the safety catch is on. Then she creeps back to the study door and knocks once more. The door remains closed and locked.

As quietly as possible she goes back into the kitchen, then stops to listen. The gate to the rose garden is still open.

A different feeling is growing inside her now, and her temples are starting to throb. Anger. There's someone out there in the rose garden, someone who's broken into her dad's property. Maybe it's happened before, which would explain why he keeps all the doors locked now. And has to take pills to get to sleep. He's frightened.

Her anger grows stronger. Usually she would think of her therapist now and use one of the techniques slightly-too-tall Bengt has taught her to control her moods. Instead she decides to use the anger to her advantage.

She takes a deep breath, opens the door to the terrace and sneaks out. The night air is moist, full of the smells of late summer. She's only wearing pyjama bottoms and a vest, so she ought to be feeling cold. But the adrenalin is warming her blood and sharpening her senses.

She imagines she can hear a faint sound from the other side of the wall of the rose garden. There's someone in there, she's sure of that. But this time she's the hunter, she's the one in control, for the first time in a very long while.

Holding the shotgun tighter against her shoulder, she lets her thumb slide over the safety catch, and keeps her eyes focused above the barrel, the way Uncle Harald had taught her. She's barefoot, and moves almost silently down the little flight of steps from the terrace, then across the gravel path towards the gate to the rose garden.

Chapter 31

Summer 1983

The city cops had fooled him, Månsson realised that now. When the court remanded Tommy Rooth in custody the previous week, he should really have been kept in the city prison rather than transferred back out here. What Månsson had interpreted as a polite gesture towards him and his officers was in fact a way for Bure and Borg to protect their own backs. This wasn't about who was going to get the glory for solving the case, but who was going to be able to avoid any of the blame in the unlikely event that they failed to secure enough evidence to raise the level of the charges against Rooth.

And now Månsson was sitting here alone, with a whole acid bath in his stomach and the unlucky Old Maid card locked away in a cell a dozen or so metres from his office. He tore open two sachets of antacid powder and tipped the contents into the glass of water on the desk.

He'd had nightmares about the pump house for the past few nights. Tommy Rooth had taken Billy Nilsson there, held him captive on that disgusting bed, he was absolutely certain of that. But even though they had spent a whole week looking out there, using four different police tracker dogs, conducting a meticulous search of first the forest, then the surrounding area, they hadn't found any trace of the boy. The Northern Forest and the ridge it straddled was over fifteen square kilometres in area. It contained ravines carved out by water, steep drops and patches of bog, as well as forest so dense that sunlight never reached the ground. Rooth knew it as well as the back of his hand. And knew where you could hide a body where it would never be found again.

The bloodstains found in the pump house and the back of Rooth's Amazon hadn't provided any clear answers. They were an unholy mix of various types of animal blood, and the lab technicians hadn't been able either to confirm or rule out that they might contain traces of human blood. Laila, who had seen Rooth try to lure Billy out of the car at the petrol station, was standing by her story, but she had only seen them from a distance and the prosecutor was sounding increasingly doubtful that a court would believe that it really was Tommy Rooth she had seen.

Just like the city cops and evidently also the courts, Senior Prosecutor Hammarlund didn't seem to appreciate that people out here were used to seeing each other from a distance. That you identified someone by posture, gait, clothing and the vehicle they drove, not just from faces. Not that it was worth trying to explain that. The incident at the petrol station was only supporting evidence, after all, not conclusive proof of Rooth's guilt.

Rooth himself denied touching the boy, but was saying very little apart from that, even though Borg and Bure had been grilling him for several hours each day. The two detectives got louder and louder, sweatier and sweatier, inside the interview room while Rooth sat silently on his chair with his lawyer beside him and that arrogant smirk on his lips. The fear that had been visible during that first interview, and later when Aronsson had peered into his cell, had vanished. And with good reason.

The last time they met, Rooth's lawyer – appointed by the court – had pointed out the deficiencies in the police's case with admirable clarity: no body, no forensic evidence, no witnesses. Nothing that supported raising the level of suspicion or would persuade the court to extend Rooth's time in custody.

The telex that Britt from reception put on Månsson's desk a short while ago indicated that the prosecutor shared that evaluation:

At 17.12 today Senior Prosecutor J. Hammarlund decided that Tommy Rooth, d.o.b. 21/10/1947, should be released from custody immediately and without delay.

Månsson gulped down the antacid solution, splashing some on the shirt of his uniform. He wished the glass had contained something much stronger.

This was his case, Borg and Bure had made that very clear. And now he was the one who was going to have to release a child killer. Rooth would remain a suspect, and the preliminary investigation would continue, formally at least, for several more weeks or months. They would carry on working on all leads without prejudice, and that was what he was going to have to tell both the boy's family and the media. He knew he was unlikely to sound particularly convincing. Everyone involved already had a good idea how this was going to turn out. Tommy Rooth would walk free and the Nilsson family would never find out what happened to their little boy.

Månsson closed his eyes and swallowed hard, feeling the antacid collide with his heartburn halfway down his chest. *Fucking hell!*

He got stiffly to his feet and opened the door. He glanced towards the reception desk. It was past closing time, but instead of packing up and going home, the two receptionists were talking in whispers to two uniformed officers. Judging from their body language and the looks on their faces, Britt had already shared the contents of the telex. Månsson turned and began to walk towards the custody unit, feeling their stares on the back of his neck.

Chapter 32

A shotgun isn't a complicated weapon. Two barrels, the same number of cartridges. You hardly need to aim, just point and fire. If the target is within ten metres of you, there's more chance of you hitting it than not. And, unlike a weapon that fires bullets, it doesn't matter where on the body you hit. The collapse in blood pressure caused by the hail of shot makes the heart stop, and your prey dies of shock rather than the injury itself.

Uncle Harald's words echo through her head as Veronica cautiously peers through the crack in the open gate. The sound she heard before is clearer now, but the crack is too narrow for her to be able to figure out where it's coming from.

She takes a deep breath and slips through the gap, taking care not to touch the gate and make the hinges creak. Once she's inside she presses her back against the wall and makes a sweep of the rose garden with the shotgun. Everything is quiet. The only movement she can detect is from the wind-chime hanging from one of the beams of the summerhouse, making sporadic metallic tingling sounds. With the exception of the deep shadows beneath the larger bushes, the summer-house, covered in its Magdalena rose, is the only part of the garden she can't quite see. She knows there's a bench in there. A good hiding place, and possibly the only one in the entire garden.

She moves forward very slowly. The Öland stone beneath her feet is cool and rough. The slabs have a reddish, almost pink tone, but they look white in the moonlight.

The sound of the windchime changes, becomes weaker, more irregular, and just as she's about to step round the corner of the summerhouse some clouds pass in front of the moon. The garden is left in almost total darkness. She stops, trying to get her eyes used to the change. But before her sight has time to adapt the clouds are gone and the garden is bathed in white light once more. The bench is only a couple of metres from the end of the barrels. The summerhouse is empty. There's no one here.

She lowers the shotgun slightly, and starts to wonder if she's imagined it all, if it's all just a consequence of everything she's been through, and that the noise she heard was actually just the windchime.

She almost manages to convince herself of that before she suddenly realises that something isn't right. The windchime is almost silent now, but the little metal bars are still swaying gently, making the occasional little sound. Apart from that, the rose garden is perfectly still, as are the trees beyond. There's no wind at all.

Something moves behind her and she spins round, then hears the gate slam shut, followed by steps running on the gravel outside.

Shit!

She rushes along the path and pushes the wood with her shoulder. It opens a crack, then stops. She sees through the gap that the catch is on. She's shut in. She swears loudly again and looks around for a way out. She spots a wooden stepladder in the corner by the cold frames.

The ladder doesn't reach the top of the wall, but it's still tall enough for her to be able to swing one leg over the wall and sit astride it. The garden is empty, but she sees the lowest branches of the fruit trees swaying.

Without thinking she swings her other leg over the wall and jumps down onto the gravel path with the shotgun in one hand. She lands heavily and the sharp stones cut into her feet, making her gasp. She loses her balance and puts her free hand out to steady herself, cutting her palm in the process. She still manages to get up quickly, and her feet feel wet on the grass. She hopes it's just the dew, but isn't sure.

She hears branches scratching against fabric and runs towards the sound as fast as she can with the shotgun raised ready to fire. She passes the sundial and the gnarled old fruit trees and carries on into the bushes. For the second time tonight her muscle memory kicks in. She knows how to move through dense undergrowth, she's done it plenty of times with Uncle Harald. Make yourself small. Move sideways on, arms and weapons close to your body. Sharp twigs scratch red lines across her bare shoulders and arms but she hardly notices the pain.

A large bramble bush is blocking her path, far too vicious for her to push through. The intruder, on the other hand, evidently didn't think that, because some of the branches are still swaying. She darts quickly round the bramble and gains several seconds.

Clouds pass in front of the moon again and she doesn't see the twig that scratches her on the forehead and then gets tangled in her hair. She stops and frees herself with her left hand. It's almost pitch black in amongst the bushes, and pushing ahead blindly really isn't a good idea. She crouches down instead, aims the shotgun in front of her and listens.

All she can hear is her own breathing and the blood pulsing in her temples. Whoever it is in front of her in the darkness has stopped at the same time as her. That big bramble must have hurt, and had probably left the intruder with some painful cuts and an inclination to be more cautious.

The clouds part briefly and the bushes in front of her rustle. She catches a glimpse of movement, then everything goes dark again. Instinctively she's already pressed the butt of the shotgun to her cheek, taken the safety catch off and put her finger on the trigger. She listens, waiting for the next break in the clouds.

She hears a shuffling sound, as if something were being dragged across the ground. Then there's more rustling in the undergrowth, scraping against fabric, but it sounds different now. Softer, less sharp.

The clouds part to let the moonlight through. She moves forwards as fast as she can, leaving the safety catch off and holding the butt against her cheek as she aims in front of her. She moves past another dense thicket, through a small clearing and almost runs straight into the rusty old wire fence at the end of the garden.

She stops. There's a deep furrow under the fence, and just a metre or so away the maize stands like a dark wall. In the distance she can still hear the sound of someone running through the field. Their head start is growing with every step, it's already far too big. She lowers the gun and puts the safety catch back on. The hunt is over.

The adrenalin rush starts to subside and she realises she's freezing. Her feet hurt, and the scratches on her shoulders and arms sting. She shivers as she looks around the clearing.

The place where Billy's shoe was found can't be more than a stone's throw from here, out among the maize. Where the intruder fled.

She shivers with cold again, unless it's from unease, as she suddenly realises that someone's watching her. From ten, fifteen metres away along the fence. She turns and raises the shotgun, releasing the safety catch in the same smooth movement.

An animal. A doglike creature with pointed ears and its head tilted. It's sitting perfectly still, looking at her. A fox.

Chapter 33

Summer 1983

Månsson opened the door to the custody unit, prompting the police officer in the little glass booth to stand up.

'He's being released,' Månsson said, gesturing towards Rooth's cell. The officer didn't seem surprised, so tattletale Britt must have let him know too.

'OK, I'll sort out the practical details.'

Månsson waved his hand dismissively. 'No, I'll take care of it. You get going.'

Månsson waited until the door had closed behind the officer before sticking his head inside the glass booth. He leaned over and pulled out the baton that was kept in a tube under the desk. He pulled the strap over his thumb, wrapped it round the back of his hand and spun the baton until it sat snugly in his hand.

Rooth was half lying on his bunk reading a paperback thriller that must have come from the meagre custody unit bookshelf. When Månsson entered the cell he looked up and closed the book.

'What an honour – the Chief of Police himself.' Rooth had regained his usual patronising tone. 'If you want to talk you'll have to call my lawyer. I'm not saying anything without—'

Månsson slammed the baton down on the bunk, five centimetres from Rooth's foot, making him jump and drop the book. The sound echoed off the bare walls like a pistol shot.

At first Rooth looked shocked, but he soon collected himself. He sat up, his eyes narrowed and his lips tightened.

Månsson looked him in the eye. He imagined Rooth inside the pump house. Imagined Billy Nilsson on that horrific bed. Raised the baton again, but for some reason he hesitated.

Rooth shifted position. 'My dad used to hit me . . . Well, hit isn't quite the right word. He used to beat me black and blue. My earliest memory of him is actually him looming over me, hitting me with his belt. I didn't think you were that type, Månsson.'

Månsson squeezed the baton, trying to make himself continue.

'He kept doing it until I learned to hit back,' Rooth said. 'So when I turned seventeen I gave the old bastard one hell of a going over, then went off to sea. I got into a fair few fights there too. Once you learn that's how things work, it's easy to carry on. But Sailor took me under his wing and made sure things didn't get too fucked up.'

He fell silent and gestured towards the baton.

'What I mean is that I'm used to being beaten up. Badly beaten up. Just so you know, Månsson. If you're planning to hit me, you're going to have to make a really thorough job of it.'

Månsson swallowed. He tried to hold on to the image of Billy Nilsson, to cling on to his rage and frustration. The hatred he felt for Tommy Rooth. But doubt had got hold of him. Was he really this sort of person? He stood there with the baton raised, glaring at Rooth. Then he slowly lowered his arm and took a step back. All of a sudden he felt sick.

'The prosecutor has decided to let you go, for the time being, anyway,' he muttered. 'But you're still a suspect. You're not to leave the district, is that understood?'

Rooth stood up and nodded slowly. 'You could have sent someone else to tell me,' he said. 'To avoid the humiliation. Why didn't you?'

Månsson took a deep breath. 'The Nilsson family are in pieces,' he said quietly. 'All they want is to know where their little boy is. Have him back home again.'

In his mind's eye Månsson conjured up images of Johan and Jakob when they were Billy's age. He lowered his voice still further, and didn't have to make much effort to sound sincere.

'You're a father, Tommy. You should be able to understand what Ebbe and Magdalena are going through. Imagine it was your boy who was missing. Ebbe's like a ghost, and Magdalena's shut herself away in her room. She hasn't got out of bed since Billy . . .'

Something changed in Rooth's angular features. A shift in expression. Rooth seemed to notice it himself, because he looked away and ran his tongue over his lips. Månsson found himself thinking of Vera Nilsson and the uneasy look in her eyes.

'Give them some peace, Tommy,' he went on. 'You're the only person who can do that for them.'

Rooth licked his lips again. He opened his mouth as if he were about to say something, then paused.

Månsson thought of the Nilsson children, standing in the window. The way Vera and Mattias had gazed down at him, waiting for him to find their little brother. Put an end to their nightmare. He held his breath.

The expression on Rooth's face changed again, and now looked almost pained. Then it slowly went back to normal. He shook his head.

'I've got nothing else to say.'

He didn't sound triumphant, just exhausted. Even so, it irritated Månsson. His anger suddenly flared up again, even stronger than before, and he could feel his pulse throbbing behind his eyes.

He thought about Vera Nilsson. About her older brother, her mum and dad. About Harald Aronsson, about Malin and the boys. About everyone in the village who was relying on him to find the truth. To bring Billy home. The throbbing became a roar.

I'm doing my best, Månsson thought. I'm trying to be a good husband, a good father. A good police officer. But sometimes ... He raised the baton, squeezing the handle so tightly that his fingers turned white. Sometimes that just isn't enough.

Chapter 34

Veronica usually sleeps soundly and wakes up late, and it takes a long time for her body and brain to start working. Not today.

Outside the fog is hanging heavy above the grass, making the field of maize and the red eyes of the wind giants invisible. The house is completely silent. No sound from either the study or the kitchen. She's been dreaming again, she knows that much. Looking for Billy, calling his name over and over, but the only response is the rustle of the wind through the maize. Unless the sound is actually someone running.

She creeps out into the bathroom. The old pipes boom dully when she turns the tap on. They clank and splutter for a while before finally releasing a weary dribble of hot water. She sits down in the old bathtub. The enamel in the bottom is yellow and rough, its smooth surface worn off by millions of leaking drops of water going back to her grandparents' day. The little hourglass still hangs from the wall, with the text: *As the sand runs down beneath, take good care to brush your teeth.*

She slowly washes off the remains of last night's chase. The water makes the grazes on her arms and feet sting. Even though she takes her time in the shower, there's something that won't allow itself to be washed away. A feeling prompted by the chase that's only grown stronger overnight, strengthened by her dreams. There's nothing to suggest that last night's events have any connection to the break-in in her flat. Yet she can't shake the feeling that they're somehow connected. That something's going on that she doesn't quite understand, a peculiar game of hide-and-seek where she doesn't know who or what she's looking for. Or even where to start looking.

Her fingers trace the scar on her lower arm. The skin there is paler, slightly harder than the surrounding flesh. It's interesting how the body heals an injury, making the wounded area tougher than it was before. The body learns from its mistakes, unlike the mind.

She dries herself and pulls on her underwear, jeans and a clean, long-sleeved T-shirt. She ties her hair up in a ponytail, then goes downstairs. It's just gone seven o'clock.

Her car starts at the second attempt. The fog is still lingering over the stubble in the fields in front of the house, swirling over the gravel road and around the headlights.

Just before she reaches the main road she spots a sign by the side of the road that she didn't notice the previous day. A company logo showing the propeller of a wind turbine. She recognises it from the papers on her dad's desk.

On her way into the village she looks more closely at the turbines she passes, and sees the same logo on them. The blades are turning incredibly slowly, as if the giants were only just waking up.

She parks the car on the patch of gravel in front of the church. The heavy, whitewashed wall resembles the one enclosing the rose garden, only one third its height.

There's almost no wind. Only the very tops of the trees that protect the dead from the wind that usually sweeps the plain are moving, just a little. The fog sits like a lid above the path through the churchyard, and seems to make the smell of boxwood stronger, a smell that always makes her think of funerals. She walks round the white church building. In a few hours' time there'll be a service. She thinks about the grinning goat's head up on the roof and wonders if it's still there. But why wouldn't it be?

Her paternal grandparents' grave is an unobtrusive grey stone in the middle of a row. Nothing remarkable, and typical of the Nilsson family. Her maternal grandparents' grave, on the other hand, is the complete opposite. It sits in its own corner of the churchyard, fifteen, maybe twenty square metres, with perfectly straight edging stones. At the top end stands a large black metal memorial. The words ARONSSON FAMILY GRAVE gleam so bright and gold that Uncle Harald must have had them re-gilded recently. Below, in the neatly raked shingle, stand three dark headstones: Grandfather's parents', his unmarried sister's, and his own and Grandmother's. LANDOWNER ASSAR ARONSSON. ALVA, HIS WIFE.

Mum's headstone stands slightly separate, just outside the family plot, right next to the wall of the churchyard. It's made of some pinkish, faintly sparkling stone whose name Veronica has forgotten.

Magdalena Nilsson, née Aronsson
21 August 1948 – 18 December 1983

On either side of the stone is a perfectly pruned rose bush. One red, one pink, just like in the rose garden. Dad must come here several times a week.

Below Mum's name his own has already been engraved.

Ebbe Nilsson
3 April 1945 –

Only the date of death is missing. But it's the gap beneath her parents' names that draws the attention. The space where Billy's name should be. Around ten years ago someone suggested that they should apply to have Billy declared dead, but her dad reacted furiously, which didn't happen often. Under no circumstances was Mum going to lie next to an empty coffin. Since then no one has dared raise the subject again, not even Uncle Harald.

Grief demands total devotion before the heartbreaking pain mutates into something more manageable. The human psyche always tries to find points of light even in the deepest darkness, searching for a glimmer of hope to cling on to. It was probably that hope that broke Mum. As long as Billy's body wasn't found, the hope and the questions wouldn't go away. *Where's Billy now? What's he doing? Who tucks my little boy in at night, who comforts him when he cries?*

Her doctors had said Mum was on her way out of her depression. Veronica suspects that she had just resigned herself to the fact that she would never get any answers, and that the stones, ice and lake were the only things that could get that hopeless hope to leave her in peace.

She crouches down beside the headstone. Clears her throat and tries to think of something to say.

'Hi, Mum, it's me.' The words sound clumsy, as if they belong to someone else, and she's struck by how stupid this all feels. They never confided in each other when Mum was alive, and trying to do so now, like this, feels like a film cliché.

She stands up, embarrassed, and brushes some imaginary stones from her trousers. She feels a sudden urge for a cigarette, and curses not blagging a couple off Mattias the previous evening when she had the chance.

Then she notices something she hadn't spotted before. A small object on top of the gravestone. A little black stone, perfectly smooth and cold in her hand, as if it had been polished by countless waves. She rolls it in her palm. She's sure it wasn't Dad who left it there. So the stone must have been put there recently, or else he would surely have removed it for spoiling the otherwise perfect symmetry.

The feeling from first thing that morning is back, now even stronger. There's something going on here. And another realisation is starting to grow just as strong, sucking energy from the little stone in her hand: that she really does need to find out what it is.

She walks quickly back to the car. For a brief, unpleasant moment, just as she's going through the gate, she gets the feeling there's someone standing by the corner of the church, she can almost feel their eyes on the back of her neck. But when she turns round the churchyard is deserted and the only things moving are a couple of magpies flying up into one of the tall trees.

She's waiting outside the grocery store on the dot of eight o'clock. Plastic floor, fluorescent lighting. Walls and ceiling that could have done with freshening up a long time ago. The smell of freshly baked bread makes her stomach rumble loudly. But the need for cigarettes drowns out her hunger, and her curiosity is greater still. With a bit of luck she might be able to satisfy all her needs in one go.

'Goodness, is that you, Vera?'

Aunt Berit comes round the counter to give her a hug. She's an old schoolfriend of Mum's. Her best friend, Berit would probably say, but Veronica is pretty sure her mum wouldn't have agreed with her about that.

Berit looks much the same as always. A bit more grey hair, a bit heavier, and with a few more cigarette wrinkles around her mouth. Sensible shoes and practical clothes, a big red cardigan with the shop's logo on the chest. She's fifty-five, the same age Mum would have been, but she actually looks a couple of years younger, which makes her pretty much unique in the village. Aunt Berit is the type who talks until she runs out of breath, which means she has to take an audible breath at the end of every sentence.

'It must be at least four or five years since I last saw you! Or is it even longer than that?'

Berit is married to Uncle Sören, a large man with a chin-strap beard, a receding chin and gentle eyes – he looks a bit like an actor who always plays kindly fathers on television. Sören sometimes used to give her and Mattias an ice cream when they went shopping, probably to give him an excuse to talk to Mum. His family has run the village shop for three generations, which means that he, Berit and their two children are always referred to by the surname Grocer, even though their real name is Möller. That's the way it works out here. You're not only your-self, you're also your parents and grandparents. Sören and Berit Grocer. Erik Carpenter. Sven Postie. Inger Seamstress. She will always be known as Vera, Ebbe and Magdalena's girl, regardless of what it might say on her driving licence or in the census.

In the space of just a few minutes Aunt Berit manages to tell her most of the important news. She herself is fine (apart from a few niggles). *Breath*. Her children, whose names Veronica can't remember, except that they start with 'L' are also fine. The boy, Ludde (that was it) lives in Trelleborg, his sister Lena still lives in the village. They're both married, of course, and have a number of children.

They also manage to deal with the unavoidable fact that Veronica hasn't had any children (such a shame), or even a husband (you just haven't met the right person). Instead of changing the subject and asking questions herself, Veronica smiles sadly and murmurs in agreement, just as she is expected to do. Because that's how Vera Nilsson, Ebbe and Magdalena's girl, behaves.

'Have you seen your uncle?' Aunt Berit asks.

She shakes her head. 'Not yet.'

'No, I don't suppose he's got time, he's so busy with all those new windmills.'

Veronica doesn't say anything, just waits for her to go on, as she's bound to.

'Ninety metres tall, did you hear? We didn't say anything when he built the others, but these new ones he's planning are almost twice the size. Great eyesores that'll be seen and heard everywhere. They'll spoil the whole area.'

Aunt Berit shakes her head, then looks around quickly as if to make sure no one's listening.

'And I'm not the only one who thinks that. There's talk of trying to get planning permission withdrawn. Has your father mentioned it at all?'

Veronica shakes her head again.

'No, well, I don't suppose that would be the first thing Ebbe would want to talk to you about. Seeing as you're not home that often, I mean.'

'No.' Veronica swallows the poorly concealed reproach as she tries to find a way of steering the conversation to where she wants it to go.

Aunt Berit seems to be waiting for some response that would give her a reason to carry on talking about Uncle Harald's wind turbines, but when nothing comes she drops the subject. Her voice grows milder.

'You're looking more and more like your mother, Vera. Just as beautiful.'

Veronica knows it's a compliment, but she still doesn't like it.

Aunt Berit sighs and tilts her head to one side. 'Magda was also an unsettled soul. You've got that from her.'

To Veronica's surprise, the woman reaches out and gently strokes her hair. She sees an opportunity, and decides to grasp it.

'Was that why Mum ran off to Copenhagen?' she says. 'Because she was an unsettled soul?'

The question seems to catch Aunt Berit by surprise. She purses her lips and tugs at her cardigan, but can't resist the temptation to carry on playing the best friend.

'Your grandfather ...' Aunt Berit hesitates, then starts again. 'Assar and your mother didn't always see eye to eye. Magda wasn't happy on the farm. She wasn't ...' Another pause. Aunt Berit probably doesn't know much more. The fact that she calls Veronica's mum Magda is enough for her to realise that. She hated being called that. Veronica decides to nudge the conversation in the right direction.

'But then Mum came home,' she says. 'Got married to Dad.'

Aunt Berit nods, and the anxious look on her face vanishes. 'Ebbe had been in love with Magda ever since school. Most of the boys were infatuated with her. Apart from my Sören, of course,' she adds, slightly too quickly for it to sound believable. 'Unlike the other boys, Ebbe never even tried to ask her out. He was too shy, mostly kept in the background. But you only had to see how Ebbe looked at Magda to understand the situation. He worshipped your mother, he'd have done absolutely anything for her.'

Veronica murmured in agreement. The fact that Dad worshipped the ground Mum walked on was hardly news. But she had to have patience, and very gently nudge the conversation towards the summer of 1983.

'Everyone was surprised when Magda was suddenly home again,' Aunt Berit goes on. 'Everything happened so quickly. The engagement, the wedding, Mattias being born . . .'

Berit gives a knowing smile and Veronica can feel her blood start to boil. She's heard this rumour before as well, that Dad might not be Mattias's father. That Mum got pregnant with someone in Copenhagen and that Grandfather and Uncle Harald went to get her and made her get married to avoid a scandal. She can even understand where the rumour came from. Mattias is a head taller than Dad, has broad shoulders, big hands, and the same prominent features as Uncle Harald. You really have to exert yourself to see anything of Dad in him. All the same, she knows it's there.

She sticks her hand in the back pocket of her jeans, finds a piece of paper and realises that it's the photofit picture. A few seconds of silence follow.

She's fumbling in the dark, she understands that. She still doesn't know who or what she's looking for. But there's at least one key figure in this story. Someone who, one way or another, must know the truth about Billy. So she decides to get straight to the point.

'Tommy Rooth,' she says. The name provokes precisely the sort of alarmed reaction in Aunt Berit as she expected, and it makes her feel slightly mischievous. 'You knew him, didn't you?'

Berit tugs at her cardigan and looks around again as if she's worried someone might be listening. The shop is still empty, and after a couple of seconds her predilection for gossip gains the upper hand.

'I don't know if knew is the right word. We were at school together, him and me and Magda. Sören, Ebbe and your uncle, too, come to that. Tommy was good-looking, but no one liked him. You never really knew what he was thinking. He was an unpleasant sort, drank a lot and kept getting in trouble.'

She purses her lips, making her wrinkles deeper.

'He broke a bottle over my Sören's head once, down in the park. We must have been sixteen, seventeen, something like that. It could have been really nasty. Tommy was being a bit pushy and Sören intervened. He had to have eight stitches, but we didn't involve the police.'

'No?'

Aunt Berit shakes her head. 'Tommy's father came over with a whole deer for Sören's parents to make up for it. It wasn't the first time he'd had to smooth things over for his son. Not long after that Tommy went off to sea. There were rumours that he'd beaten up his father.'

Veronica tries to look serious and sympathetic at the same time. She thinks about the photograph of Tommy Rooth in the paper. That dark, slightly dangerous look in his eyes. She tries to imagine him trying it on with a seventeen-year-old Aunt Berit, but it isn't easy.

'Wasn't Uncle Sören the last person who saw Rooth after . . .' She lets the rest of the sentence hang in the air.

Aunt Berit takes the bait at once. 'Yes. Heading south on the main road, the same night the police let him go. Straight to Trelleborg and a ferry out of the country. Driving that terrible old Volvo as if the devil himself was after him.' She lets out a derisive snort. 'It's a scandal that Månsson couldn't keep Rooth locked up. That he never got punished for what he did to little Billy.'

Mention of his name makes Aunt Berit's torrent of words dry up. She looks uncomfortable and starts fiddling with some cartons of coffee on a shelf. She suddenly seems extremely concerned about the layout of the goods. The topic clearly unsettles her, and Veronica can tell that Aunt Berit is about to make her excuses and get back to work any moment.

'Didn't anyone in the village use to spend any time with Rooth?' she tries, in a last attempt to find out something she doesn't already know.

Aunt Berit shakes her head, adjusts the packs of coffee once more, then straightens up.

'Only that other drunk.'

'The other drunk?'

Aunt Berit turns round. Brushes the front of her cardigan a couple of times, hard, as if she was trying to get rid of something unpleasant. Something that's clinging to her even though it's invisible.

'Kjell-Åke Olsson,' she mutters. 'Most people call him Sailor.'

Chapter 35

Veronica stops outside the shop and angrily tears the cellophane off the packet of cigarettes, and is about to light a Prince when a big black BMW with tinted windows pulls up in front of her. The door opens and a curvy woman around the same age as her gets out.

'I thought it was you, Vera!'

It's Lidija, someone she went to school with and hasn't seen for at least ten years. Longer, possibly, they don't quite agree on how long. She doesn't seem to have aged a day. She's attractive, well dressed in high heels and a trouser suit. Her hair has been blow-dried, she's got long nails, perfectly manicured. She and her expensive car both look out of place in the village, but that doesn't seem to bother Lidija in the slightest. She talks loudly, and laughs even louder.

'Look, have you had breakfast, Vera?'

'Er, no . . .'

'I was just on my way to see Dad. Tag along, he'd love to see you.'

Veronica begins to formulate an excuse, but Lidija interrupts before she has time to get going. Besides, she forgot to buy anything to eat in the shop, so she gets in her battered old car and follows Lidija's huge BMW. She's surprised at her own spontaneity. It isn't like her. On the other hand, this morning is proving to be altogether rather out of the ordinary, to put it mildly. The strange feeling she had in the churchyard is still there, and she isn't entirely sure how to handle it.

They park outside one of the pizzerias, the one with the sign saying FULLY LICENCED by the door. She remembers Lidija's dad as a big, noisy man, one of the many who were bussed here from Yugoslavia in the sixties and seventies to keep Swedish industry going. These days he's considerably smaller but no less noisy.

'Gastric bypass,' he laughs, patting his stomach. 'I lost forty-five kilos. Forty-five, that's half a Lidija.'

'Stop it, Dad!' Lidija rolls her eyes, then kisses her dad on both cheeks.

He gestures to them to sit down and, even though it's so early in the day, serves up plenty of food.

'There's no point objecting,' Lidija whispers. 'Just have a little bit and he'll be happy.'

Veronica helps herself to the food, to Branko's evident delight. He says something she doesn't understand to his assistant, then sits down at their table with them.

'It's good to see you, Vera,' he says. 'How's your dad doing? He hasn't been in here for ages.'

'Fine, thanks,' she says, surprised. Her dad eats pizza? He always says he prefers to cook for himself. And he's good at it, too.

'Has Lidija told you? She's a real Rockefeller these days . . .'

'Stop it, Dad!' Lidija says. She tries to cover his mouth with her hand.

They play fight for a while until Veronica's strained smile starts to ache. She tries to imagine her dad in here.

'What he's trying to say is that I've set up a few businesses that are doing pretty well. Hair care products, lotions, perfumes.'

'Here in Reftinge?' Veronica says, hearing the astonishment in her voice.

'Why not? Reftinge's perfect. Cheap premises, plenty of workers. We have a website where customers can order our products. My girls pack them up and post them out. We have customers all around the country.'

Lidija's dad shakes his head. 'I'm still getting to grips with the Internet. Lidija says I have to, but I don't know. You can't teach an old dog new skills.'

'Tricks, Dad. And of course you can, unless the old dog wants to drive all the way to the city to do his banking.'

They cheerfully start to squabble again and Veronica looks away. She spots some photographs on the wall and stares at them instead. Pictures of customers, and to her surprise she sees her dad in one of them. He's got more hair and the colour in the picture is a bit faded, so she guesses it must be at least ten years old. He's sitting at a table with another man, raising his beer glass in a toast towards the camera. The man with him is partly hidden by her dad's raised arm. She doesn't recognise him.

'. . . nail bars,' Lidija says, and Veronica realises she's missed the start of the sentence. 'I've already got two, but within a few years I'll have franchises in every shopping centre in the whole of Skåne. Fast Nails, it's going to be really big, I swear.'

'Great,' Veronica says. She can't help glancing back at the picture of her dad. He looks reasonably happy, but as usual his eyes are sad.

'By the way, Branko,' she says when they're about to leave. 'Do you know Kjell-Åke Olsson, Sailor?' It's a spur-of-the-moment question and she doesn't really know what sort of answer she's expecting.

'Of course. Sailor was a regular here before he went doolally. He got expelled from the pub . . .' Branko waves his hand in the air, as if he doesn't like what he's saying.

'Expelled?'

'Yes, how do you say it?' He looks at Lidija for help finding the right expression, then finds it on his own. 'Frozen out, that's it. No one wanted to drink with him. Sailor said they used to spit in his beer.'

'Because he knew Tommy Rooth?'

Branko grimaces. 'Probably. People round here never let anything go. I don't agree with that. Life's too short. If your dad doesn't have a problem with Sailor, then neither do I.'

'Dad?'

She notices Lidija tugging gently at her father's arm, but he doesn't let her put him off.

'Ebbe and Sailor were friends. They used to have a drink or two together. Take a look at this.' Branko goes over to the photograph on the wall and points to the man beside her dad. 'There,' he says. 'That's Sailor.'

Chapter 36

Ekhagen Care Home is on the eastern side of the village, not far from the church. Veronica hasn't been there since her grandfather was alive. At least fifteen years ago, probably more, she can't be bothered to work it out. She's got other things on her mind. The photofit picture is still in her jeans pocket. She reaches back with her hand and touches it gently.

Inside the home a smell of coffee hangs in the air above the grey linoleum floor. Heavy, old-fashioned wooden furniture lines the corridors where they're wide enough. Like the paintings of farms on the walls, the furnishings all come from bequests, battered leftovers from another age that no one cares about anymore. Which would also be a fairly accurate description of Sailor.

Veronica can tell from the nurse's tone of voice that he isn't one of the home's favourite residents. He's sitting in a wheelchair in his room with the door closed and a blanket over his knees, even though it must be at least twenty-five degrees. His body is shrunken and wasted. His nose and cheeks are lined with tiny broken blood vessels, a pattern she recognises from her therapy groups for alcoholics.

'You've got a visitor, Kjell-Åke. That's nice, isn't it?'

The nurse, Marie, a schoolmate whose name Veronica remembers even before she sneaks a glance at her name badge, recognised her at once. She ostensibly accepts the explanation that Sailor is an old friend of her dad's, even if the look in her eyes says otherwise.

Sailor stares at Marie, then Veronica. One corner of his mouth is drooping down, and a blob of white saliva has gathered there. His lips move slowly, making weak, wet sounds.

'My name is Vera Nilsson,' she says.

It feels odd to say the name, which is hardly surprising seeing as she hasn't used it for a very long time.

'Ebbe and Magdalena's daughter,' she adds when he shows no sign of recognition. 'From Backagården. You know my father.'

The name of the farm makes Sailor raise his head a little. Veronica sees a spark ignite in his eyes, but he still doesn't say anything. He looks between her and the nurse again. She turns and indicates to Marie that she'll be OK on her own, but the nurse misunderstands.

'As I said, Kjell-Åke has dementia. There's not much left. He drifts in and out most of the time.'

'OK.' She goes on looking at Marie, and after a few seconds the nurse finally gets the hint.

'Well, I need to get on. I'm sure you'll be all right on your own, Vera.' She sounds slightly annoyed, as if she'd have liked to stay a bit longer. 'Kjell-Åke can get a bit loud and swear a lot sometimes, but don't mind that. Ring the bell if you need anything. If not, we'll be back to fetch him for lunch.'

Veronica waits until the sound of Marie's wooden-soled sandals has faded away before pulling up a chair and sitting down next to Sailor. He smells faintly of urine and something more cloying which she'd rather not think about.

'You used to be friends with Tommy Rooth,' she says, without bothering with any small talk.

Sailor's eyes narrow. 'You're Aronsson's daughter.' The words are half hissed, half slurred.

'Niece,' she says. 'Harald's my uncle.'

'Fucking cunt,' he says. Then his eyes grow vacant and the mean look on his face vanishes. His fingers pick at the blanket.

'You and Tommy used to do business together. Hunting,' she says.

That last word seems to click. Sailor's eyes grow clearer again and the angry look returns.

'None of your fucking business. No one else's either. Nosy fuckers. I'm not saying a word. Our business. Mine and Tommy's. Aronsson's a fucking cunt.'

'You didn't like my uncle?'

The old man looks up. 'Fucking cunt, Aronsson.'

'Yes, so you said.'

She sits and waits for him to go on, but he presses his lips together.

'You and Tommy Rooth used to hunt up in the Northern Forest, didn't you? Even though my uncle had the hunting rights,' she prompts.

Sailor leans forward with a smirk. 'Maybe. Maybe Tommy. Maybe the forest, maybe . . .' The light in his eyes fades again and his fingers feel for the blanket once more.

Veronica sighs. The old man's impossible to talk to, this is completely pointless. What was she actually expecting from this visit? That the old man would be able to tell her who was creeping around her dad's garden, who put that stone on her mum's grave? An old man who never goes further than the dining room.

Outside she hears the church bells ringing to announce the service. The old folk evidently have lunch very early on Sundays.

She tries in vain to think of something else to say. Just as she's about to stand up she has an idea. A familiar feeling that makes her gasp for breath. She leans back in the chair and stares at Sailor intently. The look on his face, the way he's picking at the blanket. The tiny movements in his face.

'You're grieving,' she says gently. 'You grieving for your friend, aren't you, Kjell-Åke?'

Sailor doesn't answer. He goes on staring down at his lap, but his fingers have stopped moving.

'Was Tommy a good friend?' she says. The old man sits there in silence, but she thinks she spots what could have been a nod.

'Were you a good friend, Kjell-Åke?'

This time the nod is more pronounced.

'I helped Tommy when he first went to sea. He was only a young lad. I taught him, kept an eye on him.' He falls silent again.

She wishes she'd brought a notepad with her.

'Was Tommy a good friend?' she asks again.

Sailor looks up. 'A good friend doesn't let you down,' he says in a hollow voice. 'Tommy wasn't like that. Never. Not until that summer.'

'Do you think Tommy let you down? That he abandoned you?'

Sailor looks down again without saying anything.

'You were there for Tommy. You were a good friend, but he left you here. Left you among people who were angry with him for what he'd done, angry with you because you knew him.' She stops, wanting to make sure that she hasn't lost him.

'I was a good friend,' Sailor mutters. 'A good friend.'

'Did he ever get in touch? Later on?' Veronica realises that she's holding her breath.

'Never.' He shakes his head. 'Not a peep.'

Veronica forces herself to wait rather than interrupt with another question.

'He got what he deserved,' Sailor says abruptly. His voice is suddenly sharper.

'Who did? Tommy?'

'No! Aronsson. He got just what he deserved. He shouldn't have fucked about. He took Tommy's livelihood away from him. From his family. So Tommy did it. Tommy . . .' The words seem to catch somewhere between his brain and mouth. Sailor's eyes start to dart about anxiously.

She takes a deep breath.

'What did Tommy do?' she says.

The old man's lips make a wet sound. As if he's trying to find the words but failing.

'What did Tommy do with my little brother?'

'Sh-shack,' the old man says.

'What shack?'

'Askedalen. The hunting shack. It wasn't Tommy's fault . . .' The rest of the sentence collapses into mumbling.

She leans closer.

'Tell me about the shack.'

'None of your damn business!' Sailor suddenly cries, spraying her with saliva, and she jerks away. He starts to rock back and forth in the wheelchair. 'Secret, the shack's secret. Why didn't you say anything, Tommy? Why didn't you say what happened?'

He stops short, and his body seems to slump. His fingers start picking at the blanket again.

'Kjell-Åke?' she says tentatively. 'Sailor?'

Veronica puts her hand on his lap gently, but he doesn't react. She thinks she can hear the sound of sandals approaching.

She gets an idea, pulls out the photofit picture, unfolds it and puts it in the old man's lap. The steps outside are getting closer. It sounds like two people. Sailor looks at the picture. Then at her.

'Do you recognise him, Sailor?'

Voices now, a hand on the door handle. Veronica picks up the picture and holds it closer to the man's face. His eyes are darting about, as if he finds the picture unsettling. His lips move again.

'The truth is up there,' he mumbles. 'Deep in the forest where no one can find it. I said as much to him.'

'Who?'

The door opens. Marie is standing in the doorway with another carer. 'Time for lunch, Kjell-Åke.'

Veronica pulls the photofit picture towards her, and is about to fold it up and tuck it away when her fingers slip and it falls to the floor. Marie bends down and picks the sheet of paper up.

'Oh, so you know Handsome Isak?'

'Who?'

'Handsome Isak. Well, that's what we call him. Sailor's nephew.' She waves the picture, then shows it to her colleague.

'Has Isak been here?' She feels her stomach tighten. 'When?'

'About a month ago, something like that. Not the sort of person you forget easily, if you know what I mean?' Marie winks at her, then turns to Sailor. 'OK, Kjell-Åke. Time to go to the dining room. Stuffed cabbage leaves today, one of your favourites.'

The old man grins. There's no trace of his earlier anxiety now. Veronica is about to stand up, but just as the nurse releases the brake of Sailor's wheelchair he reaches out and takes hold of Veronica's hand.

'Thank you for listening, Vera,' he says, with unexpected clarity. 'And send my regards to your father. Tell him . . .'

Sailor stops, and seems to lose his train of thought. He goes on squeezing her hand with his old man's fingers as if he doesn't want to let go.

'Tell him what?' From the corner of her eye Veronica sees Marie lean closer to hear. His voice is weak, barely more than a whisper.

'Tell Ebbe summer will soon be over.'

Chapter 37

Y ou remember some things from childhood better than others. For instance, she can still remember all the words to Abba's 'The Winner Takes It All'. Abba split up in the January of the year Billy went missing. She knows it made her mum sad, and is pretty sure that's why she played the song so often, both on the record player and on the untuned piano in the best parlour.

Later, when Mum was in the home, Veronica used to shut herself in her room after they'd been to visit her, put her headphones on and listen to that particular song. The sad, high voice that reminded her a bit of her mum's. The words that she didn't quite understand, but which still felt right somehow.

After Leon left her she played the song again. Listened to it through whole nights instead of sleeping, convinced that it described exactly how she felt. That all she had to do was explain that to Leon, and he would be hers again.

The registration number of the green Volvo 245 that they drove to the care home in every Sunday is also etched on her memory. KBH 278. As is the institutional smell inside the old building, the number of steps from the entrance to Mum's room, and the number of shadow squares the grille on the window cast on the floor when the sun shone through the window. She can recall all this in a millisecond.

Other things, however – how to conjugate German verbs, the chemical symbol for mercury, or which year Charles XII got shot in the head by a brass button – are completely gone, even though she once made a real effort to learn them. Which really only proves that the brain lives a life of its own and can't be controlled, even by itself.

She doesn't remember much about Askedalen, except that it's deep within the Northern Forest and that there was once a coal mine there. The roads leading to the valley have long since been abandoned and reclaimed by the pine forest, and she has only the vaguest idea of how to get there.

After driving around aimlessly for over an hour she eventually finds a narrow, half-overgrown loggers' track that leads off in what she thinks is the right direction. The car bounces and jolts some five hundred metres along it before it comes to a halt.

She gets out of the car, taking the pocket torch she keeps in the glove compartment along with her mix tapes and MOT certificate. She tries to figure out which direction Askedalen is in, and how far away it might be.

She gets it half right. The direction is fine, but it takes almost three quarters of an hour of trudging through the dense forest – twice as long as she'd thought – before she comes across the first deciduous trees. By now her top is soaked with sweat and her trainers are like two lumps of clay from the mud in the hollows of the tracks left by logging machinery, which have somehow managed not to dry out in the heat.

The hike has given her plenty of time to think. The blond man has been in the village. He said his name was Isak, and he visited Sailor in the care home, so it can hardly have been a coincidence that he turned up in her therapy group.

Sailor's fragmented story seemed to confirm that Tommy Rooth took Billy as revenge on her uncle. If Isak really was Billy, that meant that Rooth didn't kill him, as everyone believed. In which case, what happened after the kidnap, and what did Sailor mean about the truth being up here? Why has Isak only just appeared, and why doesn't he just say who he is? And if he isn't Billy, as her dad and Mattias say, then who is he and what is he after?

There are plenty more questions, all just as valid, such as how any of this is connected to the events of the previous night and the smooth pebble on the headstone. Not to mention what might actually be the most pressing questions of all: why had she set off into the forest on her own, and what was she hoping to find?

When she reaches the valley she stops on the edge, crouches down and tries to get an idea of the scene in front of her. The slope is far too steep for forestry machinery, and the deciduous trees and bushes along the side of the valley form a canopy, making it almost impossible to see all the way to the bottom. For the same reason she can only just make out the other side, but she guesses that the valley must be a couple of hundred metres across.

A crooked sign attached to a tree trunk bearing the words DANGER! RISK OF SUBSIDENCE! wakes an old memory. Something Uncle Harald said about never going hunting in Askedalen in case the dogs or any of the hunters fell into one of the sinkholes caused by the collapse of the old mine workings.

She takes a few more minutes to catch her breath before carefully beginning her descent. The ground is covered by a thick layer of leaves in varying stages of decay, which makes her footing slippery and unpredictable. Halfway down she slips, and slides a few metres on her backside before managing to grab a birch trunk and get to her feet again. She can see the bottom of the valley now. A green carpet of moss, grass and ivy, broken in places by saplings and fallen trees that hadn't managed to cling on to the loose ground. She can also make out a number of sinkholes of varying sizes.

It's almost completely quiet down here. The only sound is a woodpecker far in the distance. The foliage filters the light, transforming it into an odd mixture of day and night. She looks around and estimates that she's somewhere in the centre of the valley now, and tries to figure out which way to go.

If she was Tommy Rooth or Sailor – two poachers wanting a safe place to set camp – she'd want to find ground that was as high as possible. So she follows that instinct, and heads slowly north, up the gradual incline.

The ground is soft, her feet sink several centimetres each time she puts them down. The floor of the valley is like some green lunar landscape. Most of the sinkholes are no deeper than a metre, and roughly three times as wide. The ground at the bottom of them looks much like the surrounding terrain, but she can't be sure that it will hold her weight and skirts carefully round them as she slowly makes her way upwards.

Ten minutes later she finds the first evidence of human activity. A heap of twisted scrap metal, already half consumed by rust. She can see wheels and pulleys, and guesses they were part of some sort of haulage system. She nearly trips over an almost completely overgrown concrete pad right next to the heap, presumably the foundations of one of the buildings that must have been here when the mine was active. When she looks up towards the edge of the valley she can just make out a slight depression that could be the remains of a track that once led down here. The pine forest looms dense and tall above it, suggesting that the track was abandoned many years ago, long before Rooth and Sailor started coming here.

She carries on up the valley, and eventually comes across something resembling a path. It's too narrow and indistinct to have been made by a human being so she guesses deer, and is proved right when she sees some hoofmarks in a patch of mud. There's no sign of any footprints. Nor of campfires, marks on any of the trees to indicate which ones should be felled, no shelters or anything else to suggest that anyone has been here. In theory, she could actually be the first person here since Sailor and Rooth stopped coming.

She passes a stack of half-rotted sleepers, and beside them the metal skeleton of what, to judge by the wheels, was once a mine cart. Then she comes to a large, dense thicket. The path continues straight through it, and she considers walking round to pick up the trail again on the other side, but something tells her to keep going. She pushes the branches aside and has to crouch down and bow her head, so almost walks right into the small shack hidden a short way into the undergrowth. Perhaps it was too far away when the mine was dismantled and had already been forgotten, unless the ground around it had become so unstable that they simply hadn't been able to get up here with their machinery.

Whatever, the shack is still here, even if nature is well on its way to finishing it off. There are plants sticking out of from between the planks, and up on the tin roof there's such a thick layer of moss, leaves and grass that the walls have started to bow.

She takes a step closer and feels something under her foot. Looking down, she sees an empty vodka bottle, half buried in the ground. She finds another one when she goes round the corner of the shack.

The remains of the door are lying on the ground, and the entrance is gaping open darkly. There's something hanging from the roof next to the door, something a pale yellow in colour. When she gets closer she realises that it's a windchime made out of animal bones and pieces of horn – someone's drilled holes in them and strung them up on a long strip of leather. She stifles a shudder, then walks over to the doorway and peers inside.

Chapter 38

O nce, when they were playing hide-and-seek out in the garden when she was a child, she managed to shut herself inside the old milking parlour in the cowshed. The heavy door swung closed and locked behind her, and it was over an hour before she was found and let out. An hour during she which she cried so hard that her voice broke, and banged on the door until her hands hurt.

She was playing with Mattias and three of his friends. Mattias was always better at making friends than her. Which wasn't that strange, really. He was open, kind and loyal, and good at games and sports. The sort of thing that makes a boy popular with both sexes, at least in junior and high school. Sometimes – fairly often, to be honest – she was jealous of him for that.

That day it was he and his friends who rescued her. They let her out of the milking parlour and said nothing to her mum and dad about what had happened. She even remembers Mattias comforting her later on when she used to wake up at night from nightmares about the darkness, damp and cold. The following year, when Billy was old enough to join in their games, Dad put a padlock on the door and used the room to store his winter tyres. But the smell of the milking parlour is stuck in her head. It will be there as long as she lives. A rank, raw smell, almost exactly like the smell inside the shack, and she has to stop several times and remind herself that she isn't nine years old anymore, and doesn't need to be rescued or comforted by her big brother.

It takes just five minutes to explore the shack. It contains nothing but a rusty stove, some firewood and a few empty beer and vodka bottles. There's a box of empty cartridges on a shelf, and a box of waterproof matches. Anything else that might once have been here has long since disappeared. She can't be sure that the shack is the place she's looking for, of course. But judging by the creepy windchime and the empty cartridges, it's an abandoned hunting shack, and the vodka bottles inside and out speak volumes. There can hardly be more than one hunting cabin in Askedalen, and her gut feeling is that she's in the right place. But she can't see anything that might help answer any of her questions.

She decides to make her way out of the thicket and carry on along the path, up the steadily narrowing valley. It's darker here now, the sloping sides are getting closer together as the gradient of the incline gets steeper. In places the sides are so steep that the bare rock sticks out. It's black and porous, a bit like ash, which is presumably what gave the valley its name.

A large sinkhole forces her to stop. It's over ten metres in diameter, stretching across the whole of the valley floor. In the centre of the inverted green cone is a gaping black hole.

She can hear the splash of water, and realises that the hole leads down into one of the mine tunnels. It could even be one of the vertical shafts, in which case the hole could be very deep indeed, twenty metres, maybe more, and almost certainly full of water.

The neck of yet another broken vodka bottle is sticking out of the ground a metre or so from the opening of the hole. She feels her pulse quicken. The hole would be the perfect place to get rid of anything you didn't want to be found again, and the bottle suggests that Rooth and Sailor were here.

She looks around, trying to figure out if there's any way to get a better look without going down into the sloping funnel. There isn't. The ground looks pretty stable, though, so she decides to risk it. She takes a tentative step over the edge, pushing down with her foot a few times. When nothing happens she stamps a bit harder. She shifts her bodyweight and takes another step. The ground here is less overgrown, and almost feels firmer than the rest of the valley. She moves slowly towards the centre of the funnel, one step at a time. The sound of running water gets louder, and she can detect a damp, subterranean smell that reminds her a little of the metro.

The opposite wall of the hole is clearly visible now. Densely packed earth with plant roots sticking out of it like hairy worms. Below that, black rock and darkness.

She shortens her steps and inches forward until she reaches the edge. She takes out the torch, points it into the hole and leans forward to be able to see. Gently now . . .

The hole isn't as deep as she thought. She can see the bottom, some three or four metres below. There's a heap of earth, leaves and stones, presumably a mixture of the collapsed roof and things washed down later by the rain. Surrounding the heap is a pool of water, its surface broken by the constant dripping from the edge of the hole. The water stretches into the darkness, and it's just possible to see that there's an open space down there, considerably larger than the hole itself.

She moves the torch, trying to see further into the shadows. The beam of light from the cheap torch is fairly weak, only reaches a few metres before the darkness swallows it up. When she points it to the right she catches a glimpse of something right on the edge of the beam of light. She tries to hold the torch still, screwing her eyes up in an effort to see better. A small, pale stick is poking out of a pile of rubbish. When she leans forward she realises that it isn't a stick, but a bone.

The truth is up there, Sailor's voice hisses in her ear.

The crack in her chest opens wider, letting out an icy chill. The blood drains from her head and she staggers slightly. And without any warning the edge of the hole gives way and she finds herself falling headlong into the cold darkness.

Darling,

I tried to get hold of you yesterday, I called you at home, and even went past your house. I know I'm breaking the rules, breaking our agreement. But not hearing from you is driving me mad.

I can't believe that you've abandoned me. Not now, when I need you most. I can't believe that everything you've said, all the words you've whispered, have been nothing but lies. Unless perhaps you believed them at the time, just as much as I did? Did you think the two of us really could make it?

I hate you, but at the same time I still love you. More now than ever. Isn't that strange?

Chapter 39

When she comes round she's lying on her front at the bottom of the sinkhole. There's water dripping on her face, her head hurts and she can taste soil in her mouth. She must have hit her head, but the leaves and earth seem to have cushioned the fall and to her relief she hasn't broken anything. She sits up. Apart from a few scratches and the headache, her only injury is a split eyebrow. She presses the back of her hand to her head to stem the bleeding while she tries to get an idea of where she is. The torch landed in the pool of water by her feet, and doesn't work at first. But she shakes it a few times and hits it hard against the palm of her hand, and it comes back to life.

She shines it around her. The hole, or – more accurately – the cave she has landed in is bigger than she thought. Approximately seven metres in diameter, with the heap where she's sitting roughly at the centre. Around the edge the roof is only a metre or so off the ground, but above her head it's a good deal higher. The hole up above is no longer a perfect circle, and now has a gouge along one side where the soil gave way. Small clods of earth and stones are still falling, splashing into the large pool of water by her feet.

She shines the torch into the darkness to her right and soon finds what she's looking for. The heap with the small bone sticking out of it.

The pool is only a few centimetres deep, and her shoes are already so wet that she hardly notices the water as she moves cautiously closer. The torch lights up what she had thought was a pile of rubbish surrounding the bone, revealing a pair of thin horns and the remains of fur, sinews and hooves. The carcass of a deer that must have fallen down the hole some time ago. The tension in her body eases, then turns into fear as she realises her predicament. She's in an abandoned mine deep in the forest, in a place where nobody ever goes.

She clambers back up onto the heap. The hole is much too far away for her to be able to reach it. She explores the rest of the cave, looking for something she might be able to stand on. All she finds are a couple of rotten wooden beams stuck beneath a load of stones over by one wall, and the rusted remains of a tin bucket. There's nothing here, nothing that could help her climb back up.

Panic starts to bubble in her chest, lurching into her throat when the torch flickers a couple of times before going out. The murky light coming through the hole only illuminates a few square metres of the floor of the cave. The rest is as black and cold as the old milking parlour. And this time there isn't anyone looking for her. No one's going to come.

She feels her breathing get more ragged, a warning sign that a panic attack is on its way, and she hurries back to the cone of light from the hole. She sits down on the heap, sticks her head between her knees and tries to focus on not hyperventilating.

In.

Out.

Iiin.

Ouuut.

Why the hell did she come up here, on some wild goose chase after ghosts? She's stuck down here now. Stuck, stuck, stuck . . .

Her head starts to spin, and the blood oozing from her cracked brow makes her close one eye. For a moment she thinks she's going to faint, then suddenly she hears Ruud's voice in her head.

Calm down, for God's sake, Veronica, you have to calm down! This is just a temporary setback, something you need to work through.

The hammering in her chest slows. The cave, the hole, the whole of this bloody valley are just another obstacle she needs to get past. Just like Leon, Ruud himself, and the agreement. Temporary setbacks.

She manages to take a deep, shaky breath. Then another one. The panic slowly loosens its grip.

She straightens up, then gets to her feet and tries hitting the torch against her palm again. It comes back to life at once. She wades through the pool of water and explores the cave again, more thoroughly this time. The side where the dead deer lay is towards the top of the valley, and the ground there is dry. A metre or so beyond the pile of fur, horns and bones is a smooth rock face, which might mean that this is where the mine ends, where the rock becomes harder. Perhaps that's why there's a cave here, to store things in, possibly – the rusted bucket would tend to support that idea. And if this is the end of the tunnel, then it must lead off in the opposite direction. She looks at the pool of water, and sees the way it spreads out from the middle of the cave towards the wall with the wooden beams embedded in it.

She makes her way over there and realises that the beams were once the supports for the collapsed tunnel. Water is filtering through the stones at the bottom, and it takes her just a few minutes to clear enough of them to be able to shine the torch through to the other side. The air in there smells even more strongly of subterranean damp. But she can feel a draught on her face, and realises with growing hope that there must be another opening at the other end. She removes some more of the stones and shines the torch through the hole again. A narrow tunnel leads off beyond the blockage. The light of the torch shimmers off the water covering the ground.

The wooden beams stuck beneath the stones make it possible to carefully enlarge the opening near to the floor, and soon it's big enough for her to crawl through. She turns and glances back at the comforting light from the hole in the roof. Tries not to think about the darkness of the milking parlour.

She puts the torch in her mouth and snakes through the gap. The water beneath her is ice cold, making her gasp as it soaks through her clothes.

Getting through to the other side is easier than she expected, and once she's there she finds she can almost stand up in the tunnel. The floor is covered by a reflective mirror of water, constantly topped up by the water running in from the cave behind her, as well as the hundreds of drips and trickles making their way down the uneven, shiny rock walls. It takes her a few moments to realise that the water isn't standing still. It's moving very slowly, into the darkness in front of her.

There are large, rusty bolts sticking up every so often. Presumably there had once been a set of rails that were removed when the mine was closed. She moves forward at a crouch, shining the torch before moving her feet. The water splashes around her, the ripples breaking the smooth surface and swallowing the light from the torch.

Every three metres there are rotten, almost black wooden supports wedged beneath crossbeams in the roof. She takes care not to touch the supports and tries not to think about how many tons of earth and rock are above her head as she makes her way onward.

The tunnel is sloping gently downwards, and slightly to the left. She's sure about the slope, the movement of the water is enough to prove that, but the curve is more of a gut feeling. She guesses that the tunnel runs close to the side of the valley where she fell in, and that it's one of a series of mine tunnels at various depths that have left the valley floor extremely unstable. The thought unnerves her, all the more so when she realises that the amount of water running down the walls is increasing.

About fifteen metres along the tunnel the thin covering of water has become a sluggish stream reaching up to her ankles. She stops for a few moments. The tunnel is still heading downwards, following the slope of the valley above, which means that the water level is only going to get deeper. She can still feel the faint draught, so somewhere in front of her air is getting in, through some sort of opening.

Ten metres further on the water is up to her knees and she has to move even more slowly. The sound of running water is getting louder. She can feel the pull of the water on the backs of her thighs, then her backside. When the water reaches her waist the current gets stronger and she realises what that means even before she reaches the blockage.

The roof has caved in, and the tunnel is blocked almost completely by two large boulders that must weigh several tons. She can shine the torch between them, can feel the draught and see that the tunnel curves off ahead of her. But she can't get through.

She curses loudly, mostly to fend off her growing panic. Her teeth have started to chatter and the muscles in her arms and legs are starting to twitch involuntarily. She shines the torch at the boulders again and sees that the water seems to get sucked down immediately in front of them. She sticks her hand down and feels the surface of the rock. Around knee height she finds an opening, and after more exploration she estimates that it's wide enough for her to swim through. On this side, anyway.

She shivers, and feels the spasms in her muscles turn into nonstop shaking. How long has she got before the cold gets the better of her? Quarter of an hour, maybe. Less if she dunks the rest of her body in the ice-cold water. And what happens if she gets stuck halfway? It didn't take a genius to work out the answer to that one.

For the first time she seriously considers turning back and trying to pile up enough stones from the tunnel to build a pyramid tall enough for her to be able to climb up and reach the hole. Then she realises that she's already removed the stones that would easily come loose when she enlarged the hole to get into the tunnel, and even if she did manage to loosen some more, there is no way there were going to be enough. Her only chance – unless she feels like sitting below the hole calling for help, which would almost certainly be utterly pointless – is to dive down and go through this opening, then carry on along the tunnel to wherever the air is getting in.

A sudden gust of air between the boulders carries with it a faint smell of forest. That makes her mind up for her. She switches the torch off and sticks it in the pocket of her jeans. She takes a deep breath, then bends her knees and sinks into the ice-cold black water.

The current pulls her towards the opening faster than she expected. The water's so cold it makes her head throb. The gap isn't large, and she feels in front of her with her hands, grabbing hold of a protruding piece of rock to pull herself forward. She keeps her eyes open at first but there's not really any point: the darkness down here is as dense as in the milking parlour, so she closes them and concentrates on feeling her way with her fingers.

She pulls herself further forward with her right hand, then kicks with her legs, but her knee hits the rock and the pain is so sharp that she almost stops. She feels in front of her again, trying to find something to use to pull herself forward. She manages to move a little further before she comes to an abrupt halt. She's stuck, just as she feared, and she can't pull herself loose with just one hand. The oxygen in her lungs is fast running out, used up by the cold and her racing heart.

She manages to squeeze her other hand through to help, feeling around for a new handhold, but all she can feel are smooth rocks or cracks that are too small to get her fingers into. Her lungs are burning and her vision starts to waver. Her left hand suddenly seems to have stopped working, it's no longer doing what she tells it to. It's only a matter of time before the same thing happens to her right hand.

Her body isn't moving at all, in spite of the water rushing faster and faster around her. She's run out of air now and it feels like her lungs are going to burst. Fireworks are exploding on her retinas, before slowly fading to black, like the tube of an old television. One last thought, four words pulsing through her.

You
Can't
Die
HERE!

Her anger gives her fresh energy. She reaches her right arm out as far as it will go. Her fingers are tingling, her arm is on the verge of becoming useless when she suddenly feels a definite edge. That must be the other side of the opening.

Her fingers have contracted into a claw, but she manages to get a grip and with the last of her strength uses her right arm to pull at the same time as she twists her body. The pressure around her increases and water rushes past her head, making her ears pop. Her mouth is about to open to draw a breath, filling her lungs with the dark mine water.

She clenches her teeth, straining so hard that her jaw aches as she continues to twist herself round. And suddenly she comes loose, and shoots out like a blockage from a pipe. She hits her head, then her knee. She kicks out with her legs, manages to reach the bottom and push herself upwards. She can't hold her breath any longer. Her mouth opens to take a deep breath. And she fills her lungs, not with water but cold, damp air that is scented with the forest.

Chapter 40

The air hole is just round the corner, exactly where she had thought. Part of the roof has collapsed, leaving a hole the size of her fist, with loose soil around it. Her frozen fingers are stiff and numb as she pulls down stones and lumps of earth. She shuts her eyes as the soil rains down on her face. Her body is shaking uncontrollably with cold, but after a couple of minutes the hole is large enough for her to brace herself against the wall of the tunnel with her feet and squeeze through it.

When her head and arms are above ground she grabs hold of the tussocks of grass growing at the bottom of the sinkhole and pulls herself upwards, centimetre by centimetre, until her whole body is out in the warm air. She rolls over onto her back, her body still shaking, and suddenly bursts out laughing. She laughs so much that tears start to run down her cheeks, and the spasms of laughter merge with her shivering. She must look like some sort of crazy woodland creature. A troll or a dryad, roaring with laughter as she crawls out from the underworld, filthy and soaking wet, her face smeared with blood.

The fit of laughter passes but she carries on shivering. In spite of her numb fingers she manages to pull her dripping top off, but that doesn't help much. She needs warmth, more warmth than this shaded sinkhole can offer.

She struggles out of the hollow and tries to get her bearings. She realises that she's not far from the large thicket hiding the shack. So she heads unsteadily towards it.

The logs in the basket may be ancient, but they've been under cover and the wind blowing through the gaps in the walls has helped keep them dry. Fortunately the matches she found earlier are also dry, so it doesn't take long before she manages to light a fire in the small stove with the help of some crowberry twigs. As with everything else to do with nature and the forest, she has her Uncle Harald to thank for knowing what to do.

She hangs her wet clothes up next to the stove, then sits shivering in just her bra and pants, holding her hands up towards the flames. She feels a prickly pain as the feeling slowly returns, and almost bursts into laughter again.

When she was training to be a therapist she read about this phenomenon, but has never experienced it before. Survivor's euphoria. The feeling resembles a cocaine rush, and for several minutes she feels immortal, as if she hasn't got a care in the world. But as her body temperature slowly returns to normal, so does her mood.

What has this stupid excursion actually achieved? The reply is easy. Nothing at all. She may have found the shack that Sailor and Rooth once used, but there's nothing to suggest that Billy was ever here. Nothing that either confirms that he died or indicates that he survived, which is what she was secretly hoping to find. And even if Sailor's addled brain managed to produce a few rational sentences, his mutterings about the truth were hardly reliable. All things considered, she hasn't got any closer to the answer to any of the many questions swirling around inside her head. Meaning that Isak's identity remains a mystery.

She picks some small stones out of the soles of her shoes and throws them irritably into the bushes outside the entrance to the shack. The stones are from the mine. They're small and black, and she can almost crush them between her fingers. They're made of clinker – poor quality coal that used to be ground into grit and spread on the sportsgrounds and running tracks in half of Skåne, or was simply dumped in huge heaps. She tosses another stone away. It hits something in the bushes with a metallic clattering sound.

She looks up in surprise, pulls her wet shoes on and goes outside. The bushes form a dense thicket. She throws another stone in the same direction as the last. Another clatter, louder this time. There's something in there, something hidden by the sharp brambles. She goes back inside the shack and pulls on her trousers and top – even if they aren't completely dry, at least they're warm. Then she heads out into the bushes.

Despite being careful, thorns dig into her thigh almost immediately. More scratch her arm and she lets out a yelp of annoyance.

She's been scratched plenty of times by the time her foot hits something solid. It takes her a few moments to realise that it's a fairly large object, covered by a dirty camouflage net.

She tugs at the net, feeling the tension mount as she gradually uncovers the object. A rectangular metal chest, slightly larger than a washing machine, standing on a concrete base. On top is a large handle and two metal eyes. The chest, which was probably once used to store dynamite, is large enough to hold a full-grown adult if they were curled up, and certainly a child.

The hammering in her chest is almost painful, and before she gets to grips with the lid she has to stop and rest her hands on her knees for a few moments to quell a wave of nausea. When she straightens up again she spots something on the ground beside the concrete base. The remains of a sturdy padlock, presumably originally used to fasten the two eyes on top of the chest. She picks it up. The lock has been severed cleanly, which would have required a serious pair of bolt-cutters. The cut surface is as rusty as the rest of the lock, though, so it must have been lying on the ground for years.

She stands up, takes some deep breaths, then grabs the handle and tries to lift the lid. It's heavy, at least ten centimetres thick, but after a couple of attempts the lid starts to move, and swings open on dry, creaking hinges.

The chest is almost empty, which makes her relax a little. The inside is lined with wood. Along one side there's a partition and a shelf. On the shelf is a aerosol can that she recognises, Skyttens gun-oil.

She understands at once what that means. This was where Rooth and Sailor stored the guns they used for poaching.

Rifles with silencers that they didn't have licences for, and which they didn't dare keep at home.

There's something glinting at the bottom of the chest. A brass cartridge stuck between the planks lining the base. She leans over the side and reaches one arm down as far as she can. She manages to pull the cartridge out, along with one of the planks next to it.

There's another compartment underneath. She can make out something dark and rectangular, and leans over a bit further. Her feet are dangling in the air and for a moment she almost falls head first into the chest. But she regains her balance, moves more of the planks out of the way and reaches down for the object. A green tin box, about the size of a thick book. She snatches at it, then pushes herself up out of the chest.

The box is light and when she turns it over she discovers that it's unlocked. She opens it. Empty, as she had already feared. She's so frustrated that she almost throws it into the bushes. Then she discovers that there's something stuck in the bottom of the box. A small scrap of paper which she carefully teases out. It's been folded double, and resembles a triangular pocket. When she tries to open it she sees that there's something stuck inside it. Something so fine and so pale that it's almost invisible, but it's enough to drive open the crack in the ice inside her chest.

Three short strands of blond hair.

Chapter 41

It's almost seven o'clock in the evening by the time she gets back to the logging track where she left the car. Her clothes and shoes are still damp and stink of the mine water, but the climb out of the valley and the hike back through the forest have warmed her up.

She's holding the box in a way she imagines might not destroy any potential fingerprints, and she's so immersed in thought that she doesn't see the other vehicle before she's almost reached it. A green pick-up with the Aronsson Farming logo on it.

The driver is leaning against her bonnet. Aviator sunglasses, a green trucker's cap, dark workman's trousers. A flannel shirt with the sleeves rolled up.

He's got a mobile phone pressed to his ear as he turns towards her when she emerges from the forest. 'She's just shown up. I'll call you back,' she hears him say before he ends the call.

It's Patrik, the guy she passed yesterday on her way to the farm. Patrik Brink, she remembers now. The son of Uncle Harald's foreman, as well as Cecilia's cousin.

The memory she tried to suppress before bubbles up to the surface. It's 1986, and she's about to turn sixteen. Mum's been dead three years, Abba have been disbanded for the same length of time, and Mattias lives in Stockholm. A party in someone's house. The lights are out, the air is thick with expectation and the CD player is stuck on 'Take My Breath Away'. The tongue inside her mouth tastes of tobacco and beer. A hand fumbles under her top, unbuttons her fly. She hurriedly suppresses the rest of the memory.

Patrik Brink belonged to the cool gang in those days. The guys with driving licences whose lives had probably already reached their high point, somewhere between sixteen and twenty. He's put on ten kilos of what looks like mostly muscle, and his moustache has been replaced by a neat goatee, but apart from that he looks much the same. His self-confidence seems undiminished and he has a weather-beaten look that isn't altogether unattractive. Maybe he's one of the few whose star has continued to rise, in spite of everything. He takes off the sunglasses and grins at her.

'What the hell have you been up to, Vera?'

She sees her reflection in one of the car windows and realises that it's a perfectly reasonable question. Her clothes are stained with clinker, blood and mud. Her face is streaked and filthy, her hair hanging in dank clumps.

'I fell over,' she says.

'Where? And what the fuck are you doing out here anyway?'

She shrugs her shoulders. Skips the first question and moves straight on to the second. 'I was looking for an old den we had when I was little. But I got lost.'

Patrik looks at her suspiciously, unless he just thinks she's a bit weird.

'Did you find it? The den?'

'Mm.' She's already bored with the conversation, and feels in her trouser pocket for the car key as she turns towards the door.

'What's that?' He nods towards the tin box.

'Just something I found.'

'In the den?'

She pulls the key out, unlocks the door and quickly puts the box down in the passenger footwell. When she turns round he's moved, and is standing on the other side of the open door, far too close. She's seen that smile on his face before. The look in his eyes too.

'Everyone's looking for you, Vera. People are worried.'

'My uncle, you mean. I presume that's who you were talking to on the phone?'

He pulls a face which neither confirms nor denies what she said. Then he smiles again.

'How long have you been working for him?' she says, mostly to wipe the grin off his face.

'Off and on since I was fifteen. With breaks for national service and agricultural college. He paid for everything while I was a student, he's my mentor, I took over as foreman when Dad retired. But you know all that already.'

Both this claim and his tone of voice annoy her. As if Patrik Brink is so incredibly important that she's bound to have heard all about him six hundred kilometres away. She hasn't spared him a single thought for years.

'So you do whatever he says, just like that? Following orders.' She finds herself instinctively mimicking his tone of voice. It works better than she would have imagined.

'I'm Harald's foreman, not some fucking dogsbody. Aronsson Farming wouldn't last a day without me.'

'Really? I wonder if Uncle Harald agrees with you about that.'

Patrik leans closer. The car door is between them, but his proximity still feels invasive. He looks away from her eyes, down her body. Then he looks back up again.

'You haven't changed, Vera.' His self-confidence is back. 'Just as pretty as before, but with a few more curves. More experienced than last time. You remember Jocke's party, don't you?'

She feels a sudden urge to grab the door and slam it into his chest, then yank him by the hair while he's gasping for air and beat his head against the doorframe until that smug smile disappears. She knows she shouldn't think like that, slightly-too-tall Bengt is right when he says that sort of anger never leads to anything good. So instead she shrugs, slips into the driver's seat and starts the car.

'The only thing I remember about that is that you've got a tiny fucking cock,' she says before slamming the door on him.

Exhaustion catches up with her in the car on the way home and she opens the window so the breeze will help keep her awake. Her body is protesting against its exertions and the adrenalin rush earlier, and she knows she has to fight against it. Even so, she can feel her thoughts start to wander, and her head fills with drifting fog, the same colour as the dusk light outside the car.

Her eyelids droop, then her head, and even though she's aware of what's happening on some level, she can't stop it. The car swerves across the road and hits the left-hand verge. The tyres make a crunching sound in warning as they roll across the gravel on the hard shoulder. But in her head 'Take My Breath Away' is playing, and Mum's dead, Billy's missing and Mattias has abandoned her. The car crosses the road again, sliding off onto the other hard shoulder, and weirdly enough she watches it happen, even though her eyes are almost closed. She realises she's about to drive into the steep ditch and prepares herself for the impact without doing anything to stop it.

Something appears in front of the car. Two glinting dots reflecting the light of the headlamps. Eyes staring at the car as it rushes towards them.

And suddenly her ability to react kicks into action. Her foot hits the brake so hard that her joints creak, her hands spin the wheel like mad and she manages to stop the car leaving the road at the last moment. The brakes shriek, accompanied by the squeal of the tyres and the crunch of tarmac. The steering wheel judders, then everything is quiet and still.

She sits for a while with her heart racing, her arms shaking. A smell of rubber and warm asbestos is coming through the open window, turning her stomach. She swallows hard and opens the door, then gets out to see what kind of animal she hit. In the field to the right of the car three wind turbines stand out against the sky, winking at her with their red eyes. The blades are turning slowly in the weak evening breeze, making a dull, pulsating sound.

Her stomach lurches again. She leans on the bonnet, then slowly walks round to the front of the car, preparing herself for the worst. She's seen accidents like this before. She recalls Uncle Harald muttering about sissies who didn't have the guts to kill injured animals and left them screaming to die in agony. She knows that sound. Desperate, terrified, almost human.

But the only sound as she moves round the car are the crickets and the heartbeat of the wind giants. The headlights are both intact, and there's no blood or fur, or any dents in the bodywork. Nor any blood on the tarmac around the car. She stumbles away and throws up into the ditch.

Chapter 42

It's starting to get dark by the time she pulls into the farm-yard. The lights are on inside the house, and there are two cars parked next to Dad's. One of them is Mattias's, the other a big, shiny Land Rover. She hesitates for a few moments, then decides not to take the tin inside with her.

When she cautiously opens the front door she hears a number of voices that she manages to identify fairly easily. Apart from Dad she can hear Mattias, Cecilia and their three girls. Uncle Harald, his wife Tess.

She creeps through the house to the utility room, where she washes off the worst of the blood and dirt in the large sink. She pulls her hair up into a ponytail. She finds a stack of old clothes in the far cupboard. Some jogging bottoms which must once have been hers, and one of Mattias's tops, far too big but at least it covers the scar on her arm. She pulls the clothes on, then checks her reflection in the window before she steels herself to go in and meet the others.

They're sitting in the dining room, and all of them seem pleased to see her, even though she's late. Mattias and the girls seem genuinely happy, but Cecilia's delight is as fake as her own.

Tess and Uncle Harald have one son, Timothy. The last time Veronica saw him he was tiny. Now he's five or six. He seems shy, wants to climb onto his dad's lap and hide his face from her. Uncle Harald holds him gently, as if he were a baby bird. His face glows with pride and even if the boy has dark hair and looks more like his Thai mother, Veronica finds herself thinking of Billy. She glances at her father, and can see from his face that she isn't alone in that. Especially when Tess calls the boy Timmy.

Uncle Harald is the same as usual, just a bit greyer and maybe a little heavier. Her grandfather's sharp nose and thick eyebrows are still very prominent. His eyes haven't changed. Hard, watchful. Except when they look at Timothy, when they soften and almost make him look like a different person.

'Now say hello to your cousin Vera,' he says, winking at her over the boy's head. 'She's been out having an adventure today, you know. She's been all over the place. Even underground, by the sound of it.'

Over dinner Veronica tries to make eye contact with Mattias. But he's fully occupied playing the role of good husband, father and son.

She studies her brother, trying to figure out what's going on with him and Cecilia. If they're just pretending for the children's sake. If that's true, then they're succeeding pretty well. She even spots Mattias holding Cecilia's hand at one point, a gesture that surprises her almost as much as Uncle Harald being such a proud father. But what surprises her most about dinner is that it's actually rather pleasant. They're all talking at the same time, filling the usually quiet room with chatter and laughter. Even Dad looks more cheerful, bustling between the big dining table and the kitchen to fetch more wine and refill the dishes. He smiles modestly when everyone praises his cooking effusively. Not even Uncle Harald's predictable anecdote about America bores her. Maybe it's something to do with the wine, but for a short while everything feels the way it should. Almost normal. Then she finds herself thinking about the tin box out in the car. The folded piece of paper and the strands of blond hair inside it.

Timothy thaws out during the meal, and even sits on her lap when she reads a story from one of the dog-eared Disney annuals in the bookcase. His chubby little hands are sticky from the sweets his mother keeps giving him, even though he had a double helping of dessert. When he leans his head back against her chest she can't help smelling his hair, inhaling the sweet scent small children have, which makes the ice in her chest start to creak and rumble again. The boy reaches out a chubby finger to point at one of the pictures in the book. A character with red fur and a cunning smile on its lips.

'A fox,' the boy says. 'Daddy shoots foxes. Don't you?'

Uncle Harald turns to them and pats the boy on the head.

'Absolutely. All hunters shoot foxes whenever they get the chance, Tim.'

'Why?'

'Because there's only room for one hunter in the forest.' He winks at Veronica over his cognac glass as if to let her know that he's joking. For some reason she isn't entirely sure about that.

When it's time for everyone to leave she goes out into the yard with them. It's almost eleven o'clock, the youngest children have fallen asleep and need to be carried out. She's drunk three cups of coffee and finds herself in that odd state when her body is utterly exhausted but her brain is wide awake.

When they're outside she finally manages to get Mattias on his own. 'I've got something I want to show you,' she whispers. 'Something I found up in the forest. I think it could be to do with Billy.'

'What?' His voice is wary, tense.

Before she has time to say more, Uncle Harald appears out of nowhere.

'It's good to have you back home, Vera,' he says, and sounds as if he means it. 'It's nice to have the whole family together.'

She nods, unsure of how to reply.

'No one can manage without family. Not in the long run. What do you say, Mattias?'

He slaps Mattias on the back and she notices a slightly uncomfortable look in her brother's eyes.

'By the way, have you had a chance to talk to Ebbe? There's no funny business. He just needs to sign, and we'll do the rest.'

'Sign what?' she says, a little too quickly.

Several seconds of silence follow. Neither of the men seems to want to say anything.

'What does Dad have to sign?' she repeats.

Before either of them can speak, Tess blows the car horn.

'Time to go,' Uncle Harald says. 'Like I said, good to see you, Vera. Hope it won't be so long until next time.' He turns to Mattias and slaps him on the back again. 'I'll call you tomorrow. And don't forget to talk to your dad.'

'What was all that about?' she says as they wave Uncle Harald off.

'He wants to build more wind turbines. Twice as tall. Replace the old ones out there.' Mattias gestures towards the darkness on the far side of the house. 'Dad needs to sign to say he agrees to their construction.'

'But surely he doesn't? Those turbines will block the view from the back of the house. And there'll be no way of escaping the noise anywhere in the garden.'

Mattias shrugs.

'Yes, it'll be a nuisance for you to have to put up with that when you come home once every five years.'

He doesn't sound aggressive, just matter-of-fact, and possibly a little drunk. It still makes her sad, though.

'Are you coming, Mattias?' Cecilia calls from the car.

'I need to go.' He seems remorseful now, as if he's realised he went too far. 'Pop into the station tomorrow, around nine, and we'll talk more then.'

She nods. She stands and watches the car drive off, and wonders about packing her things and setting off in her car like she'd planned, leaving all this behind. She quickly dismisses the idea. She needs to show Mattias the tin box, so he can help her piece the puzzle together. She lights a cigarette and smokes it in silence.

Somewhere far off in the darkness the solitary nightingale is singing.

Chapter 43

Veronica wakes up because she's cold. The window is open and the nocturnal damp has crept into the bedroom. She gets out of bed and closes it. Her body feels battered and bruised and her hands ache. Her knuckles and fingers are still black with ingrained dirt from the mine. The cut above her eye stings. She's slept a deep and dreamless sleep, but still doesn't feel rested.

Outside, the garden is almost still. There's a faint breeze making the trees sway slightly, a southerly breeze. Still no sign of autumn, even though August will soon be over.

When she goes down to the kitchen her dad has already made breakfast for her. Bacon, scrambled eggs, toast. Even freshly squeezed orange juice. She considers telling him about the person she saw in the rose garden the night before last. Asking him why he didn't answer when she knocked on the door of the study, and why he's started locking all the doors. And what he and Sailor talked about then they used to drink beer together in the pizzeria. But her dad's still in a good mood from the dinner the previous evening, talking about his grandchildren, smiling and stroking her hair.

So she decides it can wait until later. After she's spoken to Mattias.

'Are you staying till the weekend?' he says, apparently assuming she's on holiday even though she hasn't said anything. 'There's a harvest supper on Saturday down in the park. I wasn't planning to go, but if you're here . . .'

She says something diplomatic without making any promises. Then hurries out before she has time to see his disappointment.

The village police station smells of bureaucracy and disinfectant. She's never been here before, so she has no memories to compare it with, but the reception area where Mattias comes to fetch her looks much as she expected.

The walls of his office are covered with pennants, framed badges and police souvenirs from around the world. She wonders where he got them from, if he inherited them from his predecessor or has actually visited the various places represented. Greater Manchester Police, Miami-Dade Police Department, Polizei Rheinland-Pfalz. There's a bulky computer screen on the desk, and a police radio that crackles from time to time, then emits clipped sentences that can only be understood with difficulty.

She gets straight to the point and tells him what happened in the rose garden. Then about her encounters with Berit, Lidija and her father, then Sailor in the care home. She hurries on before he has time to interrupt with questions and doubts, and tells him about the shack and the tin box she found inside the concealed chest.

She leaves out the bit about falling into the mine, and doesn't tell him that Uncle Harald seems to have told Patrik Brink to keep an eye on her. There's already more than enough for Mattias to take in. He pulls on a pair of plastic gloves, then inspects the tin box from all sides before examining the fold of paper and the strands of hair with the help of a magnifying glass. He almost looks like an old-fashioned detective, which makes her smile.

'A corner,' he murmurs, as much to himself as her.

'What?'

'The paper. It's the corner of an envelope.'

'Oh.' She leans forward and looks at the paper, which he's carefully holding up with a pair of tweezers. She realises he's right. Silly of her not to have noticed. 'What do you think that could mean?'

He puts the piece of paper down gently. 'Well, we don't know for certain if this is Billy's hair. We need to send away for analysis. Until we know that . . .'

'But if we skip that bit for now,' she interrupts. 'If we assume it's Billy's hair?'

Mattias shrugs his shoulders. He doesn't look anything like as interested or excited as she'd expected.

'OK, if we assume that this really is Billy's hair.' He leans back in his chair. 'The police were working on the theory that Tommy Rooth kidnapped Billy to blackmail Uncle Harald. If that's right, then this corner could have come from a black-mail letter.'

'But there wasn't a letter, was there?'

'No, not as far as we know. Maybe Rooth cut off some of Billy's hair and put it in an envelope anyway. And wrote a note demanding money. But for some reason the letter never got sent. Maybe things went wrong and Billy died soon after he was taken, so Rooth got rid of the letter, leaving just this corner that somehow got caught in the tin.'

'Unless something completely different happened.' She pulls out the photofit picture, unfolds it and smooths it out on the desk in front of him. She sees the set of his mouth harden. 'A man looking like this has been to see Sailor up at Ekhagen. He told the nurses his name was Isak, and that he's the old man's nephew. They remember him very clearly. And when I showed this picture to Sailor, it was obvious that he recognised him.'

Mattias looks at the picture, then at her. He looks more interested now. He's about to say something when there's a knock on the door. A woman of around thirty looks in. The expression on her face before she realises that Mattias isn't alone makes it very clear to Veronica who she is.

'Oh, sorry. I didn't know you had a visitor.' The woman stops in the doorway. She's beautiful, with dark eyes, and skin that's almost the same bronze tone as Leon's.

'This is my sister.' Mattias sounds rattled.

'Oh, hello,' the woman says, smiling, but doesn't give her own name. Mattias doesn't introduce her either.

'Did you want anything particular?'

'Nothing that can't wait. Nice to meet you.' The woman nods to Veronica and closes the door behind her.

Mattias evades her gaze. Veronica doesn't quite know what to say to break the sudden silence. Clearly Mattias is at just as much of a loss, because he suddenly gets to his feet.

'Come with me, there's something I want to show you.'

She follows him down a flight of stairs, past a row of lockers, two changing rooms and an open door leading to a small gym. They carry along the corridor until they reach a fire door bearing a sign saying ARCHIVE.

The room is a rectangular, windowless box, and even though it's big it puts her in mind of the old milking parlour. She shuts her eyes and swallows.

The air in there is dry, and smells of printer ink, dust and paper. A central aisle runs between rows of shelves full of folders, files and boxes. She reads the years on the edges of the shelves: 1998, 1995, 1993. Mattias keeps walking, goes round a corner marked 1983, and stops. He points to the shelf by the wall. Blue folders, maybe twenty or so, all with the same case number on their labels.

'This is the Billy investigation. Nineteen full box files that Månsson left behind him. I must have been through the whole lot at least ten times. I've scrutinised every interview transcript, every memo, every note.' He runs his finger across the files. 'Whatever people say, Månsson really did do his best. He carried on looking for Billy long after the prosecutor had dropped the investigation. He kept receiving and investigating tip-offs, almost regardless of how far-fetched they were. I suppose he was hoping that Rooth would make his way home at some point.'

'And did he?' She guesses the answer before Mattias shakes his head.

'The last sign of life was a postcard with no message, postmarked in Rotterdam, sent to Nilla Rooth. That was a month or so after Rooth vanished. Sven Postie spotted it and gave it to the police. I think Månsson went to show it to Nilla. It's here somewhere, I've seen it for myself.'

He gestured towards the files.

'The postcard is of a ship, which could suggest that Tommy Rooth really did go to sea. There are notes showing that Månsson called various sailors' churches and missions in Rotterdam and other ports. Rooth was their only suspect, after all, the only person with a motive, so I can understand why Månsson was unwilling to let go of him. That he wanted to know where Rooth was, in case Billy's body was ever found and there was more evidence. But he never found anything.'

'What about the car? Rooth's old Volvo Amazon. What happened to that?'

'It was never found. Scrap by now, presumably.'

'And Månsson? What happened to him?'

'He moved back to Östergötland. To Mjölby, I think it was. Probably just as well. Most people blamed him for Rooth's release, although I don't agree with them. I'm not sure I'd have done any better.'

Mattias shrugs his shoulders.

'Is he still alive?'

'I think so. Someone said he's been ill. Stomach cancer, something like that. You remember Månsson, don't you?'

She nods. 'He always looked a bit pained, and he had an odd way of talking. An Östergötland accent, but using Skåne words. I remember thinking he had kind eyes.'

And that I lied to him about us getting home at the same time, she thinks. So you didn't get into trouble. Because back then it was you and me against the world.

'What are you trying to tell me by showing me all this?'

Mattias turns to look at her. 'Have you been in Billy's room since that summer? Or Mum's, come to that?'

She shakes her head. 'They're locked.'

'Do you know why?'

She has an idea of the answer, but decides to play along. 'No.'

'I've tried to persuade Dad to move into the village, where he can be closer to his grandchildren. Get a ground-floor flat, maybe. Uncle Harald has offered to buy Backagården for a good price.'

'But?'

'Dad refuses to move. He won't even talk about it. And that's also why he's refusing to give his permission for Uncle Harald to build those turbines.' He stops and looks like he's thinking. 'What I'm trying to say is that sooner or later we have to let go of the past. Or else we risk getting stuck there.'

They go back up to Mattias's office and he stops off in the kitchen to fill two chipped mugs with coffee. The police station is almost silent, the only sounds are the occasional crackle of the police radio and the clatter of a keyboard further along the corridor.

'I'll send the sample to the National Forensics Lab today,' he says when they're sitting down with their coffee. 'Even if those strands of hair do turn out to be Billy's, I'd be surprised if they get us anywhere.'

She nods, she's already figured that out for herself.

'And I'll talk the manager at Ekhagen and ask her to call me if that Isak character shows up again,' Mattias goes on. 'As for Dad and that person you say you chased through the garden . . .'

'What do you mean, *say*? I'm sure. There was someone there!'

Mattias puts his cup down and holds his hands up. 'Sorry, wrong choice of words. But if I understand correctly, you didn't actually see anyone. Like in Stockholm.'

'I'm absolutely certain.' She's trying not to snap at him, to not let her anger get the better of her. Sadly it's all too easy to get angry at Mattias.

'And it couldn't have been a deer?'

'A deer that latches the gate to the rose garden?'

He holds his hands up again. 'I'm only asking.'

They stare at each other for several seconds, then he capitulates.

'We had some break-ins at isolated farms at the start of the summer. Maybe the thieves have shown up again. I'll get the night shift to go past Dad's every once in a while.'

'Good,' she says. Then adds a 'thanks' in a slightly friendlier voice.

More silence.

'Are you staying until the weekend? There's a harvest supper in the park. Uncle Harald usually provides food and drink for everyone. Live music too, apparently.'

'What's happened to him? Since when did he get so generous?'

Mattias grins. 'The whole business with the wind turbines has made him pretty unpopular. So I guess he's trying to buy people off by throwing a party.'

'That would explain it.'

She tentatively returns his smile, and feels the atmosphere in the room relax.

'How are you getting on with . . .' She nods towards the door. 'Family therapy?'

His smile turns to a grimace. 'Not too well, to be honest. I'm doing my best, but it's complicated. Cecilia and I have known each other since school. We've got kids, a house together. I can't just give up.'

She thinks about Leon, and comes very close to telling Mattias what happened, seeing as he's confiding in her again.

'Do you love her?' she asks instead. And only realises the ambiguity in the question once she's said it.

Mattias shrugs. 'There are lots of different types of love.'

She nods, and scratches the scar on her arm.

'Does Uncle Harald know you're having problems?'

Mattias shakes his head. 'I've only told Dad. Cecilia and I are trying to keep it quiet. For the girls' sake.'

But also because you know what Uncle Harald will say, she thinks. That he'll put pressure on you to stay with Cecilia, do what he thinks is right. And because you'll find it hard to disobey him. Because you're a good boy. Ebbe and Magdalena's boy.

She decides to change the subject and make the most of this moment of closeness to ask something that's been troubling her for far too long.

'Do you think ... do you think Mum loved us, Mattias? I mean ...' she adds quickly, before he has time to protest, 'losing a child is the worst thing that can happen to a person. But she still had us. Why wasn't that enough?'

Why?

The word lingers in the air, and they drink their coffee in silence.

'Do you ever feel guilty?' he says after a while, shifting on his chair. 'Billy could be a fucking nightmare. Like the time he told Mum about the hawks' eggs. And Mum always treated him differently, as if he was ...'

'Special.'

'Exactly. It was like the rules were different for him.' Mattias gives her a wry smile, and something about that smile makes her feel better.

'It was Billy who started to call them Mum and Dad, do you remember? We always said Mother and Father.'

'Yeah, I remember.' Mattias lets out a laugh. 'We didn't start calling them Mum and Dad until after . . .' He tails off and looks away.

She takes a deep breath. Decides to challenge the ice in her chest.

'I was angry with Billy, that night. I thought he was hiding in one of our hide-and-seek places and had fallen asleep. That he'd made Mum worried and you'd have to pay because you got home late. That it would be like with the hawks' eggs all over again. I looked everywhere, in the barn, the cowshed, calling him all the names under the sun, out loud and in my head. Sometimes I still dream about it. Looking for him but never finding him.'

She stops, and tries to work out if she's said too much. But Mattias's face is giving nothing away.

'What about you?' she says. 'How do you feel?'

She thinks about all those files down in the basement. And the fact that Mattias has read them over and over again. Page after page, trying to spot something that no one has noticed before. Something that could put everything right, even though he knows that's impossible. Something that could explain the inexplicable. Is she the same? Is that what all this is about? She'd like to say no, tell herself that there's a difference.

'Sometimes . . .' he begins, then rubs the back of his neck. 'Sometimes I get the feeling that that summer's still going on. That we're somehow still living in it. You, me and Dad. The whole village—'

He's interrupted by the telephone. The ringtone is unexpectedly sharp, and makes him jump. The gentle expression in his eyes vanishes.

'Hello? Yes, hi . . .'

She can tell from his voice that it's Cecilia, and realises that their conversation is over.

Chapter 44

Veronica only has a vague memory of Rooth's farm. A few rundown buildings right on the edge of the Northern Forest, with grey roofs that were visible from the main road. But now, as she drives up and down several times on what should be the right stretch of road, she can't see any sign of a turning, or any rooftops. There's a huge green tractor pulling a disc harrow in one of the fields next to the road. Its driver has got out and is fiddling with the hydraulics. She stops the car and walks over to him. He's in his thirties, but she doesn't recognise him.

'Do you know where the Rooths' farm is?' she asks.

The man smiles at her and shakes his head.

'Only speak English.'

She tries again, in English, but the man's accent isn't easy to understand. Eventually he points towards the end of the field where a group of trees are growing a little way in front of the edge of the forest.

'Maybe there!'

She walks across the stubble. It's further than she thought, seven or eight hundred metres, and her bruised body protests. What little wind there was this morning has died away, the

313

sun is high in the sky, and by the time she reaches the shade of the trees she's worked up a sweat.

Despite the tractor driver's suggestion there are no ramshackle buildings among the trees. Just a clearing that looks more like an overgrown turning circle. On the far side the field of stubble carries on for a few hundred metres more before the forest proper begins. No hint of any buildings in any direction.

She curses the tractor driver out loud. But after a while her eyes get used to the low light beneath the trees and she realises that he was right after all. In the middle of the clearing the ground is still so compacted that the grass hasn't been able to take root. There are signs of stone foundations in a few places, and in one corner there's a heap of broken bricks. When she expands her search and kicks her way through the nettles she finds a few rusty tools, some chunks of wood and broken tiles. This was where Rooth's farm once stood. And now it's gone, razed to the ground, as if someone had tried to wipe it from the face of the Earth.

Something about the dimly lit clearing makes her feel uneasy, and it takes her a while to realise what. The clearing is silent. There are no birds singing, no leaves rustling. All she can hear is the tractor engine in the distance. She doesn't really know where the feeling comes from – she isn't superstitious at all – but suddenly she gets the sense that something happened here. Something that's still lingering over the place.

The tractor comes closer, but when she turns round and looks out across the field she sees that the noise is coming from a large green Land Rover that's driving straight towards her across the stubble.

She recognises the vehicle and walks towards it. It stops next to the trees and Uncle Harald gets out and stretches.

'You're off on another adventure, I see.'

'I'm trying to find Rooth's farm.'

'Yes, I thought as much.' He comes a couple of steps closer. 'Why this sudden interest in Tommy Rooth?'

She ignores the question and gestures towards the clearing behind them.

'What happened to the farm?'

'The bank took it.'

Uncle Harald takes a pipe from the breast pocket of his shirt and carefully fills it before he lights it.

'Rooth was behind with his payments. The bank was threatening to foreclose and he needed money. Which is why he did what he did.'

Uncle Harald stops and inhales deeply from the pipe. The smoke smells sweet and strong at the same time. She must have seen him smoke that pipe a thousand times.

'What happened to his family?'

'They moved away a year later. They weren't exactly popular to start with, and when Billy . . .' He leaves the rest of the sentence unsaid, but she has no trouble finishing it.

'But Nilla and the children hadn't done anything, surely?'

He shrugs his shoulders. 'Who knows what Nilla knew or didn't know? I heard that Social Services in Malmö took the kids off her. Maybe that answers the question.'

Uncle Harald takes another puff.

'And you bought the farm from the bank?'

He nods. 'Fifty acres of prime agricultural land. The best in Skåne.'

'And the buildings?'

'I had them demolished.' Another shrug, but she can hear the change in his tone of voice.

'Were they in that bad a state?'

'No, the house could probably have been sorted out if anyone had wanted to.'

'So why did you pull it down?'

He takes the pipe from his mouth and stares at her. The look in those deep-set eyes darkens.

'For Magdalena's sake.'

He clears his throat as if his voice is about to break, and she wonders if it's from anger or grief. Both, perhaps.

'My father, your Grandpa Assar, you remember him, don't you?'

'A bit, I was only eight when he died.' The sudden change of subject catches her by surprise. 'He and Mum didn't get on, I remember that much. Why?'

Uncle Harald gives a wry smile. 'No, Assar wasn't an easy man to deal with. Even though he was from the older generation he wasn't scared of new ideas, or of taking risks. He was quick to realise that the war was coming, and figured out that transportation was going to be more important than ever. Food, fuel, people. So he used all his savings and mortgaged the farm to buy some old trucks and buses and fit them with wood-gas generators.'

He bites down on the pipe and lets out more smoke. 'So when war broke out he was ready for it. He got contracts with the military and the local councils. Worked day and night. He used the money he earned to buy property and land. He'd realised that large-scale farming was the future. That you have to keep looking ahead, trying new crops, new techniques. It's thanks to your grandfather that I dared to put my money into wind turbines, long before anyone else.'

'Weren't there a lot of rumours about him?' she says. 'Something about loads of wood going missing from military stores at the end of the war, and all the new tyres being switched for old, worn ones? That Grandfather had a set of keys and was the main suspect, but paid someone else to take the hit for him?'

As she expected, Uncle Harald's smile vanishes abruptly. 'That's just gossip. Lies and slander spread by people who were envious of him. People say a lot of stupid things.'

His pipe seems to have gone out. He taps it against the heel of his wellington boot, then treads the remains of the tobacco into the ground.

'You're never here, Vera, so I don't expect you to understand. But you have to do what they do in America. Keep looking forward. Not get caught up in the way things used to be. Anyone who doesn't understand that . . .'

'You mean people who don't support your plans to turn this area into one massive wind farm?'

He lets out a snort, something between a derisive snigger and a laugh. 'Sometimes you're so like your mother that it's uncanny. Just as lippy, just as convinced you're that bit smarter than everyone else. Always convinced you're right.'

Uncle Harald shakes his head and puts the pipe back in his pocket.

'The future always arrives, Vera. Whether you want it to or not. The past, on the other hand, never comes back.' He turns to walk back towards his car.

'What if Tommy Rooth didn't kill Billy?' she blurts. 'What if something else happened and Billy's still alive?'

He stops. She's expecting him to be angry. Ask her what the hell she's talking about. But instead he just laughs.

'Yes, I heard you had a few ideas about that. Running around showing people pictures.'

He takes a step towards her, tilts his head slightly and says with a gentleness in his voice that makes it harder for her to be angry with him.

'Billy's never coming back, Vera. Tommy Rooth killed him and got away with it. And at the same time he killed your mother, my little sister. Unlike your father, I'm not the sort to plant roses. I actually thought we were on the same page when it came to that, you and me.'

Something about his tone makes her react. A note of disappointment that she doesn't really know how to handle.

'Your little brother's buried somewhere up in the forest,' he goes on. 'All alone in an unmarked grave instead of in the churchyard with his mother. And it was Tommy Rooth who put him there. And for that I hope the bastard's burning in hell.'

He comes closer and puts his hand on her shoulder. Her first instinct is to pull away, but the gesture seems genuine, as does the look of sorrow in his eyes.

'But all that belongs to the past. And now we have to look forward. You, your father, me – the whole district. Do you understand what I'm saying, Vera?'

Chapter 45

The house is locked again when Veronica gets home, but her dad has left the spare key in the usual place. The cart shed where he parks his car is empty, so he's probably gone shopping in the village. She goes into the study and calls her answerphone to check if Ruud has left her a message.

She has three new messages, but in the first two all she can hear is the faint sound of someone breathing, then a click as they hang up. For a moment she gets it into her head that it might be Leon, but obviously that's a ridiculous idea. Why would he be calling her when he's gone to such lengths to stop her contacting him?

She waits for the third message, expecting the same thing to happen again. The sound of a voice catches her by surprise.

'This is Lars. From the therapy group. I'd like to talk to you as soon as possible. Call me.' He gives his number, then hangs up without saying goodbye or explaining what it's about.

Lars, the man with the beard, the one Ruud has banned from the group until further notice. What does he want with her, and how has he got hold of her private number? She listens to the message again, but is none the wiser. As she does so she leafs idly through the papers on the desk. The documents about planning permission for the wind turbines are still there, still unsigned.

She pulls out the top drawer, and in one of the little trays for pens, paperclips and erasers there's an old-fashioned door key. She picks it up and weighs it in her hand, thinking about what Mattias said about the locked rooms upstairs. She checks the drive for any indication of her dad's car before making her mind up.

Billy's room, which used to be hers a long time ago, is to the right as you reach the top of the stairs. The key turns with no difficulty and she slips inside and closes the door behind her. The room smells of carpet and Ajax. The roll-blind in the window is pulled halfway down, casting a gloomy light across the room.

There's a large photograph of Billy hanging on the wall above the bed. The same studio picture she's got at home, the one she's seen in the newspaper articles, just much bigger. He's laughing towards the camera, showing his little milk teeth and the dimples in those soft cheeks. The twinkle in those blue eyes. She has to swallow hard to suppress the chill in her chest.

Beside the photograph is one of Billy's drawings, possibly of a rabbit, and below that, on the bed, his stuffed toys are neatly lined up against the blue wallpaper.

She steps slowly farther into the room, and starts by opening the wardrobe door. It seems a lot smaller than she remembers, as does the dark space within. The shelves are stacked with a small boy's clothes. She wonders if Billy used to check that the door was locked before he went to bed, the way she used to. She catches sight of the wooden rifle leaning against the wall between the bed and the bookcase. If she remembers rightly, Uncle Harald gave it to Billy one Christmas. Her little brother was probably also treated to Uncle Harald's horrible stories, and she guesses that he liked to arm himself as well as he could to protect against the nightmares. The thought makes her chest ache.

There are some other wooden toys on top of the bookcase. A tractor and trailer, with moving wheels and magnets to connect them. Next to them is a harrow, its blade made from the teeth of a metal comb. All three have been neatly carved and carefully painted. She knows Dad made them in his workshop, and that he must have spent many long hours getting them perfect.

Below the toys is a row of books by Gunilla Wolde that Billy inherited from her, and beside them some shells and smooth stones he must have picked on one of the few occasions they went to the beach. The sea is sixty kilometres away, about an hour by car. Even so, they hardly ever went. The sea used to worry Mum. Veronica finds herself thinking about the smooth stone on her grave again. A stone from the sea. She regrets not slipping it into her pocket.

The third shelf contains some small Lego models. They're slightly too advanced for a five-year-old, so Mattias probably helped Billy to make them. Next to the models is the portable blue plastic record player, with a record still on it.

Judging by the absence of dust on the black vinyl and the smell of detergent, Dad must have cleaned the room within the past few days. He probably changed the sheets as well. She carefully runs her hand over the pillow. The pillowcase, duvet cover and sheet all seem freshly laundered and smell of fabric softener.

There's another Lego model in the middle of the desk, not quite finished. There's a handful of loose pieces beside it, and it looks almost as if they're waiting for the room's occupant to come back and put them in the right places. Next to the Lego is a small vase containing a single white rose. It looks like it came from the bush her dad was weeding around when she arrived on Saturday. The rose is fresh, and very beautiful. She leans over and smells it, then nudges the pieces of Lego, picks the model up, and puts it back down again. She moves on to the record player. This too was once hers, a Christmas present from her parents. Then, when she moved into Mattias's room, he already had a proper stereo which he'd bought with the money he earned working in the ironmonger's during the summer holiday, so the portable record player stayed in here, where, like so much else, it became Billy's.

She lifts the stylus. The machine clicks and the record begins to turn. It takes a few seconds to build up to thirty-three rpm. She puts the needle down on the vinyl, and hears a crackle from the speaker. The story is familiar, she recognises it at once from the narrator's voice. *Klas Klättermouse and the Other Animals in Hackeback Forest.*

She sits down on the bed and listens to the story, and realises that she knows it almost off by heart even though she hasn't heard it since she was a child. She and Mum used to lie on this very bed and listen to it together.

You're my little mouse, Vera. My very own little Klättermouse.

The chasm in her chest opens and becomes a dark, icy crevasse. She lies down and buries her head in the pillow. As well as fabric softener, it smells of Billy, and Mum.

She didn't cry when she found out Mum was dead, nor at the funeral, even though everyone else – including Uncle Harald – did. But the smell of the pillow, the story on the scratchy record and the sad little room waiting silently for a young boy to come back releases something inside her.

She sobs so hard that her body shakes. The storyteller goes on relating the story about the animals in Hackeback Forest, and by the time she's finished crying and her tears have been replaced by a paralysing tiredness, the needle has reached the last track on the A-side. 'Klättermouse's Lullaby' – her favourite song.

She shuts her eyes and listens to the familiar melody. And for a moment she's five years old again. She's had a nightmare, woke up terrified. Mum's there, lying beside her, whispering in her ear. Making the nightmare go away.

Hush now, little one, later there'll be time to play. All the other mouse children are sleeping the night away.

She can feel Mum's breath on the back of her neck. The warmth of her body, the smell of her perfume. She curls up and listens to the lullaby.

Sleep soundly in your crib, I won't disturb you now.

She wants to tell her mum that she's not disturbing her. That she can stay as long as she likes. But the lullaby is so short, barely more than a minute long, and the needle has already reached the last line. The words that always make the nightmares creep back into the darkness. She shuts her eyes tight and whispers the words.

The fox is also sleeping now, tail tucked around his head.

And when the song is over Mum kisses her softly on the cheek. The bed creaks and the carpet sighs as she moves off towards the door. A faint breeze, and then she's gone.

Chapter 46

When you sleep in the room you slept in as a child, the bed feels smaller, the walls and ceiling much closer than you remember them. But at the same time the smells, the rough feel of the sheets against your skin, the way sounds echo round the room are so familiar. It's so natural, so safe. Yet still oddly unsettling.

Perhaps that's another reason why she doesn't go home – because she can't bear the idea that she no longer feels at home here, and never will again.

She's woken by the sound of the phone ringing. Her dad's footsteps downstairs, followed by a faint 'Hello?'.

It takes her several seconds to realise where she is. She gets up quickly. The record player has stopped and the needle arm has swung back to rest on its little crook. She quickly plumps the pillow and straightens the covers.

'Vera?' her dad calls from downstairs. 'Are you there?'

Shame at being found out, of doing something forbidden, burns inside her. She hurries out onto the landing, casts a last glance back into the room to check that it looks the same as when she went in. Then she closes the door as quietly as she can.

'Coming!' she calls, a little louder than necessary, and turns the key in the lock.

She takes a couple of steps down the stairs, and is just about to slip the key into her pocket when she almost collides with Dad. They stand facing each other, slightly closer than feels comfortable.

'Everything OK?' he asks. 'You look upset.'

She closes her hand around the key and tries to keep it hidden behind her back. 'Must have fallen asleep,' she says. 'Is it for me?'

She nods in the direction of the phone and tries to slip past him. But her dad doesn't move. He's looking intently at her, as if he's trying to figure out if she's lying.

'The phone,' she says. 'Is it someone for me?'

He moves slightly. 'Yes, someone from your work.'

She hurries downstairs, aware that he's watching her. He carries on up the stairs and she thinks she can hear the door handle of Billy's room being pressed and then let go of again. She sneaks into the study, opens the desk drawer and puts the key back where she found it. Then she picks up the telephone receiver, which is lying on top of one of the piles of paper. It's Ruud.

'You're not an easy person to get hold of. Haven't you ever heard of mobile phones?'

'Mm.' She tries to figure out how he's managed to get hold of this number. Did she put it on any of the forms when she started work at the Civic Centre? Possibly in the bit about next of kin. That was probably it.

'What are you doing down in Skåne?' he adds.

'Nothing special. Just a little trip.' She curses her addled brain for not being able come up with a better excuse, but Ruud doesn't seem to react.

'I've got some good news,' he says, sounding as if he's holding the phone closer. 'Bengt has submitted his report. He's recommending that you keep your job, and I've managed to persuade the HR department. Come back here and I'll tell you all about it. Can you be back in Stockholm tomorrow morning?'

'Sure,' she says. 'No problem.' She puts the phone down slowly, and realises that she should be feeling happy. She's being allowed to keep her job, will get another chance to see Isak and simultaneously satisfy the part of her that's crying out for more grief. Other people's grief, not the sort Back-agården is full of. But any sense of happiness proves elusive.

Dad makes them an early dinner before she sets off. An omelette, eaten at the kitchen table. She can sense that something's changed between them, without quite knowing what. But that she needs to put it right, whatever it is, before she leaves.

'I was at Mum's grave yesterday,' she says. 'It looked really nice. The roses . . .'

'Mm.' He nods, and carries on chewing.

She tries to think of something more to say. Anything to soften him up.

'How long would you have been married now?' It just slips out of her, but it seems to work. Her dad looks up.

'Thirty-six years on 13 January.'

'Of course . . .' She bites her lip, realising that she forgot to get in touch on the last anniversary, and starts to formulate an apology. She sees him smile to himself.

'It had snowed the night before, and there was a ferocious wind. For a while we weren't sure it would even be possible to get to the church. The council snowplough hadn't got round to clearing the road. But your grandfather got the neighbours to pitch in with their tractors.' He shakes his head.

'You must have been frozen?' She clings on to the subject.

'Like you wouldn't believe! I managed fairly well in my suit. Magdalena was wearing her mother's wedding dress, thin silk, so she must have been absolutely frozen. Her hands were ice-cold. But she didn't complain, not once.'

'Where did you have the reception?'

'At your grandparents'. There weren't that many guests, mostly family. Hold on . . .'

He stands up and goes into the study, and she hears him looking for something.

'Here, take a look at this.'

He puts a black and white photograph down in front of her. She's seen their wedding pictures before, but not this one. Not that she can remember, anyway.

It's a family photograph, taken in her maternal grandparents' best parlour at Ängsgården. The bridal couple are in the centre, with the bride's family on one side and the bridegroom's on the other. They're surrounded by vases of flowers.

Grandfather Assar looks stern and uptight standing there just behind Mum. The resemblance between him and Uncle

Harald, who's standing on the far right, was already striking even then. The same deepset eyes, pronounced brow and sharp nose. Grandmother's features were rather softer. She's smiling stiffly at the camera, her high cheekbones just like Mum's. And hers.

Her father's parents look much happier. The Nilsson family are a typical, good-natured farming family from Skåne, who all look like they were raised on goose and *spettekaka*, and the contrast with the tall, stiff and rather haughty Aronssons is striking.

Dad has a broad smile on his face and the happiness in his eyes is so obvious that it's still infectious, and makes Veronica smile.

Mum is also smiling in the picture, but there's something about the expression on her face that doesn't seem quite right. It takes Veronica a while to realise what it is. It isn't a very big photograph, and Mum's eyes are smaller than half the head of a pin. But when Veronica leans over and looks really closely, she still thinks she recognises the look in her eyes. She's seen it in her own reflection, and knows what it means. And what it means isn't good.

'She could have picked anyone,' Dad murmurs, and Veronica can't work out if he's talking to her or himself. 'But she chose me.'

By the time she leaves everything is almost back to normal. She hugs her dad, kisses him on the cheek. Promises to drive carefully and to call him when she gets home. A warm southerly wind has got up, making the giants' great blades spin in farewell as she leaves the plain behind.

Her old car doesn't cope with the heat very well, and after four hours driving she has to stop at a petrol station to put more water in the radiator. Dad gave her some food for the journey – neatly made sandwiches with cheese and ham, and a flask of coffee – so she takes a short break.

She's been hoping that the car journey will give her a chance to think, to make sense of everything that's happened over the past few days. She also needs to decide what she thinks about the man who says his name is Isak. Is he really Billy? When she drove down she was almost convinced that he was. Now she isn't so sure. The feeling she had as she made her way up towards Askedalen has faded a little, but the questions are still there.

She realises that she's been very lucky to keep her job. She's missed the grief therapy sessions, misses the kick, so the sensible thing would be to concentrate on doing her job perfectly while she waits for Isak to show up again and give her more to go on.

That sounds like a reasonable strategy, and she finishes her coffee and decides that the break is over. When she picks the flask up she discovers a little piece of masking tape stuck to its base. *Property of the Nilsson family*, in Mum's ornate handwriting. The edges of the tape have come loose, and she wonders about pulling it off but decides to leave it. Mum taught her how to write the old-fashioned way, beautifully shaped letters that – unlike the writing she uses during group therapy sessions – aren't for sucking up other people's feelings. She thinks about Leon again, and all the words she wrote to him and which she now regrets. Words she thought would help, but which actually did the exact opposite.

Maybe Tommy Rooth was thinking something similar when he sent that postcard from Rotterdam? Mattias said there was nothing on it apart from the address. No message, no explanation, not even any excuses for abandoning them. Did Tommy Rooth understand what she herself had refused to see? That sometimes there aren't any words that can help.

She packs the flask away and gets ready to set off again. She sits for a few moments with the engine in neutral. The Östgöta Plain lies ahead of her. A flat agricultural landscape, almost like home. Krister Månsson's home territory. Krister Månsson, with the kind eyes and odd way of talking.

She switches the engine off. Wonders if the roadside café has a telephone book. Then she gets out of the car to find out.

Chapter 47

Krister Månsson has just poured the batter into the tin when he hears Bella pad towards the door. Her claws clatter on the parquet floor, then an eager bark just before the doorbell rings. He and Bella are always on their own on Monday evenings. Malin's at her book group with her friends, and rather than watch television while he waits for her to get home he usually makes a cake for her to take to the staffroom the next day. He likes it when she comes home with an empty container and tells him how much everyone enjoyed his baking. Rhubarb sponge is a favourite, so he makes that one at least every third week.

Bella is still barking by the front door. Månsson hangs his apron over one of the kitchen chairs and goes out into the hall. He can make out a fuzzy figure through the patterned glass in the door.

'Quiet, Bella,' he says, but as usual the little terrier doesn't obey him, so he pushes her out of the way with his foot before opening the door.

'Hello!' The strawberry-blonde woman outside is in her thirties. In the light of the outside lamp he's initially convinced she's one of Malin's work colleagues. Bella carries on barking, and he's on the point of saying that Malin won't be home for another hour or so when he realises that there's something familiar about the woman. The moment she holds out a pink sachet of restaurant sugar towards him, he understands who she is.

'Do you still collect these?' she says.

They sit down at the small pine table in the kitchen. Bella settles down beside his chair, tilts her head and lets out the occasional whimper, and as usual Månsson gives her a treat even though Malin doesn't like him feeding the dog at the table. The cake is warm in the middle and melts on the tongue. Even so, Månsson has trouble swallowing it.

He tries to tell himself that it's good to see Vera Nilsson after all these years, and even if he doesn't quite succeed, he's genuinely pleased that things seem to have turned out OK for her. The only question is: what is she doing here, in his home, and why now?

To get time to think, he tells the story of how he and his family moved back up here in 1984. As usual, he blames the fact that Malin was offered a good job and the boys wanted to move back home, which admittedly was perfectly true. He doesn't mention the fact that Johan and Jakob were being bullied at school. That the other children kept teasing them about their dad being a bad policeman. Then he tells her about the bowel cancer diagnosis in 1986, and his treatment and recovery. His decision to change his lifestyle and career.

'So you're no longer in the police?' she says, looking at him intently. He recognises that look instantly, even though it's been many years since he last saw her.

'No. I got a job as a recreation manager here in Mjölby. It's a good job, very worthwhile.'

He reaches for another slice of cake, mostly to avoid meeting her gaze. Bella's tail swishes across the floor.

'I took early retirement last year, so now I'm a househusband. I pick the grandchildren up from preschool twice a week, make a fuss of Malin when she gets home from work. We like playing golf.'

He takes a large bite of the cake. Feels his stomach protest before he's even swallowed it.

'How about you, Vera?'

'Veronica,' she corrects. 'I changed my name when I moved away from home.'

Månsson listens as she tells him about her work and studies abroad, and how she lives in Stockholm now, and has qualified as a therapist. He listens carefully, nodding and murmuring in all the right places. But the whole time he's struck by how much she looks like her mother.

They don't get round to Billy's disappearance before the cake has cooled down and Bella has padded off to her basket. By then he's had time to prepare for it. He's dug out the stock replies he usually uses when reporters still get in touch occasionally: that the case is regarded as solved from a police perspective, that of course he's sorry they couldn't get a guilty conviction of the perpetrator, but that he put the whole thing behind him a long time ago.

He says all that, and a bit more, making the words sound both genuine and convincing. At the same time he tries to read the expression on her face, looking for any sign of anger or accusation. To his relief he can't see any evidence of anything like that. Veronica is smiling slightly, and even nods sympathetically several times, and Månsson is on the point of thinking that the danger is over, that he's been worrying about nothing, that she isn't here to get answers.

So the question she goes on to ask catches him completely by surprise.

'Do you really believe that Tommy Rooth murdered my little brother?' she says quietly, and that's all it takes for him to be transported back in time, back to Skåne, to Reftinge, and that terrible summer.

Chapter 48

Summer 1983

H e's standing at the back of the police station. The street-lamps have come on, but the one above the compound is broken and the entrance to the custody unit is unlit. The air is sharp, there's a storm approaching. He can already see lightning on the horizon.

Månsson is holding Rooth's keyring in his hand, he's put his finger through the ring and keeps spinning the keys. One of them is for the pump house, two to doors at the Rooths' farm. The fourth is the key to Rooth's red Volvo Amazon, which is parked over by the fence. There's a small piece of deer horn attached to the keyring, Rooth has drilled two holes in it. It's shiny, worn smooth by the keys and Rooth's hard hands. At the end of the piece of horn hangs a fifth key, one for which Månsson and the detectives have failed to find a matching lock.

Månsson holds it up. A typical, anonymous-looking pad-lock key that could fit any lock, as Bure or Borg pointed out when he raised the subject. And, as they also said, people always keep keys, as they had discovered when they found a huge bunch of them out at the farm – Månsson was welcome to go through those, if he really wanted to focus on keys in the middle of a murder investigation.

He understood what they meant. But there's still something about the unidentified key that troubles him. The other keys on the keyring are ones Rooth uses on a daily basis. Important keys that he's chosen to take with him wherever he goes. And he had also fastened the padlock key to a little handcrafted ornament to make it stand out from the other keys. That ought to mean something. Must mean something, in fact.

The door of the custody unit opens and Tommy Rooth saunters out. He's carrying a plastic bag containing his belongings, and fishes out a cigarette and sticks it in his mouth. Månsson watches him in silence. He's pleased he managed to control himself earlier, that he didn't give in to the impulse to beat the hell out of Rooth. Perhaps he isn't a particularly good police officer, the detectives might be right about that, but he isn't one of the really bad ones either.

Rooth lights the cigarette, stops beside Månsson and takes a deep drag. Then he blows the smoke out to the side. Månsson follows it with his eyes, and thinks he detects movement behind one of the windows of the police station. Probably a member of staff who can't resist sneaking a look, to see if the unthinkable really is happening – that they're letting a child killer go.

'Here you go.' Månsson hands him the bunch of keys, holding his arm out straight with the ring between his thumb and forefinger. When Rooth reaches out to take it he doesn't let go.

'What's this key for?'

'Nothing.' Rooth shrugs. He sounds disinterested, as if the question doesn't bother him in the slightest. Even so, Månsson is absolutely certain he's lying.

Rooth seems to be making an effort to maintain eye contact, and smiles that crooked little smile people often use to try to make out that a lie is the truth. Månsson stares at the man, trying to think of something, anything, that will enable him to lead Rooth back to his cell. To avoid the defeat and derision that are staring him in the face.

The first raindrops start to patter on the tarmac around them. Rooth's smile appears unshakeable.

'Can I go, or what?'

Månsson reluctantly lets go of the keys.

'You're still our prime suspect, Tommy. Make sure you stay in the area, OK?'

Månsson stands and watches as Tommy jogs over to his car, then looks on as the red Amazon disappears through the gate with its windscreen-wipers flailing wildly. The rain forms little trickles down his temples and neck. He clutches his stomach, pinching the skin until the pain of that drowns out all other feeling.

There's a rumble of thunder. A dull, threatening growl slowly rolling in over the village. A monster set loose.

Chapter 49

'I stood there in the police compound and looked Rooth in the eye. Perhaps I thought I'd be able to see the evil in him. Unless I was hoping to see something else. A sign of regret, of guilt. A hint that it might all have been a mistake, a stupid, drunken idea that got out of hand.' Månsson falls silent and looks down at his hands.

'But you didn't?' Veronica says gently.

Månsson shakes his head and turns his wedding ring.

He's thinner than she remembers. Less hair too, which is hardly surprising. He's over sixty, after all. But his manner is much the same as before. Thoughtful, intuitive. A decent person.

She's been using his grief ever since he opened the front door. It's grown gradually over the coffee and cake, even though he's done his best to persuade her that he put Billy's case behind him a long time ago. Now that he's finished telling her about the evening he was forced to let Tommy Rooth go, he seems to have lowered his guard. His grief is only making her feel dejected, just like her dad's does. Perhaps that's because they're quite similar men, or because Månsson's grief is too close to her own. Possibly both.

'When you left the police,' she says, and gets a slow nod in response, 'you said it was because you'd been ill . . .' She pauses and waits until he looks up. 'There must have been other reasons, too?'

For a moment it looks like he's going to disagree. So she raises one eyebrow to indicate that she wants the truth rather than another rehearsed explanation. She's used that trick before, and is well aware that it doesn't always work. But Månsson interprets her expression precisely as she hoped. He looks down again, still toying with his wedding ring.

'I left because I couldn't do it anymore. I couldn't bear the thought that I'd let Billy's killer go. I used to lie awake at night wondering over and over again if there was anything I could have done differently. Better.' He looks up. There's a hollow look in his eyes. 'Malin used to say that Billy's case was eating me up from inside, just like the cancer. And she was right.'

Veronica nods. She says nothing for a while, letting his sadness expand.

'My brother Mattias is a police officer in Reftinge now, did you know?'

He gives her a wry smile. 'Yes, I heard.'

'Mattias says he's been through the investigation ten times or more. He says there was nothing wrong with the police work. That he would have done exactly the same as you if he'd been in charge of the investigation.' She sees Månsson react, and waits for his face to relax again before getting to the real purpose of her visit.

'What if it didn't happen the way everyone thinks?' she says. 'What if Billy's still alive?'

She tells Månsson the whole story, starting with how Isak turned up at her group therapy session, then her trip home, what Sailor told her, and what she found in Askedalen.

It feels good to talk to someone who knows everything yet is still an outsider. Someone who doesn't immediately try to interrupt her, picking at details and shooting holes in her theories. Once Månsson has got over his surprise he listens intently, not least when she gets to the part about the chest, the tin box and the torn envelope corner.

She's convinced that the key on Rooth's keyring – the one Månsson has just mentioned – fitted the padlock she found next to the weapons chest. Månsson agrees, saying that would explain why Rooth had it on the keyring, and why he lied about it. The small piece of horn the key was attached to also seems to be the same sort of handicraft as the creepy wind-chime hanging from the shack.

But there's one detail that doesn't make sense. If Rooth headed up to Askedalen as soon as he was released to empty the chest of guns and the letter, why had the padlock been cut off? Did Tommy lock the empty chest after him, or had someone else already been there? Someone who knew where it was and what it contained, but who didn't have a key? The only person she can think of in that case is Sailor.

Månsson doesn't agree on that point.

'Sailor's a drunk who used to spend most of his time in the pub. Together with another idiot he even managed to capsize a boat in one of the marl pits when we were looking for Billy. I just don't think Sailor would have been crafty enough to tidy up after Tommy Rooth, not on his own initiative, anyway. And Rooth was completely isolated in custody, so he couldn't have asked Sailor to do anything.' He rubs the back of his neck thoughtfully. 'Besides, I'm having trouble believing that Rooth would have confided in Sailor. Tommy Rooth is intelligent, shrewd. Using Sailor to help out with poaching, or even when he shot your uncle's windscreen, is one thing. But making him an accomplice to kidnapping is something else entirely. An unnecessary risk ...'

Månsson frowns, then gets up to fetch the coffee pot.

'But if it wasn't Rooth or Sailor who emptied the chest, who was it?' she says once he's refilled their cups. 'Could Rooth have had another accomplice?'

'That's not impossible.' Månsson takes a sip of coffee.

He looks different all of a sudden. His back is straighter, his voice sharper, and he reminds her a bit of Mattias. She realises that she likes that, and can't help smiling.

'If your theory is correct, Veronica,' Månsson says thoughtfully, 'and if Isak *is* Billy, someone must have looked after him during the week Rooth was in custody. Giving him food and water, making sure he didn't come to any harm.'

'Nilla Rooth? Could it have been her?'

'Unlikely. We were pretty sure Billy was kept hidden in that pump house that Rooth used as a slaughterhouse.'

'Why?'

Månsson pulls a face to indicate that he would have preferred not to have to go into detail. 'There was a pair of handcuffs there, and an old bed,' he says, glancing at her to see how she reacts.

Veronica maintains her façade, merely nodding to him to go on, but inside she feels a sudden chill.

'If Nilla Rooth was involved, then she would have done all she could to keep the pump house a secret, she wouldn't have told me about it. Besides, she had children of her own, a boy the same age. I have a lot of trouble believing she would have done anything like that.'

'How did Rooth explain the handcuffs and bed, then?' Veronica is surprised by how matter-of-fact she sounds. Månsson seems to think the same, because he looks up with a surprised expression on his face.

'At first he didn't say anything, then, when he had a law-yer, he said he used to take women there. Married women whose names he didn't want to reveal. There were plenty of rumours along those lines about him, but it sounded mostly like a convenient explanation his lawyer helped him come up with.' Månsson takes another sip of coffee.

'But whoever the accomplice was, he or she could have removed Billy from the pump house after Tommy was arrested. Then, when he was released a week later, Tommy collected Billy and drove south as fast as he could,' Veronica says in summary.

Månsson nods. 'That could well be what happened.'

'Then what? After that? Why would Rooth want to take Billy away?'

'Yes – that really is the question.'

Månsson and the eager little dog accompany her to the door. After a momentary hesitation she gives him a farewell hug. He smells of cake and Old Spice. He hugs her back, promises to keep thinking about it all and says she can call him whenever she wants. It sounds like he means it, too.

Chapter 50

A city is a place for everyone who actually belongs somewhere else, but who doesn't know where.

She read that in a book somewhere, or maybe heard it on
television. There's a lot in it. She's lived in Paris, London,
Berlin and now Stockholm. Even so, she can't really say that
any of these cities has ever really felt like home.

She's had plenty of time to think about Krister Månsson
during the past few hours on the road. About how lovingly
he talked about his wife, and about the pictures of them,
their children and grandchildren hanging in the hall and living room. Månsson must have been married to Malin for at
least thirty-five years, but he seemed to be genuinely looking
forward to her coming home. Veronica misses that, misses
having someone to long for. Misses having someone at all,
in fact.

She opens the front door and listens out carefully for any
sound inside the dark flat. Everything seems quiet and still.
She switches all the lights on, and doesn't relax until she's
checked both in the closet and under the bed. Everything is
exactly as she left it, and there's nothing to suggest anyone's

been there. She opens the window to air out the stuffy smell, and looks off towards the end of the street. No smoker in sight. The moths are back, though, circling their electric sun, repeating the same mistake.

The phone is flashing at her from the kitchen counter. Four times, four messages. The first two are just the sound of someone hanging up. The third starts with silence, but just as she's about to click on to the next one, a voice starts to speak.

'This is Lars again, from the group.' His words are slurred, he sounds drunk. 'You haven't called me back. Fucking rude . . .' He stops, mutters something she can't hear, then hangs up. She wonders once more how he got hold of her number, and makes a mental note to talk to Ruud about it tomorrow.

The fourth message is from Mattias. 'Hi, it's me. Just wanted to make sure you got home OK. So . . .' She can almost feel his awkwardness. 'It was good to see you, Vera. We should meet up more often.' Another pause. 'Well, that's about it. Take care,' he says by way of conclusion. He sounds almost annoyed with himself, as if he'd wanted to say something else, something more profound.

She switches the answerphone off, then stares for a while at the red light that's now stopped flashing. No more messages.

She presses the button for saved messages. Leon's last message is still on there, and this time she listens to it from the start.

'It's over, Veronica. Can't you understand that? I don't want any more letters, or text messages, or phone calls in the middle of the night. And stop waiting for me outside the building. It isn't healthy.' He sighs. 'You have to stop. Please, Veronica. You have to stop now.'

Chapter 51

'Are you awake, Krister?'

Malin's voice surprises Månsson. He's been lying silent in the darkness for almost half an hour as the numbers on the clock radio ticked past midnight. Listening as the sound of his wife's breathing grew deeper, just letting his mind wander.

'Sorry, I was just lying and thinking about something. Did I wake you?'

'No.'

He knows she's lying, and that she's doing so for his sake, so he won't feel guilty. She's the one who has to get up early tomorrow morning. Månsson feels her roll towards him in the double bed, and stretches his arm out so she can rest her head against his shoulder.

'Is it Vera Nilsson?' she says.

'Veronica,' he murmurs.

'What?'

'Veronica Lindh, that's what she's called these days. Veronica, not Vera.'

'Yes, you mentioned that earlier. Why do you think she changed her name?'

He strokes her back. 'I don't actually know. Maybe she wanted to get away from the past.'

'And doesn't want to anymore.'

'No, it doesn't seem like it.'

'Do you think her theory could be right? That Billy Nilsson is still alive?'

'If you'd asked me that a few years ago, I'd have said no. But after meeting Veronica and hearing what she had to say, I don't honestly know. It's certainly not impossible. Rooth could have taken Billy with him when he left, then left him with someone, or maybe even looked after him himself. But then the question is, why? Why would he leave his own family to look after someone else's child?'

They lie there in silence for a short while. Malin goes on stroking his chest. He likes that, likes having her close.

'So what can you do, Krister? What can you do to help Veronica find out the truth?'

'I don't know yet. I'm wondering about trying to find out what happened to Rooth's wife and children. See if any of them has heard from Tommy at all. Perhaps they know something that could help us.'

'Good,' Malin murmurs close to his ear. 'So now you've finally figured that out, maybe we could get some sleep?'

Darling,

Once I wished that summer, the heat and the blue skies, would last forever. Then I started to long for autumn, when you were going to take me away from here.

How could I be so stupid that I believed we had a future together? There's no relief here, no mercy, just endless torment under a cruel sun before the cold and darkness devour us.

I can't go on keeping our secret alone. What we did was wrong, I know that now. And for that we need to be punished.

Chapter 52

The next day is just as warm as those that have gone before. She has a long shower, puts on a white shirt and black trousers, as usual. Neutral and professional, like the sort of person who takes their job extremely seriously.

She takes the metro to the Civic Centre, where Ruud is waiting for her. He seems to be in a good mood. He gives her a hug and says it's good to see her. They go into his cramped little office. The chairs out in the meeting room are arranged in a circle. Veronica feels her anticipation start to rise at the very sight of them. She glances at the chair closest to the door. Imagines Isak sitting on it.

In his office, Ruud tells her – with a little too much self-satisfaction – how he fought for her. That he assured the HR department that the phone call was an isolated incident. Slightly-too-tall Bengt evidently helped him. Said that Veronica seemed calm and aware of her mistake.

'Bengt wants to see you a few more times, just to be on the safe side. He wants you to book an appointment as soon as possible.'

Ruud makes it sound as if he's responsible for her treatment. Even though that irritates her, she doesn't say anything. She just signs the forms Ruud has laid out.

'So you spent the weekend in Skåne,' Ruud says when they're done. 'It's beautiful down there in the summer. Is that where you're from? There's no trace of it in your accent.'

'No.' She squeezes out a smile. 'I moved away from home when I was eighteen. I was in a hurry to get away, I suppose.'

She takes a deep breath, hopes that didn't sound odd, doesn't prompt him to dig any further.

'Really? Why's that?'

What he really means is: What were you trying to run away from?

'No particular reason,' she lies. 'Country life just wasn't for me. They usually say there are two types of people who grow up in the countryside. Those who stay, and those who leave.'

'I see,' Ruud said. 'And you're second sort? One of the ones who left.'

She nods, and keeps her smile in place until he smiles back.

'How has everything been going with Lars and the others?' she says on her way out. She really just wants to know if Isak has been there while she's been away, and Lars is a good way in to the subject. Besides, she also has to talk to Ruud about the phone calls.

'Lars won't be coming back, I'm afraid.'

'Oh? Why not?'

'On Friday morning, just after I'd opened up, I went into the kitchen to put the coffee on. When I came back out Lars was in my office. He was digging through my papers. I asked him what the hell he was doing, and he got very loud. Said he had a right to know things. He was clearly drunk, so I told him he wasn't welcome here anymore, and that I'd report him to the police if he showed up again.'

'Goodness,' is all she manages to say, which sounds a little inadequate in the circumstances. But at least it gives her a few seconds to think. 'Lars has called my home number a couple of times over the weekend and left messages.'

Ruud frowns. 'Do you know what he wanted? Was he threatening?'

She shakes her head. 'He just says he wants to talk, and asks me to call him. Which I haven't done, obviously.'

'Maybe you should change your number. Wait a few days, and if he gets in touch again let me know and we'll sort something out. I can check with our legal advisor if there are grounds for filing charges.'

She rather likes the fact that Ruud is worried about her. That he cares about her.

'What about that blond guy, Isak? Has he been back?' As soon as she sees the look on Ruud's face she realises that it was a mistake to ask. 'Actually, forget it,' she says quickly. But the damage is already done.

On the way home she thinks about Krister Månsson again, and how he tried to convince her at first that he'd left the case behind. That he hadn't thought about Billy for years. But it didn't take long for him to turn back into an investigating officer again. He's moved, changed jobs, filled his life with positive things, but on some level is still living in the summer of 1983, just like her own family. Maybe that's why she likes him?

She likes Ruud, too. It took a serious amount of enthusiastic small talk to get him to thaw out after she mentioned Isak. She'll have to be more careful in future, not give him the slightest cause for suspicion. What will she do if Isak doesn't show up again? She'd rather not think about that. Would it actually be possible for her to let go of all this?

She's just tapped in the code to open the door, and hears the lock whirr when someone grabs hold of the top of her arm and spins her round. The fingers are hard, digging into her skin.

'Here you are at last, Veronica!'

It's Lars. His bearded face is bright red and puffy from drink. She realises that she's cornered against the door, with no means of escape.

'Why haven't you called back? I only want to talk to you. Now you've forced me to come over here instead. Waiting outside your door like some fucking stalker. Don't you think I've got better things to be doing?'

He squeezes her arm tighter and moves towards her, close enough for her to smell the alcohol on his breath.

'You got me thrown out of the group, you fucking bitch. You think you're something special, but I know what you're after . . .'

'Lars, this is extremely inappropriate . . .'

'Shut up!' He holds a thick finger up in front of her face. 'Just shut the fuck up, OK, you little bitch? You think you're so fucking smart. You think you know everything . . .'

'What's going on here?'

The voice is very close, but she can't quite identify it. Lars twists his torso and looks behind him.

'None of your fucking business!'

'Are you OK?' The man takes a step closer and suddenly she realises that it's Isak.

'Get lost,' Lars snarls.

'Are you OK, Veronica?' Isak asks again, and she shakes her head hard. Isak puts his hand on Lars's shoulder. 'OK, mate. Maybe you should—'

Before he can finish the sentence Lars turns round and punches him in the face. The blow comes out of nowhere and knocks Isak off balance, and he falls backwards and lands on the pavement with a heavy thud.

For a moment time stands still. Isak is lying flat out on the tarmac, and she's still standing with her back pressed against the door. In front of her is Lars, his clenched fist raised and a contorted snarl on his face. Then suddenly his expression changes to one of surprise, then fear. He lowers his fist and his shoulders slump. He looks at Isak, who's only moving very slightly, then at her.

'I-I . . .' he stammers, without getting any further. He lowers his eyes, turns on his heel and runs off.

Veronica crouches down next to Isak. His lip is split and there's blood trickling from his nose. He's conscious, but his face is pale, his eyes glazed and he doesn't seem able to focus properly. When he turns his head she sees a dark red stain spreading through his blond hair.

'We need to call an ambulance,' she says.

He blinks several times, and seems to regain his senses. 'No ambulance, I'm OK.'

'But you're bleeding.'

He feels the back of his head. His fingers turn red.

'Can you help me get up?'

She does as he says. He's unsteady at first, then seems to find his balance.

'Shall I call the police?'

'No, there's no need. I'm OK,' he says again, this time in a steadier voice.

He's holding the back of his head with one hand and looking straight at her. Something in those blue eyes releases a wave of warmth inside her, a warmth she hasn't felt in a very long time.

'Who are you?' she says.

He smiles faintly. His face is starting to regain some of its usual colour.

'I was hoping you might be able to help me find out, Vera.'

Chapter 53

I sak is leaning back on her sofa. He's holding a bag of frozen peas against the back of his head. The wound is superficial, and looks much worse than it actually is. She's helped stem the bleeding and has put a plaster on it. His split lip has swollen up, making his mouth look slightly crooked. As if the whole situation amuses him.

She's trying to absorb what has just happened, and for once wishes she had something stronger in the house, then remembers that there's a bottle of whisky tucked away in one of the cupboards. But this is hardly the time to get it out. Her head is already spinning, full of questions, such as: What on earth was Isak doing outside her building? Is he the smoker, the mysterious intruder, or possibly something more, as she has suspected since she first saw the photofit picture? Perhaps she ought to be afraid of him, but for some reason she isn't.

'Where shall we start?' she says, sitting down on the armchair in front of him.

He shrugs his shoulders and thinks.

'I think I'd like to start by apologising.'

'What for?'

'For showing up in your therapy group instead of approaching you directly. It was a stupid idea. I'm sorry.' He pulls a face that's probably supposed to look regretful, but which is distorted by his swollen lip. 'My only excuse is that I wasn't brave enough. I did actually stand out there in the street several evenings, trying to pluck up the courage.'

She feels like bombarding him with questions, forcing him to answer them. But she knows she has to take it gently, and not risk the fragile rapport fostered by the incident out on the pavement.

'It's OK,' she says. 'I understand. But you'll have to tell me more before I can forgive you. Your name, for instance.'

He nods his head, the movement making the frozen peas rattle.

'My name is Isak Welin. At least that's the name on my driving licence. I grew up in a village seventy kilometres outside Luleå. Dark and cold in winter, midges in the summer, all that.'

He's trying to elicit a smile from her, evidently used to being able to rely on his charm.

'Dad worked at sea and was away a lot, months at a stretch sometimes. When I was ten he moved out for good. I went to visit him a few times, but that happened less and less. We lost touch in the end, and I can't really say I was sorry.' He shrugs. 'Last winter Mum got ill. Kidney trouble, there was talk of a transplant. The hospital tested me to see if I could be a donor, but it turned out that I wasn't compatible. Mum and I weren't even related. You can imagine what a shock that was.'

Veronica felt her breathing grow shallower.

'Mum was in a bad way, so I didn't want to make her explain. I searched through her flat, though. Looked in old photograph albums, and discovered that there were no pictures of me as a baby. I'd never been bothered about stuff like that before, but as I went on looking I realised there was no trace of me before I was six, seven years old. No christening pictures, no baby clothes, nothing like that. And I could remember those things I've already talked about . . .' He gestures towards her. 'A big garden, much bigger than we had at home. A treehouse, a hollow tree. A missing boy. And that name.'

'Billy,' she murmurs, unable to stop herself.

He nods slowly, then puts the bag of peas down on the table.

'In the end I had to ask Mum, but she got so upset that the nurses had to give her a sedative. So I decided to wait until she was better. The prognosis looked good. Then, in the middle of a dialysis session this spring her blood pressure crashed. They called me but I didn't get there in time.' He looks away, his eyes look moist. 'I tried to find Dad, but he'd moved away a few years ago and no one knew where. Probably went off to sea again. So I tried looking on the Internet. Mostly about adoption, that sort of thing. When I looked up the year I was born, "disappearance" and the name "Billy", all the articles about your little brother came up. It might sound like a cliché, but it was like a door suddenly opening. A door I never even knew existed.'

Her heart is in her throat, making it hard to breathe. 'So you carried on looking?'

'Yes, I went down to Reftinge. At first I just drove around to see if I recognised anything.'

'And did you?'

'I think so. But to be honest, I'm not really sure. How much do you remember from when you were five or six?'

A lot, she thinks, but decides against saying so. Her mum's face appears in her mind. The time before Billy, when she was still Mum's little mouse.

'Obviously I drove past Backagården, but I didn't dare go up to the house,' he continues. 'I didn't have anything definite to go on, after all. So I tried to find out more, hung around the pub and the pizza joints. Someone mentioned an old alcoholic who some people thought had been involved in Billy's disappearance. So I went to the old folks' home to investigate. I told the staff I was the old man's nephew.'

'And?' She holds her breath. Her pulse is thudding in her temples.

He shakes his head. 'I'd never seen him before. Well, I don't think I had. The weird thing is that the old guy reacted like we knew each other.'

He sits up, smiles and tilts his head in a way that feels very familiar.

She goes out into the hall, takes the photofit picture from the drawer where she'd put it and hands it to him.

'This is supposed to be what Billy would look like as an adult,' she says. 'But it could just as easily be you. You've seen this picture before, haven't you?'

He doesn't answer, but she knows he has. She knows he drew the same conclusion as she did, but that he isn't ready to say so out loud. Not yet, anyway.

'Then what happened?' she says when he doesn't go on.

'Er, well, I tried to find out how I could get in touch with your family. I saw your dad from a distance in the village, but I didn't dare go up to him. What could I say? And your brother's in the police, so contacting him didn't feel like a good option.'

'Why not?'

He hesitates. 'I've had a few dealings with the police in the past, stupid things I did when I was younger. I was worried your brother would find out about that if he started to look into my background. So the only one left . . .'

'Was me.'

'Exactly. You weren't easy to find. I asked a woman in the library, said I was an old friend of yours. By that time I'd been there several times, so they recognised me. People tend to like me, older women in particular. That's probably my secret superpower.'

He smiles that wry little smile again, and this time she can't help joining in.

'The woman in the library knew your dad. She told me you lived in Stockholm and didn't go home very often. And that you'd changed your name. I found a picture of you in an old school yearbook, then it was just a matter of looking up all the Veronica Lindhs in the Stockholm area in the phonebook. There are five of you in total, you were the second one I checked. And a therapist was exactly what I needed. I couldn't help thinking it was fate. As soon as I made eye contact with you I could tell there was some sort of connection between us. You feel that too, don't you?'

He looks at her, and those blue eyes go right through her. The throbbing in her temples spreads through her whole body. She doesn't reply, just gets up, goes into the kitchen and takes the bottle of whisky out of the cupboard. She pours a generous measure and downs it in one. Then she takes the bottle and another glass back into the living room with her.

Chapter 54

She wakes up when the doorbell rings, with that unsettling feeling of having been dreaming something important echoing through her head. Something about hide-and-seek, about wind giants with red eyes at night, staring out over fields of maize. The scent of roses. Even though she tries to hold on to it, the dream turns into fine sand running out of her head, leaving a bitter taste in her mouth.

The doorbell rings again. She rolls groggily out of bed, pulls on her dressing-gown and stumbles into the hall. The bottle and glasses are still in the living room, all empty. Beside them are two pizza boxes and some dirty cutlery. There's a blanket bundled up in the corner of the sofa, with a bloodstained bandage on top of it.

How much did she tell Isak yesterday? Most of it, she thinks, and already regrets it. She should have taken things more slowly, not let herself be drawn. But his story left her severely shaken. And the whisky didn't exactly help.

The doorbell rings again, making her headache even worse. She gets to the door and opens it a crack. Ruud is standing outside.

'W-what are you doing here?' she manages to say.

'I just wanted to check that you were OK.'

He gestures towards the door and she opens it and lets him into the hall. The sound of the doorbell is still ringing in her head, unwilling to let go.

'I spoke to Lars a short while ago. He's spent the night sobering up in a police cell, and is now full of remorse. He said something about a row outside your building yesterday evening. He thought he'd hurt someone.'

She bites her lip. Damn! She should have called Ruud as soon as she got into her flat yesterday.

'I'm fine.' She tries to think of a way of explaining what happened without mentioning Isak. The bell in her head is ringing louder and louder, drowning out her thoughts. It turns into an alarm.

'Good. That's the most important thing.'

She nods, and is about to invite him into the living room when she sees the bathroom door open. And suddenly she realises what it is that she'd forgotten. What that persistent ringing was trying to warn her about. It has nothing to do with her dream.

'Oh – good morning!' Isak says as he steps into the hall in front of them. He's just showered, his hair is wet and he's got one of her towels tied round his waist. Ruud stares at Isak, then at her. She looks away and closes her eyes.

A short while later she's sitting on the sofa. The headache has turned into nausea, and she keeps having to put her head between her knees to stop herself throwing up across the floor. Ruud has gone, followed shortly afterwards by Isak. Both of them without saying a great deal.

She should never have let Isak stay the night, it was a stupid decision that she can barely even remember taking. Perhaps she should contact Ruud. Tell him what's going on, tell him the whole story. That she's increasingly convinced that Isak is her brother who's been missing for the past twenty years. But what proof does she actually have to back that up?

If Isak is Billy, with the stress very definitely on the *if*, then what really happened back in the summer of 1983?

They talked about Isak's adoptive father a lot the previous evening, she remembers that now. He could have been Tommy Rooth. His age is about right, and the fact that they both went to sea. Isak has seen the old picture of Rooth online, but says his dad had a bushy beard and long hair, and was a bit overweight. He can't really see any similarities, even if he can't categorically rule out the possibility that it could be him. Either way, Månsson's question remains unanswered: Where was Billy while Rooth was in custody, and who was looking after him?

Sören the grocer was the last person to see Rooth's car. Was the fact that he set off for the south intended to mislead everyone, along with the postcard from Rotterdam? A way to get the police to look for him abroad when he had actually headed one and a half thousand kilometres north instead? Abandoning his wife and children to raise Billy with another woman under an assumed name, or leaving the boy with someone he trusted. Which still leaves the eternal question, the one you always end up having to try to answer, no matter how you rationalise and analyse everything:

Why?

Isak shows up again that evening. He stands in the doorway looking rather forlorn.

'Sorry,' he says. He holds out a fairly expensive bottle of wine. 'I didn't mean to mess things up for you.'

'It's not your fault.' She lets him in and he brushes past her into the hall. He smells good, and he moves in a way she finds appealing. Softly, like a cat, full of self-confidence. The swelling on his lip has had time to go down a bit, making his smile more symmetrical.

He opens the wine in the kitchen and pours two large glasses.

'Your job . . .' he begins, but she shakes her head.

'Never mind that now.' She's surprised at how easy it is to say that. She feels strangely happy, almost excited. Not in a sexual way, she tells herself, but because something big is happening. Something life-changing, and not just for her. The doubt she felt earlier is gone, it vanished the moment she saw the intense look in his eyes.

'So what do we do now?' he says.

She's spent the whole day thinking about that, and has even had time to do a bit of research.

'There are tests you can have done, even as a private individual. We'd each have to send in a blood sample, then the lab would compare them and see if we're related. It's no more complicated than that.'

He nods, but doesn't look entirely convinced. 'I've looked into that before. It takes time, doesn't it? The lab's in America, isn't it?'

'Around a month.'

He pulls a face. 'That's a long time to wait.'

She ought to say that so much time has already passed that one more month isn't the end of the world. But she agrees with him. She doesn't want to wait that long either. Not after everything that's happened in the past few days. To be honest, she doesn't give a damn about her job, about Ruud and his Civic Centre. She can even manage without feeding her grief addiction now. But she needs to know the truth about Billy. Now, soon. Before her head explodes.

'There's another option,' she says.

'What?'

She pauses. She can still change her mind before it's too late, but the hope in his eyes encourages her to go on.

'We can drive down to Reftinge tomorrow, together. Talk to Dad, look round the house, look through Billy's . . . look through *your* room,' she corrects, 'and see if that helps you remember what really happened.'

Chapter 55

S he changes her mind any number of times before morning. She even considers calling Mattias, but she already knows what he'd say, and that he'd be angry. So she calls Krister Månsson. As she guessed, he's an early riser. He's already been out with the dog and had time to read half the paper. She can picture him sitting at his little kitchen table.

'Veronica, good to hear from you.'

She tells him what Isak has said, and about the trip they're planning. She keeps expecting Månsson to interrupt her, ask questions, advise her against it. Perhaps she's actually hoping he will. But he just listens.

'Do you think I should put the trip off? Is this a really bad idea?'

'What do you think? What's your gut feeling?'

'That Isak is Billy.' She says this without any hesitation. 'That he can help us solve it all.'

'Hmm.' The line is silent for several seconds. 'In that case . . .' Månsson clears his throat. 'In that case you don't really have any choice, Veronica. You have to take this trip, for your own sake as well as Billy's. I wish I'd dared to trust my gut feeling when it came to that key. I should have put surveillance on Rooth, found out where he went. Who he met. Maybe things would have turned out differently then.'

'OK,' she says, for some reason unwilling to hang up just yet. She likes the sound of his voice.

'I've started trying to trace Rooth's family, by the way. I've called a couple of former colleagues. Maybe Nilla Rooth met Tommy sometime later, or at least heard from him. I was thinking that someone might have seen if he had a boy with him.'

It strikes her how different he sounds now compared to the first half hour of their meeting.

'Do you think you might come up with anything?' she wonders.

She thinks about Mattias, and the fact that he's already examined every line of inquiry, and has presumably looked into Rooth's family. But she doesn't want to dampen Månsson's enthusiasm.

'I don't know, but it's got to be worth a try,' he says.

Another silence, and she realises it's time to say goodbye. Månsson seems to have reached the same conclusion.

'Can you give me a call after the two of you have been to Backagården?'

'Of course.'

'One last thing before you set off.'

'Oh?'

'In the autumn of 1983 the farmers around Reftinge kept postponing their ploughing. No one wanted to be the person who found the remains of a little boy caught in their machinery. There was nothing to suggest that Rooth had buried Billy in a field. But people don't always act rationally.' He moves the receiver closer to his mouth. 'They won't be happy about you digging about in the past. There are still several important pieces of the puzzle missing, and there could well be people still living in Reftinge who don't want the truth to come out. You need to be careful, Veronica.'

She promises that she will be, then hangs up. She can't help smiling to herself. She isn't alone, after all, she's got Månsson by her side, and that feels strangely reassuring.

When Isak shows up at her door an hour later with a military kitbag over his shoulder and looks at her with those blue eyes, the last of her doubts vanish. Månsson is right. She has to make this journey.

'Do you know how your parents met?' she asks once they've made it out onto the motorway and are heading south. 'Did they have any wedding photographs, anything like that?'

He shakes his head. 'There weren't actually any pictures of them together in the albums I found. Just pictures of me as an older child. A few of them had Mum in them, but never Dad. He was always behind the camera. I have the impression that Mum got rid of any pictures of him when he took off. That she didn't want to be reminded of him. Unless he was intentionally avoiding having his picture taken.'

They fall silent and she concentrates on driving.

'What about your dad?' Isak asks after while. 'What's he like?'

'Dad's a good person,' she says. 'You'll like him.'

'Were they happy, him and your mum? Before . . . ?'

'I think so. Well . . .' She tries to think. 'Dad was happiest when he was with Mum.'

'She was beautiful, wasn't she?'

'Yeess . . .' She draws the answer out, hoping to avoid the question she suspects is coming, but of course it comes anyway.

'What about your mum? What made her happy?'

She says nothing for a while, and tries to summon up her mum's face. Searches for occasions when she was smiling, when she looked really happy. She pictures her in different places. At home, in church, at her desk, out in the garden.

Isak seems to think she's avoiding the question and moves on to the next one.

'Were you close, you and your mum?'

Dangerous territory, but she can't not answer. 'We were when I was little.'

'But not later on?'

'Not exactly. Mum liked to have things done in a particular way. She got upset very easily.'

She realises this isn't a particularly good description, and that there must be a better way to explain how the atmosphere at home could change in a matter of minutes. How you could feel the change in the air without anyone saying a word.

'Or distraught, maybe,' she says, but that isn't quite right either.

'That can't have been easy for you.'

She doesn't like Isak's tone, it sounds like he's judging Mum from the little she's just said, which isn't fair.

'Mum liked children a lot,' she says. 'She used to run the Sunday school at church, every week after the service.'

Tell it like it was, the voice in her head whispers. Tell him Mum liked little children best. That she lost interest in her and Mattias when they got older. When there was someone else who was easier to love. Tell him that now. Tell the truth! Tell him that the only thing Mum cared for was . . .

She can feel his eyes on her, and realises that she's going to have to look down into the icy black hole that's suddenly gaping open inside her chest.

'You asked what made Mum happy.'

'Yes.' He carries on looking at her.

A chill wells up from the hole, replacing her blood with brackish water.

'Billy,' she manages to say. She hears the tremble in her voice. 'You made Mum happy.'

They stop at a petrol station in Jönköping, top up the radiator and change places. Veronica nods off in the passenger seat and doesn't wake up again until the forest has thinned out and the landscape is flatter. She looks at Isak for a minute or so without letting on that she's awake. Notices hints of tension in the set of his jaw.

She sees the sign for the turning off the motorway. Only fifty kilometres to go. Fifty kilometres until they're home. Isak changes his grip on the steering wheel and puts one hand in his lap. He's clenching and unclenching it repeatedly. She still hasn't asked him about the break-in at her flat, the pebble on Mum's grave or if he was the man she chased. He's got a scratch on his neck that could easily have come from one of the brambles at the far end of the garden. She's been putting those questions off, telling herself that she's waiting for the right moment. But maybe it's because she'd rather not know. Not right now, anyway.

She sits up, stretching her arms in a rather exaggerated manner. 'Nearly there. Shall we swap over again?' she says, a little too brightly. He mumbles something in response.

The atmosphere gets more strained the closer they get to the village. In the end it becomes so oppressive that she switches the radio on in an attempt to lighten the mood. She finds the channel rehashing golden oldies that she listened to last time. This time the music can't drown out her thoughts. How has she actually imagined this playing out? Is she just going to ask Dad for the key to Billy's room, and let Isak in there? Hope that the Lego and wooden rifle will help him start to remember? Fill the gaps, giving them firm proof that he really is her missing little brother. It's odd – as recently as that morning she'd been certain. Maybe Isak's nervousness is getting to her, but as they drive through the avenue of chestnut trees and into the yard, an entirely different feeling is gaining the upper hand. A feeling that this is all a huge mistake.

They hang around by the car for longer than necessary before walking over to the house, in a sort of tacit agreement that gives them a chance to compose themselves a little.

The front door is locked. She starts to look for the spare key in the window box, but changes her mind. She rings the doorbell instead. She has time to hope that Dad isn't home, so she can have a chance to think everything through one more time. Then she hears his slow footsteps in the hall, followed by the rattle of the lock. Her dad's wearing a cardigan in spite of the heat. His glasses are a little askew, making him look like he's just woken up, an impression only made stronger by his dazed expression, which quickly fades when he sees it's her.

'Vera, what are you doing here?'

'Hi, Dad.'

She remains standing on the step. All of a sudden she doesn't know what to say or do.

'Th-this is Isak.' She gestures to him to step forward. 'I talked about him last time I was home. I . . . well, we think he could be Billy.' Her words sound tentative rather than loaded with any particular meaning or conviction. Not at all what she'd imagined.

Her dad stares at her, then at Isak. The surprised look on his face disappears, and is replaced by something she definitely wasn't expecting.

'Get out!' he snarls. 'Get out of here, right now!'

'But Dad . . .'

He takes a step forward and stops right in front of her face. She steps back.

'Billy's dead! Can't you understand that?' He waves his finger at Isak but doesn't seem to want even to look at him. 'This man is a fraudster, Vera. A fraudster that you've brought here. A stranger trying to exploit our tragedy!'

Some of the saliva that follows these words lands on her shirt. He turns towards Isak.

'You're exploiting a dead little boy,' he shouts, making Isak jerk back. 'Sullying my son's memory.'

'Dad,' she tries, but it's hopeless. The look in his eyes is virtually black.

'Get out of here, both of you. Or I'll call the police.' He slams the front door, the door of her childhood home, in her face.

They're left standing on the step as she tries to understand what's just happened.

'We can go round the house,' she says. 'We can take a look at the garden, see if you recognise anything.'

But Isak shakes his head. 'No, come on. Let's go.'

'But we've come all this way. We've got to . . .'

He grimaces. 'Your dad will call the police if we don't leave. And I really don't feel like talking to the cops.'

He walks over to the car, opens the door and gets in the passenger seat. She follows him reluctantly, casting one last glance up at the house. One of the curtains upstairs flutters and she sees her dad's face in the landing window. She looks away quickly.

'Come on,' Isak calls from the car.

She drives off so fast that the gravel clatters against the mudguards. There's a green pick-up parked in one of the fields, but it's too far away for her to see if there's anyone in it.

She stares at the road, and Isak gazes out of the side window. Neither of them says anything until they've driven through the village and emerge onto the main road, heading back up north.

'There's a truck stop about ten kilometres away.' He sounds subdued, almost desolate. 'Can you stop there, please, Vera. There's something I need to tell you.'

Chapter 56

The truck stop is a low-rent affair, by the side of the road roughly halfway between the village and the motorway. A petrol station, a restaurant and a motel, all in one. She's been driving far too fast, the temperature of the engine is almost up in the red and the car lets out alarming hissing sounds when she parks.

Isak finds a corner table in the café. Stained, checked tablecloths. Laminated menus with fingerprints clearly visible on them. She realises she hasn't eaten anything for hours, and that hunger is only adding to her sense of despair.

The food comes quickly, and tastes mostly of chip oil. As soon as they finish eating Isak leans back in his chair. He takes a deep breath, and for a few moments looks like he's going to start crying. Then he pulls himself together.

'There are things I haven't told you . . .' He gestures with his hand, as if to gain time. 'My name is Isak Welin, and I did grow up outside Luleå. The bit about Dad leaving us and me recently finding out that I was adopted is also completely true.' He takes a deep breath. 'But your dad's right. I'm not your little brother. I'm not Billy.'

She feels herself seize up inside, and can't get a single sensible word out. He sighs and shuffles on his chair, as if he's having to force the words out.

'OK ... I've always been fascinated by Billy's disappearance, ever since I was little. I read everything I could find. Probably because we were the same age, we have almost the same birthday. And we were fairly similar. People sometimes used to comment on it.'

Isak takes out his wallet and shows her a picture of a flaxen-haired little boy. She can see the similarity. But the photograph definitely isn't Billy. She suddenly feels sick.

'This is me when I was six years old. Just after the Welins adopted me, although I didn't know that until I looked through Mum's things after she died. She had a folder with all the paperwork in it. Birth certificate, adoption papers, the names of my biological parents, the whole lot. And my adoptive dad didn't just vanish or go off to sea. He's an accountant, he lives in Sundsvall with his new family.'

He looks away, and looks pained. Her nausea gets worse.

'Those memories – the garden, the hollow elm ... ?' she finally manages to say.

'I crept into the garden at Backagården last time I was down here. I found the remains of the treehouse and all the other stuff. I even took some pictures. I think your dad might have spotted me, because a light went on in the house and I had to rush away. But I saw enough to be able to make what I said in the therapy group stand out for you.'

She stifles a retch. 'Why?' is all she manages to get out.

He runs his fingers through his hair and stares down at the table.

'When I went through Mum's flat, I found my old box of cuttings about Billy. So I got it into my head to find out more. I don't honestly know why.'

He goes on staring at the table. She's finding it hard to take in his confession, and what it means.

'Mum and I were close, or at least I thought we were until I found out I was adopted. Perhaps all this is a way for me to deal with finding out that she lied to me all my life. I had so many questions that I was never going to get answers to. So maybe I could find out what happened to Billy instead.'

He looks up and meets her gaze for a moment.

'I inherited a bit of money from Mum, so I gave up my job and went down to Reftinge to see what I could find out. I booked into this motel for a week. Some sort of soul-searching trip, I suppose.'

He smiles wryly then goes on. She's no longer listening, just feels empty. Dad was right. Isak is a fraudster. A stranger that she's let into her life, told her secrets to. Their secrets.

'I came close to calling the whole thing off several times today. I should have done, way before we were standing outside your dad's door.' Out of the blue, he takes hold of her hands. 'I'm truly sorry, Veronica,' he says, and his eyes are still so blue that his gaze cuts right through her.

They sit opposite each other for a while in silence, each nursing a cup of coffee. What she'd most like to do right now is jump in the car, drive back to Stockholm and leave all this behind her. Never see him, the village, Dad or anyone else down here again. But she can't summon up the energy. All the strength has drained out of her, and she can't even find it in her to be angry. This whole business has all been just as much her fault. She's a trained therapist, used to listening to people's stories and working out what's true and what isn't. Even so, she's walked straight into the trap Mattias warned her about. She's ignored all the warning signs, all the gaps in Isak's story, anything that didn't support what she wanted to hear.

Sometimes we want something to be true so badly that it makes us blind to the actual truth.

Quite. She's been blind. And as a result she's lost everything.

Isak gets up and is gone for a while. He comes back with a key that he puts down in front of her.

'Room 201,' he says. 'I'm further along the same corridor if you want anything. But I'll understand if you never want to see me again. I'll make my own way out of here tomorrow.'

She stands up and walks to the room without so much as looking at him.

It's dark when she wakes up. The little fridge is rumbling quietly. She sits up and fumbles for the light on the bedside table. Her mouth and throat are dry, but the minibar turns out to be surprisingly well-stocked. She starts with a can of mineral water, then quickly moves on to the shelf of miniature spirits.

The alcohol stings her throat, exacerbating the anger building up in her chest. Isak deceived her, exploited her for his own ends. Lied to her, asked questions, got her to talk about things she had never told anyone.

Were you and your mum close?

What made your mum happy?

There's a telephone on the table next to the television. She dials her own number, taps in the code for the answerphone. Her fingers slip and she has to do it again. She's hoping her dad has called. She'd like to hear his voice, hear that everything is OK, that he's no longer angry with her. Instead her clumsy fingers manage to get the machine to play the saved message from Leon.

It's over, Veronica. Can't you understand that?

Oh yes, she understands now. Understands that Leon is yet another idiot. Someone who doesn't deserve her love. After all she did to him, he didn't even have the sense to be angry with her. Just disappointed, sympathetic, patronising, in much the same way as Ruud.

She slams the receiver down and downs yet another miniature. Then she gets to her feet. The room lurches, then settles down. She goes out into the corridor and finds her way to the right door, and knocks on it.

Isak opens within a matter of seconds. T-shirt and underpants. A surprised look on his face. She walks straight in, forcing him to retreat. She waits until the door has closed behind her.

She punches him as hard as she can in the stomach. The blow lands almost exactly where she intended. He groans, doubles over. She punches again, aiming at his face this time.

Her knuckles hit his cheekbone, sending a jolt all the way to her head. He falls back onto the shabby red carpet and she throws herself on top of him, pulling and tearing at his T-shirt until it rips.

'You bastard, you fucking bastard liar! You fucking shit . . .'

He flails his arms but she knocks them away and falls on top of him, pressing her lips against his. Biting him, kissing him. She's in charge now. And no bastard is ever going to feel sorry for her again.

Chapter 57

Afterwards they lie in his bed, close together. She hasn't said anything, hasn't explained why. He seems to understand anyway.

'Are we quits now?'

Veronica doesn't answer. His lies have torn her world apart. Her wonderful, perfect world consisting of banning orders, an impersonal flat and a low-paid job with unlimited opportunities to get high on other people's grief.

'Yes,' she mutters. 'We're quits.'

He runs one finger down her arm and reaches the long white line. Ordinarily she would snatch her arm away, hide it under the sheets. Not this time.

'A hazy reminder of an old mistake.'

'What?'

'The scar. You were going to ask about it, weren't you?' She holds her arm up in the air. 'Last year I met a guy called Leon. He was one of my clients. Things … it all got a bit complicated,' she adds after pausing to think. 'At first it was all fine. We were so in love we were planning to move in together, talked about having kids.'

'But?'

She takes a deep breath. 'But then he got bored. Started seeing other people, and didn't think he had to tell me about that little detail.'

'How did you react?'

'Not very well. Not at all well, in fact.' She runs her own finger along the scar. 'I became completely obsessed with him. Calling and texting, writing long letters, showing up at his work, I stopped looking after myself. I used to wait outside his door in the evening. In the end I broke in when he wasn't there and smashed his flat up. Cut myself on a piece of glass and bled all over his white parquet floor. I had a total fucking breakdown.'

Isak is looking at her as if he's trying to figure out if she's joking.

'Then what happened?'

She takes another deep breath. 'The police came and arrested me. I had to have a whole load of stitches. Then it went to court. I got a conditional sentence, and was banned from contacting him. I promised to have therapy to teach me to deal with my anger, and was reassigned. Now, in hindsight, it sounds crazy. And of course it was crazy. But I didn't think so at the time.'

'What were you thinking at the time?' He seems genuinely interested.

'That Leon had betrayed me. That he needed to be punished for what he had done, whatever it took.'

Isak seems to be about to say something, but a sudden noise interrupts him. A monotonous siren out in the corridor, so loud that it cuts through the walls. He jumps out of bed, pulls his trousers on and opens the door. A smell of smoke and the sound of agitated voices drift into the room.

'Fire alarm,' he says over his shoulder. 'We need to get out. Right now, this seems real.'

They follow the other guests through reception and out into the car park.

'Keep to the right,' a man in a hi-vis vest calls out, waving a large torch.

In the distance they hear sirens coming closer. There are flames off to the left of the motel. A car burning. The heat has shattered the side windows and flames are leaping from inside the car, sending thick black smoke across the car park. It takes her a while to realise that it's her car.

The fire brigade take ten minutes to put the fire out, then another twenty to go through the building and confirm that the danger is over. The motel staff have handed out blankets to the small number of guests who have gathered on the terrace at the end of the building. Even so, Veronica is freezing so badly that her teeth are chattering.

'Your car,' a police officer holding a notepad says.

'Yes.' She wonders if he works with Mattias, or if the motel is in a different district.

'Was there anything wrong with it?' he says.

'It's been overheating. I had to top the radiator up every so often.'

'I see.' The policeman wrote something on the pad. 'And you don't have any enemies? Anyone who might have wanted to set fire to your car?'

'Not that I know of.'

The policeman makes a note of her name, address and ID number. When he's done, the hi-vis man with the torch comes over to her. 'OK, we've got the all-clear to go back inside again. We really are extremely sorry about this . . .'

Isak appears at her side. He kept out of the way while she was talking to the police officer. 'So what do the cops say?'

They start walking towards the entrance to the motel.

'He just took my details. Asked if I'd been having any trouble with the car.'

'OK. Well, I suppose in a way it's lucky it happened here and not on the motorway.'

She nods. Her paralysing tiredness from earlier in the evening has returned. She should really be feeling upset about her car, but right now all she feels is exhausted and empty.

'What are you going to do now? How are you going to get home to Stockholm?'

She shrugs. 'I suppose I'll get the bus into town tomorrow, then the train from there.'

'Maybe we could keep each other company?'

Before she has time to answer he stops outside the door to her room. It's standing ajar, and the frame right next to the lock is splintered. They look at each other. He shoves the door open. Her clothes are strewn across the bed. She digs through them, then checks the outer pocket of her case.

'Fuck!'

Isak rushes out into the corridor and comes back shortly afterwards. 'My room's been ransacked as well. Wallet, keys, mobile – all gone.'

Chapter 58

When it gets to half past seven in the morning she gives up and calls Mattias. She's been thinking it over from every angle, and has concluded that she doesn't have a choice.

The police have been back, the same officer she spoke to before about the fire. He concluded that a total of four rooms along that corridor had been broken into, and that she and Isak weren't the only people who have lost belongings. That's no help to her. She's got no money, no bank card, and no car. She can't even pay for the night in the motel. She can't call her dad, not after his outburst yesterday, and she can't remember Lidija's number. And they're not really that close friends anyway. Which leaves Mattias.

He's not answering his mobile, and she doesn't feel up to phoning him at home and having to talk to Cecilia. So she settles down in reception with a complimentary cup of coffee and tries to figure out what to do.

'Vera, are you OK?' she suddenly hears a voice say.

She looks up. It's Patrik Brink, Uncle Harald's dogsbody and her own teenage conquest. Dark work trousers, flannel shirt, trucker's cap, just like last time. But at least he's not smirking this time.

'Sure, why?'

'I was driving past. Recognised your car.'

He gestures over his shoulder with his thumb towards the car park, where her burned-out car is still standing. The firemen moved it away from the building, leaving it right by the entrance.

'What's happened?' He sounds concerned, as if he actually cares about her. So she tells him about the fire and burglary.

'Bloody hell,' he says when she's finished. 'So now you're stuck here?'

'Yes, looks like it.'

'Have you called Harald?'

'No.'

'Why not?'

She sighs. She hasn't got a good answer. Because they don't have that sort of uncle-niece relationship is the best she can come up with.

'Wait here!' He goes out to his pick-up, sits in the driver's seat and pulls out his phone. She watches him talk for a couple of minutes, then he comes back.

'Get your things.'

'Hang on a minute . . .'

Patrik has already gone over to the reception desk and is saying something to the receptionist that Veronica can't hear. Isak appears out of nowhere, shaking his head.

'I haven't managed to get hold of anyone who can help us,' he says. 'How about you?'

Patrik comes back and stops in front of them.

'Is he with you?'

She looks at Isak, and can't help seeing how uncomfortable he looks. She thinks for a few seconds.

'Yes, he is,' she says eventually.

'OK,' Patrik says. 'Go and get your stuff and we'll get out of here.'

The four guest cabins are red with white eaves and windows, and are laid out on the grass right behind one of the big barns at Ängsgården. There are cars with Polish plates parked beside three of them, but the fourth is evidently empty. Patrik unlocks it and shows them round. Two rooms with bunk beds, a bathroom with a shower, and a living area with a television. Clean, pleasant, functional.

'Here.' He hands her the key. 'You can stay as long as you want. There's no phone, but my office is over there if you need to call your insurance company and so on.' He points towards one of the old stable blocks which have been turned into offices. 'There are a couple of cars up there as well, if you need to borrow one.'

She doesn't quite know what to say, but manages to come out with 'thanks', and 'this is really kind of you'.

'No problem. You have to help old friends out, don't you?'

She's expecting a mocking smile, but he looks perfectly serious.

'Harald's away sorting some things out, but he'll be back in a couple of hours. He'd like to see you, if you've got time?'

The words are phrased as a polite question, but of course she has to say yes.

'Well, I guess that's everything. I hope you'll be happy here in our little camp. The Poles can be a bit noisy sometimes at weekends, but they're not too bad. Just shout if there's anything else you need.'

He winks at her, nods at Isak, then leaves them alone.

'Nice guy,' Isak mutters as Patrik drives off towards the office. 'Known him long?'

'Since I was little,' she says, lying down on one of the lower bunks. 'Patrik's dad was my uncle's foreman once upon a time. And now he's taken over the job. My brother's also married to his cousin, so we're practically related.'

Isak puts his bag in the other bedroom. 'You uncle seems to be involved in an awful lot of things.'

'Hmm,' she murmurs, and closes her eyes.

It's afternoon by the time she walks up towards the main house. Just before lunch she used the phone in Patrik's office to talk to her insurance company and bank. She's booked a locksmith to change the locks on the door of her flat. But first she needs to get home. And to do that she needs to talk to Uncle Harald. She's prepared carefully, going through all the possible scenarios in her head, and promising herself that she won't get angry and will play the grateful niece.

She walks past the four hyper-modern cowsheds, breathing in the sweet, unmistakeable smell of cow, made even stronger by the still, warm air between the buildings. She walks round the vast green machine store, which looks like an aircraft hangar. She can't help but be impressed by what Uncle Harald has achieved. Haulage, machinery, farming and forestry, hunting trips, properties and wind turbines. And presumably even more that she doesn't know about.

Ängsgården was big even in her grandfather's day, but now it's by far the biggest farm in the area. Six shimmering silver towers loom above the roofs, twice as high as the old silo she and Mattias once climbed up. The handsome, whitewashed main house, three storeys and four chimneys, has been extended and now resembles a small manor house. As she gets closer she hears laughter and the whirr of an engine. Uncle Harald's Land Rover is parked right in front of the house with a trailer behind it, and there's a ramp leading down from the trailer. Uncle Harald, Tess and Patrik are standing watching Tim drive round and round the gravel on a motorised mini-tractor painted in the colours of Aronsson Farming. The wheels are kicking up stones and the boy is roaring with laughter. Uncle Harald is laughing as well, but Tess looks worried, and keeps telling Tim to be careful. Patrik is standing a few metres away, off to one side behind Uncle Harald and Tess. He's looking between the boy and his mother. Then he catches sight of Veronica.

'Good, eh?' Uncle Harald says, pointing at the little tractor. 'Picked it up from Eslöv this morning. Special order.'

'It's great.' She stops next to him and pretends to admire the boy's driving.

'I heard what happened to you last night.' Uncle Harald is still watching his son. 'What a business. Are you OK?'

'Hmm.' The concern in his voice surprises her, and helps stifle the anger she always feels in his presence.

'Why didn't you call your father?'

She shakes her head. 'Bad time.'

'Have the two of you had a row?'

To keep things simple she decides not to answer.

'Ebbe can be very stubborn. A family trait, wouldn't you say?' Uncle Harald gives her a wry smile, and to her surprise she finds herself smiling back.

Tim corners so tightly that the tractor tips onto two wheels, making his mother cry out in horror. Uncle Harald just laughs.

'Look, Vera! Five years old and already driving like a pro! Not scared of anything. Reminds me of you when you were a child.'

She murmurs something like agreement. Patrik has gone over to Tess. He talks to her, then waves Tim over and helps the boy to switch the engine off.

'Bravo, Tim!' Uncle Harald applauds. Then he turns to her and takes a bulky wallet from his back pocket.

'How much do you need?'

'Look, I'm really grateful for all your help, but . . .'

'Stop that,' he says, cutting off her obligatory protest. 'When you were little you and I were best friends, weren't we? Up until you were a teenager, anyway.'

She doesn't answer.

'Maybe we're just too alike,' Uncle Harald goes on. 'The same way your mother and I were. Just as stubborn as each other.'

He falls silent, then looks down and starts to leaf through the notes in his wallet.

'Will five thousand be enough?'

'I'll pay you back as soon as I've got hold of a new bank card,' she says, a little too quickly.

'No need.' His usually hard eyes seem to have softened slightly.

She takes the notes and tucks them away in her back pocket. It's easier than she imagined.

Over by the large garage Patrik is helping Tim to park the tractor next to Tess's silver Mercedes.

'Well, perhaps I should ...' Veronica gestures over her shoulder. 'Thanks again for everything. I really appreciate it.'

'I'm just glad I could help.'

She nods, and takes a couple of steps before it comes:

'By the way, could I ask a favour in return?'

Veronica stops. She's been through this scenario as well, but for a brief moment she actually believed that Uncle Harald was helping her out of the goodness of his heart.

'Sure.' She forces herself to smile, and waits for the predictable request. The wind farm, planning permission, her dad's signature. Not that she knows how Uncle Harald imagines she's going to be able to arrange that when she and her dad aren't speaking.

'The whole village is going to be at the harvest festival in the park tomorrow evening. It would make me really happy if

403

the whole family was there. I think your father would appreciate it as well.'

She has no option but to say she'll go, and in a way she likes the fact that he asked. She even feels happy about it. But at the same time she can't shake off the feeling that some sort of catastrophe is brewing.

Darling,

I can't look them in the eye anymore. They're so dishonest. Pretending their consciences are clear, that they have the right to judge anyone who's different. I hate them all, for forcing us to hide, to keep our love hidden, clutching it so tightly to our chests that it couldn't breathe.

We suffocated our love, killed the most beautiful part of us. Perhaps I tried too hard, perhaps you didn't try hard enough. Perhaps it was doomed from the very start.

But I know that everything has its time, and now our time has come. It's time to reap what we once sowed.

Chapter 59

They head over to Lidija's dad's pizzeria and each order a large pizza, which neither of them manages to finish even though they're both starving. They've hardly spoken to each other all day, only about practical things, like what and where they're going to eat. Staying on safe territory.

'What happened yesterday . . .' Veronica says.

Isak looks up. The bruise her fist left on his cheek has already started to turn yellow round the edges. He shrugs his shoulders. 'Yesterday was yesterday.'

He smiles, and she realises that she still likes his smile, even though he's been lying to her, manipulating her.

'So this was where Sailor used to hang out?' he says. 'Because they didn't want him in the village pub. Because everyone thought he was involved in Billy's disappearance.'

'Hmm.' She takes a sip from her glass of Coke.

Isak is silent for a few seconds. 'What do you think really happened? To Billy? Now that you know I'm . . .' He stops and looks embarrassed, as if he regrets raising the subject.

She puts her glass down. She'd really prefer not to say any more about it, but it's a reasonable question. And she wants to find the answer, not least for her own sake. What does she think really happened?

She briefly wonders if she trusts him enough to reply to his question, and comes to the conclusion that she does, in spite of everything. Somehow it feels as if the previous night has reset their relationship. Besides, what she thinks is hardly a secret anymore.

'The only thing left is the original explanation,' she says. 'That Tommy Rooth kidnapped him to get money out of my uncle. Something went wrong and Billy died. Rooth fled the country. Went off to sea and never came back.'

Isak frowns, evidently not quite satisfied with the answer.

'That sounds logical, but there's one thing I can't quite ignore.'

'What?'

'Tommy Rooth left his family, a wife and two children. As far as anyone knows, he never contacted them again. Was he really that type?'

She wipes her mouth with one of the pizzeria's cheap paper napkins.

'People say he was.'

'So why didn't he take off earlier? When he lost the hunting licence the previous autumn and realised he wasn't going to be able to keep hold of the farm or support his family. Why commit a serious crime to get money if he didn't actually care about them anyway?'

'Hmm. Maybe he wanted more money before he left.'

Isak shakes his head. 'I don't believe that. Rooth wasn't popular around here, but he did seem to care about his family. So why suddenly leave them in the lurch?'

'Why does anyone do anything? Your adoptive father, for instance, he abandoned his family too.'

'True.' Isak leans forward across the table. 'But he went on paying maintenance. And he did call from time to time, birthdays, Christmas. He didn't just go up in smoke.'

She looks at him. There's something about the look on his face that she doesn't like. Something that troubles her somehow.

'I don't think we'll ever know what he was thinking,' she says, and looks at the clock on the wall. 'Your bus leaves in five minutes.'

The car she's borrowed from Patrik is a green pick-up that appears to be brand new. It's an automatic, and full of buttons and controls. There's even a screen set into the dashboard to tell her she's at Reftinge bus station, in case she hadn't noticed.

She finds a parking space and switches the engine off. She feels in her pocket and pulls out two of Uncle Harald's five-hundred-kronor notes. 'Here.'

'No, you've already paid for the bus ticket. I'll manage.'

'Don't be silly. Take it.'

Isak hesitates a couple more seconds, then puts the money in his jeans pocket. He doesn't seem to know what to say.

'OK, well, goodbye, then!'

He jumps out, lights a cigarette. Slings his bag nonchalantly over his shoulder and begins walking towards the yellow bus that's waiting at the stop. He turns and waves before climbing in.

As she sits there, the feeling she had in the pizzeria keeps on getting stronger. It isn't until the bus has pulled away and disappeared round the corner that she manages to put it into words. Isak is keeping something from her, something he's either unwilling or unable to tell her. It's probably about the break-in at her flat and what happened in the garden the other night. That would at least be logical. Even so, she doesn't quite manage to persuade herself. She thinks about what Månsson said about there being some important pieces of the puzzle missing, and she can't shake the feeling that Isak is holding on to one of them.

She meets Mattias's police jeep on the drive leading to Uncle Harald's farm. He stops alongside her and winds his window down.

'I heard about happened last night. Are you OK?' His tone is curt, formal.

'Absolutely.'

'Good. And you've got everything you need?'

'Yes. Uncle Harald has been very helpful.'

A strange silence arises. The only sound is the car engines idling in neutral.

'So what were you doing here?' She nods towards the farm.

'Oh, just talking to Uncle Harald about something.'

'The wind farm?'

He snorts and shakes his head. 'I'm glad you're OK, Vera. I need to get going . . .' He starts to wind his window up.

'See you tomorrow evening,' she calls out. He responds with a strained smile.

Chapter 60

The park was laid out in the early 1900s. An open-air stage, a covered rotunda for dancing and a large party venue. August Palm is supposed to have given a speech there once, but no one knows exactly when.

Uncle Harald hasn't held back. The park is decorated with hundreds of coloured lanterns. The lottery booth has been turned into an outdoor bar with two white-clad bartenders mixing cocktails with shop-bought spirits. The rifle range has wine and beer kegs set up on it, and there are already long queues. It's a mild evening, summer is still clinging on. The weather forecast has promised thunder, but so far there's no sign of that except a faintly sticky feeling in the air. The sky is cloudless and high above the harvest moon is shining so unnaturally bright and large that it almost looks like part of the set-dressing.

Five large outdoor barbecues, staffed by the same number of sweating cooks, are spreading an appetite-teasing smell through the August evening. A jazz band is playing on the outdoor stage, then a dance band will take over in the rotunda after the food. No local group of amateurs, either, but one of the famous bands you sometimes see on television. And all over the park, at strategic intervals, are big green banners to remind everyone who's paying for all this.

At first Veronica can't help feeling that everyone's staring at her. She regrets the dress she bought on impulse in town, thinking that it feels far too short now. She keeps tugging at the right sleeve of her little cardigan to make sure her scar isn't visible. But then she runs into Lidija and some of the women who work for her, and, as the noise and alcohol levels start to rise, she begins to relax.

She bumps into Aunt Berit and Uncle Sören and receives unexpectedly warm hugs. Then she has to let Aunt Berit drag her round and introduce her to a load of people she hasn't seen in years. She doesn't even feel annoyed when someone points out for the tenth time how like her mother she is. She sees other familiar faces. Marie, the nurse from the old people's home. Sven Postie, the Strid brothers, Patrik Brink's father, Cecilia and the girls. She behaves herself, even hugs her sister-in-law and asks where Mattias is, and is told that he's still at work but will be joining them later. Her dad's with them, but he's busy shaking hands with a long row of people. She waits until he's alone, then pushes her way through to him and touches him on the arm.

'Hello, Dad.'

'Hello, Vera. So you came.' He looks surprised, but not angry.

She's been thinking about what to say. She even practised in the car on the way to town and back. At the last minute she decides to scrap all the lines she rehearsed, and keeps it simple instead.

'You were right about Isak. I'm sorry, Dad.'

He looks at her sternly. Then his face softens, and he smiles that gentle smile that never quite reaches his eyes.

'I know you mean well, Vera. Has he . . . ?'

'He's gone, yes.'

'Good.'

Without thinking, she gives him a hug. Holds him tight, as if she never wants to let go. He lowers his shoulders and wraps his arms round her, and strokes her hair.

'My little girl,' he murmurs.

She buries her head against his chest. Breathes in his smell. He says something else, she barely hears it, but at that moment it doesn't matter.

'Ebbe!' Uncle Harald's voice makes them let go of each other.

Her uncle seems to be in an excellent mood. He's wearing a Stenström shirt and a pale linen suit that looks tailor-made. He shakes her dad's hand warmly, then kisses her on the cheek. Tess and Tim are there too, with Patrik Brink standing right behind them like a shadow.

She says hello to everyone, and it suddenly dawns on her that she's surrounded by almost her entire family, and that for once she doesn't find that oppressive.

Uncle Harald guides them to the table reserved for family. Her dad is seated beside her, with Patrik Brink on the other side. The food is good, as is the wine. Uncle Harald gives an admirably short welcome speech from the stage. He manages to be funny and entertaining, and gets a loud round of applause for his efforts. Dad doesn't say much during dinner, but Patrik talks about what's become of other old friends, and behaves like a perfect gentleman. He keeps refilling their wineglasses, which almost seem to be emptying themselves.

After the food the dance band starts to play, and first she dances with her dad, then with Patrik and Uncle Harald.

'You and Ebbe seem to have patched things up,' he says. 'It's been a long time since I saw him this happy. He ought to get out and see people more often. Mattias and I are trying to get him to move into the village, to be closer to his grandchildren.'

And let you build your wind farm, she thinks, but says nothing. From the corner of her eye she sees Patrik dancing with Tess. She notices that he's holding Uncle Harald's wife a bit closer than he held her. She turns her head slightly, and sees Patrik's father watching the couple intently.

'I'm glad you decided to stay,' Uncle Harald goes on. 'It means a lot to me to have the family gathered together. An awful lot.'

The whole time they're dancing he smiles and nods at the people around them. That irritates her, makes her feel like some sort of trophy. The prodigal niece who's returned and is now being shown off to everyone.

'Yes, I suppose this matters to you. Showing that the family stands proud.'

'And what's wrong with that?' He still isn't looking at her. 'What's wrong with wanting the best for your family?'

'Oh, because I suppose a man who can't look after his family can hardly look after a whole district?' It sounds sharper than she intended, but she doesn't regret saying it.

Uncle Harald looks down at her and raises his eyebrows slightly. 'You've inherited your mother's temperament as well, I see.'

She doesn't care for his tone, nor the thought that she's become a pawn in a game. And on top of that, something else has started buzzing about inside her head. Words she thought she heard her dad whisper into her hair a short while ago. And all of a sudden that feeling from the bus station is back again.

The music fades away, until it is eventually unable to drown out her dad's voice in her head.

My little girl. You weren't to know . . .

Not know what? What is it they're not telling her? What are they keeping from her?

She lets go of her uncle. 'If you're so bloody concerned about the family's reputation, maybe you should keep a closer eye on who your wife's dancing with, and how,' she says, then turns and walks quickly towards the exit.

She's standing a short distance from the rotunda, breathing in the evening air and wishing she had a cigarette, when someone takes hold of her arm and pulls her aside. It's Mattias. He's dressed smartly and has just showered, his hair is still wet.

'Come with me.' He leads her round to the back of the building. He doesn't let go of her arm until they stop. 'What the hell do you think you're playing at, Vera?'

'What do you mean?'

'That Isak, or whatever the hell his name is. Dragging him down here with you. Are you really that fucking stupid?'

She knows he's right, but she's drunk and her dance with Uncle Harald has left her in a terrible mood.

'At least I was trying to do something, unlike you!'

'Trying to do what? What did you think you were going to achieve by confiding in a stranger? Dragging him home to present him to Dad, even though I warned you. Even though I explained to you . . .'

He shakes his head angrily, and seems to lose the rest of the sentence.

'Look, I . . .'

He doesn't seem to want to hear her explanation. And, if she's honest, she hasn't actually got one that would do anyway.

'You don't understand how things work down here. You can't just show up and stir up loads of old shit and then piss off again, leaving me to clear up after you.'

'Piss off again? You want to talk about people just pissing off? You were the one who pissed off and left me on my own here! Or have you managed to forget that?'

Mattias looks at her in surprise. Then he holds his arms out.

'For God's sake, that was over fifteen years ago. We were children. Our ideas, our dreams – they were just childish.'

'You promised,' she says. She can hear her teenage self in her voice.

Mattias sighs. 'You don't get it . . .'

'Of course I do. You promised that we were going to get away from here together.' She gestures towards the rotunda and the party going on within. 'Instead you let them keep you here. Cecilia, Uncle Harald, Dad.'

Mattias sighs and shakes his head. 'You don't get it, Vera,' he says again.

He pulls out a packet and offers her a cigarette, then lights them both. He waits until they've taken a few drags.

'No one forced me to come back here,' he says. 'It was my decision.'

She looks closely at him, trying to work out if he's joking, or – even worse – lying. She can't see any sign that he is.

'I know what you're going to say. I know what you think. That's why I find it so hard to talk to you. Because you're judging me the whole time.' He sucks on the cigarette. 'I'm actually really fucking sick of having to feel ashamed of staying here. I'm sick of having to defend myself to you.'

'Two types of people grow up in the Shadowland – that's what you said,' she snaps. 'Those who stay, and those who leave. We were going to leave together!'

'I was eighteen! What the hell did I know about anything? Leave or stay, us or them. That's how you see the world when you're young. When you haven't lived long enough to know any better.'

She folds her arms and glares angrily at him.

'If you live in the country you're automatically at a dis-advantage,' he goes on, looking away. 'You get labelled as backward-looking, you have no ambition, no imagination,

419

you're frightened of change and you're secretly racist. You have to put up with pathetic jokes about playing the banjo and squealing like a pig. As if everything real, smart and important takes place in the cities, because that's where real life is, and everywhere else is just irrelevant.' He turns towards her again. 'You think like that too, don't you?'

She doesn't answer, just goes on glaring at him. Mattias shrugs his shoulders.

'After two years in Stockholm I realised that I enjoyed life in the countryside. I like people knowing who I am, knowing my parents and grandparents. I realised this is where I belong. That's why I came back. That's why I stayed. Not because anyone forced me.'

He takes another drag on the cigarette, then blows the smoke over his shoulder.

'Obviously I should have told you. Should have tried to explain. But you were so angry, you were in such a rush to get away from here. And after that . . .'

We weren't best friends anymore, she thinks.

'This is my life, Vera,' he sighs. 'You can think whatever the fuck you like about it, but you can't just show up when it suits you, cause chaos and then have the nerve to judge me.'

She understands what he means, and feels almost ashamed. But her drunken anger is stronger that any sense of shame.

'Haven't you got a family you can lie to?' she snaps. 'How does infidelity fit with all this talk of belonging?'

Mattias treads the cigarette butt into the gravel. 'Go to hell, Vera,' he says. He sounds sad and angry in equal measure.

Out in the car park she totters a little on her heels and drops the car key on the ground. She's really far too drunk to drive, but she can't imagine there are going to be any spot checks in Reftinge this evening. Mattias and Uncle Harald will have come to some sort of arrangement about that, just like everything else. She's so tired of this place. Tired of all the unspoken agreements, all the lies and secrets.

She has no desire at all to go back to Ängsgården. No desire to sleep in a creaking bunk bed in an impersonal cabin listening to the Polish workers' drunken partying in the other cabins. She takes her shoes off, throws them on the passenger seat and gets into the car. She gets the engine started on her second attempt and drives home.

Chapter 61

Backagården is in almost total darkness when Veronica pulls into the yard. Only one solitary outside lamp is lit above the cart shed. Her dad's still at the party, which suits her fine. All she wants is to get out of this damn dress, wash the make-up off and go to bed. First thing tomorrow morning she'll ask her dad for a lift to the station, and then she'll never set foot in this dump again.

The air feels closer now, there's thunder on the way. Heavy clouds have rolled in across the sky, only occasionally letting the moon shine through. She looks for the spare key in the window box, can't find it and swears. But when she tries the front door anyway, to her surprise she finds that it's unlocked. She stands in the dark hallway for a few moments, trying to convince herself that her dad just forgot to lock up, but deep down she knows he never forgets anything. And these days he even locks the study door at night.

She listens hard, and at first hears nothing but the ticking of the old wall clock in the dining room. Then she thinks she can hear a faint sound from upstairs. She stiffens. There's someone up there. Maybe even the burglar Mattias mentioned. And because she drove up to the house with her headlights on, there's a high risk that he's seen her coming. That he knows she's standing down here in the darkness. Alone.

A shiver runs down her spine and her first instinct is to turn and run back to the car, drive off and fetch help. But out of nowhere anger takes over. The cupboard under the stairs is just a few metres away. Four silent, barefoot steps and she's there. She listens out for the sound of footsteps on the stairs as she removes the loose plank. Nothing but silence. The shotgun is exactly where she left it. She takes it out, and creeps cautiously to the foot of the stairs. Tucking the butt against her cheek, she aims the barrel towards the upper floor. She hears a faint creak from one of the floorboards up there. The intruder is still there, and has nowhere to go.

She slides her thumb over the safety catch. Then she moves softly up the stairs, one tread at a time. She avoids the fifth and seventh steps because she knows they creak. For a few moments she's a teenager again, sneaking quietly and carefully up the stairs so that she can lie plausibly tomorrow when Dad asks her what time she got home. A lie that was important to both of them, for different reasons.

Halfway up she hears the sound again. A floorboard creaking faintly as someone moves their foot. The sound is coming from the right-hand side of the house. Her heart is beating fast, but she's no longer frightened.

At the top of the stairs she stops, and sweeps the landing with the gun. She keeps her eye focused along the barrel, with her thumb on the safety catch and her index finger on the trigger. It's darker up here and it takes a few moments for her eyes to get used to it, but when they have she sees that the key is sitting in the lock of her mum's room and that the door is ajar.

She moves quietly towards it. More sounds from within. She holds her breath and listens. She can hear breathing, and the rustle of fabric against fabric. The squeak of a drawer being opened. Things being moved. Still holding the gun to her cheek with her right hand, she gently nudges the door open with her left.

The moon is shining straight through the window, bathing the whole room in silver light. The air is filled with the scent of roses, of Mum's perfume, and for a fraction of a second it almost overwhelms her.

Everything looks just as she remembers it. The double bed with its flowery bedspread, and beside it the make-up table with its mirror and stool. On one wall, above Mum's little bureau, there's a large photograph. Mum's looking into the camera, and she's probably smiling, but the moon-light in the room is distorting her face, giving it a look of infinite sorrow.

The man in the room has been so focused on what he's doing that he hasn't heard her coming. He's wearing gloves and has his hoodie pulled up over his head, and he's bent over the make-up table with his back to her, rifling through Mum's jewellery. She takes aim at his back and takes the safety catch off.

'Stand absolutely still! Or I'll blow your head off!'

The man starts. He raises his arms and slowly turns round, in spite of her command. She curls her finger around the trigger. Her pulse is roaring in her temples.

'D-don't shoot, Veronica, it's me.'

She recognises both the voice and the blue eyes before the man slowly pushes his hood back. Isak.

'What the fuck are you doing here?' is the first thing she thinks of to say when her initial shock has subsided. She holds the shotgun aimed at his chest, and raises it slightly when he seems to be about to take a step forward.

He holds his hands up towards her. 'Please, guns make me nervous. Especially when they're pointing at my face.'

He's trying to sound jokey, but she can hear that he's scared. She goes on aiming at him.

'Were you thinking of stealing my mum's jewellery?'

He doesn't answer, and slowly lowers his arms and lets them hang by his sides. 'It's not what you think. I'm not a thief.'

'Really?' She nods towards the make-up table, its drawers hanging open. 'You knew the house would be empty during the party. You knew where the spare key was. Although – how did you get here?'

'I borrowed a motorbike in town.'

'You mean you stole it?'

He doesn't deny it, just shrugs his shoulders slightly.

'You've been here before,' she says. 'Out in the rose garden. You were the person I was chasing.'

He holds his arms out in a gesture that she interprets as a yes.

'And my flat?'

He nods reluctantly. 'I saw that the window was open. I never meant to steal anything, not then, and not now.'

'No? So what are you doing here in the middle of the night?'

He takes a deep breath, then sighs. 'I'm trying to find out the truth. Find out what really happened to Billy.'

He sounds genuine, but on the other hand he's lied before, in a very convincing way.

'What for?' she says. 'If you're not my little brother, how come you're so obsessed with something that happened twenty years ago and has nothing to do with you?'

He hesitates, and seems to be thinking before he replies. 'You remember I told you that I found my adoption records this spring, after my mum died?'

He pauses again, waiting until she nods.

'It didn't come as a surprise. I knew all along that I was adopted, even if I didn't remember my biological family very clearly. My adoptive parents never wanted to talk about it, and when I found those papers I understood why. My biological mother's name was Pernilla. She was left on her own when I was five, and she wasn't able to look after us. So my sister Åsa and I ended up being adopted by two different families. I managed to track her down. She lives in Gävle now, she's expecting her first child. She remembers me and our parents well, even though she said she'd done her best to forget us. Our biological mother died of cancer in 1989, and our father . . .'

He smiles in that usual way of his, but Veronica has no trouble seeing the seriousness behind it. Then the sadness.

And she suddenly realises what he's about to say, understands which piece of the puzzle he's been keeping from her. She even understands why.

'Our biological father's name . . .' Isak goes on in a toneless voice, 'was Tommy Rooth.'

Chapter 62

Veronica lowers the shotgun, puts the safety catch back on and gestures to Isak to sit down on the bed.

'Åsa was shocked at first when I found her,' he says. 'She slammed the door in my face, and threatened to call the police if I didn't leave. After a while she calmed down. She was seven years old in the summer of 1983, and still remembers everything all too well.'

He takes off his gloves and runs his fingers through his blond hair.

'Åsa's spent most of her life trying to forget all about it, which is hardly surprising, really. Who wants to remember their father if he's a child killer?' He tries another smile. 'I had a pretty messy upbringing. Children's homes, supervision orders, a few months in prison. Mostly small stuff. Break-ins, car theft, illegal driving.' He makes a weary gesture with his hands. 'I've been involved in a few fights. But I always felt that violence wasn't really my thing. I'm more the type who gets beaten up rather than the other way round, if you know what I mean?'

Veronica catches sight of her reflection in the mirror of the make-up table, and sees that her jaw is clenched in a rigid grimace that reminds her of her mum. She relaxes her face.

429

'After seeing Åsa I started to think about it all,' Isak goes on. 'She had already thought through everything a thousand times, but to me it came as a bolt from the blue. If our dad was a child killer . . .' He stops and looks at her with a resigned expression. 'Then what did that make me? Like father, like son?'

'So you decided to try to find out more? You came down here and poked about, then you came looking for me in Stockholm.'

He nods slowly.

'Maybe it sounds stupid, but I was hoping I might find something to go on. Something that could explain why Tommy did what he did. Or, even better, something to prove he was innocent. Something Åsa and I could cling on to.'

'Why didn't you tell me this at the motel? After we . . .'

'I almost did, but I didn't dare. Sometimes it's easier to lie. Besides, I like you.'

She takes a deep breath and tries to make sense of her thoughts. Strangely enough, she doesn't feel particularly upset. More resolute, contented, almost. As if she's actually managed to accomplish something. Isak's telling the truth now, she's certain of that. She can even understand why he hid behind layer upon layer of lies. Now that his secret is out, it's possible to appreciate how exposed he must feel. How vulnerable he is. Suddenly she feels almost sorry for him. He too is a victim, just like her. Yet another person who – even though he didn't know it until very recently – is also living under the shadow of the summer of 1983.

'Why did you leave a pebble on Mum's grave?'

He shrugs his shoulders. 'I don't know. A way of showing respect, maybe. Of asking for forgiveness, from me and Åsa. I know, it sounds stupid.'

He falls silent and looks away.

'And what were you hoping to find in here?' she says.

He shrugs again. 'I don't honestly know. After what you said about the bedrooms, and your dad keeping everything exactly as it was the night Billy went missing, I suppose I just wanted to come and see them with my own eyes. One last try, maybe.'

Veronica goes over to the make-up table he had been going through, the drawers are all open. She catches sight of jewellery boxes and shiny fabrics as she closes them. There's a framed photograph of Mum on top of the table, and beside it a vase containing twelve perfect Magdalena roses set in an almost equally perfect arrangement. One of the roses is standing slightly crooked, probably because Isak happened to nudge it. She puts it back in position. The petals are as soft as velvet. The scent is enchanting. She hasn't been in here for twenty years, and just like when she was in Billy's room it's like stepping straight back into her childhood. A place where time has stood still. The door to the wardrobe is open. Inside Mum's dresses and jackets are hanging in a row. She runs her hand over the garments, then leans forward and smells them.

My little mouse. My little mouse . . .

Isak moves so quietly that she doesn't hear him stand up. She sees the movement out of the corner of her eye, turns

431

round and is about to raise the gun. But he just walks over to the window and looks out. She closes the wardrobe door, making sure to hold the shotgun in such a way that she can quickly lift it up again.

'Do you think he came from down there?' Isak is pointing to the far end of the garden. 'Tommy Rooth, my dad. Do you think he came through the maize and took your little brother that summer?'

'Maybe.' She goes and stands just behind him and looks out. The thunder has started to rumble, but the harvest moon is still peering out between the heavy clouds from time to time, turning the rose bushes below into burnished metal.

'Do you ever get the feeling that you're missing something?' Isak murmurs. 'That there's something going on right in front of your eyes, something you don't understand, no matter how hard you try?'

She starts. That description is precisely how she's been feeling over the past few days. Perhaps that isn't so strange – they're both part of the same tragedy, after all. Sharing the same sorrow.

'Some of my clients want to know how you can comprehend the incomprehensible. But sometimes there just aren't any good answers.'

He nods slowly. The moon gets swallowed by the clouds and the garden goes dark. The first lightning is already visible on the horizon. In the distance, off above the field of maize, the red eyes of the wind giants are winking.

'There's something I need to tell you. The first night I was here, I broke into the old barn. I found something there, something that worried me.'

He's interrupted by a sudden noise, the sound of a large engine approaching. Then more of them.

'You need to get away from here!' she says. 'Right now!'

Chapter 63

The yard outside is lit up by car headlamps. Doors open and close, shadowy figures move towards the house.

'Did anyone know you were coming here?' she whispers to Isak as they hurry down the stairs.

'I don't think so. But I stopped down by the park to make sure your cars were there. Someone could have seen me then.'

'And where's the motorbike?'

'On the gravel track on the far side of the maize.'

'OK. Dad mustn't find you here. Sneak out the back way and I'll try to delay them.'

He nods and takes a few steps towards the kitchen. Then he stops, turns back and looks like he's about to say something.

'Get going!' she hisses, waving him away.

She quickly puts the shotgun back in its hiding place under the stairs, and only just gets back out into the hall before the front door opens. It isn't her dad. Instead Uncle Harald and Sören the grocer are standing outside. Smart dress shirts, rolled up sleeves, hard eyes.

'H-hello – what are you doing here?' she says, unable to hide her awkwardness at having been caught out.

'Where is he?' Uncle Harald says.

'Who?'

'Your friend. Isak Rooth. Tommy's son. Where is he?'

Uncle Harald pushes past her and hurries into the kitchen. Sören grabs her arm hard and pulls her after him. The terrace door is wide open. The light from various torches is playing across the grass. She hears dogs barking, voices shouting.

'He's here! Get him!'

The barking turns into a howl, mixed with a cry of pain.

'What the hell were you thinking, Vera?' Sören says as he drags her out into the garden. 'Bringing him here and letting him in? Rooth's son. In your mother's house.'

The torches have stopped moving and are all pointing in the same direction. The dogs are barking excitedly but stop instantly when Uncle Harald bellows at them.

The long grass is wet and cold under her bare feet. She tries to pull free, but Uncle Sören just pulls her arm up higher, forcing her onto tiptoe. He pushes her ahead of him, towards the torches. He doesn't let go until they get there. The men are standing in a circle. Patrik Brink is there, holding two of Uncle Harald's largest dogs by the leash. The two Strid brothers are next to him. Hunched shoulders, bulky bodies, unused to shirts and smart trousers.

The dogs are straining at the leash, baring their teeth at Isak, who's lying curled up in the centre of the circle. One of his trouser legs is wet, ripped to shreds. Beneath it his skin has been torn open.

Veronica gasps for breath, feeling increasingly nauseous.

'Did you know?' Uncle Harald hisses. He grabs her by the arm and forces her to look him in the eye. 'Did you know who he is?'

'I-I . . .' She tries to gain a bit of time, figure out the right answer. Uncle Harald isn't prepared to wait.

'Mattias took fingerprints from the cabin at Ängsgården. He wanted to know who your friend really is. We got the results this evening. Isak Welin. A thief and an embezzler with a long criminal record. And Tommy Rooth's son. So answer me, Vera – did you know he's the son of the bastard who murdered your brother?'

'Wait . . .' Isak holds one hand up, but Patrik kicks him in the stomach, hard.

Veronica stands as if paralysed, watching as the scene unfolds in front of her. The Strid brothers pick Isak up, carry him off towards the rose garden and pin him against the wall. Uncle Harald has let go of her now, but she has no choice but to follow them.

'What are you going to do?'

'Find out why he's here. And what the fuck he wants.'

Uncle Harald suddenly looks as if something's just occurred to him. He takes hold of her shoulders.

'Has he asked about me? About Timothy?'

She shakes her head. Tries to remember. 'I don't think so.'

'You don't think so?' His grip tightens. 'Think carefully. Has he said anything about Tim?'

'Let go, you're hurting!'

'Think!' Uncle Harald's face is right in front of hers. His eyes are burning, his lips pulled back.

'Were you after Timmy, you bastard?' Patrik yells at Isak, which makes the dogs start to bark again.

One of the Strid brothers punches Isak in the stomach. Once, twice, three times. The blows are dry, muffled. The other brother makes sure Isak doesn't double over.

'No,' she yells. 'He hasn't said anything about Tim. Nothing at all!'

Uncle Harald doesn't seem to be listening. He lets go of her shoulders and beckons Sören over to him.

'Do you think he knows?'

'Why else would he be here? Like father . . .'

'Knows what?' she blurts. But the men turn their backs on her as they form a cluster by the wall.

Patrik has let go of the dogs' leashes. He's holding Isak's T-shirt and is banging his head against the wall. Isak looks like he's about to pass out, his eyes are glazed and his eyelids drooping. The only time they move is when the back of his head crashes against the wall.

Thud.

'Tell us why you're here, you bastard!'

Thud.

'Are you after Timmy? Is that it?'

Thud.

Thud.

Blood appears on the wall. The harsh moonlight makes it look black.

'Stop it!' she says, but no one's listening.

'Tell us what your father did with Billy!'

Thud.

The stain on the wall grows larger.

'Tell us, you fucker!'

Thud.

'Stop it!' she yells, and hits Patrik in the back with her fist as hard as she can.

He stops and all five men turn towards her. Their eyes are empty, almost surprised. As if they'd forgotten she was there.

'Stop it!' she screams again, with her fist still in the air. 'You're killing him!'

Chapter 64

The air grows thicker as the thunder rolls closer. The storm will soon be upon them.

Sören the grocer and one of the Strid brothers are dragging her across the yard. She sees the other men lift Isak into one of the pick-ups. His head is hanging limply and he's barely moving.

'Ebbe could be back anytime now. I don't want him involved in this any more than necessary,' she hears Uncle Harald say to Patrik.

'What do we do with her?' Sören says.

Uncle Harald throws a heavy ring of keys over to him and gestures towards the cowshed. She doesn't quite understand what's going on. Not until they drag her into the shed and over to the locked door of the old milking parlour.

'No!' She pushes back, trying to brace her feet on the ground. Her terror makes her so strong that the two men holding her eventually have to get Uncle Harald to help shove her into the darkness and lock the door on her.

She hits something and falls to the floor. It's ice-cold under her palms, the air raw and sour, just as she remembers. She jumps to her feet in panic, and throws herself against the door, banging on it as hard as she can. She screams until her lungs run out of air. None of it helps. She's locked in, just like she was when she was little. Shut in the darkness. Something brushes against her foot, it feels like soft fur, and for a couple of seconds all her nightmares merge together. The milking parlour, darkness, foxes, and she screams until her throat is burning.

She sinks down with her back against the wall. Her sobs make her body shake uncontrollably. She's trapped. Imprisoned in her own worst imaginings.

She tries to pull herself together, tries to breathe slowly.

In

Out

Iiin

Ouuut

It's harder than ever. Almost impossible. But after a few minutes the panic starts to recede slightly. This really isn't any worse than the old mine. There's no water here, no tons of earth and rock above her head. And sooner or later someone will come and let her out. Uncle Harald, Uncle Sören, or one of the other men.

They've locked her in. Left her here in the dark to get her out of the way. Thinking that she'd just put up with it, and wait nicely for them to come back. Because she's Vera Nilsson, Ebbe and Magdalena's girl, who – even though she's impertinent and stubborn – always does as she's told.

Like fuck she does!

She looks up, trying to get her bearings in the room. There's a strong smell of rubber, and when she reaches out for the object she knocked into earlier she feels the rough surface of a tyre. It must be the stack of winter tyres for Dad's car. The fur-like thing she brushed against turns out, ridiculously, to be a bundle of rope.

When she walks round the stack of tyres she discovers something else. A faint sliver of silvery light is filtering in through a hole in the wall. She feels around it, and finds planks rather than bricks. She runs her hand over them and finds an edge, a hatch of some sort, roughly in the middle of the wall.

She squeezes her fingers into the crack, trying to push the hatch up. It moves no more than a couple of millimetres. She tries again, pushing with all her strength. There's a creaking sound, and the hatch moves a couple of centimetres, letting in a little more moonlight.

She rests for a while, shaking the lactic acid from her arms. Then she tries again, and again, letting her fury pour from her chest into her arms. The hatch very gradually moves, a little bit at a time, until the gap is big enough for her to be able to crawl through.

Her dress catches and she tears it as she squeezes through the hole. The grooves on the side of the hatch are full of ancient grease that smears her hands, face and hair. She couldn't care less. Fury is burning ever stronger inside her, giving her unexpected strength, and all she can think about is getting out.

The hatch turns out to lead directly into her dad's workshop. Just like the locked bedrooms upstairs, she hasn't been in here since she was a child. The light she could see is coming from a window high up in one wall. She might be able to climb up onto the workbench, smash the glass with one of the array of tools neatly hung up on their hooks, but crawling through a broken window, then jumping out and landing on pieces of glass doesn't seem like a particularly smart idea. Especially not when you're barefoot.

She tries the door to the cart shed where her dad usually parks his car. It's bolted on the outside and won't budge. There's another door in the workshop that leads back into the old cowshed. There's a metal bar across it, held in place by a padlock. She looks around for a suitable tool. She finds a heavy, well-oiled pair of bolt-cutters on a hook and cuts the loop of the padlock as if it were a dry twig.

She emerges at the end of the cowshed. She runs her hand over the wall and finds a metal box and a switch. She clicks it, and an uneven sequence of fluorescent lights flicker into life in the roof. The cold air in here still smells sweet from the cows. The floor and walls are made of whitewashed brick, and on both sides of the central gangway low walls divide the room into stalls. The double door leading to the yard, through which they brought her in, is also bolted and locked from the outside, and the windows are all nailed shut from the inside. The overlapping planks look solid, and would be impossible to shift without a sturdy crowbar. There's one hanging in the workshop, right next to the bolt-cutters, but she thinks she knows a better way of getting out.

At the far end of the shed is a sliding door that she and Mattias used to use when they were playing hide-and-seek, and which can only be opened from the inside. She starts to jog along the central gangway. The stalls she passes are all empty except for the largest one closest to the door. There's something large and rectangular inside it, carefully covered by green tarpaulins. She guesses it's a stack of boxes or something and hurries past, but when she reaches the door she turns back. She suddenly remembers what Isak said about the cowshed just before they split up.

I found something there, something that worried me.

She looks for a gap in the green canvas. She catches a glimpse of red metal, and loosens some of the bungee straps holding the tarpaulin in place and lifts it up.

Underneath is an old red Volvo Amazon estate with dark rear windows. She realises immediately whose car it is. And all of a sudden she understands what's going on.

Mattias isn't answering his mobile. She isn't really surprised. She wonders if he knows it was Patrik who set fire to her car and took the opportunity to ransack their rooms. Because that's what must have happened, she realises that now. The fact that he just happened to be passing and recognised her burned-out car suddenly feels so extraordinarily far-fetched that she can't understand why she didn't see through it at once. They wanted to keep her and Isak there, and find out who he was, once and for all.

The real question isn't how much Mattias knows, but how much he wants to avoid finding out about. A lot, judging by the fact that his mobile is switched off.

She washes her face in the kitchen sink. Lets her hair down and tries to rinse the grit and grease from it. She doesn't bother to tie it up again. Her dress is soaked, filthy and torn to shreds, and on top of that she's got nothing on her feet. She hunts through the utility room for more discarded clothes but there's nothing left that will fit her, so she runs upstairs and opens her mum's wardrobe and grabs the first thing she sees. A red dress that fits almost perfectly.

She hurries back downstairs and takes the shotgun from its hiding place under the stairs. As she passes the hall mirror she can't help stopping in surprise. She looks almost exactly like her mum. The loose hair, the clothes, but above all one other thing: the look of fury in her eyes.

She hears noises from the yard and walks towards the front door. Opens it. Her dad is standing right outside, and stares at her as if he's seen a ghost.

'Where did they bury him?' she says with hard-won calm.

He goes on staring. He seems completely paralysed. She takes a step forward and touches his arm.

'Tommy Rooth,' she says. 'Where did they bury him, Dad?'

Chapter 65

The rain has arrived. Heavy drops pattering on the car roof, forcing the windscreen-wipers to work harder.

It's hard to see anything in the darkness and rain, but they're almost there now. The wind giants are looming all around them, and up ahead in the little turning circle the cars are parked in a ring with their headlamps on. The dogs are barking in cages on the back of Patrik's pick-up. Their noise keeps getting swallowed by rumbles of thunder.

Dad hits the brakes and Veronica is out of the car before the wheels have stopped. Her dress is drenched after just five metres. The rain is tipping down, millions of streaks slashing at the world. The Strid brothers and Sören the grocer walk towards her but she jerks the shotgun up to her shoulder.

'Out of the way!' she yells.

The men stare at her, then the gun, then back away. Behind them, in the centre of the light from the parked cars, she can see Uncle Harald and Patrik. Isak is sitting huddled up on the ground below them with his head bowed. Uncle Harald is holding a rifle, and appears to be loading a cartridge into the chamber.

'Isak!' she shouts, and they all turn in her direction.

A flash of lightning, then a clap of thunder so close she can taste it. For a moment she's convinced that Uncle Harald has fired, that she's arrived too late, that Isak is dead. Then, to her relief, she sees him move. Uncle Harald and Patrik have stopped and are looking at her, and in an instant Isak is on his feet. In his hand he's clutching a rock that he swings at Uncle Harald's head at the same time as he tries to grab the rifle. She hears a cry and sees the rifle fly out of the circle of light. Then a flurry of bodies, arms and legs flailing wildly as the three men end up in a heap on the ground. Fists rising and falling, the sound of blows, groans and grunts of pain.

She runs into the circle and points the shotgun at them. 'Stop it!' she cries. She hardly recognises her own voice. 'STOP IT!'

The tumult dies down. Uncle Harald is the first to get up. His shirt is filthy, there's dirt on his face and blood running from a cut on his forehead, only to be washed away by the rain. He stares incredulously at her as if she were a ghost. And when he opens his mouth she realises that that's exactly what she is. A ghost standing in the rain, wearing a dead woman's dress and holding her gun.

'M-Magdalena . . .' Uncle Harald stammers. 'How . . . ?'

'Tommy Rooth,' she says. 'You killed him, didn't you?'

Uncle Harald goes on staring at her. His mouth opens and closes several times without him managing to get a word out.

'All he had to do was confess. Tell us what he did with Billy. But Tommy just kept mocking us, said we'd never get anything out of him. That we could go to hell. Suddenly he just stopped breathing. That was never the intention, we're not murderers.'

'Yet you're still thinking of doing it again.' She nods towards Isak, who's lying motionless on the ground.

'He knows what we did to Tommy. He's here to get revenge. We have to protect ourselves. We haven't got a choice.'

Blood is running into his eyes and he tries to wipe it away with his sleeve. His glassy stare changes and he suddenly looks even more confused.

'I've already told you all this, Magdalena,' he says. 'At the home. When I visited you. Don't you remember?'

Veronica doesn't hear her dad approaching, doesn't have time to react when he rushes past her and punches Uncle Harald square in the face with his clenched fist.

Uncle Harald falls to the ground and Dad stands astride him, grabs him by the collar and roars in his face.

'You told her! You told Magdalena about Rooth, even though you promised not to. You killed her, Harald. Don't you get that? You killed her!'

Patrik has got to his feet and pulls her dad away. She turns the shotgun towards him, but Patrik has already let go. Her dad sinks to his knees in a puddle. Rain is running down his face, washing away the sound of his sobbing.

She tries to make sense of what just happened. What it means. But before she has time to fit the pieces together she sees the other three men approaching out of the corner of her eye. She takes a few steps to the right so she can cover them all with the shotgun.

'Stand still,' she says. The men obey instantly. Uncle Harald slowly gets to his feet. His eyes have regained their usual sharpness.

'Vera,' he says drily, and spits out some blood from his split lip. 'My beloved niece.'

He straightens up and casts a contemptuous glance at her dad, who's sitting hunched on the ground, sobbing quietly.

'Yes, I told her, Ebbe. Someone had to. Magdalena had the right to know that the monster who took her little lad was dead. That he wasn't going to hurt anyone else. She'd been in that damn home for months and wasn't showing any signs of getting better, so I figured it was time she knew.'

'She was starting to get better,' her dad mumbles. His voice is so weak that it's all but impossible to hear what he's saying. Even so, it fires an icicle straight into her heart.

Uncle Harald shakes his head and looks at her. 'Your father is weak, Vera. He plants roses and potters about in his garden. I do what needs to be done to protect the family.'

'Yes, so I can see.' She gestures towards Isak with the gun. He's lying on his back, his face and clothes covered with blood and mud. He looks lifeless, but she can see his chest slowly rising and falling.

Uncle Harald clears his throat and spits again.

'He broke into the cowshed a month or so ago and found Rooth's Volvo. He told us just before you showed up. Ebbe swore he'd got rid of that fucking car years ago, but instead it's been sitting in there all the time. I should have known better.' Uncle Harald shakes his head. 'Thanks to you and

Ebbe, Rooth junior here has figured out what happened to his father. And as usual I'm the one who has to clear up after the rest of you. Do what has to be done.'

She tries in vain to think of a response. Her dad is still sitting with his head bowed. He's always known what happened, that they killed Tommy Rooth.

Uncle Harald straightens up, then walks off into the darkness. The rest of his gang look at each other, unsure of what to do. The rain has calmed down and is falling in a steady shower. Good rain, soft rain, harvest rain. The sort of rain that's good for quenching rage.

Uncle Harald comes back into the light. He's holding his rifle in his hands.

'The best thing for all of us is if Isak here disappears the same way as Tommy. I can't think of any other solution. There's an open shaft just below the ridge there. They'll be filling it with cement for the foundations on Monday. That way he'll end up lying pretty much next to his father.' He nods towards the nearest wind giant, cocks the rifle and feeds a cartridge into the chamber. 'Kind of appropriate, don't you think? And within sight of the place where it all started. Like father, like son.'

He takes a couple of steps closer to Isak. The heartbeat of the wind giant is suddenly audible. A low, pulsing rhythm. She doesn't like that sound. Never has.

'You're forgetting something, uncle dearest,' she says. She tries to mimic his sardonic tone of voice as she raises the shotgun. She releases the safety catch with her right thumb

451

without taking her eye off the target, just as he taught her. 'You're not the only person with a gun.'

Uncle Harald stops and stares at her. The look in his eyes is wary, slightly less self-assured than just now. He seems to be trying to work out if she's serious. The distance between them is only five or six metres. It would be impossible to miss, even for someone who's not used to firing a gun.

She crooks her finger around the trigger. Her breathing is shallow, and she can feel her heartbeat through her entire body, mirroring the rhythm of the wind giants around them.

Neither of them moves.

'Go ahead and fire, then,' he says. 'Shoot me, because that's the only way you'll stop me.'

Uncle Harald grins, raises his rifle and takes aim at Isak. He staggers backwards when she squeezes the trigger just as he taught her and shoots him in the middle of the chest.

Chapter 66

The recoil isn't as severe as Veronica was expecting. The blast from the gun also sounds odd, and there's a cloud of white smoke coming from the barrel. She knows why, and hopes it's enough, but when Uncle Harald doesn't collapse and merely drops his rifle, she realises that her hopes have been in vain.

His face and upper body are covered by a thin layer of white powder. He spits, coughs and rubs his eyes.

'Salt!' He lets out a loud laugh. Blinks hard and tries to focus on her, without succeeding. The whites of his eyes are blood red, they look terrible. 'You shot me with one of Father's homemade cartridges!'

He spits out more salt crystals. Tears are streaming down his face, but he goes on laughing. His laughter gets louder, more shrill, more deranged.

The other men are looking nervously at each other. Patrik mutters something. Uncle Harald turns towards him, he still doesn't seem to be able to focus properly. Isak has come round and is laboriously trying to get up off the ground. His body doesn't seem to want to obey him.

'Well, what are you idiots waiting for? Grab the rifle and finish the job,' Uncle Harald says. 'I can't see well enough to fire, so one of you will have to do it.'

Veronica raises the shotgun again and takes aim at the men. None of them moves.

'Shoot him, I said.' Uncle Harald points at Isak, who has somehow managed to get to his knees. 'We can't let him go, you know that.'

The men shuffle but still show no sign of stepping forward.

'Don't you understand that we'll lose everything?' Uncle Harald shrieks. 'Everything we've built up round here. All the sacrifices, all our hard work will have been in vain. Our families will get dragged into the mud.'

Veronica raises the shotgun a little higher and takes aim at Sören, who's standing in the middle. She's well aware that she only has one shot left.

'You're not frightened of a girl armed with a shotgun loaded with salt, are you?' Uncle Harald bellows, but none of the men reacts. 'Bloody idiots, I'll do it myself.' He blinks hard, then takes a few tentative steps. He seems to be scanning the ground for the dropped rifle.

Suddenly Patrik walks over to him. He calmly bends down, picks up the rifle and puts it to his shoulder. He ignores the fact that Veronica is aiming the shotgun at him.

'Good, Patrik,' Uncle Harald says. 'Finally, someone who understands. Someone who has the guts to do what needs doing.'

Patrik looks like he's about to say something, but the sound of an engine stops him. A police car, approaching at speed along the gravel track, followed by a second one. Their flashing lights refract off the rain, forming tiny sparks of lightning in the air.

'Fire!' Uncle Harald says, slapping Patrik on the shoulder. 'Do it! He attacked you, you had no choice. Our word against hers. Four against one . . .'

Patrik raises the rifle a bit more, looks at Uncle Harald, then at Isak, kneeling at his feet. Then, finally, at Veronica. She's got her finger on the trigger, and is aiming at Patrik's face. The rhythm of the wind giants gets louder, becoming a roar that echoes through her body.

A siren starts to blare, and then is interrupted by a voice through a loudspeaker, a voice she recognises at once. Mattias.

Patrik is still staring at her, but she doesn't look away.

'Fire, Patrik!' Uncle Harald roars. 'FIIIIRE!'

The word turns into a gurgling scream when Patrik lowers the rifle and throws it away into the darkness.

Chapter 67

When the sun comes up she's sitting in the rose garden with her dad. The ambulances have long since taken Isak and Uncle Harald away. Mattias and his officers have taken care of the rest of the men. That leaves just her and her dad, sitting close together in the little summerhouse with the Magdalena rose arching its branches above them.

'When did you realise they'd murdered Tommy Rooth?' she asks.

'A week or so after he disappeared.'

'How did you find out?'

'Your uncle and I have known each other since we were young. I know how Harald thinks. He can never keep anything secret from me for long. He's not a particularly bad man. He thought he was doing the right thing. One of the women who worked at the police station called him to let him know that Rooth was going to be released. They were waiting for him near his farm. The rest you know.'

'Why didn't you go to the police and tell them what they'd done?'

Her dad sighs. 'Harald and your mum were very close. Magdalena was incredibly fragile, she'd already lost a child, and if her big brother were to end up in prison on top of that . . .' He makes a resigned gesture. 'So Harald and I came to an agreement. I kept his secret in return for him not telling Magdalena what happened to Tommy Rooth. Him asking me to take care of the car was his way of making sure I kept my word. It didn't really bother me.'

'But Uncle Harald broke his promise. And told Mum what he'd done a week before she was due to be discharged.'

'Yes, apparently so. The way he saw it, he'd made amends for the family.'

'But Mum didn't agree. She realised her brother was a murderer. That he'd taken another person's life for her sake.'

She can see her mum in front of her. Filling the pockets of her winter coat with heavy stones, then slowly walking off. Feeling the cold of the ice and the water beneath it. Even so, there's still something that doesn't quite make sense.

'So, after Mum . . . Why didn't you go to the police then?'

Her dad shrugs his shoulders. 'By then there wasn't really any point. Harald loved Magdalena as much as I did. Her death was a harsh punishment, and I couldn't see any good reason to make things even worse. Besides, Harald had made me an accomplice.'

'What about the Rooth family, didn't you ever think about them? Nilla, and Isak and his sister, having to grow up without their dad. Never knowing what happened.'

'Not a day passes without me thinking about them.'

He bows his head. They sit in silence for a while. It's stopped raining now, but water is still dripping from the leaves. One of the drops lands on her cheek. Her dad sits up and wipes it away with his finger.

'My little girl . . .' he says. 'You've had so much to deal with.'

She swallows a lump in her throat, leans her head against his shoulder. A gust of wind makes its way over the wall, making the windchime start to tinkle, and she shivers.

'Are you cold?'

She nods. 'I don't want to go in, not yet. It's so beautiful out here, with the raindrops on the leaves. As if the roses are . . .'

'As if they're crying.'

They sit in silence for a while longer, until eventually she gets to her feet.

'I need to go and change. Are you coming?'

He shakes his head. 'You go in, I'm going to stay a bit longer.'

She goes into the house and gets out of her wet dress in the utility room. She goes up to her mum's room to find something dry. From the window she can see down into the rose garden. She sees her dad down there through the foliage, hunched up. She's struck by how old and vulnerable he looks.

She finds a pair of jeans and a top in the wardrobe and pulls them on. The clothes must have been washed recently, but she still imagines they smell of her mum. She goes over to the little bureau. There's a single rose on top of it. A white one, just like the one in Billy's room. Mostly on impulse she opens the top drawer. It contains her mum's fountain pen and letter-writing paper, and – right at the back – a bundle of envelopes held together by a thin strip of leather. She pulls them out, and loosens the little horn clasp holding the cord in place.

She leafs through the envelopes. They contain letters written in her mum's beautiful handwriting, and she goes over to the window to see them better. The letters smell faintly of wood and earth, as if they'd been stored somewhere damp before they ended up here.

There's a corner missing from the bottom envelope, and there's something sticking out from the torn edge. Short strands of blond hair. She opens the envelope and finds a lock of hair tied with a blue silk ribbon, and her heart starts to thud against the ice. She opens the letters and reads them. One after the other, from the first to the last. And as she does so, cold black water starts to well up through the crack in her chest. Things she has seen and heard in the past few days shift and fluctuate. Only a little, but enough to give them a completely new and unpalatable meaning.

The chest up in the forest.

The severed padlock.

The bolt-cutters in the workshop.

The letters that shouldn't be here.

She could have picked anyone. But she chose me.

Billy's dead!

She still had us. Why wasn't that enough?

As if Billy was so special.

My little girl. You weren't to know.

You

Weren't

To
Know

Darling, the last letter begins.

I've made up my mind. There's no other way out. I'm sad but happy at the same time. Sooner or later he was going to leave me anyway, just like the other children. Just like you. Everyone does. Leaving me on my own.

It's better this way, better for all of us. You and me and our Billy. We'll be in a better place, somewhere there's no pain, no deception. A place where no one is abandoned. A place where we can always be together.

I hate you, Tommy.

I love you.

Slowly she goes back down to the rose garden. Her body feels heavy, every movement takes an immense effort of will. She sits down on the bench next to her dad. He doesn't say anything, just goes on admiring the Magdalena rose above them. The sun has risen above the wall now, and is turning the drops of water on the leaves into liquid crystal.

'You were right,' she says, and her voice sounds hollow. 'I wasn't to know that Isak couldn't be my little brother. I wasn't to know that Billy wasn't alive.'

She puts the bundle of letters in his lap.

'But you knew, Dad.'

He turns slowly towards her. The look in his eyes is so sad that she has difficulty breathing.

'Mum and Tommy Rooth. You knew about all of it, their relationship, the fact that he was Billy's father. But despite that...'

'Tommy made her happy,' he says quietly. 'At least at the start. Isn't that what everyone wants? For the person they love to be happy?'

'But what she did... How could you?'

'Your mum was depressed, Vera. She had been for years. She was ill and unhappy, but I loved her above everything else, and I couldn't bear the thought of being without both her and Billy.'

Veronica swallows and has to make a real effort to keep her voice steady. 'What happened when you came home that night?'

Her dad looks away again, fixing his eyes on one of the roses.

'Magdalena and Billy were lying in the bath. She'd filled it with water and given him sleeping pills. She'd crushed them and stirred them into warm milk, and had drunk some herself as well. When I came into the bathroom Billy was already beyond help, and Magdalena had stopped breathing. I managed to bring her back to life, forced her to vomit up the pills. Then I carried her into the bedroom and put her to bed.'

'Then what?'

He looks at her again. 'Then I did what I had to do in order to protect her. To protect my family.'

'You threw one of his shoes into the maize field. Called the police and told them Billy was missing.'

Her dad doesn't answer.

'What about the letters?' she says, trying to take in the enormity of what he's saying.

'Magdalena gradually started to realise that she needed help, that she was ill and that what had happened wasn't her fault. So she told me everything, including the letters. If Månsson got hold of them, he'd figure out what had happened. Magdalena would be locked up for years. Maybe she'd never get out. The police had already searched both Rooth's farm and the pump house without finding the letters, so I realised he must be keeping them in an extremely good hiding place. A place that only people he trusted would know about.'

'Sailor. He told you about the shack and the chest in Askedalen.'

Her dad nods slowly. 'It's surprising how much people will tell you if only you're prepared to listen. No one listened to Sailor. No one except Tommy Rooth. And, in the end, me.'

'Why didn't you destroy the letters?'

Her dad doesn't say anything, but she already knows the answer. For the same reason he's kept the doors to Mum's and Billy's rooms locked, and keeps everything inside them exactly as it was. The same reason that stopped him getting rid of Rooth's car.

'Because they once meant a lot to Mum,' she murmurs. 'Part of her life.'

They sit in silence for a while. The only sounds are the water dripping and the tinkle of the windchime. She understands

463

everything now, every tragic detail, each one linked to the next, forming a trail of footprints through the snow and out onto the ice.

'That was why she committed suicide. Because her big brother hadn't only killed an innocent man for her sake, but also . . .' She can't bring herself to say the last words, but they're there nonetheless. *The man she loved. The father of her child.*

Her dad looks up again. The pain in his eyes almost breaks her heart.

'Where . . . ?' Her voice shrinks to a whimper. 'Where's Billy, Dad?'

He doesn't answer, just turns away and looks at the roses around them. The pink blooms embracing them, wrapping them in their scent and hiding them from the world. And suddenly she sees a different rose in front of her. One white rose on Mum's grave, one on her bureau, and one on Billy's desk.

She gets slowly to her feet, taking the bundle of letters with her, and leaves him on the bench. It's only been just over a week since she saw him out here, but it feels like much longer. She thinks back to the look on his face when she caught him unawares. Surprise, and fear.

The chalk-white shingle under the large rose bush in the corner is carefully raked, without any irregularities at all. The roses are white, too, and incredibly beautiful. At least as beautiful as the Magdalena rose, just a bit smaller. And when Veronica crouches down and peers in under the bush, she sees a small brass plaque stuck in the ground, a long way in. Five small letters that make the ice inside her break up, once and for all, and turn into dark, open water.

BILLY

She hears the hinges of the gate creak, hears footsteps, the jangle of keys hanging from a belt. She called Mattias from the phone on the landing. She didn't ask him to come, didn't ask him for anything. But here he is anyway.

He stops next to her and puts his hand on her shoulder. Without looking up she hands him the letters. He takes them and squeezes her shoulder, but says nothing.

The windchime tinkles again, louder this time. Melancholy, metallic notes drifting over the rose garden.

'He was here all the time,' she whispers. 'But we still didn't find him.'

'You did,' Mattias says quietly. 'You found him, Vera.'

She looks up and meets his gaze. There's no hostility in it, no accusation. Just sadness. And love.

She puts her hand on his and squeezes it hard. Somewhere at the far end of the garden a fox barks. A plaintive, lonely cry that sounds almost like sobbing.

Epilogue

Malin carefully runs the clothes brush over the epaulettes of Månsson's uniform jacket. She adjusts his dark tie for at least the third time before she is finally happy with it. 'There!'

He tucks his cap under his left arm and inspects himself in the bedroom mirror. His uniform has been hanging out to air overnight but still smells faintly musty. The trousers are a little loose around the waist, and to his quiet satisfaction he's had to tighten his belt a notch. Overall he looks pretty good, considerably better than he had been expecting.

'Are you sure you don't want me to come with you?' Malin says.

'Oh, yes. You've got more than enough to do as it is.'

'But you haven't been back for so long. And funerals can be . . .'

He gives her a kiss on the cheek. 'It's sweet of you to worry, but I'll be fine. Besides, I'll have company. They should be here any minute.'

At that moment he hears Bella's small paws pad across the parquet floor, then the yapping that always precedes the

467

doorbell. Månsson takes a deep breath and looks at his reflection one last time.

'Ready?' Malin says.

He nods. 'Ready.'

Veronica Lindh hugs him and gives him a peck on the cheek before saying hello to Malin, as if they were old friends. Månsson holds his hand out towards the blond young man with her.

'You must be Isak?'

The man nods and shakes his hand. His movements are slightly slow, and he doesn't seem particularly comfortable in the dark suit he's wearing. Traces of bruising are still just about visible on his face. Månsson remembers the flaxen-haired little boy who once smiled shyly at him across the breakfast table at Rooth's farm. He feels a lump in his throat.

'I've often thought about you and your sister,' he says, then quickly clears his throat. 'Will she be coming?'

'No.' Isak shakes his head. 'Åsa and I agreed that I'd represent the family. Billy was our half-brother, after all,' he adds, as if that needed explaining.

Månsson suddenly doesn't know what to say. An awkward silence follows. Behind his back he can hear Veronica and Malin talking.

'Thanks for doing this,' Malin says. 'It means a lot to Krister that you invited him. More than he'd care to admit.'

Månsson glances at Isak, but if he heard he's sensitive enough not to let on.

'I've put together a basket of supplies for the journey,' Månsson says in the absence of anything better. 'Coffee and rhubarb sponge. My own recipe.'

Isak smiles. 'I haven't eaten rhubarb sponge for years. I used to love it when I was little.'

'Splendid.' Månsson brightens up.

'Well, are you ready?' Veronica said. 'We've got a fair drive ahead of us.'

She takes Månsson's arm and they walk off towards the car. Isak lags behind to help Malin with the basket.

'You look very smart in your uniform,' Veronica says, and for some reason it makes Månsson blush slightly. There's something different about her. Something in her eyes. He likes it.

'Funny to think I got so close,' he says. 'I literally held the key to it all in my hand. If only Rooth had told me . . . I mean, he must have realised what Magdalena had done.'

Veronica nods.

'I think Tommy really did love Mum. That he knew she was ill and for that reason couldn't bring himself to give her up. That's what the letters suggest. The fact that he kept them, I mean, rather than just getting rid of them.'

'That could well be true. What about your dad?' he adds after a short pause.

'The prosecutor has decided not to press charges. Extenuating circumstances . . .'

'That sounds sensible.'

'After the funeral Mattias and I are going to try to persuade him to move into the village. We'll see how that goes.'

They reach the car. The air is clear, and there's a flock of swallows circling high above them, round and round before they reach the right altitude for their flight south.

Månsson stops and turns his face to the sky.

'A northerly wind,' he says. 'First time in several months. You know what that means, don't you, Veronica?'

'Vera,' she says. 'You can call me Vera.'

Månsson smiles to himself. He thinks back to the first time he spoke to her at Backagården. He can hardly believe twenty years have passed since then. The moment still seems so vivid. As if it had never really left him.

Vera leans her head against his shoulder and they stand like that for a few seconds. The wind makes her hair fly up and stroke his cheek.

'What does it mean?' she says. 'A northerly wind?'

'The end of summer,' Månsson replies. All of a suddenly he feels strangely light-hearted.

Keep reading for an exclusive extract from the next book in the Seasons Quartet

DEAD OF WINTER

When fifteen-year-old Laura Aulin arrives to spend Christmas with her beloved aunt Hedda, she is also looking forward to spending time with Jack, Hedda's foster son.

But a lot has happened since last summer and Laura soon finds out that things are not what they first appear, as old faces and new seem to be keeping secrets from her. Tensions and jealousies come to an explosive finale at a party on the night of Lucia.

And when the smoke clears, all that is left is ash . . .

Coming Winter 2022

1

She hates the winter, has done ever since she was little – or almost. Once upon a time there was ice skating and sledging, campfires, a flask of hot chocolate and friends to share it with. But that was a long time ago, before the Lucia Day fire.

Now there is only the cold.

'So . . . Laura.'

Her table companion glances at the place card next to her wine glass for at least the third time. His name is Niklas, and so far he's turned out to be both dull and nervous. He's managed to spill something on his tie – or even worse, he chose to put on a tie with a stain already on it when he was dressing for dinner.

'How do you know Stephanie?'

The question is almost laughably predictable.

'We met through work a few years ago, but now we're good friends.'

Laura is trying to be polite. She doesn't say that Steph is her best friend, sadly perhaps her only friend. Except possibly Andreas.

Niklas asks her something else, but the loud alpha male opposite them, who has been holding court ever since he made his ostentatious entrance three quarters of an hour ago, says something funny and the laughter from the other guests drowns out Niklas's voice.

She should have turned down this invitation, explained that she has a headache and too much work to do, but she had promised Steph. Promised to behave herself and give nervous Niklas a chance.

'It's important for you to get back in the saddle, Laura. Find somebody new. Yeehaw!'

To be fair, Steph didn't actually say 'yeehaw', that was Laura's own addition. She takes a big gulp of her wine and decides she's being unfair. Steph grew up in the USA, and tends to speak both Swedish and English at the same time. Sometimes Laura thinks she does it deliberately, exaggerating her use of Swenglish to make her stand out from the crowd, which really isn't necessary.

She glances over at the head of the table. As always, Steph looks good in a dress that shows just the right amount of décolletage. Her blonde hair is perfectly styled, and she is sitting with her head tilted to one side in the way that makes every man in her vicinity want to be of service. Steph is two years older than Laura, but the cosmetic procedures she's undergone are so discreet and professional that no one would think she's a day over forty.

Laura, on the other hand, definitely looks forty-five. She has crow's feet at the corners of her eyes and a furrow in her brow that shows up particularly well on the kind of alabaster skin that only redheads have. She inherited her hair colour and skin tone from her father, but she alone is responsible for the grim set of her mouth.

She is wearing a long-sleeved shirt beneath a cashmere cardigan, and even though the warmth in the room has already prompted a few of the gentlemen to loosen their ties, her fingertips and the end of her nose are freezing cold. They always are, all year round, thanks to the winter fire. Or rather because of it. She feels no gratitude towards it whatsoever.

She and Steph are the polar opposites of each other in many ways. Steph is open and extrovert, she's built up her own business from scratch. Laura took over her father's company. *Handed everything on a plate,* as her mother points out on a regular basis.

Steph must have felt Laura's eyes on her; she looks in her direction and nods meaningfully. Laura gets the message. *Pull yourself together and give the guy a chance.*

She sighs and turns back to Niklas. Tries to avoid fixating on the stain on his tie.

'Sorry, I didn't hear what you said.'

Niklas blushes.

'I was just wondering if you worked in investment too?'

'No, my speciality is risk management. Mainly the soft sector.'

Niklas looks puzzled, and she realises she needs to expand on her answer.

'We assess people – to see if they're suitable to be taken on, or promoted. You might have heard of screening?'

'You mean you find out if they have a criminal record, that kind of thing?'

She can hear from his tone of voice that he doesn't understand, which is hardly surprising. Her area is narrow, to say the least.

'That's just a small part of what we do. We aim to form a more comprehensive picture of the person. Look into their finances, family relationships, talk to their former teachers, employers, colleagues. We carry out over a hundred different checks, and sometimes we even conduct in-depth interviews.'

She doesn't mention that this is in fact her own area of expertise; no point in scaring him unnecessarily. She's already worked out most things about Niklas – mainly that she has absolutely no intention of seeing him again, whatever Steph says.

'Who are your clients?'

A good question, she has to give him that. If this were an interview she would have made a little squiggle in the margin of her assessment form to indicate that he was brighter than he looked.

'Usually recruitment firms, but also companies, agencies or government bodies that are considering internal promotion to the leadership team or other key posts. Sometimes it's investors who want to know who they're dealing with.'

'Like Stephanie?'

'Exactly.'

Just as Laura is about to return the favour and ask Niklas about his job, the alpha male opposite breaks into their conversation. He must be fifty, and she doesn't need to look at his place card to know his name.

'Did you say you worked as a head-hunter?'

He already has the attention of everyone around the table, which means they are now focused on her.

'No,' Laura says curtly, because she already knows where he's going with this.

However, he's not so easily dismissed.

'I'm actually looking for a new challenge.'

Laura shakes her head. 'As I said, that's not what I do.'

He's not listening. 'I usually increase turnover by at least ten percent in the first twelve months,' he informs her. 'There was an article about me in *Industry Today* the other week – did you see it?'

Laura demonstratively turns to Niklas, but the alpha male still doesn't get it.

'The head-hunters call me once a week, if not more often,' he boasts. 'You wouldn't believe the salary they offer – but I need the right kind of challenge. What company did you say you worked for, Lena?'

Steph intervenes before Laura bites his head off.

'*Laura* runs her own business, Tobias. She assesses people like you, searches out their weaknesses. The skeletons in your closet. You need to watch yourself.'

There are odd bursts of laughter, and if Tobias had any sense he would drop the whole thing. Instead, he leans across the table.

'Do I, indeed? So how would you assess me, Laura? What are my weaknesses?'

He beams at her, showing his recently whitened teeth, and she can see that a number of the guests are on his side. Steph is giving her a look, and Laura knows she ought to keep her mouth shut, but alpha-Tobias is wearing the smug expression favoured by only a certain kind of man. He really is asking for this.

Steph shakes her head almost imperceptibly, but to no effect.

'I've met so many people like you,' Tobias goes on. 'Cod psychologists who think they can judge someone by getting them to fill in a fucking form. *Can you list your three greatest weaknesses? What colour do you associate with your personality? If you were a car, what make would you be?* Bullshit, pure and simple.'

He laughs loudly, and once again several of the other guests – mainly male – join in. Buoyed up by their support, he leans even further forward and extends an index finger with a faint sticky film covering the nail.

'Go on, Laura – give me your best shot!'

'OK, but remember this was your idea.'

She takes a sip of her wine, puts down the glass while observing Tobias closely. Follows the tell-tale redness at his hairline, down over his upper body, his hands. You could hear a pin drop around the table.

'You're married,' she begins. 'But that's not your wife.'

She nods in the direction of his companion, who is at least twenty years his junior.

'You drove here because you wanted to show her your expensive car. It could be an Italian make, but it takes time to learn to drive them properly, and you don't have the patience, so I'll go for a slightly more easy-to-handle Porsche.'

Tobias's eyes are darting from side to side.

'You've already drunk too much, but you're still intending to drive home, because you don't want to leave your precious toy parked on the street. Which means you don't really care about risks or consequences for yourself or others. Since you came by car, you don't live in town, but in Lidingö or Djursholm. Judging by the exaggerated way you pronounce the letter *i*, I'd go for the former, but the cadence of your sentences suggests that you were born and grew up somewhere on the west coast.'

She pauses, leaving him to squirm for a few seconds. She avoids catching Steph's eye. This is too easy. And so much fun.

'Your suit is Brioni, your watch Rolex, your tie Fendi. Red, of course, because you read in someone's autobiography that it's a power colour. Autobiographies are all you read, by the way. And you recently had a hair transplant.'

She leans back, trying not to look smug.

'To summarise, Tobias: you're a walking, talking, risk-taking, middle-age crisis. What do you think of my assessment?'

No one speaks. Tobias is gasping for air, as if he's about to explode.

Suddenly Steph begins to laugh, a loud, infectious belly laugh that draws everyone in, and the atmosphere lightens.

'Don't say I didn't warn you,' she says as the laughter gives way to an amused hum of conversation. 'Laura's fucking lethal.'

Tobias knocks back the contents of his wine glass.

'How the fuck did you know all that?' He sounds annoyed, but reluctantly impressed.

'Do you really want to know?' Laura says.

The conversation dies away. She gazes steadily at him.

'I read the article about you in *Industry Today*. It told me where you come from, where you live, and that you've been married for many years. But your companion this evening isn't wearing a wedding ring.' Once again she nods in the direction of the young woman, whose hands are clearly visible. 'Plus, you had a much higher forehead in the photograph in the magazine.'

And there's something sticky on your fingers which I'm guessing is Regaine, just in case the transplant doesn't succeed, because you can't think of anything worse than going bald. She decides to keep that little snippet to herself. There are limits, after all.

Tobias's face is bright red. He has got over the shock and surprise, and now he's furious, humiliated. He's probably wondering whether to call her a bitch and storm out, or pretend to turn the other cheek and be a good loser. She thinks he'll go for the latter option; anything else would be stupid.

'And the car?' the man next to her asks. 'How did you know he drives a Porsche?'

Laura shrugs.

'He arrived just after me and parked by the door. I saw them getting out of the car as I was walking in.'

Another burst of laughter. Tobias grins, looking embarrassed but doing his best to join in the merriment. A wise decision.

One of the women is laughing so much she can hardly breathe. She reaches for her glass of water and knocks it over. When she leans forward to retrieve it, one of her curls gets too close to a candle.

Laura can see what is about to happen and opens her mouth to warn the woman, but it's too late. A flash of fire, then a scream.

It's over in a second. The hiss of burning, the flame is extinguished. All that remains are agitated voices and the acrid smell of burned hair.

Everyone's attention is on the woman, so no one notices when Laura gets up and hurries out of the room. Her stomach contracts, she can feel the sweat on the back of her neck.

She just manages to lock the toilet cubicle door, turn on the cold tap and sweep her hair out of the way before she throws up in the hand basin. She swills out her mouth, blows her nose several times to try to get the smell of burned hair out of her nose, but somehow it is still there.

She looks in the mirror. Notes that she is even paler than usual, if that's possible.

'Calm down,' she murmurs. 'Just calm down.'

After a while she feels better. The voices in the dining room have died down. A slight draught indicates that someone has opened a window.

With hindsight, she realises it wasn't a good idea to take Tobias down like that. If she hadn't been showing off, the woman wouldn't have set fire to her hair, and she wouldn't be standing here throwing up in Steph's marble hand basin.

Her headache has gotten worse, and all she wants to do is go home, close the door, and not see anyone. But she can't let Steph down.

She takes out her phone. One text message, two missed calls. The first is from a contact called Andreas ex-husband/ stalker.

One of Steph's little jokes that she hasn't had the energy to correct. It's her own fault for leaving her phone unattended for a few seconds. Plus, it's not entirely untrue.

A year after the divorce, Andreas still calls her almost every day. Over the last few weeks, he's been calling even more frequently. She ought to ask him to stop, of course. Explain that they both need to move on. And yet she hasn't done it.

The other missed call is from a number she doesn't recognise. A landline with an area code that looks vaguely familiar.

She opens a search app. The number belongs to a firm of lawyers called Håkansson in Ängelholm, and as soon as she sees the name of the place, a faint warning bell begins to ring in the back of her mind. She makes the call before she has time to think, not really expecting anyone to answer at eight o'clock on a Friday evening.

'Håkansson.'

The man on the other end of the line speaks with a rough Skåne accent.

'Hi – my name is Laura Aulin. I think you tried to contact me about an hour ago?'

'I did, thank you so much for getting back to me.'

She hears the rustle of papers.

'It's about your aunt. Hedda, Hedda Aulin. Have you spoken to her recently?'

The warning bell is louder now, and the nausea comes flooding back.

'We . . . We're not in touch.'

'No?'

'No, we haven't been for many years. Has something happened to her?'

The brief silence answers her question. She swallows hard.

'I'm very sorry, but your aunt has passed away.'

'When?'

'At some point during the early hours of Monday morning, we think.'

Without warning the skin on her back begins to crawl, a painful mixture of heat and cold that she hasn't felt for many years. At least not while she was awake.

'So anyway . . .' Håkansson goes on. 'Your aunt spoke to me not long ago. She wanted to make a will. You're her only heir.'

He falls silent, waiting for Laura to say something, but she is lost for words.

'As I'm sure you understand, there are a number of practical decisions that will have to be made concerning her estate,' he continues.

'I . . . I understand,' she manages to say. 'Can I call you back tomorrow?'

'Monday will be fine – there's no hurry. Once again, my condolences. Your aunt was . . .' He pauses, searching for the right words. 'A very special woman.'

He ends the call, and Laura stands there with the phone pressed to her ear. The skin on her back is burning like fire, drops of sweat are trickling down towards the waistband of her trousers. The rest of her body is ice-cold.

RITES OF SPRING

Skåne, 1986: On the night of Walpurgis, the eve of May Day, where bonfires are lit to ward off evil spirits and preparations are made to celebrate the renewal of spring, a sixteen-year-old girl is ritualistically murdered in the woods beside a castle. Her stepbrother is convicted of the terrible deed and shortly after, the entire family vanishes without a trace.

Spring, 2019: Dr Thea Lind moves into the castle. After making a strange discovery in an ancient oak tree on the grounds, her fascination with the old tragedy deepens. As she uncovers more and more similarities between her own troubled past and the murdered girl, she begins to believe that the real truth of the killing was never uncovered.

What if the spring of 1986 claimed more than one victim?

Available now